FALLEN STAR

RUINED ROCKSTARS BOOK ONE

HEATHER ASHLEY

Fallen Star
Copyright © 2020 Heather Ashley

All rights reserved. No part of this book may be used or reproduced in any manner whatsoever without written permission except in the case of brief quotations embodied in critical articles or reviews.
The characters and events portrayed in this book are fictional. Any similarity to real persons, living or dead, is coincidental and not intended by the author.

ISBN: 9798471035706

Published by DCT Publishing
Copy & Line Editing: Outside Eyes Editing Services
Cover & formatting: Black Widow Designs

Contact the author at www.heatherashleywrites.com

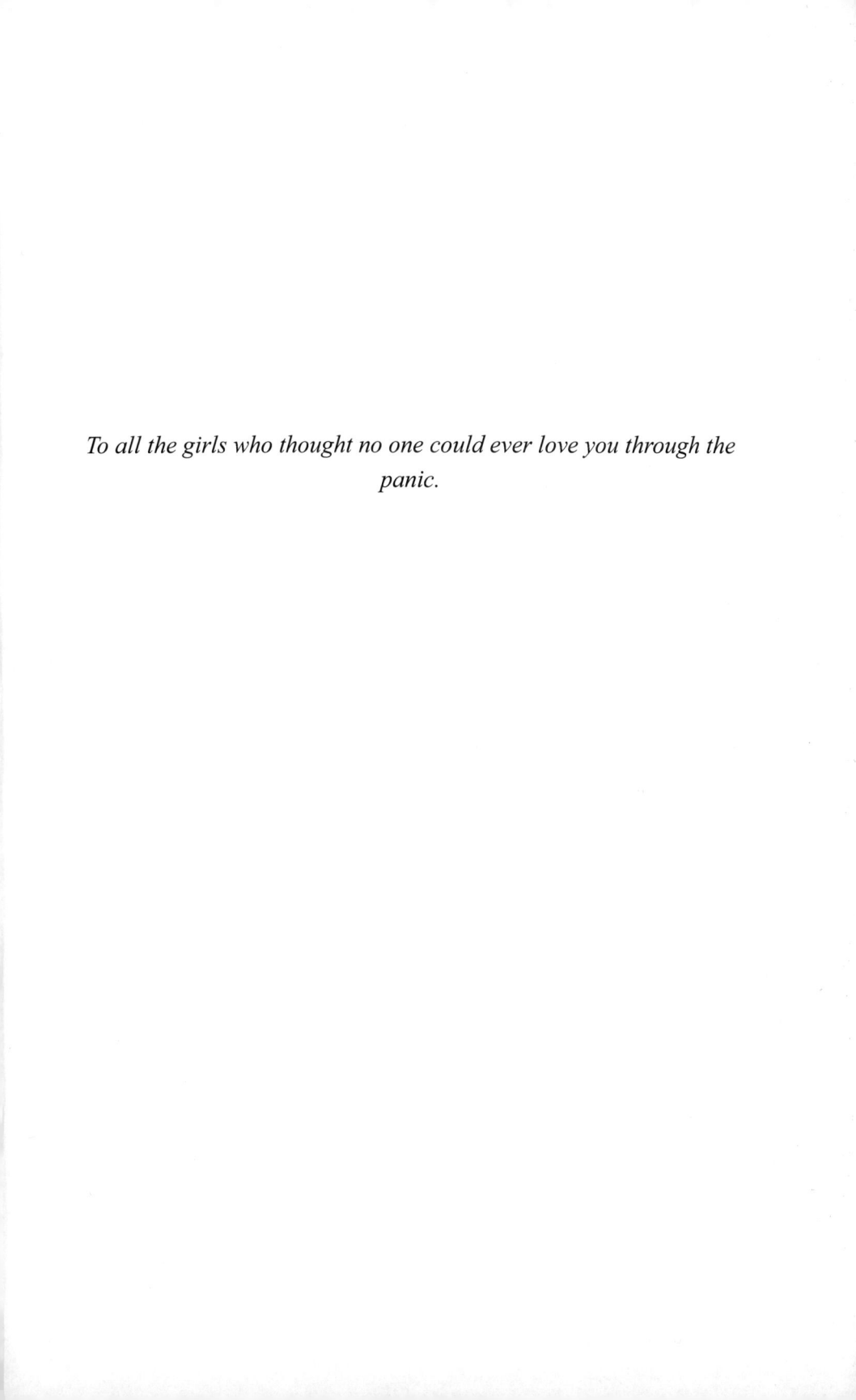

To all the girls who thought no one could ever love you through the panic.

PLAYLIST

Playlist:
Listen along here

"The Hills" – The Weeknd
"Heavy" – Linkin Park feat. Kiiara
"What Ifs" – Kane Brown feat. Lauren Alaina
"Guys My Age" – Hey Violet
"Starboy" – The Weeknd & Daft Punk
"Unapologetically" – Kelsea Ballerini
"Make You Miss Me" – Sam Hunt
"Love Lies" – Khalid & Normani
"I Know Places" – Taylor Swift
"Simple" – Florida Georgia Line

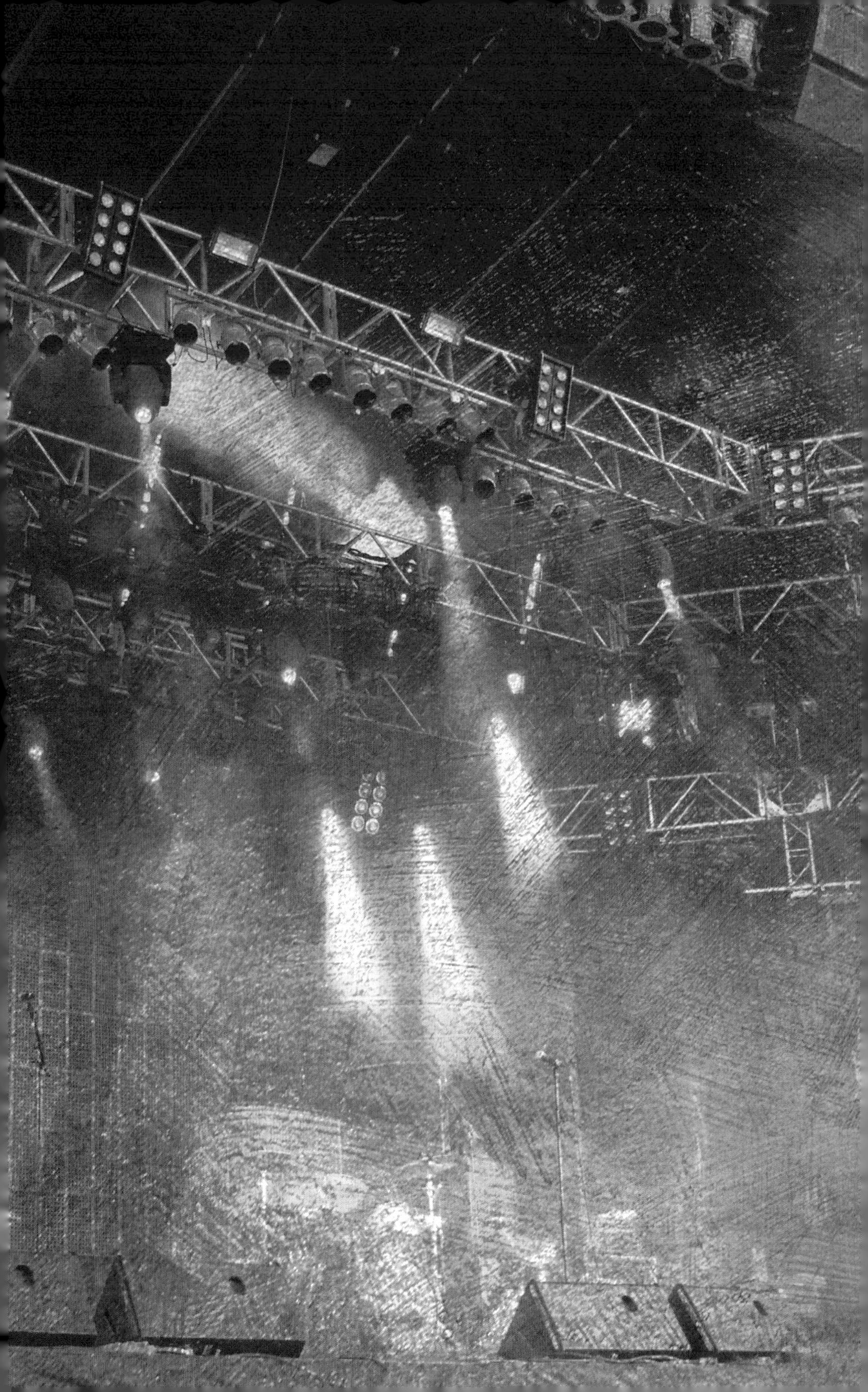

CHAPTER 1

ZEN

"LISTEN TO THE SCREAMS, man. Is there anything better?" My best friend True closed his eyes and let the distant crowd sounds wash over him. Even after ten years, every show was a fucking high for him. I wished I could say the same.

"I don't know. It's the same shit, different night," I replied with a yawn. The constant low roar of the sold-out crowd sounded like white noise to me. It used to pump me up before a show just like it did for True, but now it just blurred into the background of my consciousness.

Lately, my mind wandered all over the fucking place, and the energy I used to get before a show just wasn't there anymore. True cracked open one blue eye and stared at me, his knowing smirk showing just a hint of a dimple.

True might be one of my best friends, but he wasn't into taking advantage of the perks that came along with being a rock god. He put on a good show in the media for the sake of his image, but he was more of the fall in love forever type. It was a huge secret that he didn't like to fuck around like Maddox and me.

"C'mon, you're living the dream. Tell me you'd give this up." He opened his arms wide. "There's not a chance you'd walk away and leave this behind, no matter how cranky you are. Stop being such a downer. Maybe eat a snack." His other eye popped open, and he grabbed a bottle of water, drinking half of it in one gulp.

I rolled my eyes. I wasn't hungry and he knew it. Numb was more like it. "It's just gotten too fucking easy. There's no challenge, nothing to separate today from yesterday. How are you not bored?"

"Are you kidding? Being on stage, playing our music for thousands of fans who scream the lyrics so loud we can barely hear ourselves is as good as it gets." True practically vibrated with his excitement, he was so amped up. If I didn't know better, I'd think he was on something. "Seriously, who'd ever want that?" His voice was laced with sarcasm as he shook his head.

The other members of my band, Shadow Phoenix, strolled into the room. A bass guitar was slung over Maddox's shoulder, and he wore his usual *fuck off* glare. He was what chicks referred to as *dark and brooding*. Intense didn't even begin to describe him but calling him a grade-A asshole came close. Right now, his deep brown eyes were hard and steely. Pre-performance jitters weren't a thing for Maddox. He went on stage ready to perform every night, even if he wasn't entirely sober when he did it.

Jericho rounded out our merry band of musically talented assholes. Somehow he managed to perform in front of people even though his social skills were severely lacking. He was so quiet that people mistook his silence for some sort of shyness, but he was really the biggest dick of us all. He didn't let anyone in except True, Maddox, and me. Of all of us, he always had the biggest crowd of women trying to get his attention, probably because he never gave it to them.

He was also the most talented drummer I'd ever met. His chin lifted in greeting to True and me before he went back to tapping out a rhythm only he could hear on his thigh.

The ground trembled underneath my feet as the fans impatiently waited for us to take the stage.

I glanced over at True, who slung his guitar across his chest. He grinned at me, and I knew he couldn't wait to hit the stage. True sucked up the energy the crowd gave off, feeding off it like he'd die if he didn't get another hit. At the end of the night, he'd be bouncing off the goddamn walls, but he put on a hell of a show.

As for me? When I got up on stage and sang, I couldn't hide my emotions. Every lyric I wrote had meaning to my life or I wouldn't be able to write them. I connected with the words on a deep level, and that connection drew people into me like I was a fucking magnet. My stage presence was fucking legendary because of it, but people felt like they really knew me when they didn't. That was one part of fame no one ever told you about, how you could stand in a room full of people who knew every fact about your life, but still feel completely alone like nobody really understood you.

I started down the long hall to the stage entrance, the guys following my lead. I glanced back at Maddox, then Jericho and True, raising my eyebrow. All three nodded back at me.

I stepped onto the platform and braced myself. Rising up through the floor of the stage, I took a deep breath and exhaled slowly. I pushed the depressing thoughts from my mind, and the music became my only focus. The audience bled energy, and I tapped into it like a vampire. Their excitement would fuel me for the next couple of hours. Despite how empty I felt, they deserved one hell of a show.

Feeling thousands of eyes on me had been unreal to me at the beginning. It had once been scary as fuck, the idea that I could mess up and let down so many people. I was long past the point where I broke out in a cold sweat, or my heart beat so hard I thought the audience could hear it through my mic. I was disconnected, empty and cold except when the lyrics flowed through me. I closed my eyes as I rose through the floor of the stage into the waiting darkness. The energy crackled in the stadium as people fidgeted in their seats.

I stood still as the platform settled into a solid stage below my feet, gripping a microphone in my left hand and waiting for what would come next. In a few short seconds, the spotlight would find me like it always did, and the show would begin.

"Zen! Zen! Zen!" The crowd chanted my name as if I needed a bigger boost to my already healthy ego. Adrenaline used to crash through my body every time I stood in front of a crowd, but lately I felt flat. I plastered a cocky smirk on my face anyway, my signature look, and stepped up to center stage. As soon as True's familiar guitar strum sounded out against the quiet darkness of the stadium, I raised the microphone to my lips and began the show.

The drumbeat pounded under my feet as I moved across the stage, my voice rising above the deafening screams of the crowd. Jericho's arms moved so fast he bounced on his throne, his almond eyes focused on the snare drum in front of him and the kick drum at his feet. He never missed a beat, keeping us all on the same page.

The climbing notes of True's wicked solo, midway through our third song, almost couldn't be heard over the shrieks of the audience. The crowd loved it when he did shit like that. They ate it up. My eyes found his, and he threw me a cocky grin. He knew what he was doing and was never more in his element than when he was on a stage.

When I glanced at Maddox, his glare was focused out into the abyss of the crowd, not settling on any one spot for long. He didn't bother looking my way.

I found my mind wandering, even as my body continued to perform, like muscle memory or some shit. I replayed, again and again, the highlight reel of my career through my memories. It wasn't every day a nobody like me rose up and became a rock legend at the ripe old age of twenty-eight. By all outside observation, I was living the fucking dream.

On my sixteenth birthday, my parents decided they'd done their job and were ready to move on without me. I got emancipated and moved to LA to pursue music. Back in the day, when I met up with the guys, the four of us were horny sixteen-year-old dudes who thought we were cool as shit. Somehow our music transformed from a way to get laid to a serious dream. Twelve years ago, Jericho started a YouTube channel, and once we hit a million followers, the offers rolled in. We inked our record deal less than a week before graduation.

The past ten years blurred together like a training montage from a *Rocky* movie. Now I carried a heaviness with me all the time. I didn't know what to do about it besides keep moving forward like I'd always done. I couldn't tell one day from the next, and it was fucking with my perception of reality. I didn't know what day of the week it was, but I guess it didn't matter as long as I got up on that stage and performed. My only escape came in a bottle and burned on the way down.

Walking the tightrope between a comfortable buzz and blackout drunk was a challenge I took on with enthusiasm, one that gave me a twisted sense of purpose. Finding myself nestled between a pair of long, silky legs helped distract me from the nothingness that settled inside my chest, even if it was only temporary.

The nameless stream of conquests didn't matter. The women who had the privilege of spending the night with me used me just as much as I used them. They got bragging rights because they spent the night with *the* Zen Taylor. I handed out orgasms like I was Oprah motherfucking Winfrey. Why should I feel bad about it? My personal assistant had standing orders to round up the hottest groupies he could find and deposit them wherever the band would be. The chase didn't exist for me.

The last notes faded into the applause, and the lights went dark.

The last half of the show was a blur of old memories and melancholy it was getting harder and harder to shake.

I handed my mic off to one of the roadies and moved to the side of the stage before the audience lights came back up. Sweat poured down my face, burning my eyes. I grabbed a towel and swiped it down my face as I made my way back to the dressing room. The cheers behind me were quickly replaced by the low murmur of shouted conversations and clothes rustling as people made their way out of the arena.

My mind shifted to the after-party, the same party we had to endure every night. After high school, I thought the parties would change, and they had. The women got more plastic and aggressive, the drugs and liquor got harder and more expensive. And yet it still felt like the same damn thing every fucking night.

Tonight the party would take over my house in Malibu, just like it always did when we played in LA. It was a tradition for Shadow Phoenix to play our last tour stop in LA so we could finally go home after it was over. We all had our vices, and tonight would be filled with indulgence and distraction like always. Patrón would flow freely. Smooth, tanned skin would be plentiful and on display, ready for whatever wild scenarios my soon-to-be-drunk ass could imagine for the night. Maybe I'd take two women to my bed. It wouldn't be the first time and probably not the last either. Maybe Maddox would want to join in.

Swinging my front door open, I tilted my chin up at Jericho. He lifted his beer in greeting, the Xbox controller already in his hand, and his headphones over his ears. He wasn't into the whole party scene anymore, but he always came anyway. Women threw themselves at him, but he didn't give a shit about them. Soon a joint would be hanging out of his mouth, and he'd play until he passed out.

Despite how tired the parties had become, I wasn't sure what else to do. I accepted a shot glass from True, who looked as worn down as I felt now that the tour was over. We clinked glasses and tossed them back, not bothering to exchange words. I scanned the room, finding Maddox on the couch with a blonde girl in his lap, his hand already up her skirt. These guys were my brothers, and we'd seen each other in every compromising position you could imagine over the last twelve years. Maddox and me, we'd shared more women than I could count.

The four of us were feeling the effects of living on the surface, though. At one point, the music had been enough to fulfill us, but that wasn't cutting it anymore. The adrenaline rush of putting on a concert, to a sold-out stadium of people screaming our names, kept us buzzing until the first rays of sunlight signaled the morning. So I might as well try to enjoy it, even if I was drowning in the pointlessness of it all.

THE POUNDING in my skull started before I was even fully awake. The floor-to-ceiling windows in my bedroom suddenly seemed like the worst idea ever. I raised my arm, lifting my middle finger toward the window, as if that would somehow help the intense throbbing in my head. It wasn't my finest moment. I wondered who the fuck left the curtains open and then realized I was home. It was me, I was the asshole who hadn't closed the fucking curtains. Cracking one eye open, I groaned and slammed it shut again. Hangovers fucking sucked.

The California drought had nothing on my mouth. I blindly reached for my nightstand, feeling for the lukewarm glass of water I sort of remembered setting there before I passed out. I tried to remember what the fuck happened last night, but I only got a couple of images flashing through my mind.

Shot glasses filled with Patrón.

Swaying bodies surrounding me.

A hot as fuck woman in a tight red dress.

It must've been a good time. I couldn't find the will to care either way.

I finally found the glass and lifted my head just enough to pour the stale water down my throat. When I was done, I tried again to force my eyes open, but prying my eyelids up was almost impossible. Every throb inside my skull brought me one step closer to praying to the porcelain god. My stomach lurched precariously as the water I just drank sloshed around.

I rolled over, trying to escape the asshole sun that wouldn't go the fuck away. The weight and warmth of a body part that wasn't mine made me freeze. Squinting, I slowly moved my gaze down and sucked in a breath as I saw the red pointed nails that led to golden brown skin that was slung across my waist. My head dropped back to the pillow, and I studied the ceiling while considering how the fuck to get out of this bed, without waking the woman curled up against me.

Goddamnit. A cold sweat broke out across my brow as nausea rolled through my body again. I couldn't deal with this right now.

Tossing the blankets off, I shifted slowly away from the arm until I freed myself. I stood up and swayed, the stabbing pain inside my skull making me dizzy and threatening to take me to my knees.

Why the fuck did I keep doing this to myself? I woke up this way more often than not, and I hated it every time. When the numbness got to be too much, though, drowning it out with liquor always seemed like the best choice, consequences be damned.

I grabbed my phone off the nightstand, tapping out a message before unsteadily making my way to the bathroom. My staff would take care of last night's leftovers while I showered.

Finding a woman in my bed when I woke up happened more often than I liked, and I liked it somewhere around never. To me, the types of women who came to our parties trying to hook up played a role. They distracted me with a night of mediocre fucking until I passed out. Rinse and repeat. Meaningless sex with random women left me with red scratches down my back, bite marks marring the ink on my body, and a reputation for being as much of a god in bed as I was on stage, so it wasn't all bad.

I still had no interest in making it anything more than it was.

After the shower, I hesitated just inside the bathroom door, a towel wrapped securely around my waist, catching the droplets of water running down my chest. I peeked out around the door frame just enough to check the bed. I let out the huge breath I'd been holding, when I took in the rumpled sheets but empty bed. For some reason, the girls who stuck around always left me on edge. I couldn't take a deep breath until they left.

My housekeeper, Anita, would clean up the mess because it was her job. I hired people to clean up my messes, and no one complained. I understood why so many celebrities acted out. When no one told me no, and I never faced any consequences, I started to wonder how much I could get away with, how far I could push. It became almost a game, or at least it had back when I could still feel things.

I threw on some clothes and shuffled into the kitchen, pulling the fridge open and searching for breakfast. I pulled a container out and shoved it into the microwave. I absently pressed a series of random buttons without really paying attention. My head still throbbed with every heartbeat, so I pulled out a beer and twisted the top off, drinking half of it while waiting for the telltale microwave beep.

I picked my phone up off the counter and unlocked it, scrolling through my texts. While my eyes scanned the screen, the phone began to vibrate. *Harrison.* There were only a couple of people who bothered to call me anymore, and when they did, it was never for a good reason. My publicist was one of those people.

I swiped, lifting the device to my ear. "Hey, Harry. What's going on?"

"How many times do I have to tell you not to call me Harry?"

I pulled the phone away from my ear, wincing. "Goddamnit, Harry. Some of us are trying to die of our hangovers in peace. You don't need to scream. Besides, you know I do it to piss you off, right?"

Harrison sighed. "Mate, you've already pissed me off. Now you're just making me want to punch you right in your pretty-boy face."

I stood up a little straighter. "I woke up half an hour ago. What could I possibly have done to piss you off at this hour? And I'm not a pretty boy. I'm the *bad boy*. Tattoos, remember? True's the pretty one." I inspected the ink running down both of my arms.

"Maddox is the bad boy, you wanker. Anyway, get to my office." Harrison said. "Now." It sounded as if he was clenching his jaw.

"I'm kind of busy to—"

"I don't care if you're scheduled to meet with the bloody Queen of England herself. It wasn't a request. You're either here, or you find yourself a new publicist."

I closed my eyes as he hung up, gripping the counter so tightly my knuckles turned white and taking a deep breath, the kind that hurts your lungs. Harrison had never once threatened to quit working with me no matter what I'd thrown his way over the past five years. I pushed off from the counter, the microwave forgotten as I slipped my phone into my pocket and grabbed my keys. I wasn't ready to deal with whatever shitstorm Harrison was about to rain down on me, but I didn't have a choice. This was the life I'd always wanted after all.

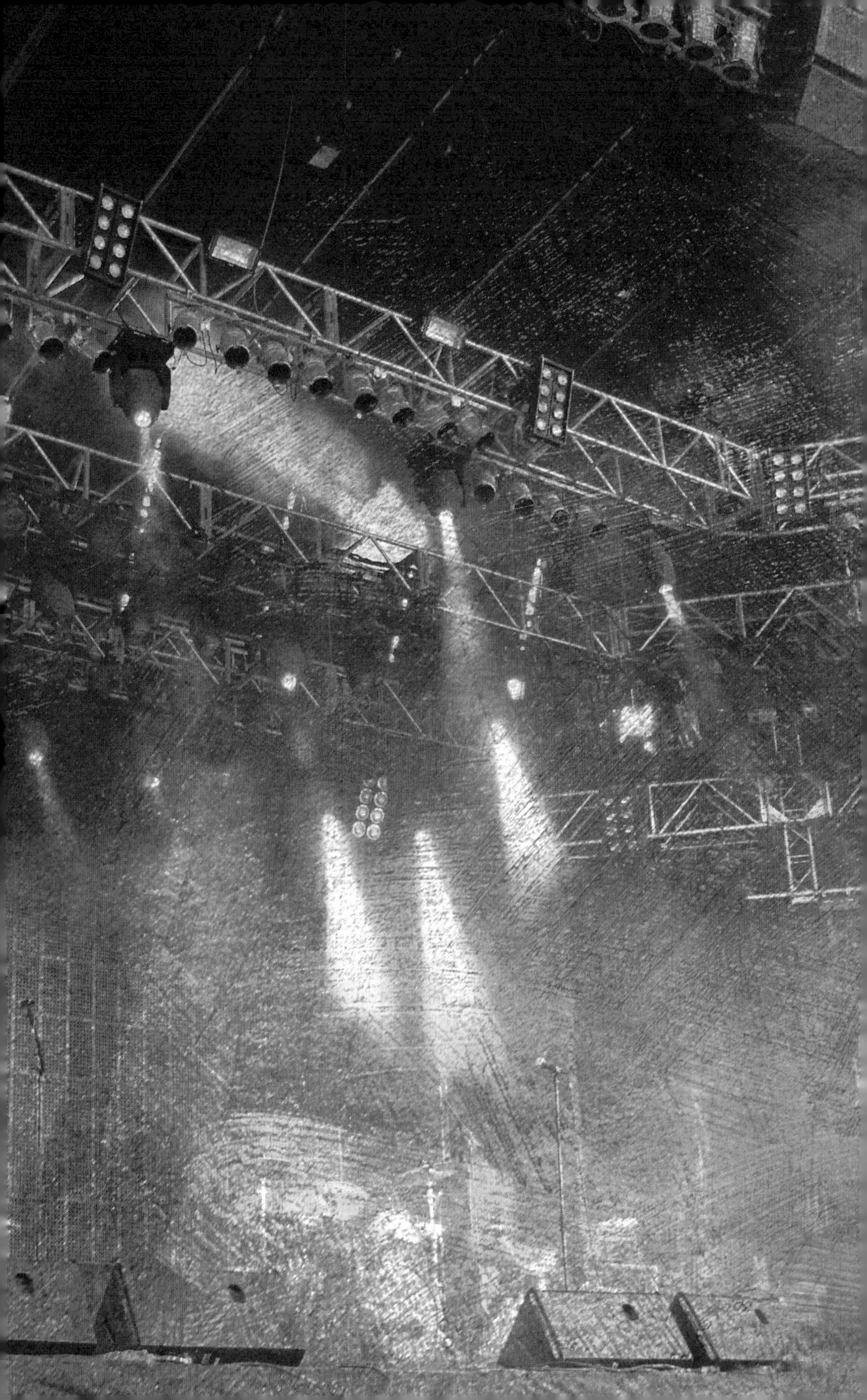

CHAPTER 2

ZEN

THE BLACK SUV I took whenever my bodyguard was with me waited outside my front door, ready to whisk me to this supposedly impromptu meeting. The fact Connor knew he needed to escort me to my publicist's office wasn't surprising. Nothing got past my bodyguard. It was why I hired him five years ago. I didn't get scared, ever, and yet a deep sense of unease rolled around in my gut at the prospect of the meeting ahead. More than Harrison's words, his tone was unsettling and hinted at something I was going to absolutely fucking hate.

It took about forty-five minutes before Connor was striding around the Tahoe and opening my door at our destination. "Thanks," I mumbled as the bright camera flashes smacked me in the face. I pulled my black hoodie down over my head. The voices calling my name and shouting fucked up questions just bounced off me at this point. I'd been through it so often that I didn't even take the time to register what they were saying. Paparazzi just came with the gig. I walked the short distance up the sidewalk and stepped through the glass door to the building that housed Frost Communications where Harry worked.

I knew Connor would expect me to wait on him before taking the elevator up, so I glanced around the office building's lobby, looking for a way to entertain myself. This building had a small bar in its lobby, and I briefly wondered whether or not I could grab a quick drink before catching the elevator. I began walking toward the bar and made eye contact with a leggy blonde drinking alone. A wolfish grin curved across her lips, and I winked at her. She could be a fun distraction for a few minutes if Connor took much longer.

Unfortunately for me he popped back up at that moment, clearing his throat beside me to let me know he was there and ready to head upstairs. He was a man of few words, but he'd been with me long enough that I knew what most of his grunts and growls meant without him having to say much. It was pretty much like speaking fluent *Jericho* with a Connor accent.

The dude was also straight-up deadly. You'd probably imagine my bodyguard as one of those huge bulky guys that's almost as wide as he is tall, but Connor's different. Sure, he was cut and over six feet, but he's also fast as fuck and I'd seen him take down guys twice his size with nothing but his bare hands. He'd also pulled me out of a lot of hairy situations. As a celebrity, having a good team around was essential. At least in my experience. You could act like a fuck up all you wanted if you had people there to bail you out and cover it up.

I shrugged at the blonde and spun on my heel back toward the bay of elevators. The ride up was silent as Connor and I waited for the twenty-eighth floor. Stepping out of the elevator, I found myself back in an office I'd been in probably hundreds of times before. It was all white with dark floors and modern lines. Someone had decorated with a few shrubs and potted plants to make the place feel less sterile, but it wasn't working.

When I strode into Harrison's glass-walled office, I hesitated when I saw my agent Montana was sitting in front of his desk, too. Shit. The only other time I'd been in a meeting with both of them, at the same time, was when the entire band had to meet because some groupie tried to extort Maddox for money when she claimed she was pregnant with his baby. It turned out she wasn't, and Harrison made it go away so the press never found out, but the whole experience had been about as much fun as being mauled by a bear and that was just me. For Maddox, he wasn't sober for an entire month afterwards and for the first time in years, he switched back to only hooking up with dudes.

I flopped down in the remaining chair in front of his desk, Connor positioning himself like a sentry outside of the office door. His body took up half the doorway so I couldn't escape if I tried. He knew me so well, the bastard. I didn't miss the knowing smirk he flashed my way, before turning to stare straight ahead and pretending like he wasn't listening to every word.

"You summoned?" I joked.

"It's not funny," my agent, Montana, snapped at me. Her fiery red hair made her seem even more terrifying than usual. She also looked like she'd been up all night, probably because of me and this mysterious thing I did.

"Never said it was."

Harrison lifted himself out of his chair, his open suit jacket fluttering behind him as he paced behind his desk. "I'm just going to come out and say it, because it's not going to get any bloody easier if I put it off."

I folded my arms across my chest and leaned back in the chair, kicking my legs out in front of me and trying to look like I didn't give a shit about whatever he was about to say, but honestly, I was starting to get uncomfortable. I wracked my brain again for the tenth time since his phone call this morning. What had I done? Outside of my regular shenanigans, nothing came to mind.

He stopped pacing and looked down at me. "There's a video."

I swallowed hard. "A video of what?"

"Of you and one of your... let's call them lady friends. Apparently, she took it when you were too pissed to notice, and it's explicit. She'd been shopping it around and found a buyer before I found out it existed."

Okay, even I'd admit this was bad. My junk was about to be plastered all over the internet. "Fuck. What does this mean? What can I do?"

Montana tapped her high-heeled foot on the ground next to me. "You can start by keeping your dick in your pants for five seconds so we can do damage control."

I sighed and ran my hands down my face. "Is this really that big of a deal? There are reality TV stars who owe their entire careers to videos like this. It's not like I have a small dick or don't know how to make a girl come, and I'm a fucking legend. This can't possibly be a bad thing, can it?"

Harrison glanced at Montana, and their eyes met briefly before she spoke up. "The label was already pissed at you guys for trashing that hotel room in Tokyo and then there was Maddox's baby mama drama a couple of months ago. They're threatening to drop Shadow Phoenix from the label, and with this fresh in the press, no one is going to want to touch you guys for months, maybe longer."

"But we're about to record the new album. The label can't do that. They already gave us the green light."

She looked like a real-life dragon, eyes blazing, and her mane of red hair flying around. Her reputation as the scariest chick I'd ever met was being reinforced right now because I had a sudden urge to cower, and I never backed down from anything or anyone. "Are you fucking hearing me? They can do anything they damn well please, Zen. They're the goddamn label. They're the ones in charge here, not you."

"This is such bullshit. So I'm filmed without my permission, and now I'm being punished for it?" My blood was starting to boil.

"That's how this works, mate. The label has to sell you guys to the public. Image is everything. It's why you keep me on the payroll." Harrison cracked a small smile but dropped it just as quickly under Montana's seething glare. "You need to go into damage control mode."

"What the fuck does that even look like? Taking up knitting? Going to church? Because I'd rather quit making music than sit through hours of people trying to convince me to believe in some made-up bullshit."

Montana shook her head. "No, you just need to lay low. Go up north, consider it a vacation while we do our jobs here. Spend time writing so that when everything is back to normal, and a new, bigger scandal comes out, you four can hop into the recording studio and give the label something to sell. In the end, all that really matters to them is the money. If they're making a profit, you'll be back in their good graces. Just keep your head down for now."

"For how long?" I asked.

Harrison sighed. "We're not sure. A couple of weeks? A month? Maybe longer? There's no way to know until the video actually comes out and we can see how much damage it does."

"Have you seen it? The video?" I wondered.

"Not yet, but I hear it's rather… explicit."

"And Zen?" Montana drilled me with her blazing green eyes. "Don't fuck this up. From now on, keep recording devices away from your extracurricular activities."

I rolled my eyes before standing from the chair I'd been hunkered down in, getting my ass handed to me. "Is that all?"

"I'll call you when I know more. Just consider this an extended vacation while we handle everything," Harrison suggested.

"Yeah, great," I mumbled. "Do the guys know?"

Harrison shook his head. "Not yet. You want me to tell them?"

"No, I'll talk to them." I sighed before turning and walking out, wondering how the fuck I let this happen.

I thought about things while Connor drove me home to grab a bag before driving me to the airport. Good thing I hadn't unpacked from the tour yet.

They'd both suggested going up north to Seattle for my extended vacation, so that's what I'd do. I usually wasn't so agreeable, but the music was everything to me. The empty parties and hookups were sure as fuck not worth throwing away my music career for. Plus, Montana wasn't wrong. I needed to write, and I'd been stuck with shitty writer's block for months now. I wondered if it was because I didn't really feel anything anymore, and my words had always come from emotions. Writing the last album had nearly killed me, and now there was just nothing.

Getting away might help. Every couple of months, I hopped on the band's private jet and flew up north to a suburb of Seattle to escape, like I was about to do right now. It'd been almost a year since I'd been there this time, because we'd been on tour and I couldn't get back.

People kept their heads down up there and didn't bother me. Theoretically, paparazzi could be lurking around, but mostly they left me alone. Sweet freedom meant walking down the street without a security detail or being mobbed. I lived for these times, and despite the shitty reason I was on my way home, I was starting to look forward to this trip.

I hadn't picked the area by accident. I grew up there. Well, at least until I turned sixteen, got emancipated, and moved to LA. Every time I visited, my shoulders loosened, and even the air smelled cleaner and more refreshing. The heaviness I carried all the time fell off my shoulders, and I relaxed. I lost track of time, and the days always flew by way too fast even if the pace up there was slower.

Climbing down the steps of the jet, I gave the driver my address.

Crawling into the back of the waiting SUV, I closed my eyes and leaned my head back against the cold leather seat. With every mile we drove more of the tension melted out of my body.

My mind drifted as it so often did when I was sober, which was why I tried to stay drunk as much as I possibly could. Who was the woman who secretly filmed me? It wouldn't be the first time I'd caught the random groupie hookups fucking with me. Once, I'd come back from the bathroom to see one of them poking holes in the condoms in my nightstand. I'd caught at least five different girls trying to break into my phone. And more than once, I'd watched as girls tried to sneak selfies of us in bed together.

I didn't date because what the fuck was the point? Women only wanted me for two things: My talented cock and my celebrity status. They didn't actually give a shit about me, and that was perfectly fine because I didn't give a shit about them either.

The idea of love made me laugh. Love? It was just some made-up fairy tale that never really existed. Men and women used each other for a variety of reasons, and when one person got bored or tired or used up, they moved on. No, love wasn't something I hoped for or thought I'd find one day. In fact, I avoided that shit like an after-party filled with last month's hookups.

The car rolled to a stop, pulling me out of my dark thoughts. I needed a fucking drink. I slid out of the backseat before glancing up at my house. I hadn't been here in about a year, but I always felt more at ease when I took in the clean lines and walls of windows that made up the front of this house.

I traveled all over the world, but I needed to feel grounded somewhere, and I kept my roots firmly planted where I grew up.

This neighborhood housed a shit ton of tech millionaires. No one gave a fuck about who I was. I didn't stand out here with my modern house and expensive cars. I wished I could spend more time in the anonymity this neighborhood provided, but that wasn't my life. At least I could pretend for a while.

Climbing the front steps, I unlocked the house and stepped inside. The lights casting a glow in the entryway were warm and inviting. My housekeeper, Maria, stocked the fridge, made sure the sheets were clean and turned on all the lights. If I was lucky, she'd leave me a plate of leftovers in the fridge. Maria gave the house the illusion of being less cold than it actually was. She was basically a saint to put up with my shit even if I wasn't around all that much.

I tossed my bag down in my enormous walk-in closet and walked out to the concrete deck, stopping to grab a beer along the way. The flames from the gas fireplace flickered orange off of the black iron railing. I turned, leaning against the cold enclosure, watching evening clouds reflecting off the inky surface of the lake behind my house. I swallowed a big sip of the cold liquid, enjoying a quiet moment to myself. My brain itched with the effort to shove down the feelings about being recorded and having it released to the world without my consent. It could be worse. At least I didn't have a tiny dick.

I pulled out my phone and typed out a quick text.

Zen: Up in Seattle. Some shit went down with Harry today and I had to get away.
True: What shit?
Jericho: What'd you do?
Maddox: Bout time one of you other assholes fucked up. Takes the heat off me.

I rolled my eyes.

Zen: Some chick filmed us fucking and sold it to the media.
Maddox: Oh shit, lol
True: Damn.
Jericho: That's fucked up

Zen: Anyway, I'm on a forced vacation. Feel free to join me if you get bored.
True: Sorry, man. If you need us, text.
Maddox: That ^

What I needed was a distraction.

My phone slid easily into my pocket as I finished off the last of my beer. Tossing the empty bottle in the recycling bin, I walked through the house, stepping into the closet to change. I threw on a plain black t-shirt and distressed jeans, my typical uniform for a night out. I liked to keep shit simple. I also knew I looked good. I spent an ungodly amount of time in the gym for this body, so I didn't have to try very hard with what I wore. When I walked into a room, all eyes turned to me the way it should be. I wouldn't say I was full of myself, just that I knew what women liked, and I was it. I'd have the pick of anyone I wanted for the night, just like I always did.

Stopping in front of the mirror, I ran a hand through my dark brown hair, messing it up just enough to look like I hadn't tried at all. I hadn't shaved since yesterday, so I had just the right amount of stubble across my jaw. Finally, I headed downstairs to my car.

Waiting for the garage door to open, I Googled bars near my house. Picking one at random, I let the GPS guide me out of my neighborhood, and soon I pulled up in front of a bar called Shots & Bottles. I'd been told to keep my head down, but no one knew I was here. There weren't photographers lurking around every corner, and I'd be careful. I had to do this because right now I couldn't stand to be alone with myself.

Tonight would be just the distraction I needed to get the fucking nonsense thoughts running through my head from today out. Before I could think about it anymore, my feet hit the pavement, and I shoved my phone and keys into my pocket. Game on.

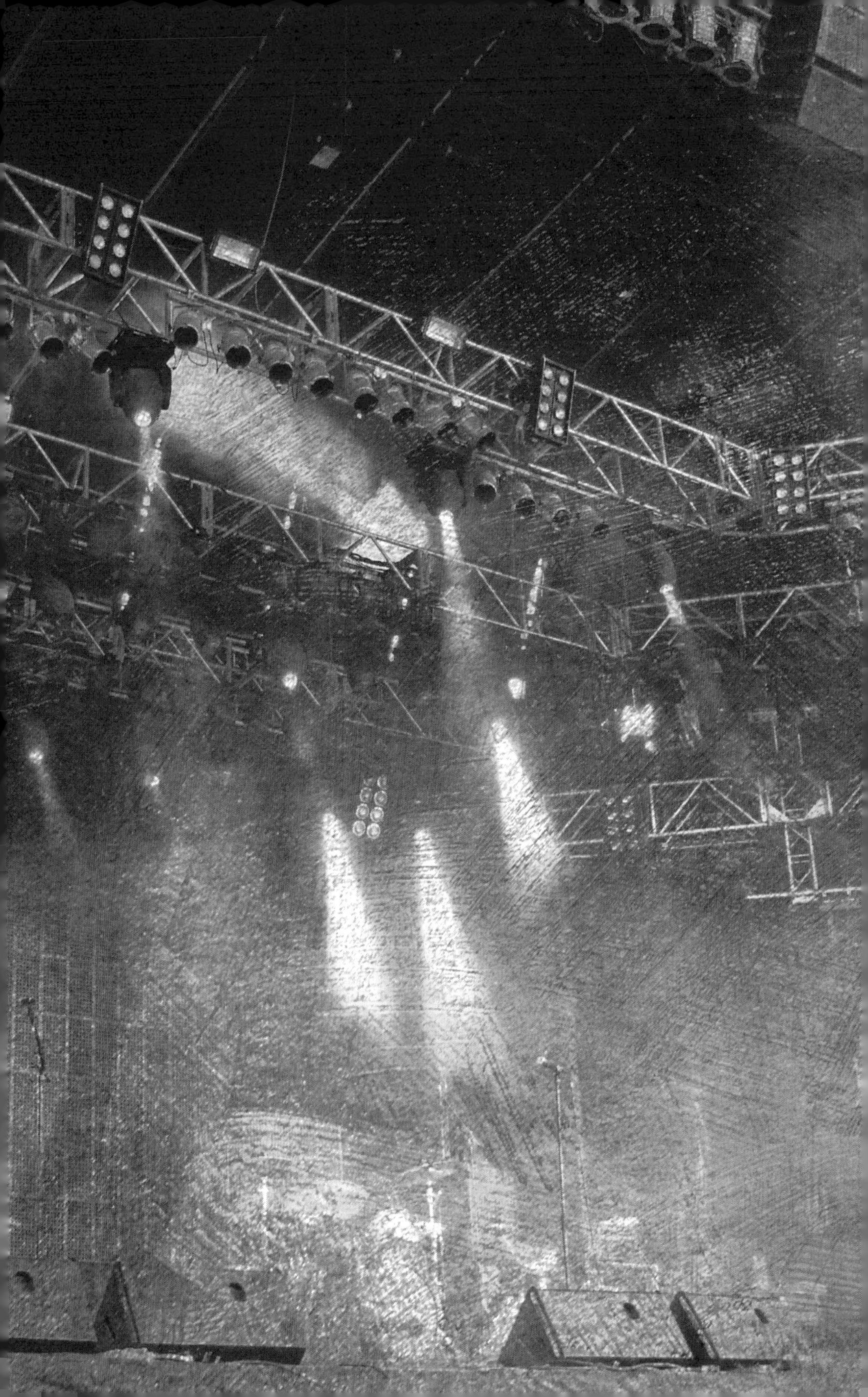

CHAPTER 3

KENNEDY

"DEEP BREATH, YOU'RE OKAY," My voice sounded about two octaves above normal and shaky as I tried to convince myself I wasn't about to die. It wasn't working.

I hoped no one around me was paying attention to my one-sided conversation. People would see me talking to myself and think I was crazy. Maybe I was.

"Yeah, crazy terrified of everything," I muttered.

My heart pounded irregularly, my eyes widened with fear, and my breath came in short gasps. I must be dying. Why did going out to dinner make me feel like this? That was a question for another day. Right now, I needed to focus.

An invisible band squeezed around my chest, and it burned with the effort of dragging in oxygen because I couldn't seem to get enough. The edges of my vision started to shimmer while I clung to reality and tried not to succumb.

I'd been through this a thousand times before. Every time it happened, I convinced myself that this was different. Maybe this time my heart would actually explode, except it never did. That worry was what kept me so terrified every single time. It kept my logical mind from taking over and reassuring me everything was just in my head; that honestly, I'd be okay. Fucking panic. My constant companion. I liked to think of it like that show *Dexter* except less murder-y. Panic was my very own dark passenger.

My eyes darted around as I wondered if anyone could tell I was in the middle of losing my shit. I strode into the restaurant with my head held high and sweat dotting my brow, marching up to the hostess with purpose. I didn't want to be here, but I'd clench my teeth and fight through my own personal hell to get what I wanted out of this meeting.

I wanted to have ordinary experiences like eating in restaurants, going to the mall, or driving a car. But I couldn't. Or at least I didn't. Restaurants scared me. Hell, everything scared me. Everything inside me screamed at me to run, to turn around and get far away from this place. Danger, danger! This meeting with one of the local city council members would help get me one step closer to getting my shop declared a public landmark. The building was old, and the city was threatening to change the zoning. I didn't own the building. I only had a lease for my shop and the apartment above it. If the owners sold, I wouldn't have much of a leg to stand on.

This meeting would be worth the hell I'd put myself through, if it meant getting one step closer to making sure my business and home were safe from the new development currently sweeping through my city.

The hostess greeted me with an overly friendly smile. "Hi, there! Table for one?"

I smiled back, though I suspected with my shallow breathing and eyes shifting around, not to mention the sweat coating my entire body in a light sheen, I looked more suspicious than friendly.

Maybe even like I was high on something really potent like meth or something. Shit, did I look like a drug addict?

With a shaky voice, I replied, "N-no, I'm here to meet Vincent Greene. Has he arrived yet?"

"Oh! Yes, follow me," she said brightly.

I tried to calm my nerves by taking deep breaths and wiping my sweaty palms on the silk skirt clinging to my thighs. I couldn't concentrate, and focused my eyes on the woman walking in front of me to keep myself upright as dizziness swirled through my body. My inner voice chanted *escape, escape, escape* and I wished I could.

As we approached the table, Vincent's eyes lifted from his phone, and he gave me a broad, genuine smile. He was in his fifties, I'd guess, with short salt and pepper hair and leathery tan skin with that orange tint that looked like he spent a lot of time in a tanning bed. He stood to greet me, holding out his hand for me to shake.

"Kennedy, so nice to finally meet you in person," he proclaimed.

"Likewise, great to meet you, Vincent."

I took his warm hand, hoping that mine wasn't too clammy, and shook it firmly. While I wished for stuff, I'd better add him not noticing my hand trembling to the list.

His dull brown eyes traveled appreciatively down my body, taking in my barely-there curves and long legs. I was pretty tall at five-nine, but I loved my height. It was one of the few parts of myself that actually made me feel powerful.

"Has anyone ever told you, you have gorgeous eyes?"

I barely contained my eye roll. I knew my bright blue eyes were framed with long, dark lashes, and because of them, people had been gasping and complimenting me since I was a kid.

"Just once or twice." I tried to give him what I thought might look like a confident smile. I certainly didn't feel confident.

Just hold it together, Kennedy. You can do this. Just a quick dinner, and then you can go home.

I exhaled slowly, trying to hide the fact that my hands were now not just trembling but full-on shaking. Vincent didn't seem to notice. His eyes rested directly on my boobs. So classy. Rather than being irritated, my heart rate actually dropped a couple beats per minute, and my breathing slowed down to maybe a sprinter's pace, because he wasn't focused on the fact I was freaking out. If I could just get him to agree to consider my proposal, I could get the fuck out of here.

I cleared my throat to bring his attention back to the meeting and off my tits. I kept scanning the room, praying to whoever was listening that the waitress got the hint and would come over to take our order. The sooner I ordered, the sooner I could get this meeting over with.

Vincent finally glanced up, not bothering to look apologetic in the slightest for being caught staring at my chest. Typical. He gave me a broad smile. "Do you want to order drinks?" Fuck no, I wasn't drinking with this creeper. It was a personal rule that I never drank to try and ease the panic, either. Sure, panic sucked, but I refused to dull my feelings even if they were awful.

"Maybe just water for me." I took the menu and quickly scanned it to find something that looked passable to my churning stomach. I wanted to be ready to order as soon as the waitress decided to grace us with her presence.

"Are you in a hurry?" he asked, frowning.

"No," I lied. "I just know your time is important, Mr. Greene. I want to make this meeting as efficient as possible."

He laughed, and then his voice dropped dangerously low. It gave me chills and not in a good way. "This is exactly where I want to be, and while I appreciate you being considerate of my time, I wouldn't mind spending a long evening getting to know each other on a more personal level."

I shuddered. Disgusting. And now I had the pleasure of dealing with this asshole coming on to me and a panic attack at the same time. Fucking fantastic.

Luckily, I had quite a bit of experience dealing with pervs just like this one. When you'd had people complimenting your looks for your entire life, you learned how to shut down unwanted advances pretty early on. I guess you could choose to embrace it, but I shut that shit down hard. I had my reasons.

I reached into the small pocket in my purse under the table, and slipped the ring I kept there for this exact type of situation onto the fourth finger of my left hand.

"Mr. Greene, while I appreciate your interest, I'm happily married. If you wouldn't mind, I'd appreciate it if we could just keep this meeting professional and discuss the options for my building."

He looked genuinely shocked as his gaze dropped to the obnoxiously huge ten-dollar fake diamond I now wore on my left hand. I barely held my laughter in, and my side was starting to ache with the effort. Maybe from now on, he'd think twice about who he came on to, but I doubted it. Why were men so terrible? They usually bought the lie and backed off, a win-win for me. It worked almost every time.

Once things had gone pretty spectacularly wrong, though. Amara, my BFF, and I were having drinks, and I used my little trick on some aggressive rando in a bar. He could barely stand up and slurred like crazy, but he'd been relentless in his quest to get me into his bed.

I told him my standard lie, that I was married but not just married, *happily* married, and wouldn't be going home with any man that night. He'd taken that as his personal challenge to get me to cheat on my non-existent husband. I fought the urge to clench my jaw at the memory. I would never cheat, fictional husband or otherwise.

In the end, the bouncer forcibly removed him. At the time, it was actually pretty terrifying. And people wondered why I didn't date and kept to myself.

Good men are impossible to find.

Finally, the waitress made an appearance at our table. She was a petite woman with a friendly smile and bright green eyes. "Hi! I'm Melody, and I'll be your waitress this evening. Can I start you off with something to drink?" she asked, leaning towards Vincent.

"Thank Thor," I mumbled.

Vincent stilled. "I'm sorry, did you just say thank Thor?"

I sighed. "Yes. Why do we always go straight to "thank God"? Why can't we pick which god to thank? I picked Thor when I was a kid, and it stuck."

He shook his head, condescendingly chuckling at me.

My attention returned to Melody. I wondered if she could sense that he had money and some little amount of power. Some women had a nose for that type of thing. I hoped she did, so she'd flirt shamelessly and let him focus on her so he'd be eager to leave to take her home. I cut into their eye fucking by clearing my throat. "Yes, I'll just have a glass of ice water with lemon. I'll also have the spaghetti, please." I wanted to be sure to get my order in. I wasn't spending one more minute in this restaurant than I had to.

Vincent peeled his eyes off of Melody long enough to raise an eyebrow at me, but didn't say anything about my order. "I'll have a scotch and the veal." He flashed his too-white predatory grin at Melody.

She smiled back, twirling a lock of her curly red hair around her finger and pushing out her breasts. "Sure thing, honey. I'll be back in a minute." She sauntered off, tossing a wink over her shoulder at Vincent.

Ew.

I leveled my full attention on the man sitting in front of me. My heart tried to pound its way out of my chest. I pretended my feet were bolted to the ground to keep myself from sprinting out of this restaurant. I was so close—time to finish this.

"Mr. Greene, I know you took this meeting as a favor to Amara, and I appreciate you giving me a chance to change your mind." I pulled a thick stack of white sheets out of my bag and handed them across the table to him.

"Yes, her father's an old golfing buddy of mine. It was the least I could do when he asked."

I plowed ahead. "The council's decision to not take up the vote on the building is a mistake, in my opinion. When modern businesses move into cities like ours, they tear down old structures and take away every bit of history. They wash away every ounce of uniqueness until before you know it, Kirkland will be indistinguishable from every other suburb across the US."

He nodded while scanning the pages before him, gesturing for me to continue speaking, and I did. I spouted off well-researched facts and spun them in a favorable way economically. When it came down to it, I just had to hope Vincent Greene actually cared, deep down, about this city and not just what I could do for him between the sheets.

"I'm intrigued," Vincent replied, a slow smile spreading across his face. "As you know, we're in recess right now until next month. I got into public service because I love making a difference in the community. But, I have to be honest with you. We've already received a rather impressive presentation from a local developer who wants to build a high rise condo building with shops on the ground floor. The council plans to debate the proposal as one of the first items on our agenda. I'm not sure they're going to want to rehash this same issue."

I deflated a little. "Sure, that sounds great."

"If you'd like, we could meet for dinner again as it gets closer. It's so nice to be able to discuss these matters face to face," he said, as his eyes dropped to my chest again. Yeah, more like face to tits.

I counted to ten, the pulse pounding in my ears almost drowning out his voice. I was barely making it through this dinner, and he expected me to do it again? Fuck. That. "Unfortunately, I don't think I'll be available."

"But I haven't even given you a time."

"No need. It sounds like the council has already made up their minds."

"For the right motivation, we're always willing to reconsider." His slimy voice and tongue running over his thin lower lip made me want to take a shower and scrub my skin until it turned bright red and hurt.

"I think I'll take my chances with the vote," I muttered.

His attention was pulled to Melody as she returned with our drinks. He went back to eye-fucking her, and I'd never been more grateful. Guess that meant I was dismissed from the dinner from hell.

Thank Thor that was over. I considered getting my food boxed up to go.

The reality was starting to set in, and my shaking wasn't about anxiety anymore. No, it was more of an all-consuming rage because Vincent had played with me, and I was no one's toy. I could lose my business and my home, and he didn't give one single shit about it. I didn't have much choice but to plead my case in an open council forum and wait for their decision at this point. The only good thing about this situation was that I wasn't angry crying, at least not yet. The night was still young.

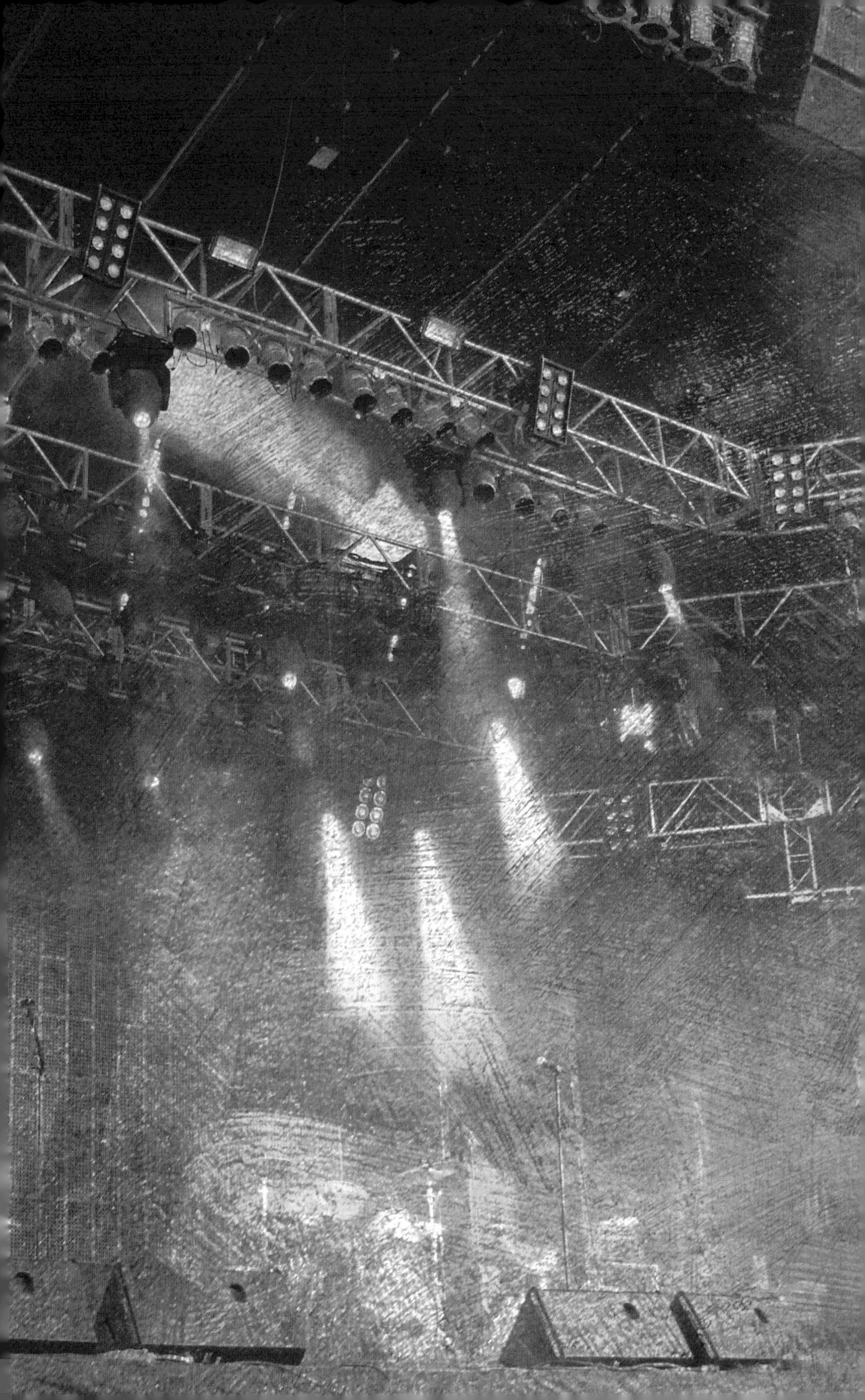

CHAPTER 4

KENNEDY

I PRESSED the palms of my hands to my eyes, trying to hold back the sting of tears threatening to spill over my eyelids. I let out a huge breath. Finally, the epic shit show I'd been dreading for weeks was over.

Walking home from the dinner meeting, I took a moment to fill my lungs with the crisp night air. I should've known what kind of man Vincent Greene was when he suggested an eight o'clock dinner meeting. Now I was left feeling like I needed a shower to scrub this whole evening off my skin. Such a douchebag.

Behind the immense relief and disgust, I could now add afraid to the list of things I was feeling. What would I do if I lost my home? And even worse, my store? Sure, a small bookstore slash bakery might not seem like a big deal to most people, but it was my own personal slice of heaven. It was my safe space, the only place I knew I could go and be comfortable and have everything the way I wanted it to be.

Someday, I wanted to experience the world, but for now, with my limitations, I was mostly content with my humble little shop and using the books I stocked as my escape.

As I strolled down the sidewalk, the tension melted out of my body for the first time all day. I allowed my mind to drift to a familiar daydream. I liked to visualize far off places, traveling to white sand beaches, old ruins, and beautiful rainforests. I wanted nothing more than to experience different cultures and see everything the world had to offer. Hopefully someday, if I could get over my shit.

Replaying this evening, my shoulders slumped. At this rate, these fantasies would more than likely stay dreams forever. Someday I'd like to hop on a plane and jet off across the world, but whenever the thought crossed my mind, my heart threatened to launch itself out of my chest. If I couldn't ever get past this panic, I'd never be able to travel.

The colorful sign hanging above my store flapped gently in the light breeze and snapped me back to reality. I was only about a block away from the storefront and the loft apartment I lived in above it. At this time of night, there weren't many people out on the street, and I could just barely make out upbeat music pouring out of the bar a couple blocks down. Nine o'clock at night, in Washington, in the summer, was a magical hour. The sun just finished sinking below the horizon, and the sky still shone with a hint of a pink glow that reflected off the surface of the lake a few blocks over.

Just before I reached my well-lit storefront, movement to my left caught my eye. I froze, my gaze settling on the black sedan parked in front of my shop. A woman struggled under the weight of a tall and muscular man who looked like he was utterly wasted. I could only hear snippets of their conversation, but she sounded frustrated and I thought I might be able to help.

My heart leaped into my throat at the idea of approaching a stranger, but I did it every day in my shop so I could do it now. I cautiously stepped over to where she was bending down and trying to shove him into her car. "Can I help you? You look like you're having a hard time."

She stiffened before turning around and glaring at me. "Just mind your own business," she snapped. I narrowed my eyes at her because fuck this bitch. "I was just trying to help. No need to be a dick about it."

Just as she opened her mouth to reply, the guy she was holding up decided to chime in. "She's a dick, isn't she?" he slurred. He tried to turn his head, and instead, his whole body swayed to one side. He had to have well over six inches and fifty pounds on the girl, and she didn't stand a chance. They both hit the ground, her body taking most of the fall. I choked back a laugh at the swift karmic retribution.

"Fuck this. He's not worth the trouble," she muttered, before shoving the man off and jumping into her car, slamming the door, and taking off with a squeal of tires. Well, shit. I looked down at the man sprawled flat on his back on the sidewalk at my feet, staring up at the sky and humming a song I didn't recognize.

My jaw fell open as I took him in because he was stunning—like sucked the air straight out of my lungs while my whole body tingled *gorgeous*. I'd never seen anyone like him before, and this intense desire to reach out and touch him pulled at me. I forced myself to close my mouth so the drool wouldn't leak out. Hey, I had my pride.

Even his unfocused attention on me had my body buzzing from head to toe, creating a longing I couldn't even begin to explain. My reaction to the super-hot stranger made my heart race out of control and heat spiral to my core. I tried to push down my body's response to him because I knew nothing about him, and I wouldn't take advantage.

He was several inches taller than I was, so he had to be over six feet tall with dark wavy hair cut short on the sides and longer on top, styled in a sexy side-swept way. His eyes were unfocused but piercing green. They almost looked like they were glowing in the minimal light. His square jaw was peppered with just enough stubble to feel rough against a girl's hand, not that I was picturing it or anything. His firm, muscular arms were covered in ink, beautiful tattoos that ran up the length of both limbs and peeked out of the neck of his black V-neck t-shirt. I wondered if he had ink on other parts of his body.

I swallowed, trying to compose myself. Had I already mentioned that forearms really did it for me? I knew I wasn't the only girl who liked them, either. There was a whole forum on the internet dedicated to sexy forearms, not that I spent a lot of time there. This guy could be their spokesperson, though. Damn.

My libido had clearly taken over from my sense of self-preservation. I made a split second and idiotic decision to take him home with me for the night. He'd just been abandoned, and once he sobered up, he could figure his own shit out. But for tonight, I had a safe place he could stay, and I would take precautions to make sure I didn't get hurt. I kneeled down beside him. "Think you can walk if we get you up?"

His unfocused eyes turned toward me. "Maaaaybe," he sing-songed.

I cocked my eyebrow, staring down at him. He'd gone back to humming, so I stood up and reached my hand out. "C'mon, let's get you inside."

I motioned for him to take my hand, but he didn't make a move for it. He looked like he'd be perfectly content to sleep out here on the sidewalk, but this neighborhood wasn't the safest at night, so I leaned even further over him and grabbed his arm, using all of my body weight to yank him up. When his skin touched mine, twirling energy sprang from the place our hands connected and raced through my body, making the tiny hairs on my arms stand up.

"Whoa," he said, stumbling to his feet before almost falling over again. I draped his arm over my shoulders. At five-nine, I was closer to his over six-foot height and didn't seem to be having as much trouble supporting his weight as that tiny bitchy girl had. There were only about fifteen steps until we got to my store, so I should be able to handle it. "Where're we going?" he asked.

"Into the store over here, okay? Just let me open the door." I leaned up against the doorframe while I dug in my purse for my keys. Swinging the door open, we stumbled our way into my store, almost falling over a couple of times in the short trip. There was no way he'd be going anywhere tonight. I wouldn't be able to move him again in his condition because he seemed to be getting worse, and it'd take him hours to sober up enough to leave. It took all my strength to keep him upright, and there was no way he could walk on his own.

I sighed. Hauling him up the stairs was going to be a task I wasn't sure I was up to, but I didn't have much of a choice. He couldn't sleep down in the store. I glanced around, taking in the tall shelves, large front window, and the small bakery and cafe area. I briefly contemplated setting him up at one of the small tables with mismatched chairs that I loved so much, but decided against it. He'd end up in a heap on the floor, and I just couldn't do that to him.

I locked the door and gripped the arm slung across my shoulders to hold him up. He smirked down at me. Carefully, step by step, we climbed the stairs to my loft apartment.

He leaned most of his weight against me, and I struggled to hold him up. My breath was labored by the time we got to the top of the stairs, as if I'd just run a marathon. Apparently, adding an extra two hundred pounds to your body made for great cardio.

I shoved open the door and dragged both of us inside, not bothering to shut it behind us, and stumbled to my bedroom. We bounced off the wall a couple of times, but I was glad for the added support. Once I decided he was too drunk to leave tonight, and needed a few hours to sleep it off, I figured the best spot to do it would be my bed. I could keep him confined to the one area and shut the door to keep him inside. It was an old building, so the door stuck. He'd have to yank on it pretty hard to get it to open, which meant it'd make noise and wake me up where I slept on the couch. So I could rest easier knowing he wouldn't be able to sneak up on me and try anything.

As an added layer of security, I'd text Amara and let her know what I was up to, too.

"Straight to the bedroom, huh?" he teased, swaying a little.

"Yep, lay back," I ordered. He flashed me a teasing grin, and his eyes were already half-closed.

He laid back on my pillows and closed his eyes the rest of the way. I pulled off his shoes and dug into his pockets to get his wallet and keys and phone out, too, because I'd have to roll him onto his stomach in case he threw up in his sleep. Plus, no one wanted to sleep on their phone.

I put everything on my nightstand and left the room to go get him a glass of water and some medicine he'd need when he woke up.

When I walked back into the room, he was snoring softly. I pulled out my phone and snapped a quick picture of him. If he was going to murder me in my sleep, I'd make sure Amara at least knew who'd done it and could get me some well-deserved justice.

I almost wished he hadn't passed out so quickly because I had questions. Who was he and why was he so messed up tonight? And why had that girl just abandoned him? Before I left, I penned a quick note that said 'take me,' leaving it next to the medicine and turned to make up the sofa.

I hesitated, taking a second to study his beautiful face. Typically, guys aren't referred to as beautiful, but he really was. He looked so peaceful, his long lashes fanned out against his cheeks. I resisted reaching out to brush the hair off his forehead and tracing his straight nose with my fingertips but just barely.

Where the hell did that come from? Good thing he'd be leaving in the morning, because I was a mess, and bringing someone into my mess seemed like the wrong thing to do. I couldn't even go out to a restaurant without losing my shit. No one needs that in their life. And that wasn't even taking into account my other issues when it came to relationships. Plus, for all I knew, that was his girlfriend who abandoned him earlier.

No, the less we interacted, the better. It'd been many years since I even considered letting a man into my life, not since my last failed relationship in high school that left scars that still hadn't fully healed. I didn't know if they ever would. I learned the hard way that men were just out to use me, and they'd crush me completely to get whatever they wanted. That was a lesson I had no interest in repeating.

I turned and tip-toed out of the room, stopping at my linen closet to grab a spare pillow and blanket. I'd be on the couch tonight, but I wouldn't be getting much sleep with my thoughts on the perfect stranger in my bed.

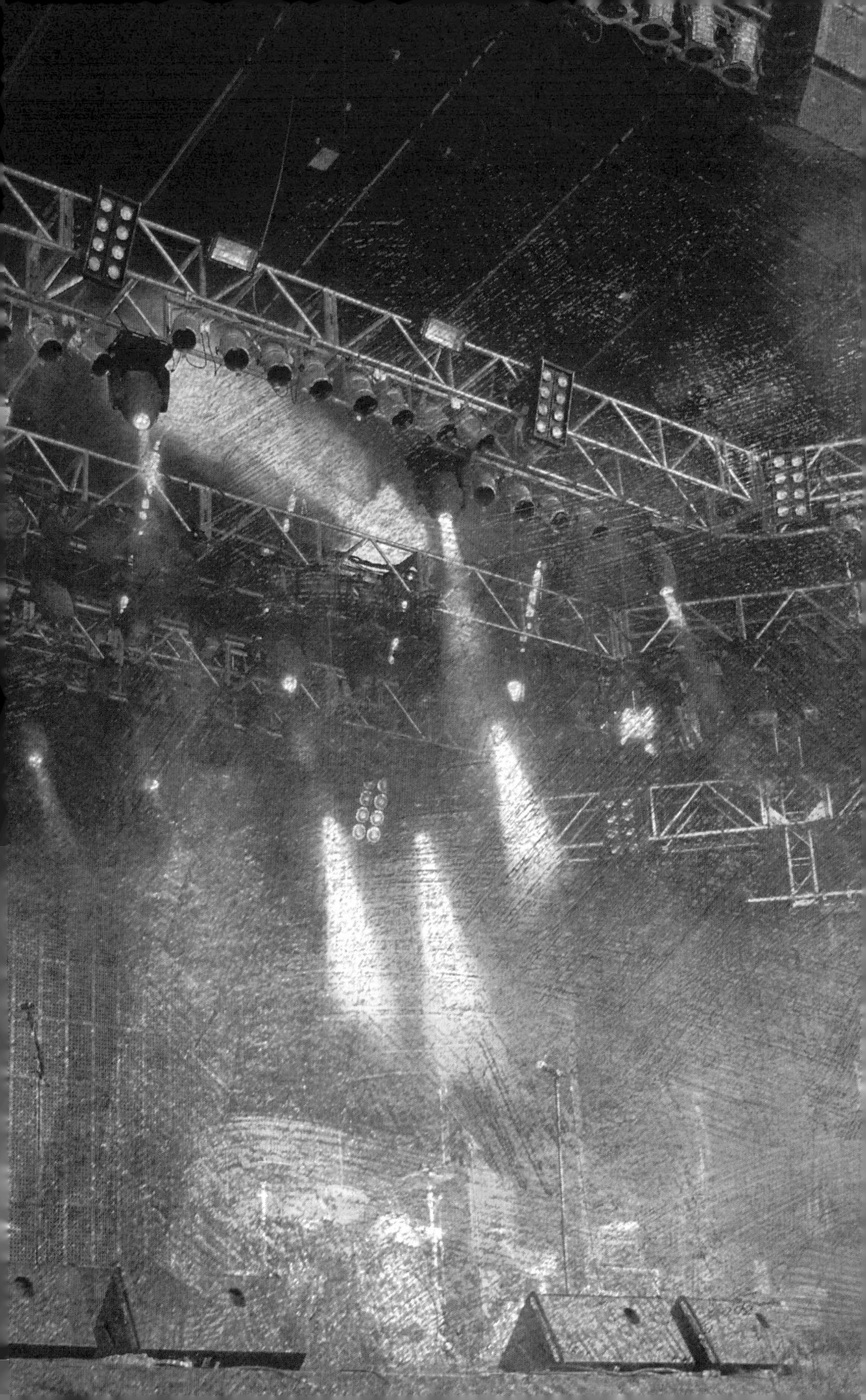

CHAPTER 5

ZEN

THE MOUTH-WATERING SMELL OF VANILLA, sugar, and coffee drifted through the air. I turned my head, forcing my eyes to open in a squint as I glanced around. I had no idea where the fuck I was. I slammed my eyelids closed, the pain of the bright room making my head throb ten times worse than it already was. I took stock of myself. Head pounding? Check. Strange bedroom? Didn't happen often, but check. Mouth dry as fuck? Double-check. Every part of my body hurt. At twenty-eight, I was getting too old for this shit.

I groaned and rolled over, again trying to remember where I was. What the fuck happened last night? I remembered walking into the bar and glancing around at the empty booths, and then my eyes slid over to the bar. My initial disappointment at the lack of prospects for the night disappeared when my gaze landed on the bartender. Her eyes ran down the length of my body before her gaze heated, and she flashed me a sultry grin. Her reaction told me she wanted me, so I figured why the hell not? Unfortunately, I couldn't remember anything after the first shot.

I wasn't a lightweight by any means. I'd built up my drinking tolerance over the years, so one shot should not have fucked me up like it did. Had she drugged me? I needed to talk to Connor about what happened last night, because if the bartender did slip me something, she needed to be dealt with. I scrubbed my hands down my face.

Maybe I was at her house. Shit. Usually, I brought girls back to my house so I could be in control of the situation. I couldn't remember the last time I'd spent the night anywhere other than one of my houses or a hotel.

I turned over and buried my face in the pillow, inhaling deeply, trying to calm my mind. It was way too early to deal with the shit I'd gotten myself into this time. The pillow smelled like it'd been line-dried in the sunshine with a hint of coconut, and it made me feel warm inside, like I was home. The kind of feeling people get when they go back to the place they grew up. Warmth spread inside me down to my toes, and I didn't want to get out of bed. I wanted to lay there and live in a cocoon of that smell and not face the reality I suspected was waiting for me.

Unfortunately, I had to because I couldn't just hang out at some random girl's house, if that's even where I was. Filling my lungs one last time, trying to commit the scent to memory and bracing myself, I slowly turned my head and glanced at the stretch of bed next to me. The blanket was smooth, tucked in tight, and the pillow looked unused. I glanced down at myself and realized I was fully clothed.

I propped myself up against the reclaimed wood headboard, and my eyes drifted to the mismatched nightstand. My phone was there, along with my keys and money. A full glass of water sat next to a bottle of painkillers. I picked up the paper lying next to the medicine. 'Take me,' it said in a curvy script. My mind tried to make sense of this morning, but I was lost. I couldn't remember anything from last night, and my brow furrowed in concentration as I tried.

Giving up, I shook a couple pills into my hand, popping them in my mouth then chasing them down with the room temperature water. I moved slowly, feeling the effects of my drunken night all over my body. My whole body ached, and I felt like absolute shit. I rubbed my eyes, running my hands through my hair. I was sure my eyes were bloodshot, my hair was a mess, and my clothes looked like I'd slept in them. I had no interest in doing my very own walk of shame, but it looked like I didn't have a choice. I could only hope that the paparazzi hadn't discovered my hideout yet. If they had, it wouldn't be the first time one of my hookups made a quick buck by selling me out.

I yanked my shoes onto my feet, knowing I needed to face the music and see what kind of mess I'd gotten myself into this time. Grabbing my phone, wallet and keys off the nightstand, I shoved them into my pockets. Stopping to listen, I tilted my head toward the closed door. Soft music played somewhere outside, so I tried to pull the door open, but it didn't budge. I pulled harder, and it flew open with a loud, scraping noise. I froze, listening, but I only heard the music coming from down the hall. I slowly walked in the direction of the soft notes.

When I stepped into the kitchen entrance, I froze again. My heart started to race. I clamped my mouth shut, which had fallen open like I was a goddamn cartoon character. The most beautiful woman I'd ever laid eyes on was in the kitchen, dancing erratically to a country music song pouring out of a speaker on the counter.

Her back faced me so I stood there and let my eyes roam freely. Her voice was off-key, but she had a blissful smile on her face as she danced around, turning enough so I could watch as she looked down at something she was stirring in the mixing bowl tucked under her arm. She closed her eyes as she moved around the room, getting into the song. Her blonde hair was wrapped up in a messy bun, and the tight distressed jeans she had on hugged her slight curves just right. As my eyes wandered back up her body, they stopped at her perfect tits, which were covered by a white t-shirt without a bra.

Fuck. Me.

I've hooked up with supermodels, actresses, and upper class socialites, and none of them could even compare to this beauty without makeup dancing in her kitchen in her bare feet.

One thing was for sure—she was most definitely not the bartender.

I needed to get my shit together and stop standing there staring like an asshole while my blood rushed south. All I wanted to do was wrap her in my arms and never let go. "Uh, hello?" I wanted to be smoother, I did. But since all of my attention was split right now, between keeping my dick in check and trying to fight off the pounding in my skull, it was the best I could do.

With her eyes closed and her voice ringing out above the music, she didn't respond to my attempt to get her attention. I cleared my throat. "Good morning," I said a bit louder. She yelped as her hand flew to her chest, dropping the whisk into the mixing bowl with a small splash. "Oh, my god! You scared the crap out of me," she said.

I laughed, holding my hands up to show her I wasn't dangerous. "I'm sorry, I wasn't sure what the protocol here was. What happened last night?" I found myself asking. I usually never talked to my hookups, but I wanted to get her talking and revel in every word she had to say. Figuring out who she was had to be high on the list, but if we hooked up, I should probably know her name so asking seemed like a dick move.

I cared less about what happened and more about who she was and where I was. I mentally patted myself on the back for a job well done at picking her last night, even if I didn't remember it. I couldn't remember the last time I'd fucked the same girl twice, but I'd make an exception for her. And next time, I sure as shit would make sure I remembered it.

She flashed me a dazzling smile, and a light, musical laugh escaped her lips. I absently wondered if I'd tasted those lips last night.

"You mean, you don't remember?" she teased as she put the bowl down.

"Obviously, I don't remember, or I wouldn't have asked," I pointed out, forcing my signature cocky grin onto my face. She just laughed harder.

"Obviously," she agreed. "Let's see, I was on my way home from dinner and was just about to unlock my door and head in for the night, when I saw your girlfriend trying to shove you into her car to get you home. You couldn't stand up and took her down in an epic tackle." She giggled, her eyes far off as she remembered. "She gave up and left you on the street."

Her nose wrinkled adorably and this weird fluttering sensation happened in my stomach. It was probably the hangover. "Your girlfriend seems like a real shit licker."

I choked on a laugh. Who the hell was this girl? Then I remembered everything else she said, and my stomach dropped harder than a Mike Tyson knockout. I'd never cared what I looked like before, but I didn't want her to see me that way. I didn't usually let myself get so hammered. It was best to walk a fine line when it came to getting drunk. I'd drink enough to numb any feelings I might have, but not enough to lose control of my ability to perform essential functions like walking, talking, or fucking. How the fuck had I gotten so messed up last night? And more importantly, why did I even care what this girl thought?

"You seemed like you could use a safe place to sleep it off, so I brought you in and put you to bed. I took the couch," she explained, pointing across the room to a cozy-looking sofa with about a hundred colorful throw pillows covering it.

"Do you make it a habit of bringing home strange, drunk men you find abandoned in the street?" I questioned, folding my arms across my chest and pressing my lips together. The idea of any other man sleeping in her house made me feel strangely pissed off, and I was practically knocked over with a fierce urge to protect her. What was she thinking? She could've gotten hurt. I knew I didn't have any right to voice my thoughts. I didn't even know her name for fuck's sake, and yet here I was, a hungover mess with my fists clenched ready to lay down the law.

"Yeah, that's a hard no. You're the first miscreant who's ever followed me home." She tilted her head to the side, and her blue eyes sparkled with mischief.

I let out the breath I hadn't realized I was holding, unsettled at the amount of relief I was feeling by her answer. She didn't seem to know who I was, or at least she wasn't letting on that she did yet. "Well, thanks for letting me stay. I'll get out of your hair." I started to turn towards the door, hoping she'd stop me before I got there. My brain wasn't working very well and I was having a hard time thinking up a reason to stay.

"Wait." I stopped, and a smile crossed my lips but I tried to hide it before I turned around. My eyes settled onto her face, taking in her bright blue eyes and her cheeks dotted with tiny freckles. "I made you some coffee and baked some blueberry muffins. I heard you shuffling around in my room, so I ordered you a ride. It'll be about fifteen minutes until it's here, so sit. After last night, I'm sure you could use some nourishment," she told me. What was this girl's deal? Women in my world just weren't like this. They were self-centered, demanding, entitled, and couldn't give a shit about what happened to me.

My stomach dropped for the second time this morning, and it had nothing to do with my hangover. Why didn't I want to go? I always wanted to get the fuck away from my hookups as soon as possible. Maybe it was the hangover, or maybe it was the smell of her bed that reminded me of home, even though my house never smelled like that. Or perhaps it was the girl standing in front of me with her wide, innocent eyes and how she'd taken care of me like no one else ever had. I tried to reason with myself. It didn't hurt that she was seriously fucking hot. I couldn't stop staring at her, and I had to clench my hands into fists to keep from reaching out and pulling her hair out of that bun and running my fingers through it while I kissed the hell out of her and branded myself on her soft lips.

"How do you like your coffee?" she asked, pouring me a mug and snapping me out of my fantasy.

"Black with a splash of cream."

She poured in a little cream and handed over my cup. I took it from her with a warm smile, my usual cockiness shelved for the moment. "Thanks."

"Sure. So, last night, is that a regular occurrence for you?" I had to hand it to her, she was straightforward as fuck with just a hint of teasing in her tone. She watched me intently with bright eyes.

I hesitated, not quite sure how to answer. "Why, you interested in joining me next time?" I flirted back, not wanting to give more of an answer than that. I didn't want her to think I was some alcoholic loser, even if the alcoholic part hit dangerously close to reality if I was honest with myself. Again I found myself wondering why I cared what she thought.

"No, I'm not sure your girlfriend would appreciate that."

"You keep mentioning this supposed girlfriend, but I'm not exactly the girlfriend type. Whoever she was, I didn't know her before last night." I wished again that I could remember what the hell had gone down at that bar.

"Oh." Her penetrating gaze studied my face before she smiled. "Well, I'm not much of a drinker. I was just curious what would be so bad in your life that you'd want to numb it away like that."

I blinked. What the fuck? I'd been talking to this girl maybe five minutes, and it was like she saw past all my bullshit. It scared the shit out of me. It was time to change the topic. "What's your name?" I asked her instead of answering.

"Kennedy. It seems funny to think we've spent the night together and don't know each other's names, even if we were in separate rooms," she laughed. "What's yours?"

I briefly considered lying. If Kennedy didn't know who I was, she would with one Google search. There weren't many guys named Zen, and none of them were as well-known as me.

If she did suspect, I'd be confirming it. I studied her eyes, and she looked genuinely curious. I decided to be honest. "Zen. Nice to meet you, Kennedy." I held out my hand, and she slid her soft palm into mine, squeezing firmly, and my skin tingled where we touched. "I don't think I've said thanks, but thank you for taking a chance on me. Who knows what would've happened to my drunk ass outside last night."

She let out another musical giggle that reminded me of tinkling wind chimes. I made a mental note to make her laugh as often as possible while I was here, so that I could hear that sound again. I tried to convince myself that she wasn't any different than the countless other women I'd met in my life, but it was fucking hopeless.

Shaking my head, I tossed back the last of my coffee and took my empty mug to the sink to rinse out. She turned around and took a tray of what looked like muffins out of the oven. "Let me wrap one of these up for you to take. You've gotta have breakfast. Then we can go downstairs and wait for your Lyft."

She handed me a hot muffin wrapped in a paper towel and I shifted it between my fingers because that shit was hot and burned my skin through the thin wrapper. Kennedy piled the rest on a tray and motioned for me to follow her. We walked toward the door, her with the tray propped up on her shoulder and me lagging behind so

I could take the opportunity to appreciate how her hips swayed when she walked, and let my mind wander.

Why wasn't she trying to get me to stay or asking for an autograph or picture? She wasn't even putting up a fight or throwing a fit when I was trying to leave. This whole morning confused the shit out of me, and I suspected I'd be thinking a lot more clearly if I didn't feel like a semi-truck ran over my skull. I wished she'd ask me to stay, but it wasn't my place to suggest it. I'd already intruded enough on her life.

Look at me, being all selfless and shit. Apparently I was capable of growth. Who knew?

Walking downstairs, I wanted to fill the silence with anything to get her to speak again, and I was curious as fuck about her. "So, was that country music you were listening to?" I asked her with a taunting sort of smirk. She glanced back at me, eyes narrowing as she picked up on my tone.

"Yes. What do you have against country music? It's pretty much all I listen to." She turned back around and continued down the stairs. I stepped closer to her, hoping to feel the heat of her skin close to mine again.

Her taste in music explained why she didn't know who I was, especially if she didn't read any gossip blogs or entertainment news sites. "I don't have anything against it. It's just not my scene. All the whining is a bit much." I suddenly needed to know if she read the news or tabloids, and I heard myself asking, "Do you read much?"

Her foot landed on the floor below the bottom step, and she stopped walking so abruptly that I almost slammed into her back. I grabbed the handrail to stop myself from running into her, but her scent moved around me, and I couldn't help the deep breath I inhaled. She turned around slowly with laughter in her eyes and a wide grin. Her body was close to mine, the heat that I'd been craving radiated off her and sank into my skin, making me want to lean even closer.

"Are you serious? Do I *read* much?" She threw her head back and burst out laughing. I glanced around her store, really seeing it for the first time. Christ, it was a fucking bookstore. Of course it was. I cleared my throat.

"Okay, that was a stupid question, but I was drunk off my ass last night and didn't remember what kind of store you had." Kill me now. How many times would I want to crawl into a hole and die of embarrassment this morning? When was the last time I gave a shit enough to even be embarrassed?

"What about the news? Do you follow it?"

She shook her head slowly, wiping a tear from her eye, still laughing softly. "No, I hate the news. It's always so negative. I mostly just read books. They're my escape. My friends think I'm crazy for ignoring the real world, but it keeps me sane to tune all the bullshit out. Know what I mean?"

Who was this girl? I struggled to wrap my mind around the fact that she was real. If I'd gone into a lab and dreamed up the perfect creature to complement me in every way, so far she'd be it. My curiosity about this stunning girl with the musical laugh who was entirely out of touch with my reality made me desperate to stick around, but I couldn't find a good excuse, and she wanted me gone since she'd called me a Lyft before I even got up. Of course, the one time I tried to stay, she didn't want me. That was a first, and it was uncomfortable as fuck.

She continued studying me, her blue eyes searching mine, but for what I wasn't sure. She quietly turned and walked to the cafe, placing the pastries she'd brought down in the display case. "Can I make you an espresso to go?" she offered with a smile. "Might help with the pounding in your head."

"No, thanks. I'm good." The Lyft had just pulled up outside. I wasn't sure what to say to her. I wanted to ask her to dinner, to see her again before I left, to actually get to know her and spend time with her which shocked the shit out of me. The last thing on my mind when I met a beautiful woman was getting her to talk *more*. Usually I wanted her to shut the fuck up and enjoy the ride, but not with Kennedy.

Not that I didn't want to explore every flawless inch of her body, but my curiosity ran deeper than that.

As bad as I wanted to, I knew I couldn't. She'd made it obvious she wasn't interested, but I wanted to get her number so I could regroup and figure out what to do next, because giving up wasn't an option. When I set my sights on something I wanted, eventually it would be mine, and Kennedy was what I wanted.

Before I could step up my game and grab her info the driver honked.

"Well, Zen, it was great to meet you." She held out her hand. Her eyes and the smile she aimed right at me were warm and sincere, and my chest tightened. My stomach flipped in that unsettling way it had earlier as I let my eyes linger on hers a second longer than I needed to.

I took her soft hand in mine, squeezing it gently. "Thanks, Kennedy. It was an experience meeting you. I hope our paths cross again." I surprised myself when the words crossed my lips since all my charm had flown out the damn window this morning. I hadn't had to work this hard to impress a girl in more than a fucking decade, and even then I couldn't remember having to try all that much.

"Really?" She looked at me with surprise.

Why did she look so surprised that I'd want to see her again? Didn't she know how breathtaking she was or the effect she had on me? "Yes, really, but I've got to run before this asshole bails on me." I pointed at the driver outside who leaned on the horn again. "I'll look you up the next time I'm in town," I called over my shoulder before stepping outside. I didn't get her number, but at least I knew where to find her.

Jumping into the Lyft, I gave the asshole driver the name of the bar from last night. I spotted my Mercedes in the parking lot, the morning sun reflecting off the chrome grille. The bar was a couple of blocks from Kennedy's store, and I wondered how I'd ended up with a random woman trying to kidnap me last night. Maybe it was time I figured out what the fuck I was doing with my life.

Pulling my keys out of my pocket, I stopped to check that I hadn't left anything behind when my brain was fuzzy earlier. I looked through everything to be sure I had my money, cards, and no one had gotten into my phone. It wouldn't be the first time some random girl robbed me or tried to break into my phone, but everything was fine. A smile stretched across my face. I knew she wasn't the kind of girl who brought that kind of drama or played those kinds of games, but those were dangerous thoughts. Letting someone into my life meant changing everything I knew, risking everything I worked for if I made a mistake and let the wrong girl in.

Was that something I wanted to do?

Fuck, it just might be.

It was time I went home and, for the first time in my life, figured out how to get a girl who didn't want me to give me a chance. I grinned. The chase was going to be fun.

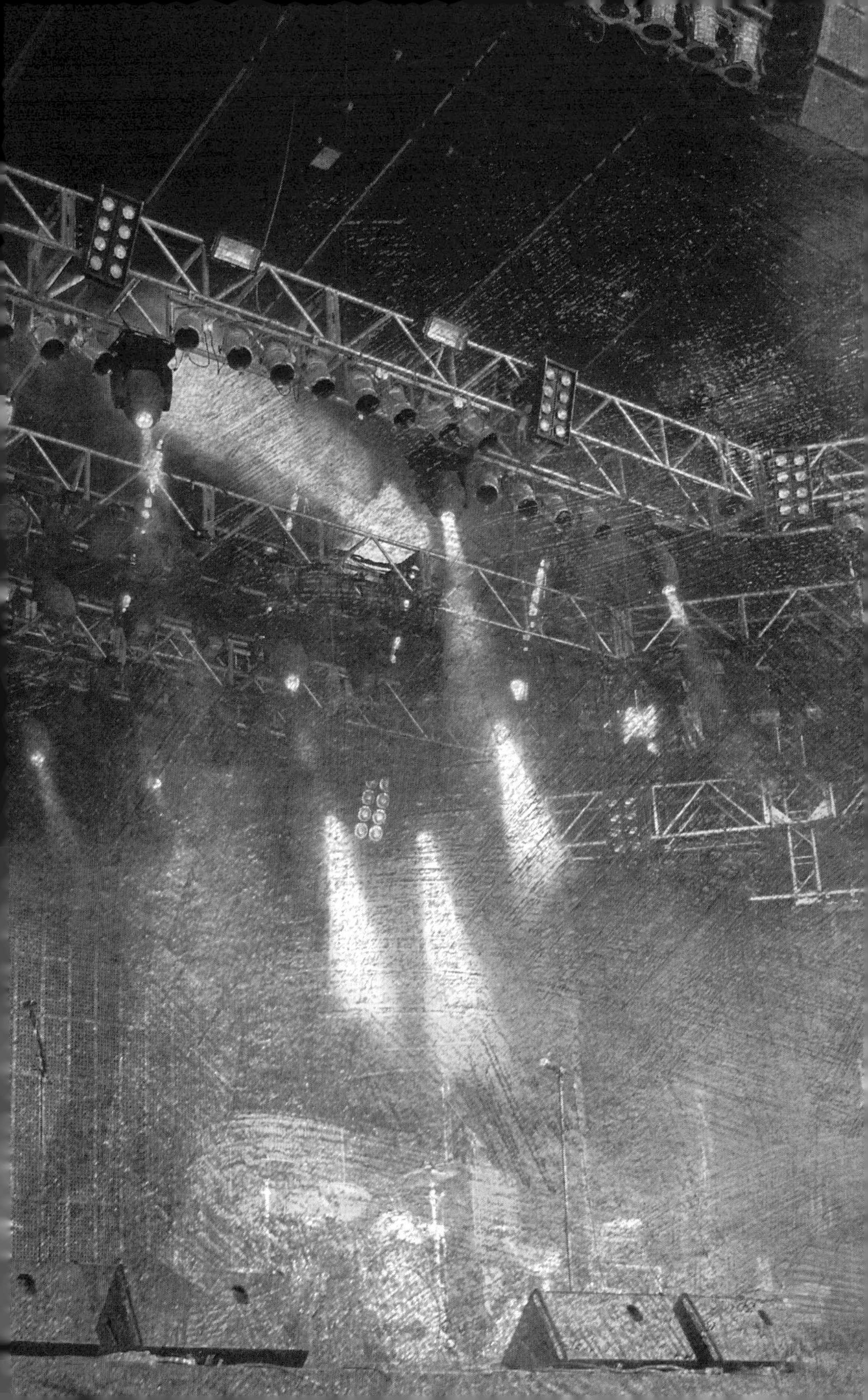

CHAPTER 6

KENNEDY

I LIFTED my turkey sandwich to my mouth, sinking my teeth into the soft bread and taking a big bite. I chewed slowly, my thoughts drifting to the man I met last night. Zen. Such an unusual name but somehow it fit his tall, dark, and fine as hell energy. Sighing, I reached for my water. Endless questions raced through my mind, none of which I had answers for. Why was he alone last night? Why was he so drunk? Why didn't he ask for my number?

At least it was a relief from my normal obsessive worrying.

I never gave out my phone number to anyone, but I wanted him to at least ask. I wasn't interested in letting anyone in, but for him, I might've considered it. The way he made me feel with just one look wasn't something I could easily dismiss. In fact, I was still obsessing about it hours later. He was a mysterious stranger, a puzzle that needed solving. Too bad I'd never see him again.

The bell over the door chimed, distracting me from my thoughts, and I turned my head towards the store entrance. The occasional straggler came into my store at this time of day, but it didn't happen often.

Amara, my gorgeous BFF and partner in crime, stepped into the shop with a massive grin on her face. "Ken! Tell me everything. How was your meeting?" She rushed the words out breathlessly, sliding into the chair across from me.

Where I was serious and weighed down by my anxiety, Amara was bubbly and fun. She helped balance me out, and I was incredibly grateful to have her in my life.

"You know, just the usual. Complete meltdown on my way there and the entire time I was in the restaurant. Oh, and Vincent Greene was a perverted jackass," I said, sighing heavily.

"You do seem to attract more than your fair share of those," Amara stifled her laugh, her hand flying up to cover her mouth.

"What did you do last night?" I asked, taking another bite of my sandwich.

"Nothing exciting. Video chatted with the team then Netflix and chilled with myself."

I laughed. "Sounds like my every night, except replace Netflix with a book and there's no *chilling*."

Amara narrowed her eyes before lifting my phone in front of her face, but she kept it low enough so we maintained eye contact. "Alexa, order the top selling personal massager and ship it to Kennedy Adams."

"What the hell?"

She laughs. "If you search vibrator, you won't get what you need. I've got you, girl. Two-day shipping."

"Jesus," I mutter, feeling my cheeks flame.

That glint she had in her eye made me sink further down in my chair. My poor sandwich was all but forgotten as my appetite evaporated. "Speaking of your love life…"

"You're such a twatwaffle."

"What? As your bestie, I have a right to know. When was the

last time you even thought anyone was interesting enough to eye-bang, let alone let them at your lady cave?"

"First, what the everloving fuck is a lady cave? Why would you ever call it that?"

She started cackling, like a legit head thrown back, deep throaty laugh. I hoped her stomach got all cramped.

"And second, we've been through this," I said, throwing my hands up.

"Remind me, it was what, high school? This has gone past the point of acceptable. It's been seven years, Kennedy—seven! You can't keep letting some asshole from high school ruin your life. It's time to get over it and move on."

I let my head fall to the table, resting my forehead on the cold surface and enjoying how it gave my heated cheeks some much-needed relief. "Look, I know you think I'm ridiculous-"

"Yep."

I lifted my head to glare at Amara, who had a smug smile on her face.

"Anyway, I've only opened myself up once because the trauma of it took years of therapy to get over. I don't think I have it in me to handle that kind of risk again. When you think a guy loves you, give him all of yourself, and then he takes it and tells the entire school you're a psycho as a way to break up with you, that's not something you just move on from. It leaves a scar."

I turned my face away from my friend, eyes brimming with tears all these years later like it just happened yesterday. The humiliation still haunted me.

Amara frowned slightly. "I know what you've been through, we've talked about it, and we don't need to rehash it. The problem is that you might be missing out on something great, just because some immature asshole hurt you way back. Please promise me you'll at least consider going on a date the next time someone catches your eye—or better yet, let me set you up."

I hesitated, inspecting my nails and picking at a non-existent hangnail to avoid making eye contact with my friend.

"Kennedy, look at me."

I lifted my chin, slowly shifting my eyes up until I met her concerned gaze.

"Promise me," Amara demanded softly.

"Fine, I promise, but no set ups." I shivered and let out a groan. Searching for anything to change the subject, I asked, "Guess what happened last night after dinner?"

"You came home and grabbed a book and went to bed?" Amara guessed, giving me a pointed stare. I couldn't fault her, she knew me and my routines so well.

"Yes and no. When I was almost home, this random guy was completely wasted, and this girl was trying to basically kidnap him. When he fell over on her, she took off and left him on the sidewalk. He could barely sit, let alone stand up and walk."

Amara snorted but didn't say anything, using her hand to gesture for me to continue.

"He was totally alone, and I felt like I shouldn't just leave him out there, so I brought him in and put him in my bed to let him sleep it off." Hearing myself recap the stupid risk I took last night made me want to hide under the table. How could I have been so stupid and done something so dangerous? That wasn't like me at all.

Inviting a strange man into my house for the night, when I knew nothing about him, was about as dumb as you could get. Apparently, my ridiculous childhood dream of being on the show Unsolved Mysteries was still in full effect in my subconscious. How else could I explain my actions? There was just something about him that made me say fuck it and bring him inside. There was something in those hypnotizing green eyes that called on me to save him from himself.

Amara's mouth fell open. "Are you kidding me? What the hell is wrong with you? Wait until I tell Grayson. He's going to flip the fuck out. I didn't realize you had a death wish."

I pointed my finger at her. "If you breathe one word of this to my brother, you'll break the girl code and it'll be the ultimate betrayal." She rolled her eyes but I knew I had her. "Didn't you get my text last night?"

She shook her head. "My phone screen shattered, and it's taking them way too long to fix it, so I'm back in the dark ages for a couple more days. Email or video calls on my laptop only."

Shit, well, it was a good thing nothing had happened last night.

"I know it was so stupid, Am, but there was something about him that made me want to help."

"What was he like? Was he super hot? I bet he was make-you-want-to-throw-your-entire-life-away-and-jump-on-the-back-of-his-motorcycle hot." In case it wasn't clear, Amara was a hopeless romantic with a bad boy fetish. Wait, was it a fetish if you were only attracted to assholes and guys you could never have?

"He was the kind of hot that made it hard for my brain to form words. But he also seemed kind of lost and helpless, sort of like a stray puppy. I felt like he just needed a break, someone to take care of him for a minute." I began twirling a lock of my hair around my finger absently while I spoke. "He was a total gentleman this morning, though. He sure as hell didn't *look* like a gentleman, but he was on his best behavior. I gave him some coffee and a muffin and sent him on his way." My shoulders drooped a bit.

"Wait, you want to see him again! Ha! This is amazing." Amara bounced a little in her seat, clapping her hands together. "And I'm going to need to know if he has a motorcycle. For science."

"I don't know, I called him a ride. Besides, I don't even think he was interested. He was nice, sure, and unreasonably hot, but he didn't ask for my number, and I didn't ask for his. I'm pretty sure he lives out of town too because when he was leaving, he said he'd look me up next time he was in town."

Amara looked thoughtful for a minute. "You never know what the future holds. Just don't close yourself off. You seriously need a little adventure in your life. Also maybe a big di-"

"Okaaay, Pervy McPerverson. Don't you have to get back to work?" I asked with a hint of a smile at the corner of my lips.

"I guess. I just wanted to see how your night went. I hate deadlines that require working on a Saturday. Text later? No wait, email me later? Ugh, I really need a backup phone."

I chuckled. "For sure."

Amara stood up and pulled me into a tight hug. "Don't do anything I wouldn't do! Love you!"

"Love you, too."

She turned, flipping her dark wavy hair over her shoulder and made her way to the door.

I tossed the rest of my sandwich into the trash and got back to work, wondering if I made a colossal mistake this morning letting the hottest guy I'd ever seen walk out of my life with nothing more than a muffin and a wave.

AS THE GOLDEN light of the late afternoon sun made its way across the tall shelves lining the walls, I looked up and wiped my brow with my shirt sleeve. Doing inventory on my entire romance section was no joke. The timer on my phone went off and I hopped up and jogged to the stairs, taking them two at a time and rushing into my kitchen to remove a tray of muffins from the hot oven and turning it off. Jogging back downstairs, I slid the tray into the display in the cafe just before the door swung open, and a couple of my regular customers poured in.

I leaned against the back counter, breathing heavily. Running my store by myself up to this point had been the right business decision, but it was getting too busy to keep doing it alone. The thought of hiring someone to help made me break out in a cold sweat, but insomnia and a pounding head that was happening more and more frequently told me my mind and body both were sounding the damn alarm. I needed some help.

Just as I was passing a still-warm muffin over the counter to a customer, the door jingled. My eyes shifted toward the entrance, and my breath caught. Oh, damn. The man from this morning, who'd been living front and center in my thoughts all day, just walked back into my store looking good enough to eat. Honestly, it wasn't fair. Men in real life just didn't look like that, did they? Yet here he was defying reality itself.

His hair was styled like the night before only neater. His muscular legs were covered by a pair of dark jeans, and a tight black t-shirt for a band I'd never heard of stretched across his well-toned chest and showed off all the ink running down both his arms. His biceps stretched the fabric to its limits and I found myself hoping it'd somehow rip right off. Maybe in a freak accident? Or maybe with my teeth.

He rocked a pair of mirrored aviator glasses better than anyone I'd ever seen. He pulled them slowly off his face, his piercing green eyes searching the room until they met mine.

Zen.

Those sparks of longing from this morning erupted into full-on flames with the heat swirling straight to my core, and a small gasp slipped past my lips. Why the hell was my body reacting to him like this? I had to look away before I embarrassed myself. My cheeks flushed, and I swear the room temperature went up by about twenty degrees. I stifled the urge to fan myself. Holy shit, how could he turn me into a puddle of neediness with just one look? It must've been his superpower.

My heart raced, and I knew I was in big trouble. I glanced back up, and his eyes were still focused on me as if he'd never looked away. He flashed me a crooked smile and slowly closed the distance between us with long, measured steps.

"Kennedy," his deep voice was low and inviting, almost a purr as my name rolled off his tongue and I shivered.

"Zen, hi. I-I didn't expect to see you again," I stammered, feeling completely out of my depth.

He frowned. "Oh? Did you not want to see me again?"

"No, no. It's not that. I mean, I don't really know you, but you seem like a nice enough guy. You just didn't seem like you were looking to make friends or anything this morning." *Stop talking, stop talking, stop talking. You aren't looking to make friends? I sound ridiculous.*

"You're wrong, Kennedy. I'm not a nice guy," he rasped, leaning in toward me and lifting his hand to twirl a lock of my hair around his finger.

"Oh," was all I could manage to squeak out. Parts of my body I'd practically forgotten existed clenched in reaction to his close proximity.

He smirked knowingly, releasing the lock of hair he'd been holding. I had a feeling Zen was no stranger to girls becoming idiots around him. "Actually, I left something up in your apartment. Mind if I run up and look for it?"

"Sure, let me just grab you my key. I can't leave the store, or I'd help you look."

I walked around the counter and bee-lined for the front register, trying not to trip over my feet while my mind and heart competed to see which could race faster. I reached into a drawer, pulling out a shiny silver set of keys and dropping them into his outstretched hand, being careful not to touch him. The last thing I needed was to give him another chance to see how tempted I was to jump on him. "Just bring me the keys back when you're done."

His eyebrows raised up towards his forehead. "You're just going to let some stranger wander around your apartment? I could rob you."

I laughed. "Somehow, I don't think you're going to be able to carry anything past me without me seeing you, since there's only one exit, and it's right there." I pointed at the door almost directly in front of me. "Also, are we strangers? We spent the night together. Doesn't that make us friends? Besides, you could've overpowered me pretty easily this morning and stolen whatever you wanted or… You know what? Let's just say I'm trusting my gut on this one and I think it'll be okay."

I met his intense stare with one of my own, challenging him to look away first, to see the honesty and openness in my eyes. For some reason, I needed him to know he could trust me. I'd show him mine to get him to show me his. If he decided he could trust me, maybe he'd let me in just a little. I still hadn't figured out when I'd decided I even wanted him to let me in.

He broke eye contact first, looking down at the keys. *Gotcha.* "Friends. I think, for now, I can do that. I'll be right back." His gravelly voice held promise that he wasn't done with me yet, and he turned on his heel and strode off toward the stairs.

For now? What the hell did he mean by that?

I watched him go, mesmerized by the firm muscles in his back as they flexed with every long stride and swing of his ink-dipped arms. In a futile attempt to forget the fact that the world's hottest guy was up in my apartment, probably digging through my underwear drawer, I forced my attention back to the register and helped the customer standing in front of me. He was a regular and gave me a curious look I chose to ignore, probably because he overheard the whole *spent the night together* part. Well, unfortunately for Thomas, my life wasn't quite that interesting.

I waved goodbye to my regular with a promise to bake him some lemon poppyseed muffins for next week, and then my distraction was gone.

What felt like hours, but was probably only a couple of minutes later, Zen was back, standing in front of me with an easy smile on his face. "Found it." He held up what looked like a silver triangle attached to a chain necklace before slipping it around his neck and handing me back my keys.

Stretching out my arm to take them from him, he caught my hand in his instead, his thumb beginning to move in gentle circles at the inside of my wrist, making goosebumps break out along my arm. I looked up and met his eyes, which had darkened. "Have dinner with me."

"Why?"

"What do you mean 'why'? You need to eat, I need to eat, and I want to get to know you better." He was still rubbing soft circles around my wrist, which made it hard to focus.

My heart started to race, and I wasn't sure if it was the closeness of him or the panic at the idea of something similar to a date. What if he wanted to go to a restaurant? Why *wouldn't* he want to go to a restaurant? He was a normal guy without all the baggage I carried around with me.

"Is this like… a date?" I asked, catching my bottom lip between my teeth.

"Do you want it to be a date?" He leaned in a little closer, his eyes dropping to my mouth and his tongue ran along his own bottom lip drawing my attention. His masculine scent swirled around me, and I had to hold myself back from inhaling until my lungs were full. He smelled like nothing I'd ever encountered before, like clean cologne and fresh air, and fuck it. I breathed deeply, inhaling as much of him as I could, before exhaling slowly as if reluctant to let it go.

Our bodies had leaned closer together, our faces only inches apart now and when I realized how close we were, I straightened and put some space between us. Zen was the type of guy who could have any girl he wanted. In fact, right now in my store no less than three women were ogling him unashamedly. No way was I going to make it easy on him and become another of his conquests. If he wanted me, he'd have to prove it.

That being said, I didn't want to miss out on a second chance to spend more time with him, so I decided to hit him with my conditions. "I don't date, but I could eat. I also don't do restaurants, so we'd have to eat here."

He leaned back a little, searching my face, but I noticed he held tight to my hand. "What do you mean you don't date?"

"Me and boyfriends don't mix. So, you want to get to know me? We do it my way and we do it as friends." *Stop saying 'do it,' for fuck's sake.* "So, if you're up for it, we can have dinner. Oh, and fair warning, I don't cook. In fact, I'm less than useless in the kitchen, outside of baking." I laughed nervously. My heart was pounding in my chest because I wanted him to agree, but also I didn't want him to at the same time. I wasn't sure which side I wanted to win.

"I don't know whether to be relieved I'm not going to have to fight anyone for your attention or pissed you're telling me I don't have a shot with you before you even know me, but you know what? I'm in. How about I cook? I'll be back in a couple of hours and help you close the store, then we'll eat. Sound good?" I was really into his whole take charge vibe right now. He was still holding onto my hand, his touch firm. Zen leaned in close and stared at me with a challenge in his eyes.

I exhaled loudly wondering what the hell I was doing. "Yes."

Amara was going to have a fucking field day.

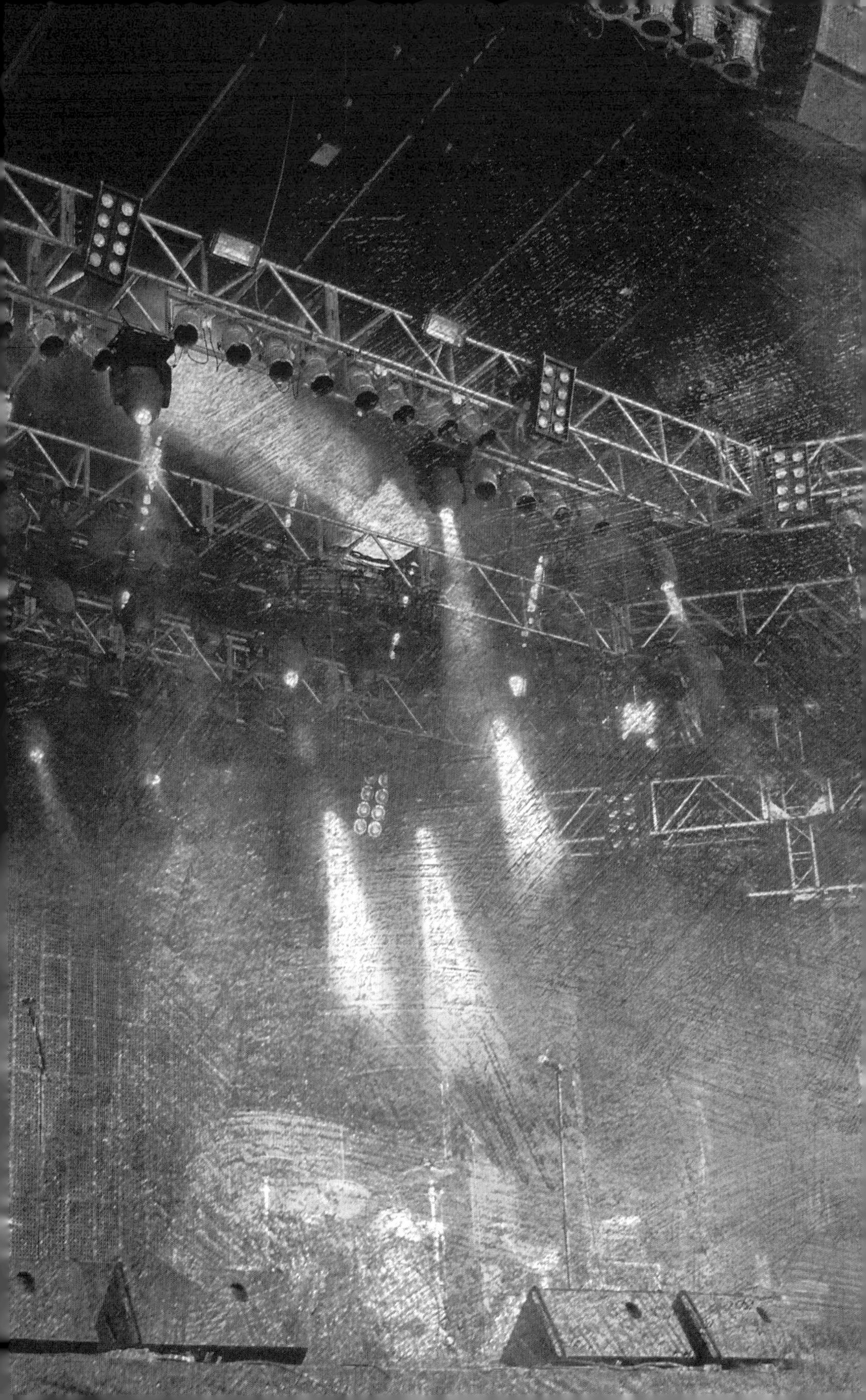

CHAPTER 7

ZEN

THE DOORS SLID OPEN SMOOTHLY and then *wooshed* shut behind me. Glancing around, I spotted a basket and lifted it, striding towards the colorful produce on display. When the hell had I last been to a grocery store on my own? Shit, it was easy to forget how many aspects of my life weren't normal sometimes. Besides, I didn't exactly fit in. In LA, I couldn't go anywhere without people swarming me and demanding pictures or an autograph, or a stupid fucking selfie, so my housekeeper did the shopping, or I ordered groceries online.

Thirty minutes later, walking out of the grocery store, I hummed a Shadow Phoenix song, one from our first album I hadn't thought about in years. My footsteps were light as my thoughts drifted to the evening ahead. I hadn't tried to date anyone in years. I just didn't see the point when I could get to the best parts without all the wooing shit. Then again, maybe no one had really been interesting enough to make me want to have more.

Kennedy made it clear this wasn't a date, but in my mind it sure as hell was. It didn't matter why she said she didn't date because I'd change her mind. There were a few things about her hesitation I liked, though.

First, even though she said she wasn't up for a boyfriend, she still agreed to a meal with me. She was definitely into me on some level. I smirked because I don't think I've ever met a woman who didn't want to fuck me at the very least. I could work with that.

Second, she didn't let men into her life easily, so there would be no competition. I was fucking thrilled about that second part.

These jealous and possessive feelings I had were a new and strange development since meeting her, and I wished I could say I didn't like them but I'd be lying. I never felt possessive over women. Why would I? There was always someone new to move on to.

Kennedy was different, though. She'd stepped up and took care of me when I was fucked up like no one else ever had, and her clear innocence was intoxicating. She was so trusting and naive, I wanted to wrap her in bubble wrap so the world couldn't taint her. She was also intoxicatingly gorgeous in a way that made me feel drunk with lust. I wasn't sure what I wanted from her yet, but I damn well knew I wasn't going to share.

Loading the groceries into the back of my SUV, I imagined what her lips would feel like pressed against mine, that moment where I would softly sink my teeth into her plump lower lip, teasing her mouth open and slipping my tongue inside to see what she tasted like. That thought led to my wondering what she'd taste like between her thighs and my cock strained against my jeans. Getting hard in a grocery store parking lot at the thought of kissing Kennedy wasn't going to help my public image problem so I tried to think about other shit, like the text Maddox sent me an hour ago detailing how he planned to get revenge on the bartender I'm about ninety-five percent sure drugged me last night.

It was in Maddox's hands now, and he was our fixer. It was hard to tell which he was better at—playing bass or getting vengeance. Whatever. He'd handle it, and she'd probably wish she'd never been born. Not that I cared how much he fucked with her. You drug people without their consent, you deserve everything coming your way. Knowing Maddox, her life as she knew it was about to come to a disturbing and painful halt.

On the drive back to Kennedy's store, I let my mind wander back toward our interactions, replaying them like a movie. How had she crawled under my skin so fast and so intensely? Keeping my mind off her was proving to be a real challenge.

I rubbed my jaw, feeling the roughness of a five o'clock shadow under my palm. Kennedy hadn't existed in my world just yesterday, but every inch I got closer to her store, my heartbeat increased. I didn't know if it was because I was excited or unsettled by what she was doing to me.

My phone buzzed, and I pushed the button on the console. "What's up?"

Connor's voice boomed throughout the cabin of the car. "Where are you? We need to talk about last night."

I glanced around the street in front of me, looking for any sign of my bodyguard. He could be stealthy when he wanted to, and I had no doubt he'd followed me up here on his own flight. It was his job even if I had fun fucking with him. "I assume you got my text."

He scoffed. "You shouldn't have gone to a bar by yourself. It was fucking stupid and look what happened."

I pulled up to the curb in front of Kennedy's store and threw my Mercedes into park. "Spare me the lecture, Connor. What did you find out?"

"The bartender roofied you. I took care of it. But if you go out drinking or put yourself in a vulnerable position again and don't take me with you, I'll make it my personal mission that you never spend even a second without a security detail. Whether you're taking a shit or fucking a groupie you'll have an audience. Are we understood?"

Letting my head fall back against the seat, I closed my eyes. The normal fight in me just wasn't there. "Understood. And Connor?"

"What?"

"Maddox is dealing with the bartender."

He chuckled. "Damn. She picked the wrong guy to fuck with, didn't she?"

"Yeah, and also I'm hanging out tonight at Sweet Stories."

"I know." He ended the call, and I shook my head. How the fuck he knew that was a mystery to me, but that was what he did. I wouldn't be surprised if he had one of his guys watching the store right now.

I took a deep breath and shook off the conversation, deciding to deal with the feelings around being drugged last night later. It helped knowing Maddox and Connor both had my back.

Turning toward the large front window, I looked over the exposed brick exterior painted in bright pastel colors outside Sweet Stories. You could see Kennedy in every inch of this place. Peering through the glass, I watched her, an easy smile on her face while she gestured wildly with her hands, talking to what I assumed was a customer. My fingers twitched with the need to reach out and touch her, to wrap my arms around her and pull her against my body. Shaking my head, I tore my eyes away, hopping out of the car and grabbing the grocery bags from the back.

When the bell above the door rang, Kennedy looked up as if she'd been waiting for me, smiling when our eyes met. My heart stuttered in my chest at the idea she was just as caught up in me as I was her. I walked over to where she was helping a customer. "Hey, gorgeous," I greeted her, leaning forward and reaching out to tuck that stray piece of silky blonde hair, that I noticed always fell in front of her face, back behind her ear. Touching Kennedy already made my list of favorite things to do, and my body begged me to do it more. "Can I have your key? I'll go put this away." I held up the bags in my hand.

"Yep, here ya go." She dropped the key into my outstretched hand.

I climbed the stairs, feeling her eyes on me as I went and getting a semi knowing she was watching me walk away. It sobered me when I realized how easily she'd handed over her key again. I was going to have to talk to her about not handing her key over so quickly to people she'd just met. She trusted too much, and she needed to knock that shit off before she got hurt.

The thought of someone hurting her had me grinding my teeth and clenching my jaw. I unlocked the door and went to the kitchen, putting everything away and trying to ignore my weird and fucking irrational feelings toward Kennedy.

I decided I'd head back downstairs to see if I could help her until the store closed. Hanging around her store gave me an excellent excuse to spend time around her, something I craved more and more with every passing minute. Spending time in public went against what my team told me to do, but I couldn't help myself. When it came to Kennedy, her light drew me in like I was a damn moth, making me want to get closer. Maybe in this case I was more like Icarus, flying dangerously close to the sun, but if I got burned, well, I had a feeling it might just be worth it.

Her sincerity and goodness called to the darkness inside me and made me want to consume it, to surround myself with it, to bathe in the glow of her innocence. Being around Kennedy made the risks worth it.

I stepped into the store, and the hairs on the back of my neck stood up as electricity sparked through my body. It was like I was already attuned to Kennedy, feeling the positivity she radiated.

My eyes fell over her lithe form, the evening sun's golden hue hitting her and making her look like an angel with the sunlight at her back. She animatedly chatted with an older guy, holding up a book and gesturing to the cover. Her eyes lifted and met mine, as if she could sense my gaze on her, giving me a small smile. Kennedy turned her attention back to her customer, and a heaviness settled in my chest at the loss. I'd never been jealous of someone over fifty before, but I wished her bright blue eyes were focused back on me instead of him. I fought the urge to stalk over and throw my arm around her waist and pull her against me, showing everyone who she belonged to. But she wasn't mine. Not yet.

I pulled out a chair and lowered myself into it, my eyes locked on her as she wrapped up the transaction. Handing the bag over the counter, she thanked the man and turned toward me. My eyes traced the length of her body as she closed the distance between us. I wanted her to jump into my arms, press her tight body against mine, wrap her legs around my waist....

My cock and I were in agreement. We needed to sink inside Kennedy and never come up for air. I shifted, not wanting to give away just how much she was fucking with both heads right now. She looked down at me and flashed that warm smile of hers, the one that pushed back my darkness. "Did you get everything you needed?"

"Yep, it's all put away. I thought I might help out down here until you're done for the day, if you'll let me." I chuckled, the idea that she wouldn't want my help striking me as funny. How many chances would she get to have a world-famous singer working behind the counter of her shop? Not that she knew who I was. "How long until the store closes?"

She cocked her head to the side and raised her eyebrow. "You want to help me with the bookstore?"

"Sure, why not? I'm not totally useless."

"Okay, well, we don't get a lot of cafe customers at this time of the day, but it would actually help a lot if you could hand out pastries if anyone comes in. We've got about half an hour left until we close."

"Perfect. Pastries I think I can handle," I said with a wink, before turning and making my way behind the counter. I could feel her eyes on my body, watching me walk away. I grinned, fucking thrilled she seemed to be just as affected by me as I was by her.

Moving behind the counter, I turned to meet her gaze, locking my eyes on hers until she blushed and turned to go to the cash register.

After the last customer left for the day, Kennedy locked the door, falling back against it and closing her eyes. She sighed with a small smile. "I'm starving. What's for dinner?"

I laughed. "Something ridiculous and fancy."

"Really?"

I chuckled. "No. C'mon."

I held out my hand, and she took it. I didn't waste any time lacing my fingers with hers before climbing up the stairs to her apartment. The place was cozy and already familiar. I'd kept the keys from earlier, so I took them from my pocket and pushed the key into the lock, turning it until it clicked. The door swung open, and we moved inside.

Shifting into the kitchen, I laid her keys on the counter but didn't let go of her hand. Her skin was warm, and her hand fit perfectly in mine. No longer being hungover, I glanced around her space with a clearer mind. I could walk from one end of the apartment to the other in just a few long strides, but she'd made it homey. Bright colors and green plants decorated every wall and surface. It gave off warmth and was bright with life just like her.

"Do you want a glass of wine?" I offered, grabbing the bottle of white out of the refrigerator.

"I'd love one, thanks." She smiled, sitting down at the island counter and looking at her fingernails, tapping her foot against the floor. With my back to her, I grinned from ear to ear. Her nervousness was adorable. I wondered if she thought this was a date despite what she said this afternoon. Between her body's reaction to mine, the way she smiled at me, and what I saw in her eyes, her attraction to me wasn't a question. Not that I had any doubts she'd like what she saw when she looked my way. I could tell she wanted me just as much as I wanted her, but she'd built a wall around herself to keep assholes like me out.

I would bring that motherfucker down.

I handed her a glass of pinot. "Here, Sunshine," I said with a smirk. She reached out and wrapped her long, delicate fingers around the stem of the glass, lifting it to her lips and taking a small sip.

"Thanks, but don't call me Sunshine." Her eyes flared, and she flattened her sweet plump lips into a line. I coughed to hide the chuckle trying to escape my throat. She was fucking adorable with her eyes narrowed, and her cheeks tinted pink in irritation at my impromptu nickname.

I held up my hands in mock surrender and finally released my laugh, "Sorry." I wasn't sorry at all.

I pulled open the refrigerator door, grabbed the ingredients out, and made my way around her kitchen. Kennedy's eyes never left me, quietly watching me work and taking the occasional sip of her wine. I liked that she was watching me. Her eyes followed my every movement as I worked, and it turned me the fuck on.

Her musical voice interrupted my thoughts. "What are you making anyway?"

"Lasagna. Is that okay?"

"One of my favorites. I can't wait to taste it."

I can't wait to taste you.

"Honestly, I'm a terrible cook, but I could try and help if you need it," she said.

"Nah, I've got this. Just get comfortable and tell me about yourself. Let's start easy. How long have you had your store?" I asked, continuing to chop vegetables while waiting for her to respond. I surprised myself when I realized I actually cared about her answer.

"I've had it for two years. When my grandma died, she left me a small inheritance. After college, I knew I wanted to run a bookstore. It's really all I've ever wanted to do, live in a world of books. Well, that and run a bakery. I can't cook, but for some reason, I can bake. I'm not a Michelin-starred pastry chef or anything, but I hold my own okay." She chuckled. "I think it's something about the chemistry of baking that makes sense in my brain."

She drifted off thoughtfully. Then she shook her head before continuing. "Anyway, I used what she left me to rent this place and open the shop. It's my own little piece of heaven, although it's been starting to get a little overwhelming." Kennedy rubbed her forehead before sighing and taking another sip of her wine.

"What's the problem?"

"I shouldn't complain," she laughed softly, and the sound made my lips turn up in a slow smile. "There are a couple of different things going on. The city is considering whether or not to allow rezoning. If they do, a developer is going to buy the building and force me out."

"What the fuck? They can't do that, can they? Just kick you out?" I questioned, already feeling my blood pressure rise.

"I have a lease, but yes, once it's done, they can. So, I've tried appealing to the city council, but it's been useless so far. There's one last meeting, but I don't know if it's even worth it to go." She sounded so defeated, I reached across the counter and squeezed her hand.

"You can't give up."

"I don't plan on it." She gave me a small smile, and I reluctantly let go of her hand. I wanted to tell her I'd fix this for her, deal with the asshole developer myself, but that meant admitting who I was and I wasn't ready to pop our bubble with the truth yet.

"On top of that, business has gotten a little too good, and sometimes it's hard to manage it all on my own. I'm gonna need to hire help soon, and I'm sort of a control freak."

She furrowed her brow and looked down as if she was afraid she'd revealed too much. Control freak? My cock twitched as my mind started to drift into dangerous territory, ways I could show her to relinquish control....

Then she lifted her head up, meeting my gaze. "How about you? What do you do?"

My shoulders tensed. I'd been expecting this question and still didn't know how I should answer. Getting Kennedy to tear down the wall she'd built around herself wouldn't work if I lied to her. I knew that. But how honest should I be? I needed to show her I was worthy of her trust before she knew the truth about me, which was a fucking conundrum. She was kidding herself if she thought there wasn't something between us. I was commitment-averse, and even I could see it. Getting her to admit to herself how much she wanted me before she found out who I was exactly would be crucial. Her body was already there, but her mind needed more convincing.

"I'm in the music business. I travel a lot for work, but I'm based out of LA. I try to come up here when I can, but it's not as much as I'd like." I hedged, deciding to be vague but as honest as I could be without giving away too much.

"Oh, that's pretty cool. I've never met anyone in the music business before, but I bet it's exciting. I'm jealous you get to travel for work. I've always wanted to travel," Kennedy said, with a wistful look in her eyes. I let out a huge breath, glad she hadn't decided to press me further on the details of my bullshit.

As I slid the lasagna into the oven and set the timer, I turned and walked around the island to where she was sitting. I grabbed her hand, tugging until she stood up. I planned on touching her as much as I possibly could get away with, without coming off as a creep. Touching her lit up my nerve endings like I'd never experienced before. She was like a new drug that only I had access to. Every place my body brushed hers or my fingers ran across her skin felt warm and electric. She squeezed my hand gently and smiled up at me as we walked toward the couch.

I sat, pulling her down next to me even though I really wanted to put her on my lap. I needed to keep my shit together and not freak her out. "That's better." I smiled, not letting go of her hand. I began tracing circles on her knuckles with my thumb, not missing the fact she hadn't pulled her hand away. "You said you've always wanted to travel. Why haven't you?"

Her shoulders tightened, and her voice came out in a whisper. "I don't know how much of my crazy I should let you in on. As soon as you know what I'm really like, you're going to run away, and I don't want you to go." She looked down, refusing to meet my eyes, like it took a lot for her to admit all that to me but I was fucking beside myself. This was going better than I expected—Kennedy admitting she wanted me to stay was huge.

But then the rest of her words sunk in. What the hell? How could she possibly think I'd bail once I got to know her? Admittedly, it was a dick move I probably would've pulled on any other chick in my past. She was different, and so far I didn't think I'd done anything to show her I'd bolt.

I clenched my jaw, fighting back an absurd wave of anger at some nameless person from her past that put the stupid as fuck idea in her head that she wasn't allowed to be human and have flaws. Whoever made her feel she wasn't worthy of anyone sticking around once she let them in had just rocketed to the top of my shit list. Everything she'd shown me so far made me look at her with nothing short of reverence. Anyone who'd tarnished her light would suffer if I ever found out who they were.

Struggling to calm myself down, I let go of her hand and reached underneath her chin, tilting her face up until her ocean eyes met mine. I could get lost in their depths. "Whatever you're about to tell me, know you'd have to drag me out of here to get rid of me no matter what it is. I want to know you, the real you. If you don't feel comfortable opening up to me yet, that's okay. We'll get there. But we are going to have this conversation at some point, so you might as well get it over with now." I smiled, trying to reassure her that I was sincere, never letting my eyes waver from hers.

She looked back at me with uncertainty, but I saw the moment she decided to let me in. A resignation crossed her gaze, and the storminess in her eyes was replaced with fear. "You're going to run," she whispered.

"Try me. I bet every dollar I have I won't," I challenged. It was a *lot* of dollars, but she didn't know that.

"You have no idea how hard this is for me. I don't let people in. Not ever."

"You can trust me."

She laughed a humorless laugh. "Yeah, I've heard that before." She sighed, grabbing my hand as if it was a lifeline. I smiled and gave her fingers a gentle squeeze.

She let out a shaky breath. "You asked for it."

"I did," I smiled again, leaning back into the couch and making myself more comfortable.

"Okay, well, I've never traveled because I can't. There's a lot of things people would consider normal that I just can't do. That's why we're eating here tonight instead of going out."

My brows furrowed and I frowned. Kennedy seemed completely normal to me. I waited patiently for her to continue, lifting my hand to tuck that stray piece of soft hair behind her ear to let her know I wasn't running away.

"What I mean is, every time I try to do any of those things, I lose my shit. I have a panic attack. I don't know if you even know what that is, but it's not cute. It's not fun for anyone in my life to deal with, and it's pure hell for me, but I don't know how to stop it. I look like a complete psycho and it basically controls my life. Staying in control of everything I can is how I keep my day to day life somewhat normal, but if I deviate from that at all, my asshole anxiety kicks in and makes me think I'm going to die. I don't take risks, I don't try new things, I don't let people in. Ever. It's how I keep things even, how I keep the panic somewhat in check." She sagged, as if she carried a crushing weight on her shoulders.

"Pretty much my whole life is a shitastrophy."

I choked on a laugh. "What the fuck is a shitastrophy?"

"Basically a shit storm and a catastrophe all rolled into one colossal fuck up." Her eyes were still wary but a little grin tipped up the corner of her lips.

I sure as fuck hadn't been expecting all that to come out of her mouth, but I didn't think she was mental or unhinged. I'd seen that shit in some of my fans and it didn't look like Kennedy. If anything, she struggled with control and fear, but to me, she came across as someone who was strong and capable. I had no doubt she'd figure out how to get past it when she was ready.

At the moment, I felt oddly protective of her. There was an ache in my chest at the shitty way she saw herself. How many times in one day could I want to wrap my arms around her and push the world out, take her fear away, and shield her from everything?

But keeping her locked up wouldn't be fair. I saw the determination in everything she did, from the passionate way she talked about books with her customers, to how she danced in her kitchen and sang off-key to country music. This girl deserved the world, and I was going to help her take it for herself.

"Don't freak out," I told her, and she tensed next to me, bracing for the rejection she probably assumed was coming. "I'm not running," I reassured her, squeezing her fingers again. "I want to help you."

She sighed, her shoulders relaxing a little. "I appreciate that you're not running for the hills. Really, I do. But I've seen therapists off and on for years, and none of them have done anything for me. In fact, I'm pretty sure I'm worse now than ever. What makes you think you can do any better?"

"I don't know just yet, but I'm going to," I vowed, feeling a renewed sense of purpose for the first time in years. "I need to. Maybe you've never had the right motivation." I flashed Kennedy my cocky smile, the one I used when I wanted to project confidence on stage or make a girl's panties hit the floor. "Will you trust me?"

She exhaled slowly. "I don't know, I'm scared," she admitted, biting her lower lip.

"I know, but for some reason, I believe in you. We've only known each other for a minute, but so far, the woman I've seen is pretty fucking incredible. She's smart, beautiful, clever, passionate, and doesn't take shit from anyone. C'mon, let me help you." I wasn't above begging. I also didn't know what the fuck I was doing, committing to helping this girl. I barely had time to deal with my own shit, let alone take on someone else's. But right now, I didn't care. Something inside pulled me toward her and wouldn't let me ignore the fear in her eyes, so I'd make the fucking time.

She held my determined gaze for what felt like forever before finally sighing. "You know what? Why the hell not? I've tried everything else at this point. Yes, Zen. I'd really appreciate your help."

I smiled and pulled her towards me, wrapping my arms around her in a tight hug like I'd been dying to do since the first time I saw her. Taking a second to appreciate how perfectly her body fit against mine, this sense of completeness rolled through me like I didn't think I'd ever felt before. I made a mental note to research panic attacks and formulate a plan later tonight because I sure as hell wasn't about to let her down. Right now, though, she relaxed into my arms, and I turned my head into her neck and breathed in deeply. She smelled like the outdoors on a sunny day and coconut, the same scent surrounding me on her sheets this morning, the one that reminded me of home.

Kennedy pulled back, her eyes brimming with tears. One tear slid down her cheek, and I reached up and wiped it away with my thumb. "Hey, what's with the tears?" I teased gently to cover up the fact that it absolutely fucking killed me to see her cry.

"It's just tough for me to open up about this stuff, and the fact you haven't left yet, it's hard for me to process," she admitted, wiping at her eyes. "I'm still waiting for the other shoe to drop and you to act like every other dickhead who's pretended they cared about me."

Sighing, I pulled her back against my chest and held her even tighter. "I'm not going anywhere," I mumbled into her hair as she held my shirt tightly in her fist.

"I think I believe you."

We sat in comfortable silence for another few minutes before the timer went off, breaking the spell. I stood, crossing the room to get our dinner out of the oven, and Kennedy followed. We moved around the kitchen like we'd done this a thousand times before. I knew I should probably have been freaked out by how quickly and easily she'd slipped into my life, but I wasn't. It was as if we'd known each other for years instead of hours.

Sitting down at her small table, she took a bite of the lasagna, and her eyes fluttered closed. She moaned appreciatively. "Oh, yum."

I stopped my fork midway to my mouth, eyes wide. Her little moan had my cock hard in record time. Fuck. Me. "Kennedy, you can't make those noises, or I'm going to skip dinner and go straight to dessert." I narrowed my eyes at her, daring her to do it again. I wasn't bluffing. I knew she wanted me, and it already took all my restraint to not make a move because I didn't want her to be like every other girl. Damn, though. I wasn't a fucking saint.

She looked at me with wide eyes. "What?" she squeaked.

"You heard me. No more moaning when you eat unless you want me to bend you over this table and show you just how much fun it is to scream my name. I promise it'll happen if you keep that up."

She cleared her throat, grabbing her wine glass with a shaky hand, taking a sip to try and steady herself. I saw her cheeks turning pink, and before she glanced away, I caught what looked a whole hell of a lot like desire flash in her eyes. "Okay, well..." she drifted off. I could only assume she was trying to think of something to clear the electric tension out of the air. "Tell me about your friends."

I threw my head back and laughed. "I'll let you change the subject for now, Sunshine, but we're going to circle back at some point because in case you haven't realized it yet, this," I motioned between her and me, "is inevitable. Friends, let's see..." I said, considering again how much information to give her. "I have three best friends, True, Maddox, and Jericho. We've known each other for years, since high school. They're like my brothers."

She tilted her head slightly, eyes softening as she studied me. "You love them, I can tell. I'm glad you have them."

"I'd say it's more of a love-hate relationship, like we're real brothers. We'd do anything for each other, but we also piss each other off all the time. Maddox, in particular, likes to get under my skin and I want to kick his ass almost every day. True, he's the sweet one. He's a closet romantic and the peacekeeper of our little group. And Jericho mostly keeps to himself, but when he does open his mouth we all pay attention. He comes across as shy, but he's not. He's more like a reserved psycho who's careful about when he lets the darkness out, but he's also a sarcastic asshole with his own set of issues."

"They sound awesome—well, maybe except Jericho. He sounds terrifying. But it's cool you have such a tight group and have managed to not only keep in touch but stay close after you graduated." It was refreshing to be able to talk about the guys without her knowing who they were or having an opinion about them before now. Plus, no one ever bothered to look past the persona I put out, one I'd worked to perfect, so her open curiosity was refreshing as hell. I needed to watch what I said around her, though, because she picked up on everything.

"Maybe you'll get to meet them someday."

The rest of our dinner passed with a mix of casual conversation and comfortable silence. When we finished, Kennedy helped me carry the dishes to the kitchen. She turned to me, her eyes twinkling. "Do you want to stay and watch a movie?"

Fuck yes, I wanted to stay. "What movie?" Not that it mattered. She could've wanted to watch a documentary on veganism that featured a shit ton of slaughtered animals and I'd have happily agreed.

"I don't know, we can pick something on Netflix. What kind of movies are your favorite?"

"I don't really watch a lot of movies." I didn't have time, but I wasn't about to tell her that.

She frowned. "Oh, well, neither do I. We don't have to watch a movie, though. We can binge a couple episodes of a show if you want. There's a new show I've been dying to watch about a group of kids and some supernatural stuff. It looks awesome," she said, her eyes dancing.

I laughed at how adorable she was when she was excited. Or anytime, really. "Let's do it," I agreed, taking her hand and leading her back to the couch.

Two episodes later, Kennedy's head rested on my shoulder, her warm body curled up against me, totally asleep. I didn't want to move and wake her, but I needed to go home and figure out how to help push her past her anxiety. My new passion project. I gently pressed my lips to her forehead. "Kennedy? I'm going to carry you to bed, okay? Just wrap your arms around my neck."

"Zen?" she quietly breathed my name, reaching up and doing what I told her to with clumsy movements. My chest constricted at the sound of my name on her lips.

I picked her up and carried her into her room, gently setting her on the soft mattress. Covering her up, I leaned over to kiss her on the forehead. Just as I was turning to leave, she reached out and grabbed my arm. "Come back in the morning. I want to take you somewhere," she murmured.

She didn't know it, but I already planned on showing up at her doorstep first thing in the morning. If I weren't trying to be better than I actually was, I'd convince her to let me stay the night. But Kennedy deserved the best version of myself, even if it was bullshit. There was nothing good about me. "I'll be here," I assured her.

Dating was a completely foreign concept to me, but this evening hadn't ended at all like my typical nights out did. I fucking loved every second of it, right down to the chaste kiss I'd left on the smooth skin of her forehead.

I turned and made my way to the living room, picking up her phone and programming my number into it. I snapped a selfie and set a unique ringtone just for myself, a slow smile spreading across my face. I knew she'd be familiar with the song, and I wanted to convey a message to her about my intentions with the lyrics. I'd only known her for a short time, but I already knew I wasn't about to let her go. It scared the shit out of me, but I never shied away from fear. She challenged me and pulled me out of my own darkness, even if just for a little while. She made me feel alive. The desire to help and protect Kennedy, not to mention the insane attraction I had to her, was overwhelming all my other senses and I already knew I was a goner.

I sent myself a quick text from her phone so I'd have her number and then left the house, keeping her key so I could lock the outer shop door. For the first time in as long as I could remember, I wasn't drunk and didn't want to be. I had a mission to make Kennedy whole and then I'd make her mine.

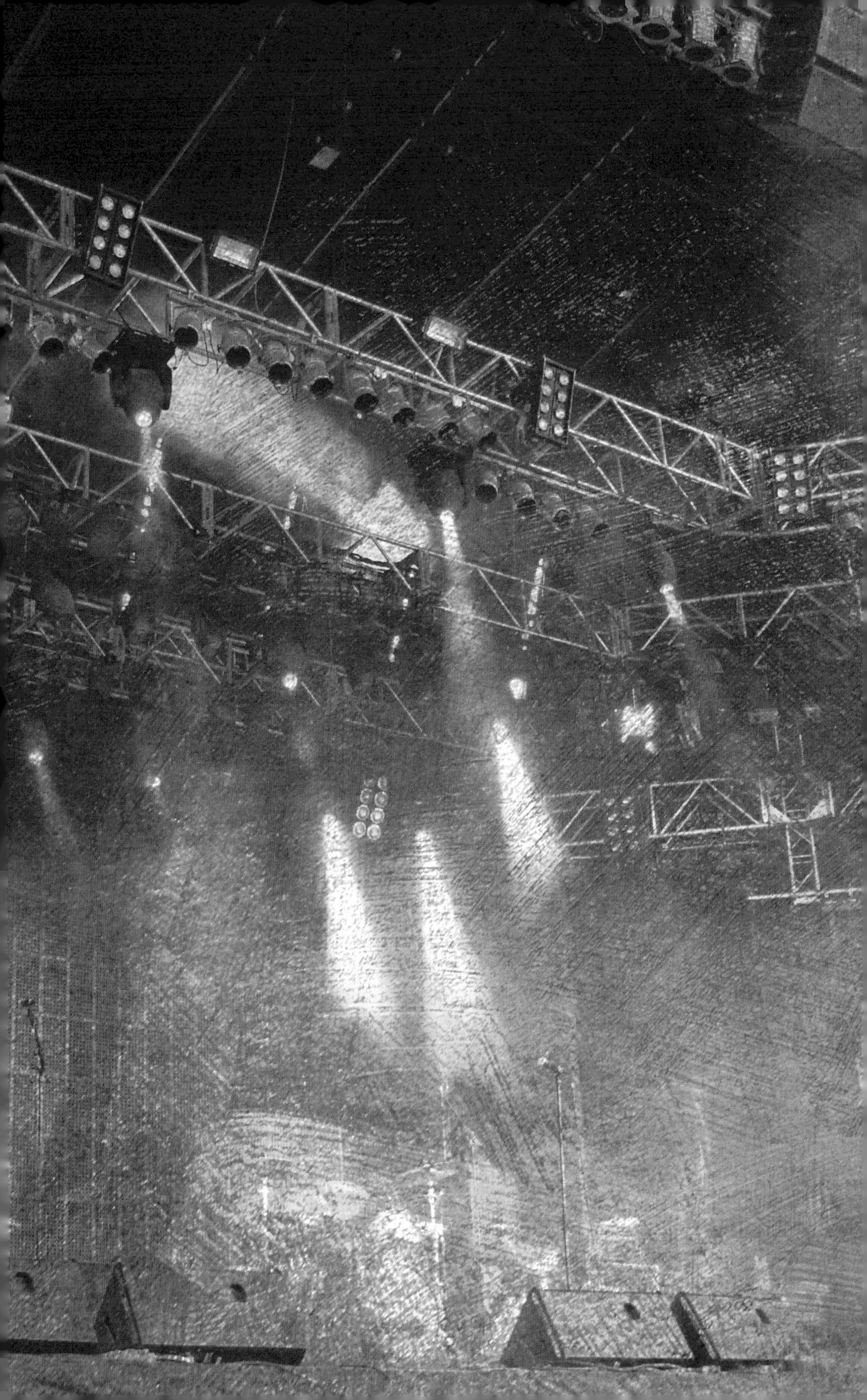

CHAPTER 8

KENNEDY

STRETCHING MY ARMS OVERHEAD, I arched my back against the soft cotton sheet underneath me. I reached my hand out to find the bed next to me empty. A flash of disappointment caught me off guard. Waking up alone every morning was my norm. This morning, for the first time, I wished things were different. A stupid grin took over my face as I remembered my night with Zen. Now he knew my biggest secret, the one I kept from everyone except the people closest to me. I felt so comfortable with him already and I didn't know why, but now my fucked up-ness was out of the bag.

Surprisingly, he stayed even after he knew. He stayed with me, sweetly lifting me into his arms and tucking me into bed before leaving like a perfect gentleman. For two nights in a row, Zen was the last thing I thought about before I fell asleep. A girl could seriously get used to that. My mind was occupied with questions and fantasies about the green-eyed, inked up mystery man who'd shown up practically on my doorstep.

Fighting the gravitational pull toward him felt impossible. My walls were crumbling, and for once, I didn't want to put them back up. Remembering his promise to come by this morning, the butterflies in my stomach took flight. Zen was so hot his very presence did things to my body—tingly, buzzing things that made me want so much more. He barely had to look at me, and I was a turned on mess with ruined panties who could barely remember her own name. His threat to bend me over the dining table last night? I had to bite my cheek to keep from saying *yes, please*. I just hoped a cold shower would be enough to get me through today without coming off like a horny teenager.

The last thing I wanted was to be just another girl who threw herself at Zen, because I was sure it happened all the time. I wasn't jealous *at all*. Not even a little.

I snorted because I was such a fucking liar.

Sundays were my free days when I closed down the shop, and I planned to make the most of this one. Zen wanted to know me, and now that I was saying fuck it and letting him in, the real me was what he'd get.

Notes of a familiar song played softly from down the hall, barely reaching my ears all the way back in my bedroom. I pushed off the blanket and hit the ground running, wondering where the music was coming from in the living room. My phone screen illuminated with Zen's grinning face. I checked the time.

Eight a.m.

I hesitated for a second, listening to the song he'd programmed in as his ringtone. *What Ifs* by Kane Brown.

He couldn't have known this song was one of my favorites. No way. What made him pick it? He knew I loved country music, maybe it was random, but somehow I doubted it. The song was romantic and beautiful, describing the kind of love story I'd always hoped to find. The lyrics described exactly how my anxious brain worked, with all the what-if questions that continually ran through my mind but in such a perfectly sweet way.

He couldn't possibly mean those things... could he?

Even if he did, knowing about my crazy and seeing it in action were two different things. It was all fun and games until the psycho came out to play. Before the phone stopped ringing, I picked it up, smiling. "Hello?"

I heard the smile in his voice as he said my name, his voice low and gravelly. "Kennedy. Good morning, beautiful." I shivered, but not because I was cold.

"Yes, it is. A good morning, I mean." My voice sounded steady even as my heart raced.

"Did you sleep well?"

"I did. Thanks for putting me to bed last night." I missed him. I couldn't wait to see him again, and it had me rattled. Letting people in was dangerous, especially someone who potentially had the power to break my heart. Zen looked like he had the whole *heart-breaker* vibe down to a science.

Who even was I right now? Amara was right—I needed to get past my relationship hang-ups, no matter how scared I was. I pushed those thoughts away to figure out later.

He chuckled. "It was hard to resist crawling in there with you. You looked so comfortable."

"What can I say? I'm a deep sleeper and also an excellent snuggler, so maybe next time," I flirted, feeling lighter than I had in weeks and also wondering what the hell I was doing. Making my way to the kitchen, I propped my phone between my shoulder and ear and started making coffee. "Do you have plans today?"

"Yep, with you. You asked me to come over this morning, remember?" He asked with amusement coloring his voice. "I was just calling to say good morning and ask what time you want me there. Oh, and I kept your key last night. I had to lock the door when I left, so I figured I'd bring it back this morning."

"Oh, perfect. Thanks for that. I'm usually not that irresponsible. I've just been running around like crazy lately, and I guess it's catching up to me." I sighed. "Anyway, give me an hour? Then I'll have everything ready."

"Is this a date?" he practically purred with that voice of his that I swore could make the devil himself cry, it was so sensual.

"Um, no. I don't date, remember? We're friends doing an activity together." Why had I made that stupid no dating rule a thing? I really, *really* wanted this to be a date.

He cracked up, and damn it, even his laugh was sexy. "Sure, keep telling yourself that, Sunshine. I'll see you in an hour." He hung up before I could give him shit about that nickname. I'd never admit that every time he said it, my stomach flipped and a thrill ran down my spine.

I bounced from foot to foot, my pulse quickening. I couldn't wait to spend the day making Zen smile, watching the way his green eyes crinkled up when he laughed, or listening to his sultry voice as we got to know each other better. He made me feel at ease, reassuring me, and comforting me with small gestures like holding my hand, or hugging me when I needed it most. I was sinking into dangerous territory with him, the kind that made me feel like I didn't want to be alone anymore. The kind that made me want to depend on him and lean on him when I struggled.

See? Dangerous.

I ran to take a quick shower. Even though this technically wasn't a date, I wanted Zen's jaw to drop when he saw me. He wasn't shy about the fact he thought I was hot, but I wanted to make him look at me like I was the only girl in the world. Glancing in the mirror, I noticed the pink tint of my flushed cheeks. My golden hair fell around my shoulders in soft waves, but makeup wasn't really my thing. I added a little mascara and lip gloss and called it good. Mascara made my bright blue eyes pop, and I wanted to highlight my best feature.

Pressing my lips together, I rested my hands on my hips and took in the chaos of my closet. I wished Amara was here. Jeans and t-shirts were my thing. Date outfits weren't a thing where I was concerned, so I was totally lost. Not that this was a date.

Running my hand along the soft cotton and rough denim material hanging along the wall, nothing jumped out at me. I put my hand up to my face and closed my eyes, taking a steadying breath. I could do this.

Reaching into the very back of my closet, I pulled out a blue floral print knee-length dress with a sweetheart neckline. Perfect. I threw the dress on and added some nude colored wedge heels I found in a box shoved underneath a pile of scarves in the corner.

Being a tall girl meant next to never getting to wear heels, so finding these in my closet was a pleasant surprise. Usually, I didn't bother buying anything taller than a flat, so I wouldn't draw attention. Like with so many things, Zen was different. I *wanted* to draw his attention. He towered over me, and I reveled in it. The only other person in my life that made me feel petite and feminine was my twin brother Grayson since he was well over six feet tall.

Twirling once in my dress, I grinned, bouncing on my toes and catching myself on the kitchen island as I almost fell on my face. I hoped I didn't make a fool of myself in these shoes. Grabbing my picnic basket and a tote bag, I started shoving everything I thought we'd need into the canvas bag. It overflowed with picnic essentials as my arm shook with the effort of pushing more and more on top of the already huge pile spilling out the top.

I set the overflowing tote bag aside and grabbed a bunch of lunch ingredients out of the fridge, spreading them out on the counter. Assembling sandwiches took no time, and I started packing everything tightly in a cute little wicker picnic basket I'd snagged at a thrift store for five bucks. I knew we'd be passing by my friend Oscar today, too, so I made a couple extra sandwiches and set them aside. Just as I was tucking the last of the food into the basket, a couple hard taps sounded against the wood of my front door before it swung open and in walked the most gorgeous man I'd ever seen.

My heart sped up when our eyes met, and my mouth actually watered.

Damn, he was sexy. How was it possible I'd somehow already forgotten just how much he affected me when he was up this close?

Zen made me feel alive. No one else had ever come close to lighting me up inside like he did, and I barely knew him. Even though I didn't want to get attached, because I knew he could and probably would break my heart someday, I couldn't keep myself from feeling pulled into his gravitational field. He was captivating and mysterious—and I fell a little bit more every time I saw him. Being around Zen made it hard to breathe in the best way.

A crooked smile flashed across his face as he made his way over to me, wrapping me in his arms. He buried his nose in my hair and inhaled, almost like he couldn't get close enough to me. "Morning, Sunshine. Is it too soon to say I missed you?"

"I hope not because I'm right there with you." I laughed nervously. "I... I missed you, too," I stammered, biting my bottom lip and feeling my cheeks heat up. My heart slammed frantically in my chest as I admitted the truth to myself. I'd missed him like crazy, and wasn't that some shit?

He stepped back with a massive grin on his face like he knew what I was thinking. Then, he put his finger under my chin and lifted it up until my eyes met his. "Really? So, does that mean you want to see more of this face?" he teased, gesturing to his face with his other hand. "Or this body?" His hand traced down the planes of his chiseled chest and flat stomach and my gaze was fixated on the motion. My nipples had turned into tight little peaks inside my bra and when I shifted, I stifled a moan as the fabric rubbed against them.

Biting my lip, I tried to hold my reaction in check but if the way his eyes dilated was any indication, I'd totally failed. "Ego much? Excuse me for being honest."

He laughed at my obvious embarrassment, this warm, tantalizing sound that had my toes curling inside my wedges. "So you admit you think I'm nice to look at?" he pressed.

I sighed. "You know you're hot--like insanely, ridiculously gorgeous. I've had to pinch myself, like, five times since I met you just to be sure you're actually real. Just looking at you does things to my body no one else ever has, and I'm pretty sure if you were to touch me I might actually burst into flames." He lets out a low chuckle, but I'm not done. "Here's the thing. I'm a firm believer in being honest. I don't want to play games, I don't want to have to work our way through miscommunication and misunderstanding. So… yes. I like looking at your face… and the rest of you and I will freely admit it." I tilted my lips up into a smirk that I hoped looked more confident than I felt after my impromptu confession.

He stared at me for a second, his eyes searching my face, but for what I wasn't sure. If I had to guess, I'd say no one had ever been so upfront with him about how they felt before. He blinked, and then he threw his head back and laughed.

Ignoring his laughter and pretending like I wasn't dying inside, I stepped away from him, making my way around the kitchen island to pick up the picnic basket and the mess of a tote bag, grunting under the weight. I slid my oversized sunglasses on top of my head and asked him, "Do you still have my key?"

His sparkling gaze met mine. "Yeah, I do. I let myself in, remember?"

I rolled my eyes. "I remember, I just wondered if you'd set them down or anything. We need them to go."

"Yeah, I've got it."

Zen followed me out, taking the bag from me as we made our way down. It was weird how comfortable I felt with him, how my usual racing heart and mind filled with every horror that could possibly go wrong during our short walk were absent. Tugging the front door closed behind him, he slid the key into the lock.

"Do you want this back?" he asked, holding out my key ring.

"Well, do you think you're going to keep coming around?" I asked shyly, sliding my sunglasses down over my eyes, trying to hide the ridiculous hope I bet was shining right through. Having him around gave me warm fuzzies that I never knew were possible outside of the books I read, and I wanted more of them.

His gaze settled on my face, holding eye contact while I searched for a clue as to what he was thinking.

"Yes, I am," he answered firmly, leaning forward to kiss me softly on the cheek. I never knew a simple peck on the side of my face could send waves of heat straight between my thighs before.

I couldn't help the smile that broke out across my face. There was no hesitation, no games in his answer. Just straightforward honesty, from a man who knew exactly what he wanted and would do whatever it took to get it. It seemed like he was taking a play out of my book.

And what he wanted was me. My heart pounded against my chest. The sensation of falling was scary as fuck but also made me want more. Of all the scary shit I'd been through, trusting Zen was near the top of the list.

Today, I was determined to enjoy getting to know him better. I wanted to know everything about him—the kind of person he was deep down, who he was when no one else was looking. What did he dream of? What did he hope for?

He held out his hand, and I grabbed it, weaving our fingers together. He gave me a crooked grin before turning to start our walk. I could look at that smile all day.

"Where are we going?" he wondered.

"One of my favorite spots on earth. I've never taken anyone there with me, but when the weather's nice, I like to go. Sadly, it rains here so freaking much that lake days are few and far between.

Doesn't matter, though. I think it just makes the ones I do get more special," I laughed. I sometimes rambled when I talked—a nervous habit.

"And you're sharing it with me?" He glanced at me with a surprised expression on his face.

"Yep. Don't make it weird." I laughed, speeding up and pulling Zen along with me.

Just down the block, we came across a man leaning up against one of the storefronts. He held up a cardboard sign asking for change but when he saw me approaching, his face transformed with his wrinkled smile. "Hey, Oscar! I brought you a couple of sandwiches. How was your week?" I asked.

"Miss Kennedy! It's good to see ya. You got good timin', I'm starvin'." Oscar rubbed his rough hands together after folding his sign and tucking it away in the pile of his stuff behind him.

"Well, I'm glad I brought extras, then. Here you go." I handed over the sandwiches. "They're turkey so don't let them sit out all day, okay?"

"Thank ya kindly. Now, who's this ya got with ya today?" Oscar smiled at Zen before unwrapping a sandwich and taking a bite.

"This is my friend Zen." I gestured to where Zen stood beside me. "We're headed to the lake."

Zen blinked down at the man, his face carefully blank. "It's nice to meet you, Oscar." A slow smile curved his lips as he held out his hand for Oscar to shake. I melted a little more when Zen didn't recoil from Oscar's hand or look down his nose at him. He treated Oscar like a human being, and I liked him even more for it.

"Nice to meet ya, too, Zen. It's a great day for the lake. Ya kids have fun." Oscar winked before turning his attention to his sandwich.

"See you next week, Oscar!" I waved before turning.

I retook Zen's hand, tugging him forward. "C'mon, slowpoke.

We've got to get there soon to get a good spot." He didn't budge from where his feet were firmly rooted in place.

He just stared at me and I could feel a flush creeping up my neck and into my cheeks under the intensity of his expression. "What?"

"You're fucking incredible, you know that?" He pulled me against his hard body as he wove his fingers into my hair and tilted my head back, staring at me with unrestrained desire in his eyes. That dark look of his ignited something in me, and my breath caught in my throat. I leaned into his touch as he brought his lips to mine, and for a few magical seconds, he kissed me. I practically melted into a puddle of need on the spot as he nipped at my bottom lip and deepened the kiss, his tongue swirling with mine. My entire body buzzed as he broke us apart and whispered, "Fucking incredible," against my lips. His warm breath ghosted over my skin, and I leaned forward, not ready to stop kissing him. I blinked as he leaned back with a cocky grin that said he knew I wanted more, and I tried to clear the Zen-induced haze from my brain.

I blushed because, brief as it was, that kiss was bordering on indecent for the middle of a busy sidewalk. "What do you mean?"

He wove our fingers together, and we started walking toward the lake. "How often do you do that? Bring food to homeless people?"

"A few times a week if I run into them on my walks. I see people suffering all the time, and everyone else just passes them by. They're humans, too. Sometimes people just need a little break, just a bright spot in their lives to remind them life is worth living, that it's not all bad. I try to be that reminder. I know what it feels like to lose hope, to feel like you've got no one. If I can help someone not feel like that, I'm going to." I shrugged.

We stopped again, and Zen's eyes searched mine before he wrapped his arms around me and kissed the top of my head, just holding me against his body. His scent was everywhere and while maybe I should've been questioning how fast things were moving between us, instead I closed my eyes and rested my forehead on his shoulder.

This was different from the kiss a minute ago. This was Zen being soft and sweet. "Fuck, you know what? I'm going to prove I'm worthy of you. Just wait." His voice came out so quiet I almost couldn't hear him make the promise. When he let me go, I missed the warmth of his body pressed against mine. I took his hand and leaned closer to him as we walked side by side, not wanting the contact to end.

After walking a block together in comfortable silence, our joined hands swinging between us, his gruff voice cut through my inner thoughts. "I want to know who made you feel like you had to guard yourself against the world." I glanced up at him, and his jaw ticked. He looked… pissed.

I sighed. "That's a… really long and painful story."

"I've got all day."

I swallowed and looked down at my feet. "Let's find a spot to set up first."

The mid-morning sun shimmered off the lake's surface, and I looked up, studying the landscape. Zen squeezed my hand before letting it go to set down our supplies. "Fine, but I'm not letting this go."

I stayed silent, picking out a spot underneath two trees in the shade. A sandy patch on the lake's shore in front of this place would be perfect for laying out our blanket. I got to work setting up the hammock between the two trees, tying the ropes around their rough trunks. Pulling the blanket out of the tote, I spread it out and plopped down. Zen sat down next to me, stretching his long legs out in front of him and leaning on his elbow. He lowered his sunglasses to look at me. "You need to tell me," he demanded before I'd even had a chance to sit down. It looked like he wasn't going to forget about our little conversation from a few minutes ago like I'd been hoping.

"Why is this so important to you?"

He pushed his sunglasses back onto his face and sat up. He reached out and tucked that stray piece of hair that drove me crazy behind my ear, and then cupped my cheek with his palm.

"Look, I know we haven't known each other for very long, but you're not like anyone I've ever met. I'm different around you, and it's surprising as fuck but I *like* who I am around you. I don't act like this. Ever. I don't try to get to know people, and I don't let anyone in. I've got my brothers, and until now that was enough. Maintaining a healthy distance from anything that could have relationship potential has been a necessity because people always want to fuck with me. I've been hurt by it in the past, too. The recent past even. You wanted honesty? Well, here it is: I wasn't looking for you or for this." He ran his hand through his hair. His thick, dark, silky hair.

"Finding someone who takes my breath away, who's as beautiful inside as out, and who genuinely cares about other people without an ulterior motive? You're a goddamn unicorn, baby. I didn't think someone like you existed. You're a bright star in a field of blackened night sky, and you don't even realize it. There you were, rescuing me when I couldn't take care of myself. You didn't have to do that. Anyone else would have just walked by or worse, taken pictures and posted them on the internet. You, Kennedy, are my own personal superhero." He chuckled.

He was right, though. There were always those assholes who stood by watching while something terrible was happening, filming that crap on their phones and sticking it online to see if they could go viral. Those people were what I liked to call shit lickers, and I thought they were some of the worst kinds of people.

"Now, you've caught my attention, so you should probably hold on because I'm an all or nothing kind of guy. I want to know everything about you. It pisses me the fuck off that someone made you feel the way you do about yourself, hurt you, and made you feel like you didn't deserve the whole fucking world. No one gets to dim your light; never again."

His jaw clenched again.

"So, I want to know who the fuck made you feel that way and what happened, so maybe I can prove to you that you have a chance at the happiness you deserve—and just to be clear, that's with me. But I can't if you don't let me in, if you don't show me what I'm up against."

His eyes burned with conviction as he waited to see how I'd react. Sharing how he felt so openly was refreshing. No one had ever been straightforward like this with me before. Another little piece of my wall crumbled. Shit. I didn't stand a damn chance against this man. I was done for the moment I laid eyes on him, it just took my brain a while to catch up with my heart.

I took his hand in mine, and he rubbed comforting circles on my wrist with his thumb that set off a chain reaction of hunger through my body like a virus. Not one inch of me was spared, and I shifted where I sat. A knowing smirk cut across his face and I sort of wanted to glare at him and deny how I was feeling just to get under his skin.

But then the reality of what I was about to confess washed over me and the lust quickly faded. Bowing my head, I took a deep breath. Was I really going to confide in him? The only other people who knew were Amara, Grayson, and my therapist. Well, if the panic didn't make him run, this would do it for sure.

My voice was flat as I began, my free arm wrapped around my middle as if I could protect myself from my words. "When I was in high school, I had a boyfriend. My junior year boys asked me out all the time, but no one ever interested me, so I always shot them down. I was more interested in books and always had my nose in one." I smiled wistfully but it slid off my face just as fast.

"At least until this assgoblin named Brock transferred in. Everyone wanted to be his friend, and all the girls wanted him. You know? That whole new student thing where everyone gets excited about it. Not me, though. I couldn't have cared less. I wasn't attracted to him right away, but he aggressively pursued me. Looking back, maybe that was my appeal to him. I'm pretty sure I was just a challenge or conquest, but at the time it felt like he actually cared about me."

I shifted my eyes down, plucking a wildflower out of the grass and pulling the petals off it one by one. "I turned him down over and over, but he was persistent. He'd show up at my locker and carry my books to my next class. He'd offer me rides home that I always turned down. But he didn't give up. He showed up at my house with a new release book I'd been waiting months for, so I finally agreed to go to a school dance with him."

My eyes started to sting, and Zen moved closer to me on the blanket but said nothing. He ran his fingers through my hair and I laid flat, putting my head in his lap and closing my eyes.

I let out a shaky breath.

"We went to the dance, and then when it was over, we were officially," I made air quotes with my fingers, "dating. We hung out every weekend and most days after school. If I had free time, Brock was there making me laugh or being sweet. I thought I was falling for him, and he led me to believe he felt the same. I confided in him about my fears and quirks because even back then, I struggled with panic attacks, and he acted like he understood. He told me it didn't matter to him, he was happy just to be with me in whatever way he could.

"After a couple of months, he started pressuring me to have sex. I hadn't done it before and wasn't in any hurry, but like before, he wore me down. He made me feel safe."

I let out a humorless laugh. "One weekend, I finally gave in. I'd like to say it was fun or enjoyable, but it wasn't. The asshole wasn't gentle or careful with me at all. He just wanted to get what he'd been working on for all those months. The payoff."

"Jesus," Zen bit out, his body tensing underneath my head had me cracking an eye open to see a storm gathering behind his eyes. "I want his full fucking name. It shouldn't have been like that. It should-"

I smiled sadly, cutting him off before he could promise violence in my honor. I'd never let him dirty his hands over someone so insignificant. What if Zen got in trouble because of my past? Nope, not happening. "I know, but it is what it is. That's not even the bad part." I whispered, tears starting to fall down my cheeks.

"Christ. There's a part worse than that?" Zen reached down to wipe away my tears with his finger.

"So much worse. So we sleep together, and I'm underwhelmed, but I figure it's going to get better. Everyone's first time is terrible, right?" I laughed humorlessly again. "I went back to school on Monday, and it felt like everyone was staring at me and whispering behind my back. At first, I tried to ignore it, but I was really starting to get self-conscious by the time lunch rolled around." Zen tightened his hold on me as I started to tremble, but I kept going. Now that I started, I wanted to get it all out.

"I went to the bathroom to escape because I was on the verge of panicking, and I didn't want anyone to see me like that." I let out a shaky breath. "I'm in the bathroom, and I'm trying not to hyperventilate, just trying to calm down, and this group of girls comes in. First, they're doing that whole bitchy mean girl thing where they know all the sordid details of my weekend with Brock. Yep, my supposed boyfriend was actually dating one of the cheerleaders and the whole thing was something they planned together. A fun game for them, I guess."

"Names, Kennedy. I'm going to need names." The malice in Zen's voice made me shiver in the best way, despite being in the middle of reliving my trauma.

"The girls surround me, and they start taunting me, calling me a psycho slut. I had no idea what they were talking about. Me? A slut? They had to have the wrong girl. I'd had sex exactly one terrible time. But then they started pushing me, shoving me back and forth between them, slapping me, tearing at my clothes. I begged them to stop but they only laughed harder with their phones out recording the whole thing."

Zen wrapped both arms around me, but I couldn't stop shaking. He stroked my hair, trying to calm me down.

He held me while I took deep breaths.

"They didn't stop. They brought scissors with them and then cut off my clothes. They cut my hair. They scratched me and kicked me and punched me until they left me in a bloody, bruised, naked heap on the bathroom floor. And I laid there until the janitor found me after school because no one bothered to come into that bathroom for the rest of the day. I found out later, one of them put an 'out of order' sign on the entrance."

Zen's grip on me was so tight it bordered on painful, but I felt safe enough to keep going. "Apparently, Brock told the entire school that I had gone to his house, stripped off my clothes and told him I wouldn't leave unless he fucked me. He said I was literally sex-crazed, a lunatic who needed to be hospitalized because I'd forced myself on him. The girls were not only jealous but petty and mean, and it didn't take long for the bathroom video to go up on social media. They were determined to show the entire school that I really was what he said I was. In the video, I was naked and crying and begging, and it only made me look worse. It was his word against mine, and everyone loved him. The entire school treated me like a pariah after that. They spray-painted psycho across my locker, threw pills at me, and I wish I could say that incident in the bathroom with those girls was the only time that happened. I got constant notes telling me I should kill myself, that the world would be better off without me. Guys would slap my ass or proposition me in the hall, shove me into janitor's closets or bathrooms or empty classrooms and feel me up without my permission. I learned to retreat into a safe space in my head when it happened, and even now sometimes when the panic gets really bad, I go there. Everyone thought I was nuts, and it didn't matter that they'd all known me for years and knew that I didn't act like that. They believed some asshole jock who was new in town over me."

I swiped at the hot tears streaming down my face. I thought I was done crying over this shit years ago. I guess not. "They tore me down because it was fun. They destroyed me for entertainment, and I've never been the same since."

"Kennedy-"

"Wait, I'm still not done."

"For fuck's sake," he muttered as his jaw tightened.

Might as well get it all out, since I already opened Pandora's box. He would, for sure, run once he heard the next part.

"That summer, everyone abandoned me. People I thought were my friends, people I had years of history with, completely deserted me. I was alone. I sank into this dark place where the panic was constant, and before I knew it, depression had kicked my ass. My parents were never around, but my brother came home from some baseball tournament he had and found me unable to function, huddled in the dark in my room where I hadn't eaten anything in days, and took me to the hospital." I studied the stem in my hand as if it was the most interesting thing I'd ever seen. Tears streamed down my cheeks. Talking about this sucked donkey balls.

"I ended up spending my entire summer in inpatient therapy, working through the trauma of it all. When I went back my senior year, I kept to myself. They tried to start with me again, but when their favorite punching bag didn't bother reacting, they gave up and moved on to fucking up someone else's life. I graduated and moved the hell away. I tried to shut that part of me down, to never look back. Except when I did, I also stopped being open to letting people in."

I looked up at him through watery eyes.

He wiped away my tears and kissed my forehead, his strong arms wrapped around me, making me feel safe like everything would be okay.

"What I mean is," I continued, "I have only ever been with someone that one time. I've never let anyone else even get close. I get hit on all the time, but I always shut it down. Can you see now why I'm hesitant to let you in? I can't let my heart get shattered again, I can't handle the humiliation. It took months of therapy for me to work through it last time, and parts of me still feel broken." I sniffled.

"Oh, Sunshine." He sighed, rocking us gently back and forth.

This was the moment he'd walk away, I just knew it.

I wanted to let him hold me for a minute before I looked into his eyes and saw the revulsion he'd inevitably have toward me now. I needed this moment with him to feel like I was worthy because that's how Zen made me feel, like I deserved to be loved. If he walked away now, at least I'd have that feeling to hold on to and maybe, just maybe I could start to move forward instead of just standing still.

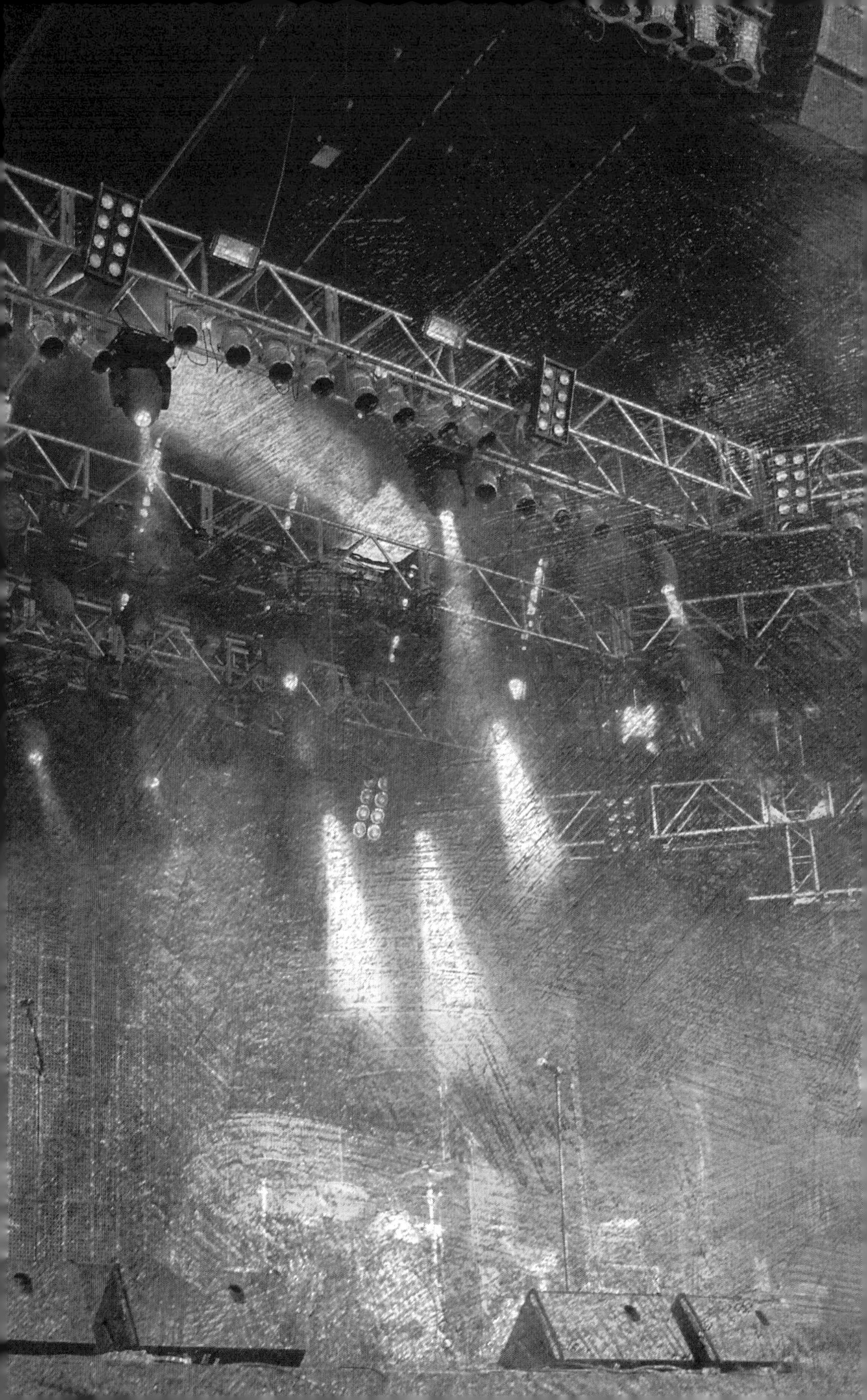

CHAPTER 9

Zen

KENNEDY LAID IN MY LAP, sniffling softly. I marveled over the fact this amazing and brave woman trusted me enough to open up. There were no words to describe the amount of rage bubbling inside me at this Brock asshole. Okay, maybe I had a few words, mostly things like *murder* and *torture*.

Maybe Maddox could track him down with the little bit of information I have from Kennedy's story. Fuck, I already knew I'd ask him to try.

How could anyone throw this incredible woman away like she was nothing? I made myself a promise right then that she'd never feel like that again. In fact, my new mission was to show her exactly how exceptional she was.

I pulled back to look at her face, which was a little red and puffy from crying. When she finally met my eyes, hers were filled with fear and uncertainty. They were guarded like she thought I was about to take off on her after hearing the ugliest parts of who she believed herself to be. The problem was she was so much more than that. She was *everything*.

I wanted—no *needed*—to make her feel safe and secure, like I wasn't going to abandon her, but I wasn't sure what to say. Instead, I leaned down and captured her soft lips with mine, pouring everything into the kiss that I didn't have words to say. This wasn't like our kiss earlier on the street. This was slower, deeper, and more consuming.

She relaxed into me, moaning softly, and reaching up to tangle her fingers in the hair at the back of my neck. I teased her mouth open gently with my tongue, tasting her and filling my senses with all things Kennedy.

I groaned, gliding my hand up her back to grip her neck and pull her even closer. She felt fucking incredible, warm and soft, pressed against me with little whimpers escaping her every few seconds. My cock strained against my jeans as I fought the urge to pull her up so she straddled me.

Fuck.

She tasted sweet and minty, and I couldn't get enough. I knew I'd never be the same after this kiss. It was wrecking me in the best way. My fingers tangled in her hair, and I tugged her head gently back, giving me better access to her mouth.

The world fell away, and all that existed were Kennedy and me. Completely lost, I reveled in the feeling of her fingers tugging my hair, my arms wrapped around her. Finally, she pulled back, both of us breathing hard. My dick was so hard it pulsed with every beat of my heart, pressing uncomfortably against my zipper.

"Well, I didn't expect you to react like that to my story," she murmured with a small smile. Her lips were pink and swollen, and her eyes were bright but hooded. Everything in me screamed at me to kiss her again. She was magnetic and I was helpless to the pull.

Instead, I stared down into her bright blue eyes. "I'm going to show you how much you deserve, how worthy of love you really are. You'll see." Words were pretty, but Kennedy had been burned by them before. She needed to see what I'd do and time to pass without me fucking her over to really start to move on. I knew that, but I had to start somewhere.

Kennedy looked away, trying to hide the tears pooling in her eyes. The darkness crept in along the edges of my vision, the need for retribution nearly overwhelming. I grounded myself with my fingers sifting through the golden strands of her hair, her head in my lap, and the peaceful expression she now wore. Vengeance could wait, at least until I set Maddox on this Brock douchebag. I only needed enough time to send a text and it would be handled, my hands would be clean, and if Kennedy ever wanted to know what happened to her high school tormentor, only then would I ask Maddox to disclose the details. It was how we worked—he fixed, we stayed out of it.

She didn't say anything, but she didn't have to. We sat in comfortable silence for a while, letting the moment wash over us. Finally, I spoke up. "I don't know about you, but I'm getting pretty hungry. Want to eat?"

A slow smile spread across her face. "That's like asking if I want to kiss you again."

"Or we could just skip lunch and-"

"No! If I don't eat something soon, you're going to see my hangry side."

"Your hangry side?"

She laughed. "You know, hungry and angry? Hangry?"

I chuckled. "I bet you're adorable when you're hangry."

"Oh, trust me when I say cute is the exact opposite of how I am. I'm sort of a monster, actually. A magnificent bitch, if you will."

I cracked up as a debate waged within my mind—hold out on

feeding Kennedy and tempt her hangry side out, or make sure she never suffered in even the slightest way in my presence. My need to take care of her ultimately won out.

"Gimme the food," she said, reaching her hand out and wiggling her fingers, ending my internal struggle.

I handed it over, and she set up our lunch. Kennedy didn't try to hide how she ate in front of me or eat some tiny bullshit salad. No, the girl devoured her food and watching as she moaned and savored every bite that passed her kissable lips turned me the fuck on. But what didn't with this girl?

Groups of people placed themselves on blankets around us, some setting up nets for volleyball, some lighting barbecues, and others stretching out and enjoying a rare sunny day. Because Kennedy and I were now surrounded, I started to worry that someone might recognize me. I made sure to keep my sunglasses up and my head down as much as I could without acting like a fucking weirdo and tipping her off.

Even trying to be incognito, I stood out. The ink on my body alone set me apart, but even if I didn't have that, I was always the center of attention no matter what I did.

I planned to tell her soon what my real life was like. Honesty wasn't negotiable. Kennedy was crystal fucking clear about her expectations. If I wanted to be with her, I'd have to tell the truth. My stomach already knotted with the guilt of hiding who I really was from her. Besides, she needed to know what she'd be dealing with if she became mine like I wanted. I'd had a taste now, and I couldn't let her go. In my mind, she already belonged to me. I just needed a little more time before reality set in.

"Come relax with me." I grabbed her hand and lifted her up off my lap and then stood up, leading her toward the hammock.

"Ready for a post-picnic nap?" She stretched, smoothing down her hair.

"Something like that," I murmured.

Really, I just needed to hold her closer against me, feel her body draped over mine. I was getting fucking addicted to the way she felt in my arms.

I laid down in the hammock, steadying myself and holding my arms open. Kennedy crawled in beside me, giggling when she almost toppled us over.

"Shit! Sorry," she said, throwing her arm out in front of her to try and balance.

I chuckled, wrapping my arm around her waist. "I've got you."

She tucked herself into my side, slinging her arm across my chest and her leg across mine so she was halfway on top of me. Kennedy settled in with a contented sigh before laying her head on my shoulder. One of my hands absently played with her hair, letting the silky strands fall between my fingers.

She ran her fingers up and down my chest, setting off sparks under my skin that shot straight to my dick. That wasn't what she needed right now, so I tried to will my semi-hard cock to go down. Kissing the top of her head, I pulled her closer before letting my eyes drift shut. For the first time in longer than I could remember, I felt totally at peace and content. The pressures of performing, of writing our next album, of wondering if a video of me fucking some meaningless stranger was going to pop up—all of it was gone. The only thing that mattered was Kennedy and this moment.

We must've fallen asleep, swaying gently in the warm breeze, because when I opened my eyes she was breathing evenly, still wrapped around me with her eyelashes fanned out against her cheeks. I studied her face, the small freckles that dotted her upper cheeks and nose looked like the sweetest constellations.

My stomach twisted with guilt—I was hiding from Kennedy, but I'd deal with that shit later. No way would I ruin this perfect day. It'd taken a lot out of her to tell me about her past. I welcomed the quiet to process everything she'd told me. What a fucking asshole. Brock held a solid place at the top of my shit list. The truth was he wasn't that much worse than me, and it pissed me off to admit it. I'd never played games, but I didn't exactly treat the women I'd hooked up with like they were special or important. I wondered how fucked I was going to be when Kennedy learned the truth.

Keeping secrets never ended well.

I worried that once I told her who I really was, she'd either be so pissed off I hadn't told her right away that she'd shut me out completely, or she'd think she wasn't ready to handle being with me because my life could be a giant shitshow sometimes. Fuck, I wasn't prepared to face either of those outcomes. No, I had to get her more attached, more confident in her feelings for me first. I needed to make sure we had an otherwise solid foundation before telling her who I really was and rocking said foundation.

Shit, I really was fucked, wasn't I?

Resting my cheek on the top of her head, I breathed in the sweet smell of her hair and breathed out all the bullshit running through my mind. Her scent did things to me, something I didn't want to dig into too deeply right now. How had I gone from wanting nothing but random hookups to wanting to fix and protect this amazing but damaged woman? To make her mine?

This entire weekend confused the shit out of me. I knew one thing: I wanted Kennedy, and I planned to fight for a future with her. With her, my world suddenly came into focus.

When the shadows grew longer, and the air cooled down, I gently ran the tip of my finger down her nose and over her cheek, sweeping off the tiny strands of hair the wind was blowing across her skin. She slowly opened her eyes and smiled up at me. "As much as I don't want to, we should start packing up, Sunshine."

She yawned and stretched, pushing her lower lip out in an adorable pout that made me want to bite it and pull her on top of me until she straddled my hips. Instead, we climbed out of the hammock and started packing up our picnic.

As I folded up the blanket, a tiny chick with short, spiky black hair and dark blue eyes approached us with her eyes locked on me.

Oh, fuck.

I knew that look. She wanted something and could easily expose me to Kennedy. Honestly, I'd been lucky to avoid this so far. I glanced quickly over to my girl, who had her back to me as she packed up the hammock. Small fucking mercies.

This girl walked right up to me as if she didn't give a shit that I was a celebrity. I had to respect the set of metaphorical balls she must have.

"Are you Zen Taylor? *The* Zen Taylor?"

She looked young, maybe about twenty with pale skin and a petite build. A Shadow Phoenix t-shirt with a massive print of my face on it hugged her chest.

Of course.

"Last time I checked. Listen, I'm out here with my friend right now, so...." I hoped she'd take the hint. She didn't.

"Oh, cool." She blew a pink bubble with her gum and popped it with a smack of her lips. "Hey, can I get a selfie?"

I rolled my eyes, folding my arms across my chest. The last thing I needed was her tagging my location. I'd have the paparazzi up my ass so fast, there'd be nothing I could do to shield Kennedy from it. This girl needed to go the fuck away. The price of fame never bothered me much until this moment. Suddenly, I hated that people like her thought they could interrupt my time, asking me for shit I wasn't obligated to give.

"Sorry, not today. Maybe next time." I turned and picked up the basket. I peeked over at Kennedy, who now looked my way, her eyes flicking to the girl behind me. She obviously hadn't listened to a fucking thing I'd just said.

"You're as much of an asshole as the tabloids said. Good to know," she huffed before turning and stomping off.

Pissed off fans talking shit on the internet weren't new, but it'd been a while since one did it to my face. Thankfully, she hadn't made more of a scene. Once, I refused a fan who threw an actual tantrum like a goddamn toddler. How grown-ass people could act like that confused the shit out of me.

I usually had Connor with me all the time in LA to prevent shit like this. I hadn't run into many fans out here. The fact Connor wasn't here right now just showed it wasn't generally a problem, since he'd never let me come out to the lake today without him if there was much of a chance I'd get swarmed. To be fair, up until I met Kennedy, I hadn't really gone out in public much when I visited this area. Now that Kennedy was involved, I wondered whether I should start bringing Connor to handle shit up while we were out, but decided to deal with it later.

Bringing Connor along meant answering questions I wasn't ready for yet.

I sauntered toward Kennedy, keeping my expression indifferent as her eyes shot questions at me.

"Was that a friend of yours? She looked pretty pissed off." Her gaze over my shoulder followed the girl's retreat.

"No, I don't know who she is." *The truth.* "She wanted directions, and when I told her I didn't really know the area, she got upset." *A lie.*

"Oh, what a shit biscuit." I coughed to try and cover my laugh. Some of the most unexpected shit fell out of Kennedy's mouth and I never knew what she might say. "A lot of tourists visit in the summer. GPS is free on your phone, for fuck's sake." She had the most adorable scowl on her face on my behalf, accepting my lie because she fucking trusted me, and I wanted to kick my own ass for lying to her again.

A dazzling smile broke out across her face as she leaned up on her toes to press her soft lips against my cheek, but I turned at the last second and caught her lips instead. It was a quick kiss, but I couldn't seem to help myself around this girl. I let out the breath I hadn't realized I'd been holding and smiled back. She seemed to buy my story, but I wouldn't get away with that shit again. It was only a matter of time before another fan recognized me, and Kennedy deserved better than to find out that way.

What would she think when she found out the guy she'd started dating, or not-dating as she called it, was massively famous and had a sex tape making its rounds on the internet? The heat on me needed to die down before I dragged her into my world, assuming she'd even want to stick around.

I shook myself, my attention snapping back to Kennedy. I took the bag from her, handing her the lighter basket in exchange, and she held out her hand for mine. It made my whole fucking day. She reached for me now as if it was the most natural thing in the world. Whatever barrier she'd thrown up between us when we first met seemed to have disappeared during our talk this morning.

She'd let me in. Kennedy showed me a part of herself that no one else got to see and I still didn't understand what she saw in me to make her open up. My chest tightened. I needed time to figure out how to protect her from what being with me would mean. Her whole life was going to change and she didn't even know it yet. She looked back at me, her smile lighting up her entire face. I'd do anything to keep her smiling.

"You still with me back there?" she asked, looking more relaxed than I'd ever seen her.

"Just admiring the view." I flashed her a cocky grin.

She grinned and turned back around.

Oscar saluted us on our way back. It stunned me how much Kennedy genuinely cared about people. I'd never met anyone like her.

The colorful bricks of Sweet Stories came into view as a guy who looked like he'd just left a music festival, douchey man bun and all, came jogging over to us. I knew the type. I'd headlined quite a few of those douche-fests.

I tensed, positioning myself in front of Kennedy. Who the fuck was this guy? She leaned around me and smiled at him warmly. I really fucking hated how his eyes lit up and lingered on her body a little too long.

"Hey Ken, what's good? Enjoy the lake today?" he asked, seeming way too familiar with her routines and I narrowed my eyes at him.

I officially hated this guy.

"Hey, River! The lake was awesome. This is Zen." She rested her hand on my arm, and I relaxed under her touch.

River.

What a tool.

Wrapping my arm around Kennedy's waist, I pulled her closer to my side in a move that was nothing short of possessive.

"Hey, man," I grunted, shooting him a glare that said, *stay the fuck away, she's mine.*

River eyed me up and down, no doubt judging whether he wanted to test me. I thought a spark of recognition flared in his eyes and I tensed, but then it was gone. He must've seen something in my cold glare or my coiled body language that told him to back the fuck off, because he gave a nervous laugh and stepped back.

"Well, you seem like you're busy. Let's talk in class this week. See you tomorrow?" he asked hopefully, glancing sideways at me.

"Yep, see you in class!" she chirped, before resuming our walk.

Once we were out of earshot of River, I asked, "Friend of yours?"

She stopped and turned to study me. My jaw muscle twitched as I clenched my teeth together so hard I could've cracked one. I hated how relaxed and familiar she seemed around him, and River definitely wanted to fuck her. Her knowing eyes saw right through my bullshit.

"Sort of. I mean, we take yoga classes together with a bunch of other people. It's something one of my therapists recommended to help me deal with my panic attacks. His name is River, obviously, and he one hundred percent wants to get in my pants." She laughed.

I raised my eyebrows. "Most girls don't admit they know when a guy is regularly eye banging them."

"Oh. Yeah, I guess that's probably true." She bit her lower lip, and I fought the urge to pull it out of her teeth with my thumb and replace her teeth with my own. "I learned how to spot guys like that a long time ago. I couldn't let anyone get close, and after what happened I needed to know when someone had ulterior motives for being my friend. I'm pretty good at picking up on the cues at this point. That's where my 'husband' comes in. I haven't told you about that yet." Her eyes sparkled with mischief while I was standing here dying a slow death inside.

Husband?

No, she fucking hadn't. Had I missed the part where she belonged to someone else? I really wasn't opposed to using every tool at my disposal to take her from whoever he was and make her mine if it was true.

This girl surprised me at every turn. She leaned up and kissed me on the lips, placing her hand on my chest. I instantly relaxed as I wrapped my arms around her, trying to keep the tote from banging into her side.

"Okay, now I have to know. Who is this husband, and do I need to kill him?"

She laughed and shook her head. "It's something Amara and I came up with. Whenever someone is interested or tries to hit on me, I lie and tell them I'm married." She laughed again. "I even have a fake ring I carry in my purse."

Fake. Husband.

My shoulders relaxed as the tension drained out of me.

"There have been a few times where guys see it as a personal challenge or something, but mostly it gets them to back off and stop seeing me as a sexual object."

I burst out laughing.

"What?" she asked, one eyebrow raised.

"Sunshine, no man who's ever laid eyes on you stops seeing you as a sexual object when you tell them that lie. You're fucking stunning. They just work to hide it better."

Her eyebrows furrowed as her cheeks flushed. "I... You think I'm stunning?"

I grinned. "Fuck, yes. You're the most beautiful woman I've ever seen."

"Oh."

"Oh? That's all you've got to say?"

She shrugged. "I'm used to men thinking I'm hot, but I'm not used to liking it. I'm not really sure what to say."

This girl.

"I'm just glad the husband thing works. I want the guys to leave me alone, so I don't really care how it happens. Anyway, River asked me out, and I shut him down pretty hard with that lie. Ever since, he's just really friendly. He probably thought you were my husband." She chuckled. Why did I not immediately want to tear myself away from her and run away screaming at that idea? "He's not one of the creepy ones, though. And you don't have anything to worry about. Yoga bro doesn't do it for me." She grinned up at me.

I chuckled. "Yoga bro?"

"You know, tank top, man bun? Yeah, not really my scene."

I looked down into her eyes, her blue locked with my green. "And what is your scene?"

She stared right back up at me, not breaking eye contact even to blink. "I'm starting to think sexy as hell, green-eyed bad boys with lots of tattoos."

Pulling her body flush against mine, I crashed my lips down on hers. I took her soft bottom lip between my teeth like I'd been dying to do for the last five minutes. The perfection of Kennedy pressed against my body, all soft curves and smooth skin. I pushed our hips together so she could feel exactly what she did to me. Peppering kisses down her jawline and neck, I gently licked and sucked the slope where her neck met her shoulder and she shivered in response. Her skin was sweet and salty on my tongue, and I'd never tasted anything better.

As her body trembled under my touch, I gently pulled back with one last kiss. I didn't want to push her too far. Her eyes popped open, and her pupils dilated. She whimpered and leaned toward me, like she didn't want me to stop. Like she wanted more.

Well, shit.

What the fuck was I supposed to do when she made that sound? I'd never wanted anyone more, and yet something told me I needed to tread carefully. She had to come to me when she was ready, and I refused to push her. My dick threatened to punch through my jeans, but I stepped back anyway. It was probably a first for me, and I shocked the shit out of myself.

"Why'd you stop?"

I smiled and kissed the tip of her nose. So fucking adorable.

"Because you're not ready to take this further, even if you feel like it right this second. We've got all the time in the world, no need to rush."

I leaned down to press one more soft kiss to her lips. I couldn't stop kissing her even as I tried to convince her we should stop.

She sighed and leaned against me as I draped my arm around her shoulders.

"Let's go in. Can you unlock the door? Oh, and you can keep that key for when you're in town. I have a spare," she told me casually, as if it was no big deal.

It was a huge fucking deal.

How did she trust me so fully already? I puffed out my goddamn chest. I probably would have beaten my fists on it, too, if I hadn't thought it would make me look like a complete asshole. I hadn't expected her to let me into her life so completely, so soon, but I sure as fuck wasn't going to make her regret it.

"Are you sure?" I needed to know that she was really okay with me being able to come and go whenever I wanted. Another pang of guilt stabbed me in the gut but I shoved it down to deal with later.

"Yep. You haven't run, you've heard my darkest secrets and stuck around. I know it seems weird, but there's just something about you that calls to me. I believe you're meant to be in my life. The first time I saw you on that sidewalk," she pointed to a spot near where we were standing, "I just knew I wanted to know you, even if it was only for that night, to help you when you looked like you needed it most. Ugh, I sound crazy right now."

She took a deep breath.

"I just mean, I like you. I want to get to know you better, and I get the feeling your schedule is unpredictable. I want to see you whenever I can, and I feel like this is the easiest way to do it," she continued. "So, yes. I'm completely sure I want you to keep the key and drop in whenever you can."

I searched her eyes for any indication that she was hesitant or afraid, but only certainty reflected back at me. I smiled and hugged her.

"Thank you for trusting me. I won't let you down," I murmured into Kennedy's hair, kissing her forehead before letting her go, and pushing down my traitorous thoughts that reminded me I'd already lied to her. She might not want me to stick around once she found out the whole situation.

We walked into the store hand in hand, dropping the bags once we were inside. I didn't want to come on too strong, so it was time to go for the night. For the first time in a long time, lyrics floated around in my brain, and my fingers itched to write. While this sex tape bullshit played out and I kept a low profile, I planned on writing the next Shadow Phoenix album if I could find the motivation. Spending time with Kennedy had me bursting with inspiration.

Nothing had ever felt as right as having Kennedy in my arms. I never wanted to let her go, but I knew I had to. I had to get home and back to my reality—back to Shadow Phoenix. But at this moment I wanted to pretend to be normal, just for a minute. I held her just a little bit tighter, breathing in her sweet sunshine and coconut scent, trying to commit it to memory until I saw her again, which needed to be soon. I sighed, leaning down to kiss her, knowing I'd be walking away in just a minute.

She bunched my shirt in her fist, pulling me in even closer, her soft lips moving against mine. I let my hand roam along her curves, tracing the delicate lines of her hips and moving up to the swell of her breast, kissing her hard and dirty before pulling away with a smirk. "I'm never going to leave if you keep kissing me like that," I murmured against her lips.

She gasped. "You've discovered my genius evil plan." She pulled back and tried to wink at me but instead blinked both eyes.

I laughed. She was so fucking cute. "Did you just fail at winking?"

She giggled. "Yeah, I'm not great at the art of seduction."

She had no idea how fucking seductive she could be. Every guy that came near her fell under her spell. The fact she didn't know it just added to her appeal.

I took a deep breath, running my hand through my hair, giving in to the inevitable. "I should go. I'll text you later tonight."

"That sounds perfect." She sighed, leaning back into me for another quick but heated kiss.

I stepped back, softly dropping one last kiss on her forehead before turning and grabbing my keys to leave. I gave her one last smile, and she waved with a wistful smile back.

As I walked out the front door, I headed over to where I'd parked at the sidewalk. I hopped in, but before putting my keys in the ignition, I slipped her key onto my ring, floored by her trust in me. At the same time, it felt like I was leaving a piece of me behind.

I'd be back as soon as I could, but she needed space to sort through everything that was happening between us. Kennedy had been through a lot, and I needed her to be sure about me. Calling Maddox was also at the top of my to-do list. I needed her, and I'd be spending as much time as I possibly could showing her she could depend on me, even if it meant putting my wants on the back burner for the first time in my life.

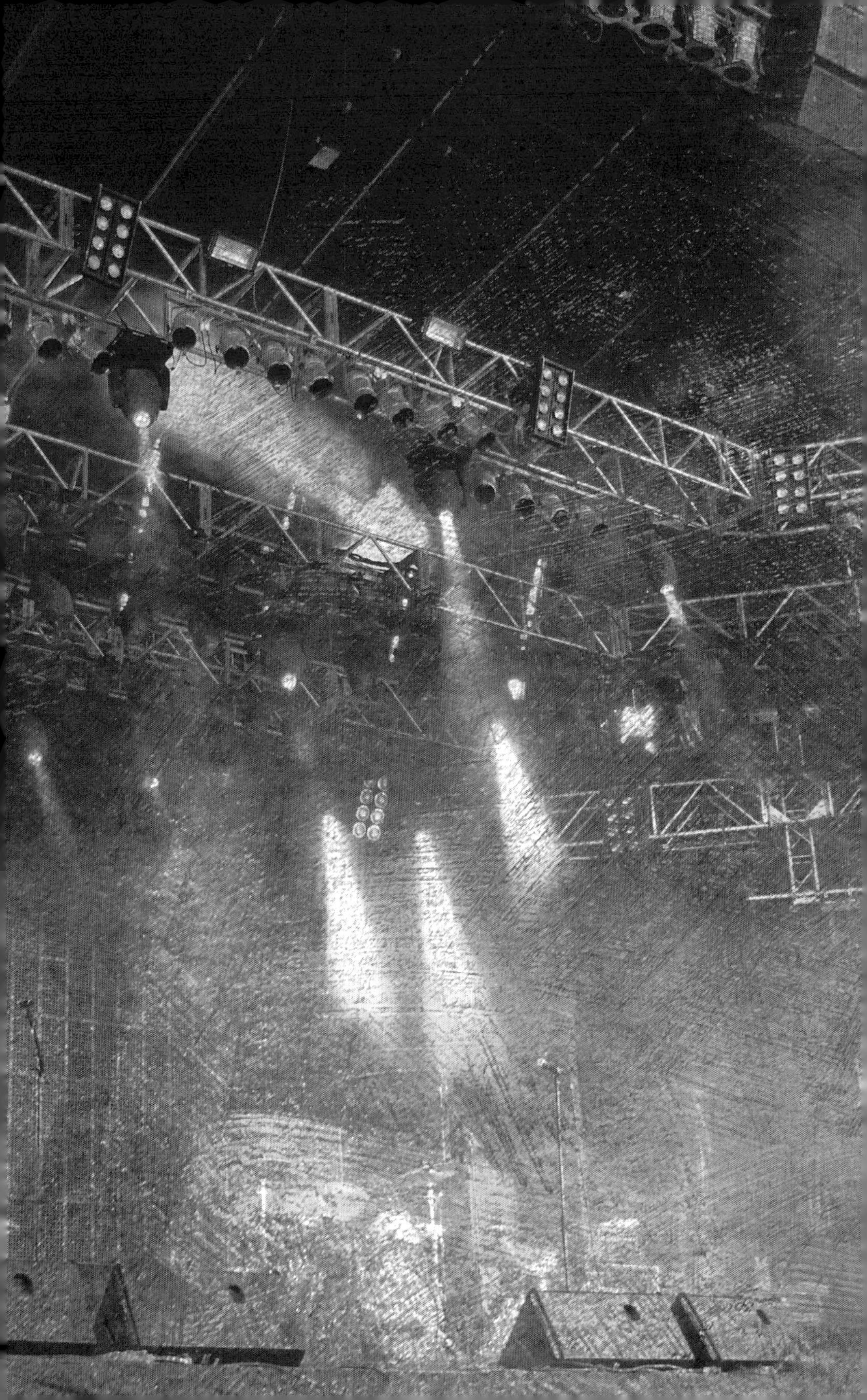

CHAPTER 10

KENNEDY

I GRINNED like an idiot as I re-read the text from Zen.

Zen: I can't stop thinking about you

My chest ached as if a piece of me was missing, and I'd just seen him about three hours ago. As soon as I opened up to him about my past and he hadn't called me crazy or run away screaming, I decided to give him a chance. The only thing I had to lose was my heart.

No big deal, right?

I sighed. Getting over my anxieties wouldn't be easy, but I had to start somewhere. Letting Zen in would at least be a fun and sexy first step.

I hoped.

Even if it ended horribly, I was ready to try. Zen was the first guy I'd ever met that caught my attention enough to consider taking the risk. My body reacted to him, whether I wanted it to or not. He drew me in with a magnetic pull I couldn't ignore.

We had this attraction to each other, and when I looked in his eyes, I could see down to a soul-deep level. I didn't know much about him yet, but that didn't matter. Deep down, he was kind, caring, and protective; I could tell. Learning the little details that made him who he was on the outside would come in time.

Kennedy: If only you knew where I lived and could do something about that

I was shamelessly flirting back and giddy as hell about it. My stomach swooped and my heart picked up its pace. Before Zen's message, I planned to curl up with a book in the pile of soft pillows on my couch with a glass of wine before going to bed.

Sadly, alone.

I swallowed down a lump of emotion. I didn't get lonely. At least not until Zen fell into my life.

I pulled out my phone, unable to resist the temptation, and fired off a text.

Kennedy: What are you up to?
Zen: I already told you, Sunshine. I think I might have a problem. How about you?
Kennedy: Getting ready to go to sleep. I just wanted to say goodnight...
Kennedy: Too bad you're not here to tuck me in.
Zen: I can be there in ten minutes. I'll even let myself in. ;)
Kennedy: Stop teasing. It's not nice
Zen: You don't think I would?
Kennedy: No, you've got too much going on, remember?
Zen: The fuck I do. I'd drop everything right now if you asked me.

Kennedy: I'd never do that. But seriously, how long until I can see you again?
Zen: This weekend. I'll be there on Friday night if I can wait that long. I need to try to be good so I can get shit done.

I sighed. Five more days until I'd see Zen again. This week was going to drag.

Kennedy: I kinda hope you're bad, though...
Zen: Just say the word, Sunshine.

I pulled my knees to my chest, hugging my arms around myself. Butterflies fluttered in my stomach and warmth spread through my body all the way to my fingers and toes.

Kennedy: It means a lot to me that you'd do that for me, but it's okay, I'll survive until Friday.
Kennedy: ... Probably.

Shit, what was it about sending messages that made it so much easier to admit to my feelings?

Kennedy: I'm going to bed. Talk tomorrow?

My phone played the ringtone Zen set for himself and flashed with his grinning face. "Hello?"

"I wanted to say goodnight," Zen said in a husky voice that did devious things to my body and my toes curled into the rug under my feet.

"You know, it kinda sucks that you have so much self-control," I mused, having fun teasing him but also not really kidding.

He let out this low, dark chuckle that shot straight to my core. "I think you're the first person to ever be upset about my self-control.

It's a new thing I'm trying out. You know if you really need me, I'm there, right?"

I nodded but then realized he can't see me. "Yeah, I know." And I did.

He sighed. "I have to get back. This is going to be the longest week of my damn life."

I twirled a lock of my hair around my finger absently. "Text me tomorrow?"

"Count on it," he said. "'Night, Sunshine."

"Sweet dreams." Sunshine. I don't know when I got over my issue with him calling me that, but now I loved it. I reluctantly hung up, wishing he was here.

I put my book down because my eyes traced the same sentence three hundred times while my mind drifted to the past weekend. Finally giving up, I made my way to bed. I couldn't wait to get the week started. I tried to tell myself it wasn't because I couldn't wait until Friday, but that would be a big fat lie. The crisp cotton sheets were a welcome sensation against my skin as I slid between them and clicked off the lamp on my nightstand, closing my eyes and willing time to fly by.

Mondays in the store always dragged. The slow start to the week was usually something I welcomed so I could get caught up from the busy weekend. Tonight I'd be meeting up with Amara and Grayson for our weekly trivia game, and I usually needed the time to prepare myself mentally for going out.

When I stepped into the bar several hours later, it only took me seconds before my gaze met an identical pair of ocean blue eyes across the room. I waved, closing the distance between my twin and me. He grinned, opening his arms for a hug, which I sank into. This place was like a second home and the tiny *safe zone* I lived inside to keep the panic at bay thankfully extended to here.

"There's my baby sister," he cooed, patting my head.

I stepped back and glared up at him. "Baby? You're two minutes older than me."

He puffed out his chest. "Two minutes and eleven seconds. The seconds count."

I held my glare until Gray's lip twitched and I cracked up, his deep chuckle joining my laugh. Shit, bested by my brother again.

"Is Amara here yet?" I asked, scanning the room.

"Not yet. She texted me saying she was running a few minutes late. Let's get you a drink, kiddo," Grayson said, signaling for the bartender.

Before I knew it, a beer sat in front of me on the bar, dripping condensation onto the coaster beneath it. I lifted it and took a small sip while Grayson turned to let down some poor woman who had just hit on him. I swore we couldn't go anywhere without women throwing themselves at him. See, my brother was a bit of a manwhore, but he knew the rules. Trivia nights were sacred. No hookups allowed.

Despite being twins, my brother and I were total opposites. I shied away from attention from the opposite sex, but Grayson was the definition of a fuck boy. Women flocked to him, which just added to his confident swagger.

He turned back to me with an obnoxious smirk. "Sorry about that, can't keep them away from all this." Grayson ran his hand down his fit body and I gagged.

I lifted my eyes to the ceiling as if I were praying for strength. "Thor help the woman who finally tames you, Gray."

He snorted. "Never gonna happen."

If Gray had girlfriends in the past, he never brought them around me. My brother lived for the single life, but always made Amara and me his priority. We were family, the three of us. Nothing got in the way when either of us needed him. Amara was like our adopted sister. Grayson and I came into this world together and had been attached at the hip ever since. Most people thought we were weird for being so close, but neither of us gave a shit. It was a twin thing.

While my brother ran to the bathroom, I took out my phone to check my messages like I'd been obsessively doing since yesterday. The glare of the woman Grayson shot down burned into my back from where she sat across the room, but I ignored it. He and I looked alike, but not so much that people automatically knew we were twins. Sometimes women assumed we were together. Like together-together.

Talk about vomit-inducing.

Staring down at the screen, my stomach fluttered when a new message from Zen, a sweet reminder that he was thinking of me, popped up. I had to admit, with all the tattoos and the shadows behind his eyes, I never would've pegged him for the sweet type. Grinning down at the phone like a maniac, I typed out a quick reply. I wasn't fast enough, though, because Grayson caught me and tried to snatch my phone out of my hand.

"Who are you texting? And why are you smiling like that?" he questioned, eyes narrowed on the phone I was holding out of his reach.

Before I could respond, Amara stomped up to the bar.

"Ugh, finally! I swear, people around here don't know how to drive," she grumbled. "What did I miss?" She gave Grayson a quick hug before turning and throwing her arms around me.

"Kennedy's texting some mystery person, and I was just about to start grilling her to find out who it is," Grayson explained, lifting his beer to his mouth but keeping his eyes on me.

"Ooh, who is it? The kidnapped guy?" Amara asked, eyes sparkling with mischief because she knew exactly what she just did.

"Kidnapped guy? What the fuck?" Grayson practically yelled, slamming his beer on the bar.

I sighed. I knew better than to check my phone if I wasn't ready to spill the details. Really this was my own fault. Grayson and

Amara were both notorious for getting all up in my private business.

"Okay, fine." I tore at the label on my beer bottle. "I know how this works. You'll be relentless until I cave. Just know I didn't want to talk about this yet." I narrowed my eyes, but both of them matched my glare with expectant expressions. I let out another sigh.

"Yes, it's the guy I rescued." I glanced at my brother. "Some girl tried to force him into her car when he couldn't even stand up. I think she might've drugged him. Actually, maybe you could learn a thing or two from the situation, Gray."

He chuckled. "Oh, Ken. I'm a big boy and am plenty capable of taking care of myself. Besides, I don't do anything against my will, ever. But thanks for your concern." He winked at me, and I rolled my eyes.

"Anywaaaaay," Amara dragged out. "What happened after?"

"We hung out over the weekend, and he's kind of amazing."

"Wait, you voluntarily hung out with a guy this weekend?" Grayson asked, sitting up straighter.

"Yeah, after she rescued his drunk-slash-drugged ass from his kidnapper. Keep up," Amara snapped.

Grayson's eyes narrowed. "Watch it, Am." He turned back to me. "He was drunk?"

I shot Amara what I hoped was a withering glare. "Was it really necessary to

tell him that part?"

"Sorry," she said, looking at me pleadingly. "I know Gray's overprotective, it just slipped out. But now that he knows, tell us the rest."

Amara was practically bouncing on the balls of her feet.

"There's not much to tell. He asked me to dinner, but you know I couldn't go out, so I suggested we eat in. He cooked, and we hung out. I asked him to come back yesterday, and we had a picnic at the lake. It was just really nice. Nothing happened, we just got to know each other a bit," I finished, trying to make it sound really casual, even though it felt like a piece of me was missing since he left yesterday. Zen shifted my entire life on its axis and now I didn't know which way was up.

"Mmhmm, and tell us everything about him. What does he look like? What's his name?" Amara asked. Grayson watched our exchange but stayed silent.

"His name is Zen. He's hands down the hottest guy I've ever seen," my brother snorted, and I flipped him off, "but more than that, he's got a good heart. I think it's hard for him to let people in, but when he does, he's fiercely loyal and protective."

"Zen? That's a weird name," Grayson observed.

I shrugged. "It fits him."

"He's that gorgeous?" Amara lifted her eyebrow. "You've had guys throwing themselves at you for practically your entire life, and not one of them has turned your head. I've got to see what he looks like. Did you happen to sneak a picture when you were hanging out last weekend?"

She leaned over to grab my phone out of my hand, but I held it up so she couldn't reach. Towering six inches over my best friend had never been more helpful. She jutted her lip out in a pout.

"Yeah, I snuck a picture and sent it to you but thanks to your broken phone, you never got it. Hold on," I looked down, scrolling and tapping until I found it. "Here."

I shoved my phone in Amara's face. Grayson leaned over her shoulder to get a better look, too.

Amara's face went pale as she gasped. I looked at Grayson, and his eye twitched a little. My heart rate sped up. Did I pull up the wrong picture? I took my phone back, looking down to double-check. Zen's crooked grin stared up at me.

"What the hell is wrong with you guys? What's wrong with him?" I demanded. A cold sweat broke out across my forehead as my heart pounded against my ribcage. I wasn't sure what to make of their reaction, but my fight or flight response was right there ready to burst on the scene like the damn Kool-Aid Man.

"I... I'm not sure what to say here," Amara hesitated, looking to Grayson for help.

He cleared his throat. "You can't see him anymore, Ken. Sorry, but I'm your big brother, and it's my job to protect you. Trust me on this."

I stared at my brother for a second, processing what he'd just said and getting more pissed off by the second. "Are you fucking kidding me, Gray? First of all, it's not your job to protect me. I can protect myself."

I crossed my arms over my chest and narrowed my eyes at him, daring him to argue. "Second of all, tell me what the fuck is wrong with you two right now." I was close to stomping my foot and had to take a deep breath to steady myself.

"I don't know how to tell you this," Amara rubbed her temples. "But Zen? He's basically the hottest rock star on the planet right now. A legend actually. He's the lead singer of Shadow Phoenix."

I threw my head back and laughed. Okay, they were definitely fucking with me. "No, that can't be true. Zen's a totally normal guy. If he were who you say, he'd be stuck up or weird or unapproachable. He'd have bodyguards and get swarmed by fans whenever he leaves the house."

If I thought about it, some of the things he'd said made more sense in the context of this new information. My knees went weak, and I fell onto the stool next to Gray.

"Wait, he did tell me he's in the music industry, but it can't be true. I... I can't believe it." My voice came out a whisper.

"And how many guys do you know named 'Zen'? It's not exactly a common name," Amara added, her voice gentle as her hand came down on my back and she started rubbing soothing circles.

For the second time in less than a week, my world tilted. I closed my eyes and took a shaky breath. "What do I even do with this information? I can't reconcile who he is when we're together with some world-famous celebrity. There's no way."

"Wait, doesn't he have a sex tape out right now, too?" Amara unhelpfully asked. I felt like I might throw up.

Grayson glared at her. "Not helping."

I had a sudden urge to run. Maybe vomit first, then run. "Sex tape?" I squeaked.

"If it helps, I heard the girl who put it out did it without his permission." Amara kept rubbing my back soothingly.

I gripped the edge of the bar as my head spun. "I don't think that helps, but thanks for trying."

Grayson took that as his opportunity to enforce his self-appointed big brother duties. "Stop talking to him right now, ghost the fucker. This is not going to be good for you, Ken. Maybe he's a great guy despite what all the tabloids say about him, and that's fine for someone else. But there are huge strings attached when it comes to dealing with his lifestyle. What are you going to do when the paparazzi find out about you? When the women on his social media find out about you and decide they hate you simply for existing? There's no way all of that is worth it. I don't want to see you go through all that shit again."

I lifted a shaky hand to my forehead, pressing hard to try and ground myself. If what my brother and best friend were saying was true, why hadn't Zen told me about this? If I was being fair to him, it made sense. Once people found out he was famous, I'm sure they treated him differently. But I didn't want to be fair. I wanted him to be honest with me, treat me differently than he did everyone else. Slowly, anger washed away the confusion.

I didn't give a shit what Gray wanted me to do. I needed to talk to Zen.

"What if you guys are just confusing him with someone else?" I asked as the anger faded long enough for stupid, stupid hope to take its place.

Amara took out her phone, tapped the screen for a few seconds, and then held it out. There were headlines about Zen's sex tape, his picture front and center, and the girls he'd been with listed on only the first search page.

So. Many. Girls.

My stomach rolled. I couldn't do this. I needed to get the fuck out of this bar before I panicked. My eyes stung with the effort to hold back the tidal wave of tears threatening to fall.

"I can't be here." I reached for my purse and threw some bills down on the bar. "I'm going home."

My heart raced, and I couldn't breathe. Grayson saw the look in my eye and knew what was coming.

Panic.

As twins, we had almost a sixth sense about how the other was feeling.

"I'm going to walk her. Rain check for next week?" Grayson turned to Amara and asked.

"Sure, of course. Ken, text me and let me know you're okay," Amara said, pulling me into a tight hug.

I nodded, unable to speak, and grabbed my phone, slinging my purse over my shoulder. I practically ran for the exit, and Grayson followed me out.

When the cool evening air hit me as I stepped outside, I breathed deeply, trying to calm myself down. My pulse pounded in my ears, and I pressed my palm to my chest to try and hold my heart inside since it felt like it was about to hurl itself out. Lifting my phone with a trembling hand, I dialed Zen's number. It rang a few times and went to voicemail.

"Hey, it's Kennedy. I just heard something, and I need to know if it's true. I'm sort of freaking out. I don't know what to believe. I wish you'd told me." I hated how shaky my voice sounded.

Grayson caught up with me, but the panic was starting to get overwhelming so I couldn't focus. I knew I needed to calm down and turn off my phone for a few minutes. The temptation to keep calling or search the internet was too much, and it would only make things worse. I couldn't handle the fear of what Zen might call and say. I threw the dark phone into my purse.

My brother walked beside me with his hands shoved into his pockets, not saying anything. He gave me space but stayed near me in case I needed him in silent support. He really was the best.

"Jesus, Gray, I can't believe I was so stupid. Why am I drawn to guys who treat me like shit? What the hell is wrong with me?"

I paced the sidewalk outside my shop with tears streaming down my face. No matter how much air I dragged into my lungs, I couldn't catch my breath, and my hands were getting tingly. I vaguely wondered if I was about to pass out.

Grayson stepped in front of me and grabbed my upper arms, forcing me to look him in the eye.

"Ken, look at me. Breathe. You're fine. Nothing is wrong with you. Not a single damn thing. It's clear you really like this guy. Maybe I jumped to conclusions in there." He sighed and raked his hand through his tousled hair, turning around and stalking away before coming back to stand in front of me again.

"I know what I said before, that there are a shit ton of strings, but if he's a good guy, maybe... you should hear him out. Fuck, I don't know." He sounded like it pained him to say the words. "You think you're so weak because of this," he gestured to all of me. "This panic thing you've got going on, but you're not weak. You're the strongest fucking person I know. You deal with this shit day in and day out and never get down about it. You wake up every morning and see the good in people, the good in the world. Just talk to the guy, hear him out. Maybe there's a good explanation for him not telling you. But right now, you need to just breathe."

I kept my eyes locked on his face and my palm on his chest, following along with his breathing. Soon, I started calming down. When my heart rate slowed down, I could think more clearly.

"You're right, Gray. I need to think this through. The truth is, I don't know if I can handle being with Zen, with what comes along with that part of his life. But, I do know I can calm down and try to figure it out. I owe it to myself and to him to hear what he has to say." I gave him a watery smile as tears slid down my face. "Will you come stay with me for a little while? I don't really want to sit in my house alone right now."

"Of course. You know I'll be there for whatever you need," he said, throwing his arm over my shoulder and giving me a squeeze.

"Thanks, Gray."

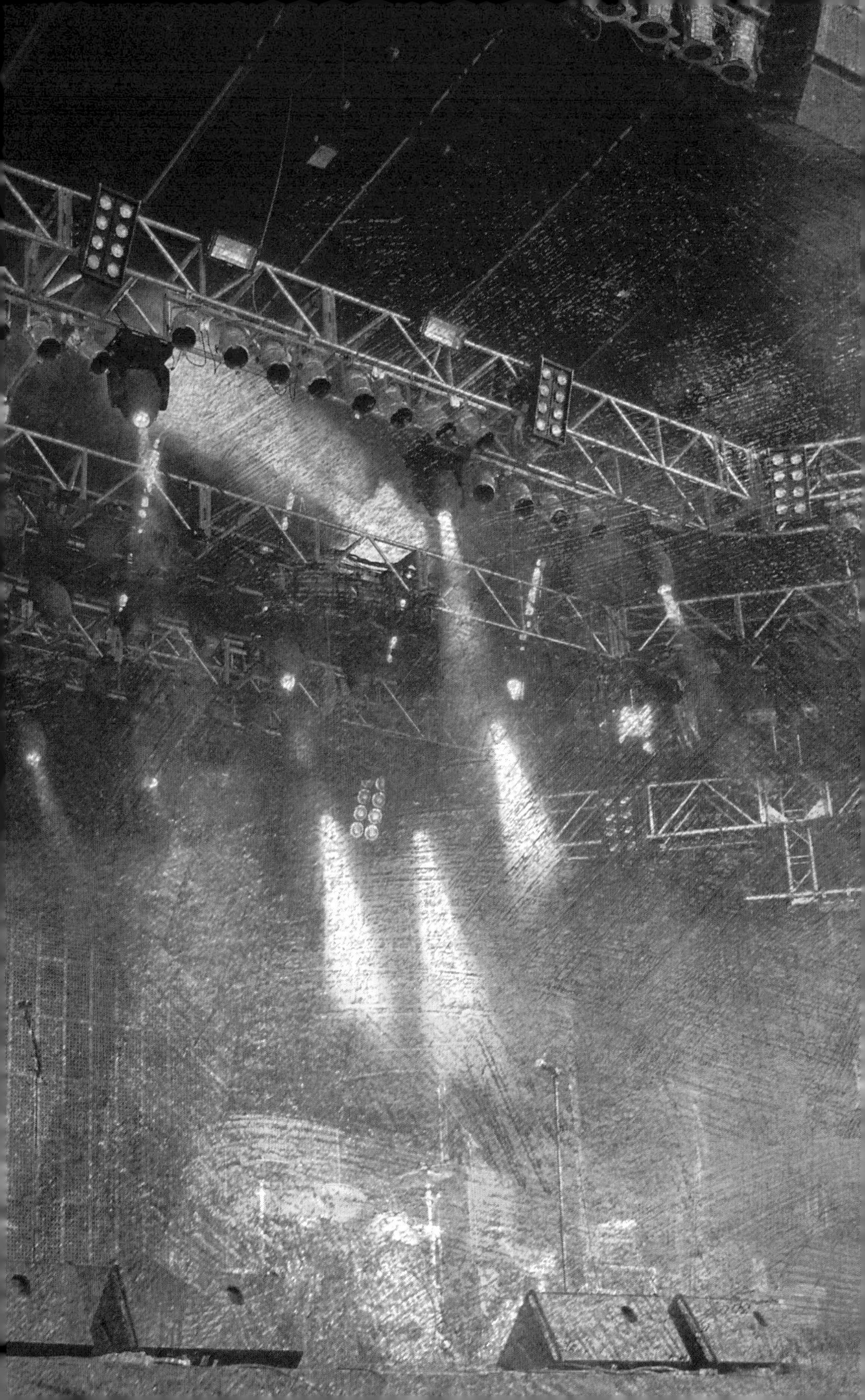

CHAPTER 11

ZEN

I WISH *you'd told me.*

I kept hearing Kennedy's voice over and over, that fucking voicemail she left taunted me. She found out who I was, which was the last fucking thing I wanted to have happen but I knew it was inevitable. I'd hoped I'd get the chance to talk to her and explain everything about my life to her, before she found out from someone else, but I should've known better.

Fuck.

I needed to fix this.

There was no way I could let her go, not now that I knew about the little sounds she made when I kissed her or the way her eyes sparkled when she found one of her customers the perfect book.

I wish you'd told me.

The recording studio in my basement was like a soundproofed dungeon, and I'd been down there when she tried to call me. Since I met Kennedy, lyrics had been pouring out of me. She was officially my muse. I didn't sleep last night because the words wouldn't stop demanding to be written.

As I paced the hall outside of the studio, I dialed Kennedy's number, and got her voicemail for the tenth time. My fingers clenched around the device so hard it creaked ominously.

"Please call me back, Sunshine," I begged. "I'll explain everything. Just call me. I'm so fucking sorry." My voice cracked as I fought a losing battle against the despair threatening to overtake me.

Fuck, why wasn't she answering? And why the fuck was I standing around here waiting for her to make the next move when I knew where she lived?

I ran my hand through my hair, trying to steady my shaking breath and calm my racing heart. What if I lost her over this? I shut that fucked up line of thinking down as soon as it crossed my mind. I wouldn't let that happen.

I couldn't.

True stepped into the hallway and I felt his eyes on me, probably wondering what the hell was wrong with me. He flew up to Washington this morning to work on the music to match my lyrics because, despite the fact I'd been exiled, the label still expected us to record a new album.

"What's wrong with you?" True leaned back against the wall and crossed his arms over his chest, an amused smirk on his lips.

"None of your goddamn business," I snapped, in no mood for his bullshit.

True just chuckled, the asshole. "Fine, don't tell me, but you know I'm going to find out eventually. You might as well just come out with it."

My glare was enough of an answer.

He pushed off the wall and moved toward me. "Dude, what the hell? Since when do we hide shit from each other?"

I knew he was right. The guys were like my brothers, and it wasn't like me to not tell him everything. But I couldn't talk about how badly I fucked up until I fixed it. "We don't, but I need to fix it first."

True folded his arms across his chest and studied me before nodding in understanding. "You want to get back in there and get this done?" He was giving me an out, not pressing for more and it was one of the things I appreciated most about him.

I didn't think I had it in me to finish the song we were working on. Not tonight. I turned away, grabbing my hooded sweatshirt off the back of the chair where I'd spent the last several hours working. The need to go to Kennedy was staggering, and I couldn't focus on anything else.

"No, I can't. I have to go. I'll be back tomorrow." I pulled my keys out of my pocket.

"You're seriously bailing on me right now? She better have a hot friend so when you fix this you can make it up to me." True shook his head and laughed his ass off at me. "Don't forget we're on a deadline, bro. The label will have our balls if we're late on top of all the other shit going on."

"I'm well aware." I slipped the hoodie on and checked my pockets to make sure I had all my shit, ignoring his *hot friend* comment.

"Want me to come with you? You might need some backup."

"Nah, I'm good." Like me, True was guarded with who he let into his life, but unlike me, he wasn't an asshole about it. He really would go with me if I wanted him to and help me rectify my fuck up.

"I'll order takeout and leave the leftovers in the fridge for when you drag your drunk ass home." Shit, was I really that bad that he expected me to go out and get shit faced tonight?

I let out a long exhale. "You were right. I met someone."

"I knew it." I wanted to punch the huge grin off his face because I was agitated as fuck. Talking about Kennedy in any way felt so wrong when I didn't know where we stood. "What's she like? When can I meet her? Tell me everything."

I should've known he'd be a fucking girl about this. He was the kind of guy who believed in true love and soulmates and shit. "I knew I shouldn't have said anything, not yet."

The smile dropped off his face and he twisted his nose ring. "What'd you do?"

"I told you I don't want to talk about this right now. I've already wasted too much time. I have to go. I'll fill you in tomorrow."

True walked over to the couch I kept down here, for the long nights I sometimes spent working, and flopped down. I knew he'd do anything I asked him to, even if he didn't like it. "I think I'll make use of your studio. I've been playing with some new music, since I've got the studio to myself tonight."

"Do whatever you want." I checked my phone one last time. Nothing.

"Maddox and Jericho aren't going to be happy if we risk our contract by pissing off the label."

"We'll get it done," I said. "I was up writing all last night, and it's the best shit I've penned in years. Give me tonight and tomorrow you've got me all day."

"Call me if you need me," True said as I turned and was already making my way down the hall toward the garage.

"Hopefully I won't see you until the morning," I threw over my shoulder at True on my way out the door. I needed to fix this right the fuck now, and if all went well, I didn't plan on coming home tonight.

Hopping in my Mercedes, I made the short drive to Kennedy's loft. My foot bounced on the SUV floor while my chest tightened, and it got harder and harder to breathe every mile closer I got. I couldn't hold still, and wanted to crawl out of my fucking skin. I wondered if Kennedy felt like this during one of her panic attacks.

In a way, I was glad she hadn't picked up the phone. Explaining in person would be so much better. I could touch her and look into her eyes when I told her everything and see how she was reacting so I could handle whatever she was feeling. I just hoped she'd hear me out. At least in person, it'd be nearly impossible to ignore me.

I knew she'd be upset and hurting after what she told me at the lake, and as much as I felt like an asshole for being the one to hurt her, I didn't want her to go through the pain without me there to comfort her. Yes, I was aware it was fucked up. It killed me that I might've hurt her or betrayed her trust. It was a big fucking deal that she opened up to me in the first place, and right about now I'd bet she was cursing the day I fell into her life.

Shit, I already broke the promise I made myself, and it'd been less than a week. It was official--I fucking sucked.

I parked in front of her store, taking a steadying breath before using my key to open the door, saying a silent thanks when it unlocked. At least she hadn't changed the locks yet. When I got inside, everything was dark and quiet so I made my way up the stairs to her apartment. When I got to her door, I knocked lightly.

"Kennedy? It's me. I'm coming in," I called, before using my key to open the door.

The silence greeted me. A light over the stove cast a faint glow into the apartment, and I walked in the kitchen and set my keys and phone down on the island.

"Kennedy?" I called out.

She didn't answer right away, so I turned toward the living room, and I froze, not wanting to believe my eyes.

What the actual fuck was this?

Curled up in a pile of throw pillows, Kennedy rested her head on some guy's shoulder, asleep in front of the TV. My heart started to race as anger tore through my veins. I thought she said she hadn't been with anyone in seven years. I clenched my jaw, my breath beginning to come faster. She wouldn't manipulate me, would she? She wasn't that type of girl, or so I thought.

It wouldn't be the first time I misjudged someone.

I moved towards her and repeated her name, this time louder.

"Kennedy, wake up."

She slowly started to stir before her puffy eyes popped open and settled on me. "Zen? What the hell are you doing here? You scared the shit out of me!" she yelled, pressing her hand to her heart and closing her eyes, taking a deep breath.

Her shout woke the guy next to her up, and my hands balled into fists at my sides. My eyes narrowed to slits as I glared at this guy who dared to touch my girl.

"Whoa, buddy. You need to calm the fuck down," the guy cautioned, holding up his hands. I guess he'd taken in the murderous look on my face.

Who the fuck did this guy think he was?

"Who the fuck calms down when someone tells them to?" I asked in a low voice drenched in malice while I took a step forward.

"This is not what you think, and you're going to make a complete ass of yourself if you keep this shit up," the guy tried to reason with me, the corners of his mouth turning up slightly into a smirk that had fantasies of dismemberment flashing through my head.

"Tell me what the fuck is happening," I growled.

Kennedy sighed. "Zen, this is my twin brother, Grayson."

Immediately, my muscles relaxed as the tension left my body bit by bit, and then I winced. Fuck, I was an asshole.

Had she mentioned she had a brother? I couldn't remember.

"Wow, that was something to see, really. I can honestly say that's a first for us, Ken. A guy being jealous of me." Grayson threw his head back and laughed.

Kennedy shrugged, her usual vibrancy completely fucking gone and I knew it was all my fault. "Happens to me all the time. A girl at the bar earlier looked at me like she wanted to kill me for being there with you."

Now that I really stopped to look, I saw all the similarities between them. The same blonde hair, the same blue eyes. It checked out and I shoved my hands in my pockets.

"Sorry for acting like a possessive asshole. That's not usually me, I just…." I trailed off, unsure what to say.

"I get it, but you don't have to worry about me putting the moves on your girl. At least not while your girl happens to be my sister," Grayson laughed before growing serious again. "What you do have to worry about is what I'll do to you if you ever hurt her again." Grayson's tone became threatening, and he stood up, standing directly in front of me now. Toe to toe, we were similar height and build, and when I sized him up, I wasn't sure who would win in a fight if it came to that. He had that slightly unhinged look in his eye, like he wouldn't mind beating me until I was bloody and might not stop even then.

Him and Maddox would probably get along great and bond over the best way to torture someone.

Believe it or not, I liked Grayson despite our rocky introduction. I liked that Kennedy had someone nearby watching out for her when I couldn't be there. And based on that look in his eye? He'd handle shit if it came down to it.

I deflated a little. "Good, I'm glad Kennedy has you around watching out for her."

"Oh, I'll always be here for her." He crossed his arms and somehow his words sounded like a threat.

"You know I'm right here." Kennedy waved from her spot on the couch. We both mumbled apologies.

"I know you want to talk to my sister, but can I have a word with you first?" Grayson asked. "Outside."

I exhaled slowly. The need to talk to Kennedy was overpowering every other thought and sense, but I'd humor him if it got him to leave faster so I could be alone with my girl.

"Fine, but only for a minute."

Grayson pulled her into a hug and told her to call if she needed anything, shooting me a warning look over her shoulder. Then he walked outside. Kennedy looked up at me. "Just go talk, I'll be here when you get back. I'm not going anywhere." She sounded exhausted, but as I turned to follow her brother, she said quietly, "I'm happy you came."

My chest tightened, and my lips tilted up. Maybe I could still fix this. I'd made the right choice by dropping everything and coming to see Kennedy in person.

We stepped outside, and the crisp night air soaked into my skin. I looked up at the sky. The nearly full moon brightened the street.

Grayson's voice cut through the silence. "Look, you've got this entire life that I don't really understand, and honestly, I don't give a shit. Kennedy's my family, pretty much all I have and she's what I care about. We're not just siblings, she's my best friend. I won't let anything or anyone hurt her, least of all you."

He ran a hand down his face. "I don't know how much she's told you, but she has issues that aren't easy for people to handle. I bet your life is chaotic on the best day, and you need to stay away from my sister unless you're ready to be there for her when she needs you. Or to fucking protect her from any of the bullshit that's going to cause her stress. You may not think it's my business to get involved, but she never lets anyone in and the fact that you're here, that she told me about you, that she got upset tonight when she found out who you really were. It means something."

"I respect that you're looking out for her, but what's between me and your sister isn't really any of your fucking business. You're right about that." I watched as he bristled but I held up my hand and continued. "That being said, I'm never letting your sister go. She's stuck with me now, even if she doesn't know it yet. So, you have nothing to worry about, Grayson. I'd rather rip my own heart out of my chest and stick it in a blender than do anything to intentionally hurt Kennedy." My chest hurt like a motherfucker; like he'd stabbed me with a knife instead of hurled words at me. I rubbed it, trying to relieve the sting, but it didn't help.

Grayson deflated, some of his anger dissipating at my confession. "As long as you don't fuck up again, I'll butt out."

There was an awkward silence, but there was no one who understood Kennedy better than her twin brother, so I admitted, "She told me about what happened to her in high school and her panic attacks."

Grayson's eyebrows shot up. "She did? She's only ever told Amara and me, and even then only because we tell each other everything and she wouldn't be able to hide it."

"Yeah, she did. I have a pretty good idea of what I'm getting myself into, and you know what? She's worth every struggle, every fear, every hurdle. There's nothing your sister could throw at me that would make me turn my back on her, because Kennedy is the most incredible person I've ever met. I dropped everything tonight, to be here and make things right with her—risking my career and everything I've spent the last decade building—because that's how important she is to me."

Grayson let out a heavy exhale. "Do me a favor and really think hard about this shit. You just met. You have no idea how bad it can get, and if it turns out you can't handle it, I'm going to have to pick up the pieces you leave behind. If you can't be fucking honest with her or yourself about your lives and how they can work together, walk away now. If you get in any deeper with her, she may not recover if you decide to walk away. And then I'll have to fucking kill you."

Grayson stared straight into my eyes, jaw set, and arms crossed, daring me to see the truth in his words.

I pushed harder against my chest, trying to ease the ache. I was so fucking angry with myself for hurting her by not just telling her the truth. Never again. If I was going to help her deal with her issues, I needed to man the hell up and deal with my own, too.

Shit, no one had made me want to look in a mirror and be a better man for as long as I could remember. What the hell was Kennedy doing to me?

I leaned against the brick wall, pushing my hands into my pockets. "I told you I'm not going anywhere, and I'm not. Spending the day up in my head isn't going to change shit. I'm not making any public declarations yet. We haven't even talked about what we are to each other, so I'd appreciate you not saying anything until I can talk to Kennedy. I'm letting her set the pace for what we have going forward. I just want you to know, even though she doesn't know it yet, she's mine and I'm sure as fuck hers."

Was it fucked up that my confession was to Grayson instead of Kennedy for the first time? Maybe, but it felt good admitting this shit out loud to someone, and owning up to my feelings eased the pain in my chest.

Grayson stood back and eyed me skeptically before blowing out a breath. "What about the other women? The tape? Groupies?"

I rubbed the back of my neck. "Other women stopped existing for me the minute I saw your sister. And as for that fucking tape, there's nothing I can do. I'm laying low here until it blows over. It was recorded and sold to the vultures without my permission."

"That blows, man. And I can't imagine one of my hookups recording me and putting it out into the world." He shuddered. "If you really mean everything you just said, I'm glad she found you, and I hope she gives you a chance. I won't stand in your way, but I sure as fuck will be watching." His lips quirked up into a grin. "Oh, speaking of her finding you, what the fuck did I hear about her rescuing you from a kidnapper?"

"Yeah, I was out having a drink and the bartender drugged me and then tried to take me… somewhere. Whatever the hell she was going to do with me, I have no idea. But Kennedy stepped in and told that bitch to fuck off. She saved me."

Grayson chuckled, and I gave him a weary smile. "Truthfully, I was a mess until your sister found me. I didn't realize it, but I had a hole in my life I was trying to fill with alcohol and women that wasn't leading anywhere good. I'm just starting to figure shit out, but it's a long story, and right now, I just want to go upstairs." I suddenly felt exhausted. "Give me your number. I want us to be able to reach each other if anything ever happens and I'm out of town."

Grayson grinned and handed over his phone. "What would happen if I posted this on social media? The private cell phone number of *the* Zen Taylor?"

I tapped at the screen for a second before sending myself a text and handing it back. "I'd get a new number," I deadpanned.

Gray laughed. "Fair enough."

"Please don't. I've had enough headaches this month to last a lifetime."

The joking expression on Grayson's face twisted into something much more serious. "I'd never betray my sister like that, and by extension, you. If she's picked you, that means you're one of us."

"Thanks. Now I'm going upstairs to fix my mess with your sister if she'll let me. I appreciate you being there for her when I wasn't."

Grayson nodded once. "I always will be."

Watching Kennedy's brother walk away, I took a deep breath and ran my hand through my hair. I said a silent prayer to any god or demon who may be listening that she gave me a chance to say what I needed to and didn't throw me out when I was done talking. I needed to find a way to make her understand that she could trust me despite my colossal fuck up.

Needing someone was a foreign concept to me. I'd never really needed anyone until Kennedy, and it happened so quickly with her that I was still trying to catch my breath. I liked needing her—a lot. Probably more than I should. I shook my head, trying to clear out my racing thoughts, and turned to go inside and face

Kennedy with the truth. No matter what happened, she deserved the truth.

Walking up the stairs, my stomach filled with dread. I hated to admit it, but I was terrified that once we had this talk, I'd never see her again. Me, the guy who wasn't scared of shit.

I could stand on a stage in front of thousands of people with millions more watching at home and not feel a damn thing, but outside the door of this girl's apartment my knees were shaking.

Fuck.

I'd do whatever it took to protect her from my life if she'd let me, but it wasn't my decision whether or not she stuck around once she knew everything. Maybe walking away from me would be the best thing for her.

I'd never been through this with a girl before, I'd never cared enough to try.

Pushing open the door, I stepped inside and closed it softly. "Kennedy?"

"Still in here," she called from the direction of the living room. Just the sound of her voice made my body buzz with the need to be close to her.

My feet carried me across her loft quickly, and I sat on the couch next to her. My hands itched to touch her, but I didn't know if she'd be okay with it so I kept my hands to myself instead. She looked over at me with tired and red-rimmed eyes that lacked their usual brightness, and my goddamn heart cracked. I'd done this to her.

"I didn't think I'd see you until Friday." The corner of her lips lifted slightly.

I smiled because she was at least in a good enough mood to joke with me. That had to be a good sign, right? "I told you I'd drop everything if you asked, and that also goes double if you need me or aren't answering my calls when there's something wrong." I reached out and pulled her hand into mine, lacing our fingers together.

"I'm so fucking sorry I didn't tell you exactly what I do sooner," I murmured, looking down at her hand clasped in mine as my stomach twists. "I've never had anything like this happen before, with people not knowing who I am. I've never given a shit what anyone else thinks or needs to know."

She watched me as she listened, moving closer until our thighs touched. She leaned her head against my shoulder. I breathed out like I was trying to blow down the goddamn building, the knot in my chest loosening at the contact. My cheek fell to the top of her head before I kept going.

"I haven't had a girlfriend or anything since we formed the band. I've just kept things casual because I never saw the point and shit gets too complicated with our schedule and the fans. Girls always wanted something from me, to use me for my body or my fame, and I used them, too. No one ever actually gave a shit about me and so I didn't care about them, either."

I'm sure I sounded bitter as fuck, and I guess I kind of was. It wasn't until I said it out loud that I realized how much. "It's made me suspicious of people's intentions when I meet someone new. It's why I didn't tell you right away who I was. Then when you told me about your past and how important honesty is to you, and I hadn't been upfront with you right away about my life, I was scared out of my mind to come clean because I couldn't handle you walking away from me, from what this could be."

I pulled away so I could look into her eyes, and I cupped her cheek with my hand. Against my palm, her skin was warm and soft, like velvet. "I'm not above begging here. Don't give up on me. I fucked up, and I'm sorry for not being honest with you about this, but I promise I'll never keep anything from you again. I can't lose you." I didn't mean to admit that last part out loud, but fuck it. It was the truth.

She closed her eyes and leaned into my touch. "After I calmed down from the shock of everything, I realized you must have had a good reason for not telling me, or at least I hoped you did. I can't imagine what your life is like, and what it must be like to have people always wanting something from you or always judging you. I thought a lot about it and talked it out with my brother. I'm not mad at you for not telling me. I was at first, but I get why you did it. But from now on, you have to be honest with me no matter how much you think you have to protect me. I may be afraid of everything, but I'm *not* weak."

She sat up and looked me in the eyes, hers filled with fiery determination. "If I let you in, if we have any hope of actually being together and making something of whatever this is, we've got to be partners. I want to be able to lean on you, sure, but you have to also be able to lean on me. You're not in this alone anymore, okay?"

She smiled, the brightest fucking smile I'd ever seen. It lit up my insides like the pyrotechnics on our last world tour. I ran my thumb along her lower lip, and her gaze dropped to my mouth. I couldn't take it anymore, resisting Kennedy was impossible.

Leaning forward, I kissed her hard, groaning at the jolt of lust the contact shot straight to my dick. I was desperate to taste her, and she clung to me like she felt the same. She was mine, and I'd make sure to remind her of that after how close I came to losing her. She moaned into my mouth as we devoured each other and I swallowed it down, greedy for all her pleasure. It wasn't a gentle kiss, but a kiss filled with emotion—hurt and forgiveness—and more than a little hunger. I kissed her once more softly, the sight of her swollen lips making my cock harden even more and my fingers tighten in her hair. She wasn't ready for everything I had planned for her yet, so I reluctantly pulled back.

"Okay, deal."

She laughed and the sound made my chest warm like the sun was shining directly on me. "That easy?"

"Yep. When it comes to you, it's that easy. I don't know if you've noticed yet, but I've gotten sort of attached, Sunshine. I'd do anything not to lose you." I exhaled, pulling her a little closer, feeling a constant need to reassure myself she's still here in my arms, that I hadn't lost her. It should've been unsettling as fuck to get so attached to her this soon, but somehow it wasn't.

Now that everything was out in the open, exhaustion settled down over me like a weighted blanket. "Now I'm fucking exhausted, and you look like you are, too. Do you mind if I stay here tonight? I probably shouldn't drive, but I can call a ride if you want some space."

"You never have to ask, Zen. You can always stay. Let's go to bed." Despite how tired I was, her words were a shot of white-hot heat straight to my cock. I reminded myself now wasn't the time but it was getting harder and harder to put on the brakes. This was the longest I'd ever waited to take things to the next level, but I knew Kennedy would be worth it. She needed to take things slow, but slow was the last fucking thing I wanted. She stood up and pulled me up with her, leading us back to her bedroom.

"I don't have to sleep in here with you if it makes you uncomfortable," I hesitated, not wanting to push her. "I can take the couch."

Please don't make me take the fucking couch.

She raised an eyebrow. "Afraid you won't be able to keep your hands to yourself?"

"Fuck, yes. Have you seen you?"

She eyed me like I was crazy, but she'd get used to me drooling over her. She really had no idea how gorgeous she was. "Just come to bed."

"Yes, ma'am." I walked over and lifted her chin to meet my eyes before placing a soft kiss on her lips. Then I stepped back and pulled my shirt over my head. With the fabric out of the way, I caught her heated gaze roaming my body before she noticed me watching her and looked away, blushing.

I smirked and ran my hand down the planes of my chest, wishing it was hers instead. "See something you like?"

"Duh. Have you seen you?" she tossed my words back at me.

Touché.

I fucking loved that I caught her looking at me like she wanted to eat me. If she wasn't careful, I was going to get used to spending nights like this and she'd never get rid of me. My jeans came off next and fell into a heap on the floor before I climbed into her bed, the smell of sunshine and coconut all over the sheets. It was the scent of her, the smell of home and I sighed, content for the first time in forever.

Kennedy went into the closet to change and came out wearing tiny shorts and a tight tank top that showed off the tight peaks of her nipples, standing at attention like my own personal ovation.

Holy shit.

"You're—" I swallowed hard. She wasn't going to make this easy on me. "You're wearing that to sleep?"

She looked down at her shirt and then back up, an adorable wrinkle forming between her eyes. "Yeah, why? You don't like it?"

"Like it? I fucking love it, but I'm going to have a hell of a time keeping my hands off you." I raked my hand through my hair. "Come here."

She climbed into bed and pulled the blankets over herself before I reached out and dragged her to my chest, wrapping my arm across her waist. She snuggled into me and I stifled a groan when she wiggled her ass right against my semi-hard dick. No doubt she could feel it, but there wasn't anything I could do, and it's not like I was ashamed of the way my body reacted to her. Breathing deeply, I tried to get my now raging hard-on under control, but instead all I did was inhale the scent of her. It was a lost cause at this point.

When she shifted again, I tightened my hold and dropped a kiss to the back of her head. "Go to sleep."

"Goodnight," she whispered before pulling my arm even tighter around her and lacing her fingers with mine.

"Goodnight, Sunshine."

I laid in her bed, holding her warm body as close to mine as I could get it, until her breathing grew even and deep. Kennedy shocked the hell out of me tonight, and the fact I was in her bed right now was beyond even my wildest dreams when I imagined where tonight might end. She took my truth in stride, and we'd work through whatever came our way together. She wasn't going to kick me out and crush my heart because, make no mistake about it, she was the only one on this earth that had the power to do so. My mind was on our future as I fell into the best sleep I'd had in years.

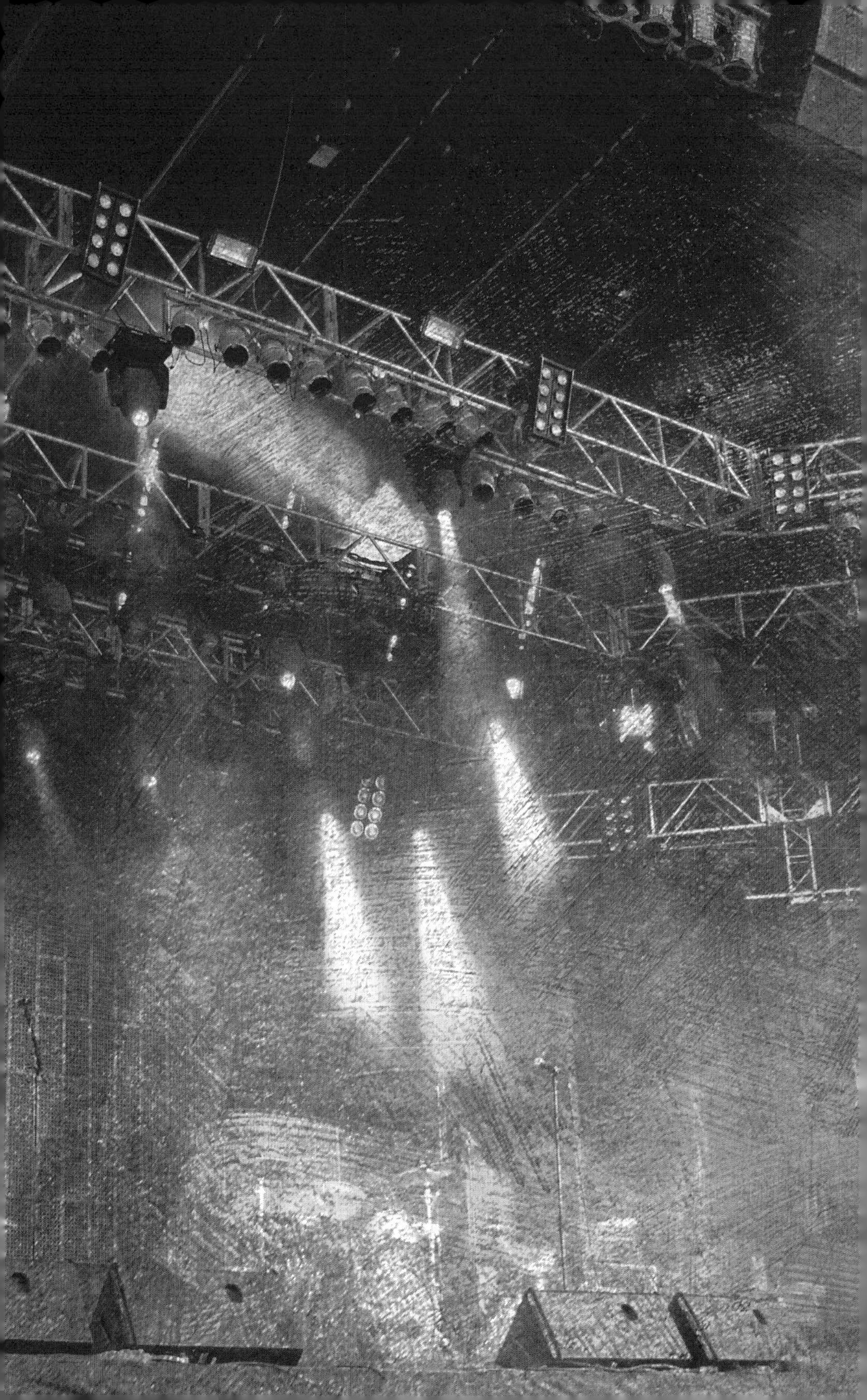

CHAPTER 12

KENNEDY

I WOKE up wrapped around Zen.

Thor, help me.

His breath came in soft little puffs against my hair. Turning onto my back, I watched him sleep as my fingers itched to trace the rough stubble lining his jaw. He looked younger, more relaxed and at ease than I'd ever seen him.

My lips curved into a grin as warmth filled my body down to the tips of my toes. With Zen's arm wrapped around my waist, pulling me against his hard body, I was safe. I'd never slept so well.

Losing the battle not to touch him, I reached up and gently moved a piece of hair off of his forehead before caressing his cheek. The stubble peppering his jaw scraped against my palm, and I wondered how it would feel on other parts of my body. My mouth seemed to have a mind of its own as it gravitated toward his sleepy face. I placed soft kisses on his cheek, his nose, his forehead, and finally, his lips. This was a view people paid thousands of dollars for, and I was staring my fill for free.

I could seriously get used to that.

"Mmm, good morning, beautiful." Zen pushed his hips against me, evidence of how he felt waking up with me in his arms pressed against me, and I swore every nerve in my body came to life.

His lips hovered over mine for a fraction of a second before he kissed me softly. Soft wasn't going to cut it this morning, though. Nope. I'd spent the night twisted up with his gloriously chiseled body, and I might actually have combusted from how hot I was. My body burned in a way I'd never felt before, and I hoped Zen knew how to put out the fire ignited low in my belly.

My fingers had a mind of their own, reaching around his neck, gripping his dark hair, and yanking him back to my mouth when he tried to cut the kiss short. His body shook with laughter as my tongue pushed into his mouth. I was determined to take what I wanted, even if all I wanted was more of him.

Zen rolled over on top of me until the weight of his body pushed me deliciously down into the mattress, and I felt the hard ridge of his cock against my thigh.

A very un-Kennedy-like mewl climbed up my throat before I could stop it, and my fingers dug into his scalp, tugging on the strands of his hair to bring him impossibly closer. Electric sparks rushed through my entire body, as if some forgotten part of me suddenly burst to life, craving everything she'd missed out on and wanted to make up for it right here, with this man, all day long. Unable to get the friction my body demanded, I rocked my hips against him and got a low growl in return.

Zen's calloused hand drifted down along my chest, tracing every curve and I shivered at his rough touch. His fingers worked their way underneath my thin tank top, and I arched into him when he ran his thumb across the sensitive peak of my nipple. He swallowed my gasp when the sting of a pinch gave way to waves of pleasure that settled in my core. My mind had gone blissfully numb for the first time ever, and all I wanted was to wrap every inch of my body around his.

There was no fear, no what ifs.

There was only Zen and me and the inferno raging between us.

Every kiss was like gasoline, stoking the flames higher and hotter.

Every touch was a burst of oxygen, pushing the temperature up so high, it might burn us alive.

If all he left behind was a pile of ashes, I'd happily rise as someone better—someone worthy of him.

He peppered kisses down my neck and across my collarbone, peeling my shirt off and throwing it across the room. Zen slid his tongue lower, tracing a fiery path over my breasts, taking extra time to tease my nipples with his mouth. Arching my back off the bed, I gripped the sheet in my fist.

"Fuck, you're good at that," I moaned.

"I know," he said, his lips moving against the skin of my stomach before he flashed me a wicked grin. My gaze locked on his as the smile dropped off his face and his teeth dragged along his bottom lip. I couldn't have looked away if I wanted to, he had me so transfixed.

His long fingers slid into the sides of my sleep shorts and he tugged them down. Lifting my hips, I helped without an ounce of self-consciousness about my nakedness. Once I was bare, he ran his nose along my inner thigh, breathing me in.

"I can't wait to taste you," he murmured against the sensitive skin of my inner thigh before shifting to my other leg and carving a path upwards with his tongue. My knees fell apart in invitation, even if I'd never done this before.

It was feral.

Wild.

Instinctual.

I nearly cried when his lips found my hip bone, and then the other, never giving me what my body needed.

"You want me to lick you, Sunshine?" he rasped. "Want my tongue to slide inside of you? Circle your sweet clit? Make you come on my fingers with this tiny little clit in my mouth?"

Had anyone ever come from dirty talk before? Because I was in serious danger of it happening right now.

I couldn't form words, so I flung my legs over his shoulders and wiggled forward so his face was between my thighs. He chuckled, but it wasn't filled with humor. No, it was seductive and low and vibrated through my body.

"I'm going to make this pussy mine, Sunshine. Grab onto something, because there's no turning back now." With that warning, he dove in, his tongue feeling like it was everywhere at the same time. He lapped at me, and then shifted and twirled his attention all around my clit but missing it on purpose. Right when I was about to grip his hair and force him to go where I wanted, he flattened his tongue and I forgot my own name as he pushed me toward oblivion.

"Zen." His name fell off my lips as a whispered prayer, but what I was asking for, I couldn't say.

My body tensed, my inner walls squeezing around emptiness as I burned hotter and hotter with every flick of his tongue, brush of his lips, and graze of his teeth.

Zen pulled his mouth off of me and I rolled my hips, trying to follow him. "Is this pussy mine?"

When all I did was writhe beneath him because I couldn't comprehend words, I was so out of my mind turned on and ready to explode, he asked me again. "Is this pussy mine, Sunshine? Or does she need more convincing?"

"Yes! Yes, it's yours. Please make me come," I begged and Zen shot me a smug smirk before attacking me with pure determination.

"Oh, shit," I whimpered as he slid two fingers inside me. It was a tight fit, but I was soaking and quickly found myself wanting more.

When he slowly drew his fingers out and then pushed them back in, twisting to hit a spot inside I didn't even know I had, there was no stopping the detonation as I was blown away, completely destroyed by the most powerful orgasm I'd ever had. Sparks flashed behind my eyes and I didn't think I even breathed while the pleasure destroyed me.

"Christ. That was by far the hottest fucking thing I've ever seen." Zen's husky voice is drenched with sex and makes my thighs clench together around his head while he sucks his fingers into his mouth.

"I've-" I blushed, suddenly feeling shy. "I've never done that before. I don't ever do that."

"You need to get used to it, because I want to wake up that way every damn day."

Zen wiped his mouth on his t-shirt and I stared, helpless to the embers flaring back up knowing he smelled like me. A possessive sort of satisfaction made my stomach swoop like a roller coaster drop, and before I could blink, he kissed me softly before hopping up to get dressed. I could taste myself on his lips, and a flush spread across my cheeks.

His body was on display, all inked perfection and toned muscles, and I sat up to get a better view, tilting my head to the side so I didn't miss even an inch. My tangled blonde hair fell into my face and I brushed it away so it didn't ruin the show.

"Won't it bother you to walk around like that all day?" I asked, gesturing at his impressive length, barely hidden behind his tight, black, boxer-briefs. I swallowed hard, wondering how it would feel to have him between my lips. How far could I take him into my mouth? How did he taste? I licked my lips, and his eyes dropped to my mouth, following the movements like a predator hunting prey.

The sheet I'd pulled over myself when he stood up slipped

down, and cold air brushed across my breasts, making my nipples tighten. The raw hunger in his eyes made my breath catch, but then the moment broke when he shook his head and pulled his jeans up, covering all my newly discovered favorite parts of him.

"It's going to be torture, but today isn't about me. There will be plenty of time for us to explore, but right now I'm on a deadline and you need to learn you can trust me. Those are both more important than me getting off."

My eyes misted a bit at his words, and I didn't think my heart had ever been fuller. Somehow, despite our rocky start, he'd already gone a long way towards earning my trust. "Are you sure you have to go? We could have breakfast or something?"

The mattress dipped as Zen lowered himself beside me, tugging at the sheet to make it drop further as the corner of his lip tilted up. "True's waiting for me, and he's already pissed. He's been blowing up my phone all morning, and I may be a dick, but I'm also a professional so as much as I don't want to leave, I've gotta get home."

"True? He's the…" I bit my lip while I wracked my brain trying to remember. "Drummer?"

Zen grinned like he just won the lottery and I had no idea why. "Guitarist," he corrected. "We write the music together, and he's helping me with our next album."

"Oh. Well, he probably won't mind if you stay a few more minutes, will he?" Yeah, I sounded needy. I also didn't give a shit. Zen gave me a life-changing orgasm, and I wanted to return the favor.

He stood then, backing up a few steps like he needed to physically put distance between us, but his chest was rising and falling rapidly with his breaths and his eyes had darkened. "If you don't cover up, I won't be able to go. I'm this close to jumping back into bed with you right now." He held up his hand, his thumb and index finger an inch apart.

Tugging the sheet down the rest of the way, I displayed my body to him in all its naked glory, even as the flush on my face deepened, and my heart pounded under his heated stare.

"Jesus," he muttered as I watched as his head fell back and his eyes closed. "You're trying to fucking kill me, aren't you? Death by blue balls."

"Okay, okay. I'll play fair." Temptation failed, I grabbed my discarded shorts and panties off the floor, pulling them on. Zen's attention was now fixed on me as I hopped up, crossing the room to grab my top and pulling it over my head.

Covered up now, I rushed over to him, wrapping my arms around his body and resting my forehead against his chest, breathing in the fading smell of yesterday's cologne. He pulled me in tighter, wrapping me up.

"When will I see you next?" My words were muffled by the soft cotton of his t-shirt.

"Friday, probably late. We're gonna be holed up in my basement all week getting this shit written and samples recorded. True flew up just for this, so I have to take advantage, but the other guys are breathing down my neck so even if I don't sleep this week, it has to get done."

I blew out a breath, feeling ridiculously morose considering I came less than ten minutes ago. "Friday feels like forever from now."

"I know. I promise I hate it as much as you do, and I'll be lucky if I can stop thinking about you long enough to write anything worth using." I moved my head back enough to tilt my chin and look up into his striking blue eyes. "Maybe we should do an album of ballads," he muses, the corner of his mouth twitching before he sobers. "I'm going to miss the hell out of you."

"I'll miss you more," I whisper, feeling both ridiculously cheesy and sad at the same time. I was officially one of *those* girls who got all sappy over a guy. Yay me.

Zen dropped a kiss to my forehead, and his lips lingered a second or two longer than a simple peck. "If I kiss you again, I won't be able to stop."

I watched as Zen walked to the kitchen, picked up his keys and phone and glanced at me one last time. "See you Friday, Sunshine." The side of his mouth lifted before he walked out the door. When it swung closed, I leaned against it and sighed.

After the last twenty-four hours, I was more determined than ever to make the changes I'd been putting off for too long. Starting today, I was going to become the Kennedy I'd always wanted to be, the one deserving of a world-famous rock star's attention. As I was, I couldn't keep up with his lifestyle, but I sure as hell wanted to.

My heart sped up at the idea of change, the familiar fear always there, starting to invade my mind, telling me I couldn't do it, that it was too hard. But if I made a plan, took it step by step, I'd make progress.

Right?

Right.

I'd start with breakfast, but then I'd get to the hard stuff like hiring help for Sweet Stories. While I explored whatever was between Zen and me, I couldn't close the store down. I had bills to pay and regular customers who depended on me. I'd been putting this off way too long, and it was time I stepped up and did what needed to be done.

An hour later, I placed a *Help Wanted* sign in the front window for the first time ever. I pulled out a chair in the cafe and sat, placing a blank notebook onto the tabletop in front of me. I tapped my chin with the pen I'd just picked up, considering the responsibilities a new employee would be expected to handle, but was interrupted when my phone buzzed.

Zen: I can't stop thinking about that delicious breakfast I had this morning.

My cheeks heated up, and a slow smile spread across my face.

Kennedy: I'm still mad you let me go hungry.
Zen: I'll make up for it double next time. Forgive me?
Kennedy: You're forgiven. You know, I think you're my new favorite distraction.
Zen: What am I distracting you from?
Kennedy: Doing something I've been dreading for years.
Zen: ?
Kennedy: Looking for my first employee. Suddenly I find myself in need of more free time.
Zen: Hmm, good idea. Maybe you should hire two so I can have all your time.

My face could split in half right now with the size of my grin.

Kennedy: Is this where I'm supposed to play hard to get?
Zen: Fuck, no.
Zen: Oh, and don't make plans this weekend. We're going on our first date.

As if he can sense my panic at the unknown, another message comes through right after the last one.

Zen: I'm not telling you what we're doing, but I'll be there to hold your hand.

My heart began to race. I forgot I told Zen he could help me with my panic attacks, which meant putting myself in uncomfortable situations. I didn't know if I was ready, but I had to try.
Shit.
I took a deep breath, trying to steady myself.

Kennedy: Okay.

Zen: I know you're freaking out, but I promise not to let you die. Focus on Friday.

Zen: Going to be in the studio between now and then, but I'll be missing you.

After setting my phone down with trembling fingers, I gave myself a pep talk.

I could do this.

I *would* do this.

My heart slowed down as I picked my phone back up.

Kennedy: Tell the truth, you can read minds, right? Have a good session, text when you can. Miss you like crazy 'til Friday.

I set my phone down and tried to get back to my list, but my mind kept wandering to Zen and what he could possibly have planned for this weekend. Throwing my pen onto the notebook and rising up out of the chair, I decided it was useless to keep trying. My mind and body were focused on one thing, and one thing only—Zen.

As I carried the notebook back behind the counter, the bell above the door rang. A girl with dark spiky hair, fair skin, and muted blue eyes walked inside and up to the counter, lifting her chin. She stood at least six inches shorter than I did, and I glanced down at her, noting she looked really fragile, like a real-life porcelain doll.

"Welcome to Sweet Stories," I greeted the girl, forcing a relaxed smile onto my face. "How can I help you?"

"I saw the sign in the window, help wanted?"

"Oh, right! What's your name?"

"Chloe."

"It's great to meet you, Chloe. I'm Kennedy. This is my store." I gestured around as sweat pricked down my spine and adrenaline saturated my body. "Do you have a resume? And time to talk now?"

Her smile brightened as she reached into her bag and dug around, pulling out a piece of paper and handing it over. "Yeah, of course. I wasn't sure if you needed a resume, so I went home and grabbed one before I came in."

"Great, let's go sit." I led her to one of the tables with mismatched chairs and pulled one out and gestured for her to sit before taking the one across from her.

Chloe sat down, waiting for me to look over her resume, which wasn't awkward at all.

Psych.

Shifting in my seat, I cleared my throat. "I see you used to manage the Barnes & Noble store before it closed."

"That's right. That's why your sign caught my eye. I love eBooks, don't get me wrong, but there's something about holding a physical book that I'm addicted to. The online bookstores have really hit brick and mortar stores hard, and when I saw your shop, I knew it was a sign. I had to come in and talk to you," she gushed. "Sorry, I tend to ramble."

I let out a soft laugh. "It's fine, I'm happy to meet a fellow book lover. I could go on forever about books."

"Me, too."

"Your experience looks great. I'll have a list of responsibilities that you'll need to handle, and I'm looking to hire someone full time to be here Tuesday through Saturday. Will those days work for you?"

Chloe bit her lip while her fingers drummed the table. "I'm sure I'll be able to handle whatever you throw at me and more. And those hours work perfectly."

"I'll just need a list of references, but as long as those check out, I'd love to hire you." I didn't think I was going to find a better option, but I wasn't stupid enough to hire her without checking her out first.

"Can I have that back?" Chloe asked, nodding at the resume on the table in front of me and I slid it across to her. She twisted and dug in her purse, pulling out a pen and scribbling onto the paper, tapping at her phone every now and then.

When she pushed the paper back across, there was a list of three people.

"Great, I'll give them a call this afternoon and if everything's good, I'll give you a call. Just so I know, when can you start?"

It couldn't be this easy, could it? Was there something else I should ask or do? I'd never done this before, and I was so far out of my comfort zone. I had no idea what I was doing.

"I can start tomorrow if you need me to. The only thing I've got going on is my failed attempt to become a celebrity blogger. I even moved to LA to try and make it work and it was a total bust. The only thing I've learned is that I suck, so it's not going anywhere." She giggled.

"Really?" I frowned, wondering how anyone could be shallow enough to care about famous people enough to make it their career. Then again, hero worship was a thing and I shouldn't be such a shit-stirring a-hole. "Anyway, I'm so excited to have your help, I can't even tell you. Will ten tomorrow work?"

"Yep, I'll be here."

"Great! When you start, I'll have a key made for you so you can open and lock up."

"That works. It was fantastic to meet you, Kennedy. I'll look forward to your call."

Chloe stood and held out her hand for me to shake, and I slid my hand into hers. She squeezed almost painfully tight, so I quickly let go. She laughed. "I'm sorry, my dad used to always tell me not to squeeze so hard when I shook people's hands, but I have the grip of a boa constrictor or something."

I chuckled as I massaged my hand. She was stronger than she looked. "Don't worry about it."

As the door closed behind Chloe, I exhaled slowly as a smile broke out across my face. That wasn't nearly as hard as I thought it'd be. Next up, I needed to call her references and talk to Gray. Grabbing my phone, I sent him a text.

Kennedy: Can you come to SS? It's not an emergency, but I need to talk to you.

Grayson: Be there in twenty.

Once that was sent, I got to work making the calls that would hopefully buy me more free time.

GRAYSON STROLLED INTO THE STORE, walking behind the counter and grabbing a muffin out of the case. He plopped down at one of the tables to eat it.

"Well, how'd your night with the rock star go?" he asked, wiggling his eyebrows suggestively at me.

I shot him a look that said *none of your damn business* as I sat across from him.

"It went great. He's a lot more than I expected and kind of perfect. I really like him, Gray."

Grayson stopped chewing mid-bite. "Are you up for dealing with the circus that comes with dating him now that you've slept on it? The paparazzi, the fans, the girls throwing themselves at him constantly? The sex tape?"

Sighing, I closed my eyes and massaged my temples. "Zen knows that if he wants to be with me, he has to be upfront and honest. No more hiding shit from me because he thinks it might scare or hurt me. I have to trust sometime, Gray. This is the first time I've wanted to take a chance on someone, so I have to believe it's going to work this time."

"You know I've got your back, so if this is what you want, I'm in. I actually really liked the guy when I talked to him last night. If he's just trying to get in your pants, he's putting in a lot of effort but I don't get that vibe from him. He seemed scared you were going to tell him to fuck off, and that healthy level of fear goes a long way in my book as your big brother."

My eyes narrow in his direction. "Seriously, Gray. You're two minutes older. Knock it off with that big brother bullshit." We'd had this argument at least five hundred times before.

"Two minutes and eleven seconds."

I rolled my eyes.

"As your older brother," he grinned, "I told him if he hurts you, I'll hurt him worse."

Deep, deep down, under layers of annoyance, my chest tightened. Both of these guys were on my side. They were both firmly in my corner, and I felt stronger because of it.

"Enough joking around, Gray. I had a serious reason for asking you to come over. I think I hired my first employee today, a girl named Chloe."

Grayson raised his eyebrows. "You think?"

"Yeah, her references checked out and I think she'll be a good fit. I called her to make it official, but it went to voicemail, but as soon as we talk she'll be the first employee of Sweet Stories."

Gray leaned back in the chair so far, it was balancing on only two legs. "Damn, about time. I've been bugging you to do that for months. I wonder why you've had a sudden change of heart."

"It's not that sudden," I snapped, feeling defensive as he smirked knowingly. I reached across the table and grabbed a chunk of my brother's muffin, popping it into my mouth. "It's a lot of work running Sweet Stories. It's gotten overwhelming."

He motioned for me to continue as crumbs fell out of his mouth.

"Jesus, Gray. Could you be a messier eater?" I tossed a napkin at him.

"Maybe I should try it." He laughed, chewing with his mouth open in the most obnoxious way possible. "Continue."

"There's Zen, and he's sort of a force to be reckoned with, you know? I want to have more freedom to have a personal life. Plus, he wants to help me deal with my panic attacks, and I'm ready to let him try. Essentially, I need more free time."

Grayson flashed his bright white smile while dropping the chair back onto four legs. "I'm going to have to thank him for pushing you, aren't I?"

I shook my head, a small smile on my lips. "Save your thanks until I actually accomplish something, 'kay? But I need your help this weekend so I hope you don't have plans. Can you watch the store on Saturday? Chloe will do most of the work, but I can't just leave her on her fourth day. I need to be sure I can trust her, and she knows how to work everything. Please, please, please."

I wasn't above begging.

"What's the big deal about this weekend?"

"You're going to make me say it, huh? Can't just be there for me without any questions?" I jutted out my bottom lip and widened my eyes, blinking a few times.

"Whoa there, you know that bullshit doesn't work on me," he laughed.

"Fine," I snapped. "If you must know, I have plans with Zen this weekend. I'm facing my fears and going on a date."

Grayson's eyes widened and he reached across the table and knocked his knuckle gently into my jaw. "I'm so proud of you, kid."

I scowled at him.

"I'll help, but only if you text me immediately after and let me know how it goes. Better yet, text me a play-by-play minus anything X-rated. No wait, anything R-rated." He shuddered.

I snatched another piece of his muffin off the table and popped it into my mouth.

"Sure. Don't be surprised if I call you to rescue me off the side of the road when I jump out of Zen's car in a panic."

Fuck butterflies, a whole herd of elephants were stomping around in my stomach and hadn't stopped since Zen stumbled into my life.

Three more days until I'd see him again.

Three more days until I'd have to be brave.

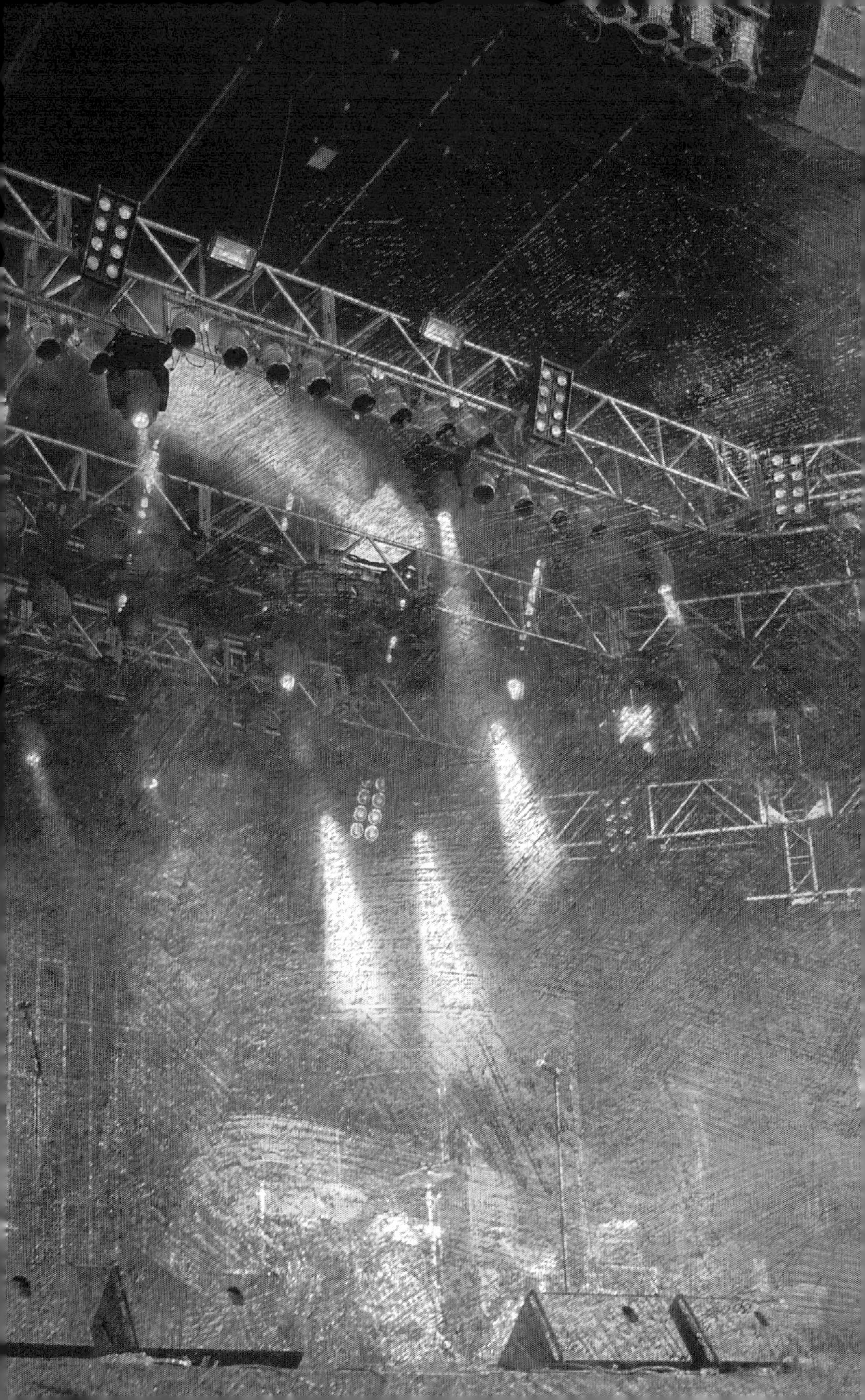

CHAPTER 13

ZEN

SMASHING *my phone into the wall won't help.*

I repeated it over and over like a mantra.

Running a hand through my hair, I tugged at the ends. Maddox's raised voice in my ear grated against my last nerve and if I could've punched him in the face, I would've just to shut him up.

"The bassline is wrong, and the tempo sucks. It's simple."

I pinched the bridge of my nose. "Take up the tempo bullshit with Jericho. The bassline fits the melody. If I change the bassline, I have to rework the entire fucking thing. It's not happening." I swore sometimes he picked on little shit like this because he thought fighting with me was entertaining.

"Fuck off, Z. I'm not recording samples until you change it."

I contemplated whether I could play the damn bassline myself on the recording.

"Fine," I seethed. "I'll change it, but send me your goddamn file today. I'm not fucking around, Mad. I have shit to do."

"Right, the mysterious *shit to do*. Wouldn't want to keep you from that."

"Why are you such an asshole?"

"Wouldn't you like to know," he said before cutting off the call.

Smashing my phone into the wall won't help.

My head throbbed, and I balled my hands into fists as I walked down the hall to the garage. I carefully set my phone down, and instead started throwing my fists into the heavy bag hanging there for times just like this. My only focus was punching until my knuckles split or I couldn't lift my arms anymore.

True strolled out into the garage, eyeing me. "I take it the call didn't go well?"

I grunted and hit the bag again.

"You can't let him get under your skin."

I panted, and sweat dripped down my forehead. True tossed me the bottle of water in his hands.

"I'm fine, he got his way, so he's fine. He's just such an asshole sometimes."

"Truth." True smirked. "So, what are we doing while we wait on his slow ass to send us his files?"

I sat on the weight bench next to the bag, taking a long pull from the water bottle. "I wrote a song."

True slow clapped. "Congrats, you did something you've done hundreds of times before. I could get you a medal or something."

I narrowed my eyes. "I need new friends."

He threw his head back and laughed. "I'm just messing with you, Z. Tell me about the song."

"You believe in romance and love and all that shit, right?"

He looked from side to side. "Not so loud, but yeah, and all that shit. Someday I'm going to meet the girl that makes everything worth it."

"Promise not to bust my balls?"

"No."

I glared at him.

He sighed dramatically. "Fine."

"I met someone, and I haven't been able to get her out of my mind. The words poured out of me onto the page, and suddenly I had a song. The melody's in my head, but I could use your help laying it down."

True smirked. "Maddox is going to have a field day."

"Would it be too much to ask you not to tell him?"

"And miss out on the endless mocking? I thought you knew me better than that."

I let out a heavy sigh, crinkling the now empty bottle between my hands. "Fine, if that's what it takes for you to help."

He clapped me on the back. "I'm going to tell the guys about the song, but I'm gonna need all the details on this girl. Who is she? Does she have a hot friend who believes in fairy tales?" True lifted his hand off of my back, wrinkling his nose. "Gross, you're all sweaty."

"Yeah, that's what happens when you beat the shit out of a punching bag. Does that fairytale bullshit actually work for you?"

True lifts a shoulder and drops it back down. "Never tried it, but I'm serious. You know the stream of groupies has never been my thing. It's too shallow, and now that I'm older and ready to start looking for the girl of my dreams, she's nowhere to be found."

Looking at my friend, I noticed how tired he looked. There were dark circles shadowing his eyes, and he looked like he hadn't had a good night of sleep in years, which if he was anything like me he hadn't.

"You'll find her, dude. I'll help."

"Yeah, there's no way that could go horrifically wrong. Ugh, you stink. Go shower, then meet me in the studio, and we'll get your song done."

Grinning, I stood and stretched out my stiffening muscles. "Give me ten minutes."

A couple of hours later, I had a song that might be the best I'd ever written. Climbing the stairs to the kitchen, I took note of the moonlight shining across the hardwood floors.

"Want to go get a drink?" True asked, stepping into the room on my heels.

"Nah, I've got plans."

He raised an eyebrow. "Oh, yeah? With your girl?"

"Yep. See you Monday."

"Wait, before you go, I have something to say."

I turned to face him. "What?"

"That song is incredible. Let us put it on the album."

I shook my head. "I don't know, man. I wrote it for Kennedy, and that shit is personal."

"Kennedy? Is that her name?"

Shit.

I let out a long exhale. "Yes, her name is Kennedy. I've never met anyone like her, T. I never thought I'd feel like I do, and I sure as fuck wasn't looking for her. She rescued me in more ways than one."

True's eyebrows furrowed. "Rescued you?"

I leaned over, resting my elbows on the counter. "The first night I got here, I hit up a bar. After the first shot, I don't remember shit. Connor looked into it, and the bartender roofied me. Then, she tried to kidnap me."

He choked on the water he'd just sipped. "What the hell? Like actually kidnap you?"

I nodded. "Kennedy caught her trying to shove me in her car, and she stepped in. The girl was a bitch and left me lying on the sidewalk high out of my goddamn mind. Kennedy took pity on me and let me sleep it off in her apartment."

True chuckled. "And you asked me if I believe in fairytales? Dude, you might as well have slipped your foot into a glass slipper."

"Whatever. It's been a long week, and I need a fix."

He twisted the hoop in his nose absently. "Yeah, go. I'll even hold off on telling Maddox about your girl until they get here on Monday."

I rolled my eyes and lifted off the counter, standing up. "Thanks."

Of all my friends, I was glad it was True staying here with me. I could actually talk to him about this shit, and he wouldn't fuck anybody in my bed. If Maddox was here, he'd have a goddamn threesome in the middle of my bed and not bother changing the sheets. Fucker.

"I'm going out. Want me to drop you off at her place?" True offered.

I blew out a breath. "Yeah, that'd be great, man. Thanks. Let me just pack a bag real quick."

I ran upstairs and threw some clothes, a notebook, my phone charger, and some headphones into a bag and ran back downstairs to grab a ride with True.

The best part about the drive to Kennedy's loft this late at night was the lack of traffic and how easy it was for True to pull up front to drop me off. I hopped out of the car with a quick *thanks* and used my keys to let myself into her store. Locking the door, I made my way upstairs to her apartment with only the lights from the street below shining through the window to light my way. I quietly unlocked the door and let myself in. My blood heated with every step I took closer to her.

I turned my phone off, not wanting anything to intrude on my time with Kennedy. Setting my keys and phone down on the kitchen island, I looked around. A night light plugged in near the stove cast the only light into the room. My eyes adjusted to the dark as I made my way to her bedroom.

Kennedy's blonde hair was spread out on her pillow in the most beautiful chaos. The blanket was kicked off of her and tangled beneath her legs as she breathed evenly. The sight of her made me feel whole again, like a chunk of me was gone when we weren't together. She lay on her side, her knees bent, and she was wearing nothing but a t-shirt.

I kicked off my shoes, set down my bag, and stripped off my clothes until I was in my underwear. Crossing to the bed, I lifted the blanket and slipped in behind Kennedy, pulling her warm body against mine. My dick was about to throw a fucking rave being this close to her, but I willed it to behave. My lips found her skin, kissing the back of her neck while I breathed in the scent of home.

"You're here," she sighed happily, as if my being here was all she'd ever wanted.

"I got here as soon as I could, I'm sorry it's so late." I leaned over to steal a quick kiss from her lips but she wouldn't let me get away so easily and her fingers wound into my hair to hold me in place.

I chuckled against her lips. "Oh, Sunshine. I'm happy to make you come a time or five before you fall asleep, but if you're too tired, stop now and we'll go to sleep." I ran a finger down her cheek, caressing her throat before wrapping my fingers gently around it. Her eyes fluttered open, a mirror of my own hunger as she looked up at me. She shifted until she was lying on her back and pulled my face back down until I kissed her.

I guessed I had my answer.

The kiss was intense—tasting her was like a hit of the best drug flooding my veins, the biggest crowd singing my lyrics, and the spotlight shining down on me all at the same time. Carnal energy crackled between us as my free hand roamed down her body, exploring every inch of skin bared to me as her t-shirt rode up. My fingers tightened around her throat as she dug into my back with her nails, dragging me so close there was no escape.

When her lips were swollen and my cock was about to stage an intervention if it didn't get inside her immediately, I pulled back.

Kennedy deserved everything and right now I was so fucking tired, I thought I might pass out with my face buried in her pussy if I let this go any further.

Death by pussy didn't seem like a bad way to go.

As much as I wanted to spend the night balls deep in Kennedy, I wasn't going to have our first time together be when she was half asleep, and I had practically sleep-walked in here. I'd do this thing with her right if it fucking killed me, and with all the blood in my body now pulsing its way through my dick, it just might.

Pulling big spoon duty, I curved myself around her and ran my fingers through her hair. "Tomorrow, Sunshine." I promised, already feeling my dick deflating as my eyes got so heavy I couldn't keep them open anymore.

ROLLING OVER THE NEXT MORNING, I reached out my hand and met only cold sheets, almost like Kennedy was a dream. I sighed and pushed my face into the pillow, inhaling deeply.

Her smell would never get old. I'd bottle it if I could and take it everywhere with me, and any hotel room I was holed up in would feel like home. Sunshine and coconuts. I stretched and sat up, glancing at the clock on the nightstand. When was the last time I was up this early? I didn't want to waste any of the time I had with Kennedy this weekend.

Getting my lazy ass out of bed, I dug through my bag and found a pair of grey sweats, slipping them on. Kennedy was probably in the kitchen, so that's where I went.

Jesus, she was breathtaking.

My breath caught in my throat when I saw her, this woman who had the power to make me feel again after a lifetime of numbness. I watched her quietly while she hadn't realized I was there. Kennedy had her back to me just like the first time I saw her in this very same kitchen. Country music played low, and she swayed her hips to the beat. Her long legs were on display because she was wearing my discarded t-shirt and it only hit her upper thighs.

I wanted to peel that shirt off and spread her out on the counter for breakfast.

Even as my stomach growled, my mind conjured visions of Kennedy laid out on the kitchen island with syrup and whipped cream dripping off her body, and my breath grew shallow as the fantasy played out. My dick throbbed almost painfully. Telling myself no was never a thing I'd done before, but I'd heard delayed gratification was a thing so I was trying to make it work. Someday, though. Someday soon, Kennedy and I were going to act out every depraved, dirty, and debauched thought I'd had since we met.

Unable to keep my hands off her any longer, I walked up behind Kennedy and wrapped my arms around her waist. Pressing my lips to the place where her neck met her shoulder, I sucked at the skin there, hoping I'd leave a mark. With my lips against her skin, I murmured, "I really fucking like you in my shirt."

She smiled, turning her head to the side to grant me better access and I took full advantage. "It smelled like you. It's good you like me in it since you're never getting it back."

"How about if I bring you over more? In fact, I don't think you should ever wear anything else." My right hand drifted down, my fingers reaching underneath the hem of my shirt to stroke the skin of her upper thigh as she trembled at my touch.

She spun in my arms and slung her arms over my shoulders, running her fingers through the hair at the back of my neck. "If you eat your breakfast like a good boy, we can talk about my wardrobe choices. Now, there's coffee and bacon. Oh, and muffins if you want one."

"You're going to spoil me, and if I'm not careful, I'm gonna gain fifty pounds eating this way every morning."

Her laugh was infectious, and I swore I felt it down to my bones. I loved that sound.

She swatted at my chest, pushing away and grabbing a plate. She started piling on the food and then slid it across the counter towards me. "I've seen videos of your concerts, and I'm pretty sure you burn like ten thousand calories every show, so a little bacon and a muffin won't hurt those abs I fantasize about."

I almost spit out the bite of bacon I was chewing as I laughed. "Someone's been a naughty girl, checking me out online. Does that mean you're gonna become president of my fan club now?"

"And what if I am?" she challenged as she stared at me over the rim of the mug she sipped from.

"Baby, I can't think of anything better. Well, that's a lie because I've got a whole list of ideas that I think will be better, and almost all of them involve you naked. But if you want the job, it's yours. I've gotta warn you, keeping the crazy bitches in check is a full time job."

She studied me carefully, her blue eyes searching my face. "I'm definitely not loving that you call women 'bitches' but setting that aside for now, what do you mean by 'crazy bitches'?"

I sighed, pushing my plate away as my appetite vanished. "I'm sure you understand that being who I am, doing what I do, I have fans. Some of those fans, well, they take things way too fucking far. It can be intense. I've had girls try to get a video of me in private situations to sell to the tabloids, girls break into my house in LA to steal shit or crawl into my bed and wait for me to come home, all sorts of crazy shit. Hence 'crazy bitches.'" It felt good being able to talk openly with her about this shit instead of trying to hide it.

She sipped her coffee thoughtfully. "Okay, I'll give you a pass because I agree, they sound like crazy bitches to me, too. I hope I never have to meet any of them. They sound really unstable, and that's coming from me with all of my issues." She had a teasing tone, but her eyes were clouded. I fucking hated that she referred to herself as crazy—just another issue to work on.

I'd gotten an up close and personal look at crazy, and Kennedy wasn't it.

Connor's warning from a month ago flashed through my mind, and I briefly wondered if I should talk to Kennedy about it now since we were on the subject. He suspected I had another stalker, someone good at covering their tracks.

People thought celebrity life was all glamorous—fame and fortune. It had its perks, but mostly, I dodged photographers and crazed fans while trying to keep my life as normal as possible. Don't get me wrong, making music was my first love, and the attention let me keep doing it. But when I wanted some privacy? It fucking sucked. How would Kennedy deal with that?

I didn't know yet.

After Connor's warning, I came home and found my clothes piled in the middle of my bedroom floor, slashed apart Freddy Krueger-style.

What kind of sick fuck did shit like that?

There were also the disturbing handwritten love letters—if you could call the threatening tone and obsessive language love—in my mailbox without any postage.

Connor would handle it. He was ex-military and didn't fuck around. I trusted him literally with my life. I had more important shit to do, like making sure the girl in front of me knew how fucking special she was. I wanted to give her her confidence back.

"Hey, where'd you go?" she asked, startling me out of my thoughts and back into the present.

I shook my head slightly, tilting my lips into a crooked smile.

"Sorry, I was just thinking about the last time I had a stalker."

A frown formed on her gorgeous mouth and a pressing need to reassure her weighed down on me.

"Don't worry, Sunshine. Connor's got a system in place for when it happens."

"Who's Connor?" she asked.

"My bodyguard." I pulled her into my arms, wrapping my arm around her waist. "If something comes up, he'll deal with it, so don't waste time worrying about it, okay? I know I don't." Or I didn't until I met Kennedy.

Fear and uncertainty crept into her expression as her body stiffened, and I reached across the counter, tilting her chin up so she had to face me.

"I promise you I'll never let anything hurt you. As long as I'm around, you're safe." I leaned forward and pressed my lips to hers before pulling back and rubbing my thumb along her sweet bottom lip.

"I wouldn't have even brought it up, but I promised you I'd be honest and tell you everything, so this is everything. It's not pretty, but it's part of my life."

She stepped around the counter, leaving her half-eaten breakfast behind and leaned into me, resting her cheek on my chest. "Thanks for telling me."

I wrapped an arm around her and changed the subject to something much more fun. "I've got plans for us this evening that you're not getting out of, but what do you want to do today?"

She leaned back, grinning at me. "Well, since you're forcing me out of my comfort zone tonight, I thought I'd do the same to you today."

"Uh-oh. I don't like that look in your eye." I groaned, hiding my smile.

"I thought you could come to yoga class with me. I haven't been able to go on a Saturday in... ever? Have you ever tried it?"

"Can't say that I have."

"There's an awesome Hatha class that's great for relaxing. We can go get relaxed and stretched before the stress of tonight. You in?"

I could think of about fifteen things I could do to her body to help her relax better than any yoga class, but she was practically vibrating with excitement.

Kennedy in skintight pants, bending and twisting herself into all kinds of new positions?

Fuck, yes, I was in.

I had a feeling I was about to take my first yoga class hard as a fucking rock. Maybe I could convince Kennedy to put on a private naked yoga class soon. Images of Kennedy, ass in the air as I plunged inside her flashed through my mind and my dick got hard all over again.

Trying not to press my cock against her, I took a deep breath, willing it to go the fuck away.

She waited for my response, and the silence got awkward while I pictured her doing naked, sweaty yoga on the floor in front of me.

I cleared my throat. "Hell yes, I'm in. What time? I want to swing by my house first."

"It's at noon. I'm going to shower now, and then we can go."

Before letting go, she kissed me hard, and I matched her until our teeth clashed together and I might've bruised her lips, but she didn't seem to care and neither did I. I wanted to devour her, to consume her so completely there was no way to tell where she ended and I began.

Kennedy needed me to go slow, but I needed Kennedy. The war between my brain and my cock raged, but right now, my cock was winning. Every stroke of her tongue against mine destroyed me a little bit more, piece by piece, until all that was left was a hunger so intense, it was blinding.

Her hands slowly roamed down my chest, exploring every dip and rise of muscle, every swath of exposed skin, and no matter how deeply I breathed, I couldn't pull in enough oxygen. Every nerve ending was tuned in to her touch, the places her fingers brushed over my skin, and a surge of heat reverberated through my body.

Breaking our kiss to watch Kennedy watch me was hot as fuck, and her lust-blown pupils soaked in every detail hungrily. Suddenly, every hour I'd spent beating my body in the gym was worth it.

Before I could take things any further, her phone rang, breaking the spell.

Her hands dropped from my body and she stepped back. "That's my brother. He's supposed to open the store," she explained, running to the bedroom to grab her phone.

Kennedy walked back into the room, pulling some cutoff denim shorts on under my shirt. They made her long, tan legs look like they were a mile long, and I couldn't tear my eyes away. She pressed her phone to her ear and grinned at me.

"Okay, okay, Gray." Kennedy rolled her eyes. "I'll be right there, just calm down."

She ended the call and tossed her phone on the counter, grabbing my keys.

"I've got to go let him in the store, and he's throwing a fit because he's been out there for fifteen minutes looking for his key, which he somehow lost. I'll be right back."

She hurried out the door and jogged down the stairs, the thumps of each of her steps echoing back into the apartment. Putting on a t-shirt seemed like a good idea since her brother was on his way up, so I walked to her room and pulled one out of my bag and got dressed. If I was going to have to interact with Grayson, I needed to be fully clothed. The last thing I wanted was to get into a fight with her brother.

As soon as I finished, Kennedy walked through the front door, followed closely by her brother. I stepped out of the bedroom, and Grayson's eyes narrowed.

"Good morning," he said, eyeing me up and down.

"Yeah, it is." I smiled wide at Grayson, giving him a look that said *what the fuck are you going to do about it?* and pulled Kennedy to me, wrapping my arm around her waist. She rolled her eyes but leaned into me, snuggling herself closer into my chest. A satisfied grin curved across my lips and I dropped a kiss on the top of her head.

"Gross," Grayson said, looking between us with a curl of his lip. "When is this new girl you hired supposed to get here? I plan on standing around managing someone else, so I'm not opening until she's here."

Kennedy sighed. "Fine, Gray. Do whatever you want. She should be here any minute. Her name's Chloe."

"Got it," he said.

"She's only worked for me for a couple of days, so I don't know much about her, but she's a fast learner and a good worker. I'm sure you'll be fine, but don't spend all day up here, please. I need you to actually make sure my store's not burning down."

Grayson saluted her in a mocking way that made me want to punch him for being an ass to his sister. I took a few deep breaths to keep myself in check.

"Sure thing, kid." His eyes softened. "Seriously, don't worry. You deserve some fun, Ken, and I'm happy to help."

The front doorbell rang in the store below us.

"Shit, time to put my boss hat on," Grayson said, turning and making his way downstairs.

Kennedy began to pull herself away from me, but I wasn't ready to let her go yet. Instead, I grabbed her hand, twining our fingers together, and followed her out the door. Whatever she had going on, I wanted to be by her side.

When we reached the bottom of the stairs, Kennedy walked over to the pale-skinned, dark-haired tiny girl who greeted her warmly.

"Hey, Chloe. This is my brother, Grayson. He'll be here in the store with you today. If you have any questions, he's your guy."

Grayson stuck out his hand, and Chloe took it, her eyes barely flicking to him before taking his hand in a halfhearted shake. "Nice to meet you, Grayson."

Chloe turned her eyes from Kennedy to me. Something about her nudged my memory, but before I could figure out what it was, Kennedy's voice pulled me out of my thoughts.

"And this is my…" She drifted off, clearly unsure what to label us but I sure as fuck knew exactly what I wanted us to be.

"Boyfriend, Zen," I finished for her, staring right at her and waiting to see what she'd do.

"Okay, then." The look she gave me was everything, and I felt like I was suspended by a wire soaring above a crowd, defying gravity and I never wanted to come down. "We've gotta go. I'm trusting you, Gray," Kennedy shot her brother one more warning look before pulling me back upstairs. Once we were back in her apartment, she closed the door, leaning against it and letting out a sigh.

"What's wrong?" I asked, not liking the look on her face.

"I've never left my store alone for an entire day before and I'm obsessing about what could happen. It's just an anxiety thing. I always figure out the worst-case scenarios and then ruminate about them."

Grabbing her hand and pulling her away from the door, I hugged her and tried to infuse as much calming energy as I could into my touch. Too bad I couldn't carry all her worries for a while so she could have a break, but life didn't work like that.

"How about we take this one step at a time? Go take a shower. You haven't technically left the building, so if they need you, they can come up here or call. When you're done, we'll take the next step."

"We?" she teased, smiling up at me as a flash of desire sparked in her eyes.

"Hell, yes."

All I could think about was Kennedy's wet, soapy body pressed up against mine, and I adjusted myself because grey sweats didn't hide a hard cock very well. She could no doubt feel it against her soft stomach.

"If only we had more time." She stepped out of my arms and backed up, biting her lower lip before sauntering off to her bedroom, leaving me with a view that'd never get old and a cock harder than steel.

Damn.

Guess my shower would be a cold one.

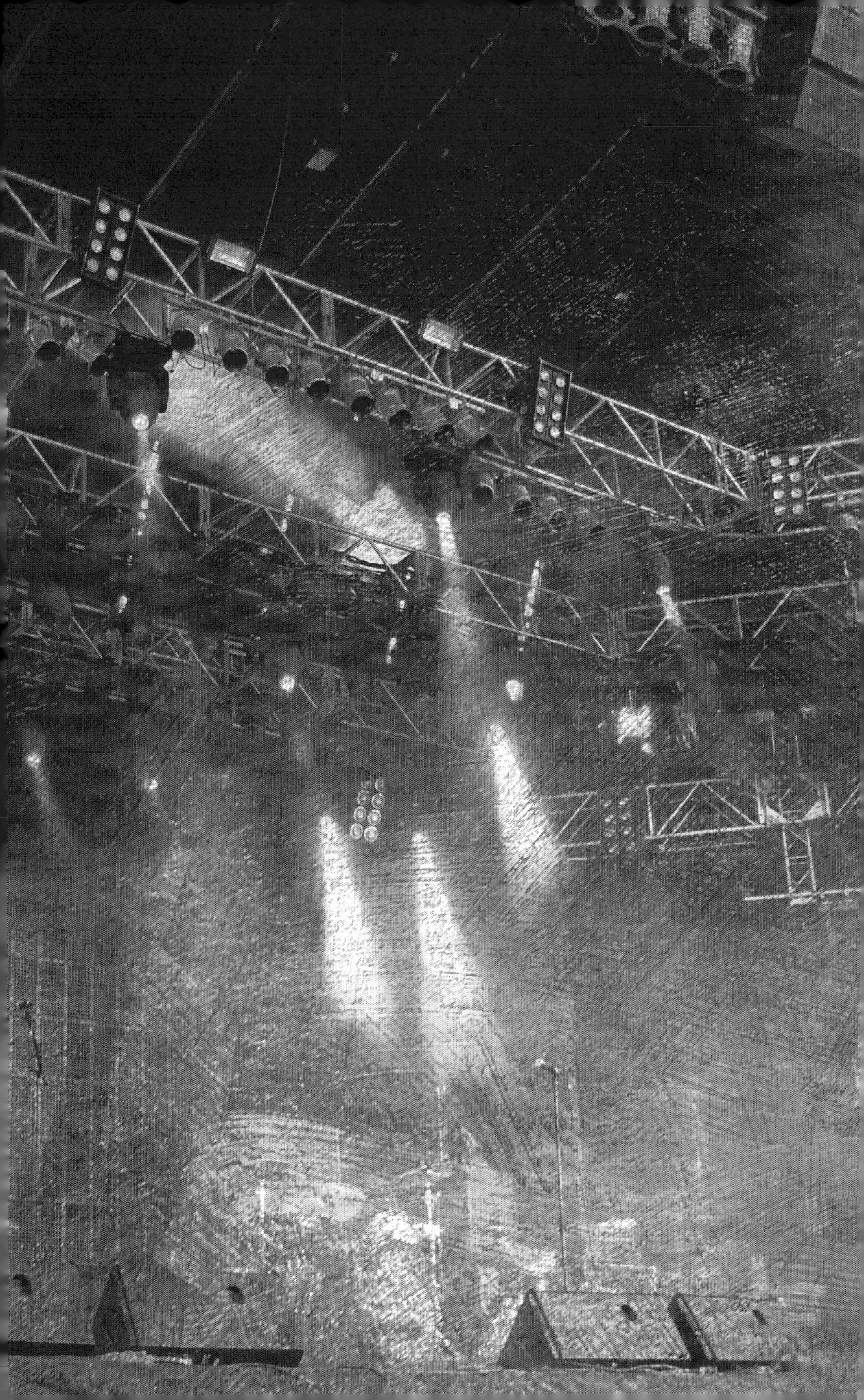

CHAPTER 14

KENNEDY

STEAM BILLOWED out behind me as I stepped out of the bathroom wrapped in a towel. Grabbing my favorite black ankle-length yoga pants and a strappy sports bra, I slipped them on and then threw on a cropped white tank top. I towel dried my hair and let it hang loose and wavy around my shoulders, making it look like I'd just come from the beach.

I grabbed my yoga mat bag and tossed in my spare, and headed for the living room where Zen sat scrolling through his phone. Black headphones covered his ears as he tapped his foot against my coffee table. He glanced up, his eyes roaming up my body, getting more and more heated with every second. He took off his headphones, setting his phone down.

"You're actually going to wear that out?" he questioned, a scowl on his face.

"Uh, yes. It's yoga, you need flexible clothes." I rolled my eyes, but he reached up and grabbed my top, pulling me down into his lap. I couldn't help the squeal that escaped my lips. "What are you doing?"

He peppered my neck with wet kisses. "Trying to convince you to stay in with me instead. I don't want anyone else seeing you when you look this fucking delicious."

"Delicious?" My voice squeaked out.

"Mmm." He nuzzled against my neck and inhaled.

At this rate, we'd never get to yoga. I had trouble remembering my own name when his mouth was on my skin.

Even though I knew we needed to go, I couldn't help sliding my hands up his chest and grabbing his face between my palms. I kissed him hard, wishing I could escape into him and live there forever. His hand moved down my back and gripped my hip, and I groaned, pushing away from him.

"We have to go," I insisted, sliding off his lap.

"How am I supposed to do downward facing dog with a permanent hard-on, Sunshine?"

"You'll figure it out," I laughed. "Ready to go?"

Zen groaned but gathered his phone and headphones and a notebook he'd been scribbling in and shoved them into his bag. "Do you drive? Or should we order a ride?"

I looked down at the ground and pulled my lip between my teeth. "I can drive, but I don't. It makes me too anxious."

"Okay, no worries. I'll call us a car, and when we get to my place, we'll grab my car. I'll drive for now."

I didn't miss the *for now* in his statement, but I'd deal with it later. We were taking today one step at a time, which meant living in the now. Letting myself spiral wouldn't help me get through this day.

My heartbeat quickened, and my legs were a little shaky, both telltale signs of impending panic.

Zen must've sensed the change in me, because immediately he dropped his bag and asked, "What's wrong?"

He walked over and took my hand in his, concern in his eyes.

"I got through the first step, but this one is harder. This time I'm leaving the store." My chest rose and fell quickly as I tried to catch my breath which was an impossible task.

"Okay. It's okay." Rubbing his hands up and down my arms, he stared into my eyes. "I've got you. Let's take some deep breaths until you feel better, and then we'll make the steps smaller. Can you do that?"

I nodded.

He smiled. "Good girl. Breathe with me."

Zen lifted my hand and placed it over his heart and held it there. The rise and fall of his chest under my palm gave me something to focus on, to shut out the intrusive thoughts. I tried to match my breathing to his.

"You're doing so good, Sunshine."

Soon, my breathing calmed, and I relaxed.

He pressed his lips to my forehead. "Better?"

"Much better, thank you." I smiled.

"Let's talk steps then. The next step isn't to leave, it's going downstairs. We'll go downstairs and see how Grayson and Chloe are handling the store. I bet once you see that everything is fine, you'll feel calmer, and then we can talk about what comes next."

Tugging me into his arms, I was surrounded by Zen. I inhaled his clean scent before resting my head against his chest, tucked under his chin. I grabbed a handful of his shirt because it anchored me. His calm heartbeat reminded me of sitting on the beach and hearing the waves crash into the shore, a peaceful and steady rhythm. The tension melted out of my body, and I slumped against him.

"You're like magic, and you make me want to be brave," I whispered, the confession floating in the air between us like fog over a mountain. My eyes stung as I fought off the tears that wanted to fall, but they weren't sad tears—more like overwhelmed.

How could this perfect man possibly want to put up with my shit? He could have anyone he wanted. Why would he want me?

Reaching under my chin, he tilted it up, so our eyes met, and as if he could read my thoughts, he said, "Don't ever question how incredible you are. I don't do shit, this is all you. Most people only have to face their fears once in a while, but you face yours every fucking day. You're the bravest person I know, and it has nothing to do with me. I'm just along for the ride."

He wiped the lone tear that fell down my cheek away with one of his long fingers.

"Think you can take the next step?" he asked.

I let out a breath and then nodded.

He reached down and picked up his bag before grabbing my hand. "You're going to kick ass today, wait and see." A watery chuckle was all I could manage as he led me out the door, down the stairs, and into the shop. My brother was at a table eating a muffin like he didn't have a care in the world as we approached.

"How's everything so far, Gray?"

Grayson finished chewing the bite of muffin in his mouth before he spoke. Small miracles. "I'd tell you to stop worrying but I know it's a waste of breath. Everything's fine. Chloe could probably handle the whole day herself. She already knows where everything is, and she made me this coffee that tastes perfect. We've got this. Plus, we both know you'll be harassing the shit out of me via text all day."

He looked up at Zen with a smirk. "You might need to throw her over your shoulder and drag her out of here, man. Seriously."

Zen chuckled. "I'm not above doing that, but the goal is for her to take the steps on her own. Me forcing her isn't going to help." A cocky grin spread across his face before he looked down at me. "Though I might consider doing that later in class if yoga bro is there with you looking like you do in that outfit. I don't think my inner caveman will be able to handle it."

Grayson raised his eyebrows. "Yoga bro?"

I grinned, the stupid nickname making me forget my nerves for a second. "Just this guy from my yoga class, River. He's one of those man-bun wearing, full of himself type of guys. The nickname fits."

"Okay, if you say so." Grayson shoved another bite of muffin in his mouth.

"I think I'm ready to go," I admitted with one last lungful of air.

"Perfect timing." Zen rested his hand on my lower back and guided me to the hired car parked outside.

I hoped that my store would still be standing when we got back.

Holding the door open, Zen waited until I was safely inside the car before sliding in behind me. He grabbed my hand, weaving our fingers together and tingles shot up my arm at his touch.

"Tell me about this yoga class. What's it like?" he asked as his thumb drew soothing circles on the back of my hand.

I appreciated his effort to distract me. "It's relaxing. There's a lot of calming stretching and breathing. It's definitely not hot yoga." I laughed.

He raised an eyebrow. "Hot yoga? Isn't yoga already hot with the tight pants and short shirts and, you know, flexibility?"

His hand teased my bare stomach, sending shivers down my spine and my thighs rubbed together at the raspiness of his voice, the same tone he used when seducing people with his songs on stage.

"Not the same kind of hot. The studio keeps the room temperature up, so you sweat buckets. It's not the sexy kind of hot, it's the sweaty kind of hot."

"I don't know, I think you in this outfit all sweaty could be really fucking hot, the sexy kind," he said, leaning in to swipe his tongue across my neck. Tilting my head to the side, I invited him in hoping he'd take advantage. He smiled against my skin, pressing another kiss there and then sucking gently.

A soft moan escaped my lips, and Zen abruptly stopped, sitting up with a cocky smirk on his face.

"Why'd you stop?" I realized I was whining, but I didn't care. I never wanted him to take his mouth off my body. Ever. Zen's touch lit me up like pyrotechnics, and it only took a small flicker to set off a reaction.

His voice was that same low, raspy tone that made my insides flutter. "Because if I didn't, I'd start to take off your clothes right here in the back seat of this car and do dirty, dirty things to you. Seeing you that way is for my eyes only."

His eyes flicked up to the driver.

I looked up at him through my eyelashes while I pouted, sticking out my bottom lip. Maybe I *wanted* him to lose some of that control, and a thrill ran through me at the thought of a wild, deviant Zen saying *fuck it* and giving in to his primal appetites.

"Christ, Kennedy. Don't look at me like that. I'm trying to be the good guy for once, and you're making it really fucking hard," he growled. "In more ways than one."

I met his gaze, and his eyes were dark and heated. I dropped my eyes to his lap, where his pants bulged.

Squirming in my seat, I blew out a breath. "Maybe I want a bad boy."

His chuckle was dark and menacing, coated in danger and lust, and my nipples tightened while my pulse pounded in response. "You've already got him. Now be good, or you'll find out exactly how ruthless I can be."

He pressed a kiss to my temple and I squirmed, wanting to push him and see what he might do, but also knowing he had a plan and wanting to see it through. This ache between my legs was completely torturous, but in a pleasurable way that I only wanted to feel more of.

We pulled up to the security kiosk outside a gated community, and Zen looked at me with hesitation in his eyes. This was the first time I'd really stepped inside his world, and I gave him my warmest smile in return. Rolling down the back window, he spoke to the attendant, and the gate swung open as the car crept slowly inside.

My eyes widened more and more the further down the road we drove. The lush landscaping and babbling creek that ran down the side of the street was breathtaking, and all too quickly, my body rocked forward as the car stopped.

Leaning across Zen's lap to look out his window, I saw a stunning house with three stories and tons of windows looming over us. It looked like three boxes stacked on top of each other at different angles, modern architecture at its finest. The concrete bottom floor housed the garage. The top two stories had so many windows it looked like the house was almost entirely made of glass except for a few spots of wooden plank siding.

Following Zen out of the car, I took in the full unobstructed view. "This place is incredible, Zen."

"Thanks. If you like it here, you should see my house in Malibu. It makes this place look like a shack." He laughed.

I rolled my eyes. "Rich people problems."

He chuckled before leaning over and pressing a too-brief kiss to my lips. "I believe I owe you a little something."

Grabbing my hand, he led me through the now open garage, pressing a button to shut it behind us. Swinging the door open, we walked into the house and up the stairs until we stood in the kitchen.

Stepping fully inside, my eyes traveled around the room. Charcoal gray cabinets and a solid marble island kept the modern theme going. I'd never seen a place this nice, but it was cold, too. Impersonal even. A giggle escaped my lips when I took in the light fixture hanging over the island. It was white and looked like a piece of art, but mostly it looked like an everlasting gobstopper from the Willy Wonka movie.

"What's so funny?" he asked.

"Nothing."

"Yeah, that's not gonna work for me. I'll torture it out of you if I have to." His eyes darkened as he took a step toward me.

"Torture? You wouldn't." I narrowed my eyes, considering his threat.

"Oh, Sunshine. You have no idea what I'm capable of. You'll be screaming out the information I want in less than a minute. That's a motherfucking promise." Zen took another step.

Swallowing, I stepped back as he took another step forward. Suddenly, he stood right in front of me, his sculpted chest pressed against mine. Leaning down, Zen crushed his lips into mine, grabbing a fistful of my hair and tugging my head back with a mix of pain and pleasure. The kiss turned impossibly deeper.

His mouth moved to my neck as he sucked and nipped his way down to my collar bone. With his other hand, he pulled my shirt and bra up, so my top half was naked in front of him. My nipples hardened from both the sudden rush of cold air and my arousal.

Holy shit.

I'd never been so wet in my life.

"You're fucking irresistible." Picking me up and setting me on the island, Zen groaned. I wrapped my legs around his waist as he pressed his hardness where I needed him most. I rocked against the ridge in his pants, trying to relieve the pressure he'd built up.

I gasped as he pressed harder into me. "Please keep doing that."

While he pulled my nipple into his mouth, I threaded my fingers into Zen's hair and held him against my chest. He pulled back, teasing me with his tongue, swirling it around and around before gently running his teeth over my newly stiff peak.

If I didn't get some relief soon, I might actually die of sexual frustration.

I threw my head back and grabbed the back of his neck to pull him closer.

He chuckled and pulled back. "Nope. That's all you get unless you tell me why you were laughing."

I growled in frustration. "You. Are. The. Worst."

"Two seconds ago you begged me not to stop. That's the best, not the worst." He ran his finger down my neck, and I shivered.

"Fine, I laughed because your light fixture over the island reminds me of the gobstopper candy from the Willy Wonka movie."

His gaze flicked up to the fixture and then he broke out into a laugh. "How the hell did I never notice that before? Now that you pointed it out, I can't un-see it."

"There, now you know. How about we pick up where you so rudely left off?"

He chuckled, his eyes slowly lowering to my mouth, his gaze darkening. Reaching up, he ran his thumb over my pouty bottom lip, pulling it down and pushing his thumb into my mouth. I sucked gently, then nibbled the soft pad with my teeth. I wanted to make him as desperate as he made me. Zen's breath hitched, and he pulled out of my mouth, lowering his head to my chest.

Just as he began swirling his tongue around my nipple, a click sounded from behind us, and he jumped up and pulled me against him protectively. I buried my nose into the hard planes of his chest, inhaling deeply. He smelled like the ocean and sandalwood. It was a deliciously masculine scent that had me closing my eyes and forgetting everything around me. Also, I was trying not to lick him.

My peaceful moment was snatched away as my eyes flew open. I peeked over Zen's shoulder at a man looking everywhere but at us. He cleared his throat.

"Get the fuck out," Zen growled at him.

"Shit, sorry. I didn't realize you were back," the man said, before turning and leaving through the door he just came through.

I rested my forehead on Zen's shoulder. "I guess we should take that as a sign we need to get ready to go."

Lifting my head, a small smile tugged at my lips. He caressed my cheek, sighing and placing a kiss on the tip of my nose.

"I'm going to go take a shower. A really fucking cold shower."

I grinned. "I'll be here snooping through all your stuff."

"Go for it, I don't have anything to hide."

"You know I was kidding, right? I wouldn't do that. At least I wouldn't tell you about it first."

Shrugging, he stepped away from me, and I immediately missed his hard body pressed against mine as I pulled my shirt down and adjusted my clothes. "If you want to, you can. I'll be back in a few minutes."

Watching him walk up the stairs was a treat for my eyes. Defined muscles moved under his clothes, and I tried not to drool. I couldn't wait to see everything he had under those clothes later.

Drawn to the modern yet cozy concrete deck, I stepped outside and leaned against the black iron railing, breathing fresh air deep into my lungs. I stepped away from the fence, walking around the deck while taking in the view. It rained so much here that an uncovered deck made no sense. Zen's was covered, protecting the plush outdoor furniture I found myself sinking into with a contented sigh. Just off in the distance, the lake shimmered with the midday sun.

This house wasn't what I'd been expecting from a rock star. There weren't bottles and drugs scattered all over the place. It was comfortable yet masculine, modern, and clean. Plus, you really couldn't beat the view.

I was leaning against the cushy sofa back, letting my eyes drift over the lake's surface when his arms wrapped around my neck, and he pressed a kiss to my temple.

"That was fast." I closed my eyes and leaned back against him, breathing in the clean scent of his body wash.

"I didn't want to make you wait. Plus, it's not exactly fun taking a cold-as-fuck shower." He kissed down my neck.

"You actually took a cold shower? I thought you were kidding."

"Fuck, yes, I did. My dick has been rock hard since I woke up this morning, and I needed to calm myself down. Unless you want to say fuck it and stay in?"

His voice had gone husky, and I almost gave in as he pressed open-mouthed kisses down my neck. Almost. But Zen was right. Building a solid foundation meant more than a quick fuck to satisfy my suddenly out of control libido.

"Not a chance. C'mon, we're going to be late."

Standing, I turned around, and my eyes dropped and slowly raked back up Zen's body. He looked like every girl's hottest fantasy, and I gripped my hand in a fist to keep from fanning myself because I was suddenly burning up. I never knew just looking at someone could turn me on before, but here I was, pressing my thighs together and feeling grateful as hell I'd worn black yoga pants.

His gray joggers hung low on his hips and didn't leave much to the imagination. If the bulge on display was any indication, Zen was fucking huge. A black sleeveless top hugged his chest, straining against his defined pecs, and I wanted to trace the tattoos covering his arms with my tongue.

Zen looked good enough to eat. I blinked a few times, trying to snap myself out of my lust-fueled daze.

"Could you be fucking me with your eyes any harder?" His eyes twinkled mischievously.

I swallowed hard. "I…" I cleared my throat. "No, I don't think I could."

He chuckled. "If you make it through everything I have planned, I'll show you what's underneath later. Every. Single. Inch."

I was practically panting, my heart going about four thousand beats per minute. I sucked in a ragged breath.

"Right. What were we doing again?" My eyes were unfocused, my mind still overwhelmed with thoughts of Zen, sweaty, stripping off his clothes and running his hands down my body.

Was it weird I wanted to lick the sweat off of him? Was that a thing people did? Watching a drip make its way down his throat onto his chest, running my tongue along his neck, tasting the salty-sweet flavor unique to him exploding on my tongue.

I fought off a moan.

Zen studied me and then reached out, tucking a stray hair behind my ear. He smirked when I quivered under his fingers. "Yoga class. Remember?"

"Yoga, right. Yo-ga." I shook my head, trying to clear the overwhelming Zen craving.

He led me back to the garage, where I enjoyed the uninterrupted view of him walking in front of me the entire way. When he opened my door, I stepped into his Mercedes SUV. The smooth leather was cold against my overheated body. This was the most beautiful car I'd ever been in by far. Zen walked around to the driver's side and got in, closing the door behind him.

Playing with the music app on the console, I found a country station. A smile crossed my face because I knew Zen hated country. Glancing to the side, I noticed him giving me the side-eye.

"What? I love this song." I cranked up the volume and started singing along completely off-key. Singing was *not* my forte, but it had never stopped me from belting out all my favorite songs before, and I wouldn't hide who I really was in front of Zen. He wanted to know me? Well, this was me.

He laughed, and it was warm and comfortable, like wrapping my insides in a fuzzy blanket. My stomach fluttered, and I realized I was in serious danger of completely falling for this man.

Shit.

If he walked away now, it'd hurt more than anything ever had before. I couldn't stop myself from wanting him, though. The risk was worth it.

A smile tugged at his delectable mouth. "Wow, you're a terrible singer."

"Can't hear you! Too busy singing!"

A couple songs later, we pulled up in front of the studio. Zen parked, and we went inside.

"Hey, Ken!" I cringed as River crossed the room toward me, his eyes darting over my shoulder to Zen. His eyes narrowed briefly before he recovered himself. "Zane, wasn't it? You look familiar."

Zen's jaw clenched. "It's Zen."

"Right, sorry, man. So, you're the infamous husband I've never seen around." I tensed at how *so* not *in*famous Zen was but said nothing, wondering if I needed to bail him out and confess to my lie.

"I travel a lot for work," he answered with an appraising glare in River's direction but shocked the hell out of me by not denying the whole husband thing.

I needed to stop the interrogation. Yoga was supposed to help relax me, and River was fucking up the vibe.

"Sorry, gotta go find our spots." Without even a glance in River's direction, I grabbed Zen by the arm and tugged him across the room.

"I hate that guy," Zen hissed.

"I know. Let's put our mats over here." Unrolling my mat, I stepped toward the window and laid it on the floor.

River seemed to be forgotten as the instructor led us through the starting poses. I couldn't help the giggle that escaped me when Zen struggled to contort his body from downward dog into chaturanga. He was fit, but he wasn't flexible, and I loved it. Somehow, the tiny flaw made him more human.

At the end of class, I looked over at Zen. Sweat ran down his face and neck, and I laughed at how completely shattered he seemed to be. His face was flushed, and he was breathing hard.

He grinned. "That was not at all what I expected."

"What, the great Zen Taylor thought yoga would be a walk in the park?"

"Pretty much." He laughed. "Who thought stretching could be so hard?"

I raised my hand.

"I do love a challenge, though." He shook his head.

"Does that mean you liked it?"

"I did, and not just for the view." His palm slapped me playfully on the ass as he winked. Between his hand on my ass that he still hadn't removed and the sweat dripping off his body, it took everything in me not to jump on him right here in class. I squeezed my legs together.

"Will you come back with me?"

"Really?" he asked, his eyes hopeful.

"Not to sound like a total fucking psycho, but if I had it my way, I'd spend all my time with you. Every free minute." Playing games wasn't going to work for me. Better to be honest with him about how I was feeling.

"Next time you go, I'll be here with you. And for the record, I feel the same. I just didn't want to scare you off by admitting how obsessed I am with you already." He grabbed my hand and placed a soft kiss against the inside of my wrist. Inside I was melting. He was obsessed with me? Well, the feeling was mutual. "Ready to get out of here?"

"Yep, let's go get ready for this mysterious date night." My smile faltered as that herd of elephants started stomping around in my stomach again.

Tonight would be fine. I could do this.

Could I do this?

Worst case scenario, I'd jump out of the car and call Gray to pick me up. The corner of my lips tilted up at how ridiculous that would actually be.

Zen stopped walking and turned back, his green eyes settling on my face. "What's going through that pretty head of yours, Sunshine? I can see you overthinking."

I took in a shaky breath. "I just realized it's here. The date. I'm trying not to start freaking out like I always do, but I'm failing pretty epically."

Zen put his arm around me and stroked my hair gently with his other hand. "It might feel scary, but your anxiety isn't going to kill you. You're strong enough to do this without me, but tonight I won't let you out of my sight, and we'll take things one step at a time, like we did this morning. I mean, look at you. You're fucking killing it today. You've been out of the store for a couple of hours and this morning you didn't think you could do it. Have you thought about the store once since we left?"

Shocked, I blinked a couple of times. "Wow, you're right. I haven't."

Zen was the perfect distraction.

Maybe I could do this after all.

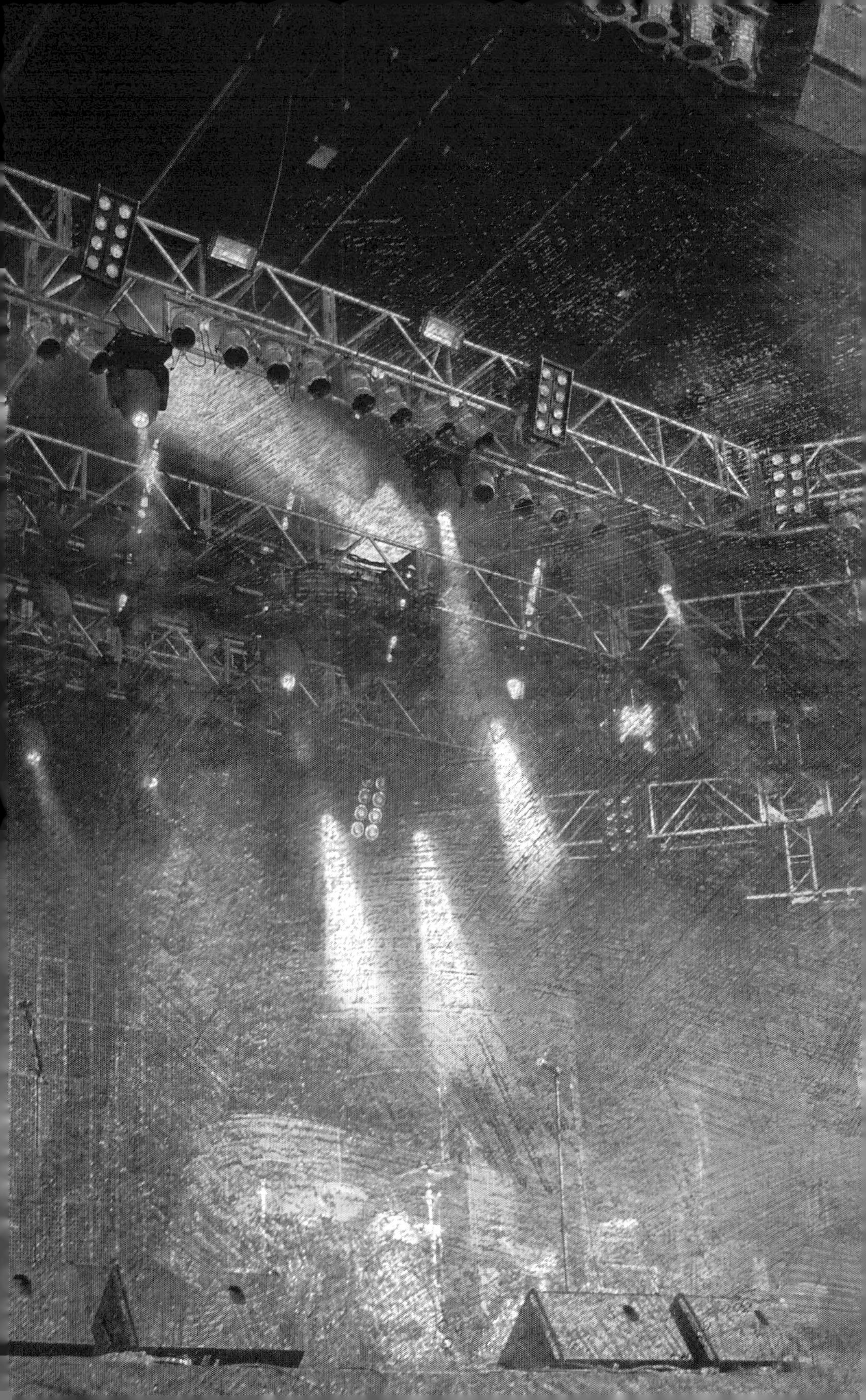

CHAPTER 15

ZEN

DROPPING Kennedy at her apartment after yoga made me feel sick to my stomach and empty at the same time. Like I shouldn't have left her behind. My possessive instincts when it came to her were out of control. I was officially addicted. When I told her I was obsessed, I wasn't kidding.

I needed an hour to get ready for our date, but fuck if I didn't miss her already. I knew tonight would be really fucking terrible. My goal was to make her as comfortable as I could, even if I knew it was futile. It didn't matter. I had to try because the thought of Kennedy in distress made me want to rip my hair out.

Reaching into my closet, I pulled down a backpack and started shoving supplies for tonight inside. A knock sounded on my door frame, and I glanced up to see Connor standing just outside.

"What?" I snapped. I didn't need the interruption right now. Kennedy depended on me, and I sure as fuck wouldn't be letting her down.

Connor cleared his throat. "I wanted to update you about the security protocol, both for the house and for tonight."

"Fine, but hurry the fuck up. We're leaving in a few minutes." I didn't even glance over at him.

"I've installed motion-activated cameras surrounding the entire property. There's a guard here doing regular patrols twenty-four seven. I've also talked to the front gate security, but there isn't much they can do because it's not just your house they're guarding."

I scowled. "So, what you're telling me is the gate is useless because they'll let anyone in."

Flicking my gaze to the ceiling, I crossed my arms before turning my glare on him. "Fix it. I pay you to deal with this shit so I don't have to."

"I know, but you need to know what's happening even if I'm guarding your cocky ass." Folding his arms across his chest, he frowned. "I've been with you a long time, you know I take my job seriously, but that doesn't mean things don't happen."

Connor leveled his steely gray gaze on me, meeting my glare with a hard stare of his own. He wasn't backing down and didn't put up with my shit. It was why I hired him in the first place, why I liked having him around.

"Nothing touches Kennedy." I was not above getting my hands dirty if necessary, and if Connor fucked this up, I'd have to step in.

Connor leaned against the door frame. "Not on my watch. You still need to pay attention to this shit."

"Noted. Anything else?" I threw my headphones in the backpack and zipped it up.

"I'm bringing someone else in from my team, to guard the house outside of the guy on perimeter duty. I can't be in two places at once, and I don't trust anyone else with your safety. You should know some of your stuff has been moved around when you weren't here. Someone's been getting in."

Ignoring the blood pounding in my ears, I tried to block out the terror I suddenly felt overcome with. Not for myself, for Kennedy.

No one would lay a fucking finger on her as long as I was breathing. This person was a threat I couldn't ignore.

Connor pushed off the door frame, arms still folded across his massive chest. "I'm taking care of it, but it's going to mean I'll be tagging along with you more often, and you need to be more careful when you go out in public with your girl."

Running a hand through my hair, I sighed. "I'm so fucking sick of this shit. I don't care what it takes, what you have to do. I'm not even worried about myself, but I swear to god if anything happens to Kennedy, I will lose my shit, and you don't want to see what that looks like. Fix. It. Now."

"Done. We'll be ready to leave in about twenty minutes. Everything's set up."

"Good." Slinging the bag onto my back, I followed him out of the room.

Fuck, I hated all this shit.

When was the last time I actually just went somewhere without having to clear it first? The lake with Kennedy, but even then, I knew I shouldn't have gone without Connor. But I didn't want her to know about how fucked up my life could get yet. Try explaining a bodyguard to someone you've just met, while wanting to come off as a regular guy. For once, I wanted to experience a couple of hours of being normal. Except I wasn't normal.

Climbing into the back of my Mercedes twenty minutes later, a slow smile spread across my face. I was going to see Kennedy in a couple of minutes, and I couldn't fucking wait. I wasn't sure what to expect out of tonight, but I armed myself to go into battle. We'd fight her demons together, side by side. She may not know it yet, but I was already her most relentless protector, even ready to save her from herself. Ultimately, I hoped she'd save herself.

Parking in front of Sweet Stories, Connor moved out of the car and opened the back door, waiting for me to climb out. Bringing a bodyguard made me stick out, but I wouldn't put Kennedy at risk. People on the sidewalk nearby were already craning their necks, trying to figure out who I was.

Fuck.

"Could you try to look less conspicuous?" I hissed at Connor.

He tilted his aviator sunglasses-covered eyes in my direction and shot me a smirk before folding his arms across his chest. "No. The whole point is to intimidate people into staying the fuck away. You'll thank me when you and your girl get home safe tonight and nobody fucks with you."

Cocky asshole. Unfortunately, he had a point.

I stepped into the store, and Connor followed on my heels; the jingle of the bell above the door announced my arrival. I glanced around, eventually locking eyes with the new girl, Chloe. Her eyes widened for just a second in recognition before quickly regaining her composure and slowly walking over to me, almost like a cat stalking its prey. It was fucking unsettling.

She got uncomfortably close. There were just inches between us as she lifted her chin until her eyes bored into mine. I took a step back, trying to distance myself.

What the fuck?

Did she have shitty social skills or something? Apparently, Chloe didn't understand the concept of personal space.

She took another step forward, again getting too close and making me want to take a huge step away from her. Out of the corner of my eye, I saw Connor moving toward us.

"It's Chloe, right?" I smiled at her tightly, wanting to keep my distance, a distance she didn't seem to want to give me. Usually, people took the hint and backed off, but not this girl.

"Yep, that's me," she said brightly with her wide eyes locked onto my face. "I'm sorry, but I have to ask. Are you Zen Taylor? From Shadow Phoenix?"

I ran a hand through my hair, exhaling. "Yeah, that's me. But, can we keep it just between us?" The last thing I needed was this chick putting on social media that I spent time here with Kennedy.

"If you sign this for me, I'll take your secret to the grave. Promise." She twisted a pretend key at her lips and tossed it over her shoulder before holding out the paper I hadn't noticed in her hand.

I glanced at Connor, who'd stepped up to my side so our shoulders touched. He handed me a Sharpie and I side-eyed him. How the fuck did he always anticipate the shit I'd need?

"Do you want me to write something?" I asked her, grabbing the paper and tapping Connor so he'd turn around for me to use his back as a table.

Chloe clasped her hands together under her chin, almost like she was about to say a prayer. "How about 'To Chloe, the most beautiful girl in the world. Love, Zen.'"

The girl was fucking pushing it. I couldn't write that shit. I scribbled out a quick *To Chloe, you rock. Zen* before handing it back. My handwriting was practically illegible, so hopefully, she wouldn't notice.

She held the paper up against her chest, almost like she was hugging it. "Ohmygod, thank you so much."

"Sure." I handed the marker back to Connor, who was watching Chloe intently. "Have you seen Kennedy?"

"Oh, I think I saw her go upstairs." She waved her hand in that direction absently before practically skipping off back to the counter, where she stared at me as she helped a customer.

So fucking weird.

Chloe creeped me the fuck out. Pushing the interaction from my mind, I turned to move up the stairs. "I'll be right back," I told Connor, who had followed me to the bottom of the stairs. "Stay."

His jaw tightened. "Fuck you," he grunted in the way only Connor could, but he stood at the bottom of the stairs with his eyes trained on the store. I had more important shit to do than worry about that Chloe chick. That's what I had Connor for. My job was to get Kennedy through tonight.

I opened the door to Kennedy's apartment. "Kennedy?" I called out.

She didn't immediately answer, so I walked toward the kitchen, but a quick glance around told me she wasn't there either. The living room was empty, too. My heart started to beat faster.

Where was she?

Hoping she hadn't run away, I walked a little faster back to her bedroom. I breathed out a sigh of relief when I saw her pacing back and forth in front of the bed. My stomach sank because she looked terrified.

She looked like she was freaking the fuck out. She was pale, and when her eyes met mine, they were wild with fear. It sounded like she was hyperventilating.

"Fuck, baby. Come here." I sank down on the bed and pulled her onto my lap. "Shh, it's going to be okay. Breathe with me." Stroking her hair, I held her against my chest. I took deep breaths, counting out loud to four as I inhaled, holding my breath for a few seconds before slowly exhaling and counting that out loud for her, too. It was the "box breathing" technique I learned about in my research. "Just breathe with me."

Her whole body was wound up, her muscles tense and shaky. Kennedy clung to me, wrapping her arms tightly around my neck as if she were holding onto a life raft, and if she let go, she'd drown. She started to breathe more slowly, following along with my breathing pattern. After a few minutes, her grip relaxed, and her muscles began to uncoil.

"Talk to me, Sunshine. What's got you so freaked out?"

"I'm going through all these worst-case scenarios over and over again. I hate that I'm like this. I can't have a fun night out with you because it turns into this." She buried her face in my neck, and the tears running down her cheeks soaked into my shirt. I tightened my arms around her.

"Do you trust me?" I asked, resting my cheek against the top of her head.

Her voice came out muffled. "Yes, I do."

"No matter how you're feeling tonight, know that nothing will happen to you. Nothing. I promise you, you'll be completely safe with me." I willed her to believe me. "Let's do this like we did this morning, okay? Just small steps. You can walk outside and lock the door, can't you? We'll do it together."

She nodded, sitting up and wiping her eyes before giving me a small smile. "Yes, I can do that."

Moving off of my lap and standing up, Kennedy smoothed out her dress and grabbed her purse. Looking at me, her eyes were still unsure and filled with fear.

Oh, my sweet Sunshine.

We would get through this night even if I had to carry her. By the end of tonight, Kennedy would know how strong she really was.

I raised myself up off the bed and grabbed her hand, rubbing my thumb in soothing circles over the back. "Do you have everything you need?"

"Yeah, I think so," she squeaked, her voice small and shaky.

Grabbing my keys, we stepped outside the door, and I locked up. "Step one is done. Still with me?"

She nodded, and I squeezed her hand. "The next step is going down the stairs. Ready?"

Kennedy nodded again, giving me a little squeeze back.

"Breathe, Kennedy. Deep breaths," I reminded her, and her warm breath hit the back of my neck as she exhaled.

Good girl.

At this moment, Kennedy surrendered herself entirely to me, and I'd rather throat punch myself than let her down.

At the bottom of the stairs, I turned back to her. "This is

Connor," I gestured to the man standing off to the side of where we stood. "He's my bodyguard."

"Nice to meet you, Miss Adams." He nodded his head once at her politely. It was the kindest I'd ever seen him be, and I tried not to gape.

"Hi, Connor. I feel a little better that you'll be with us tonight, so thank you." Kennedy's voice was quiet but sincere, and I swore I saw Connor shift his body, as if he was uncomfortable with her kindness. But that was just Kennedy. She was a fucking saint.

"Do you want to go check out with Chloe on your own, or do you want me to come?"

Her wild eyes pinned me with a look that said *if you let go of my hand for even a second, I'm getting the fuck out of here*. I chuckled and gripped her hand tighter as we walked over to Chloe.

"Hey, Chloe." Kennedy's voice shook as she nervously twirled a strand of hair around her finger.

"Hey. Leaving so soon?" Chloe's eyes flicked between Kennedy and me, and she bit her lip to try to hide her smile.

"Yeah, we're on our way out. If you need anything, call Gray." Kennedy lifted her hand and pointed to the cafe where Grayson had his face buried in another muffin. I narrowed my eyes in warning as Grayson's gaze met mine. I might be new to Kennedy's life, but her brother better take this shit seriously. If Kennedy had to worry about the store tonight, she wouldn't be focused on healing herself, and she needed this.

He gave me a slight nod before lifting his coffee cup to his lips and turning back to his phone. As long as we were on the same page, Kennedy would be fine.

"Sure, boss. Have fun." She waggled her eyebrows at Kennedy, who laughed.

"Oh, we will." I inserted myself in the conversation and wrapped my arm around Kennedy's waist.

Kennedy's new employee seemed to be fitting right in, and

despite my weird-ass encounter with her earlier, my girlfriend was on her way to making a new friend. Still, an unsettled feeling nagged at the back of my mind when it came to Chloe, and I made a mental note to ask Connor to look into her.

As Chloe walked away, I turned to Kennedy. "See? That's three steps down already. You're doing great," I whispered in her ear before placing a kiss on her temple. "The next step is walking outside of the store."

Swinging the door open, the chiming of a bell sounded above us, and then we were outside. The sun was still bright, casting warm light down on us. Connor stepped around me and opened the back door, stepping back and waiting for us as he scanned the sidewalk for any potential threats.

Stopping just outside the store, Kennedy bumped against my back. "Let's stop here for a second and take a couple of breaths. Okay?"

She nodded tightly, squeezing my hand so hard she was definitely cutting off the circulation. I didn't give a shit. She could rip my hand off if it made her feel better.

I turned and smiled, dropping a kiss onto the top of her head. "Step four done. I'm so fucking proud of you."

She burrowed her face into my chest, and I heard a muffled, "Thank you."

"Next step is getting in the car. I know this is a big one, but I've got a surprise that I think will help distract you. You have to get in the car first, though." I stepped back and tugged her hand toward the door Connor held open.

She stood frozen on the sidewalk staring at me, eyes darting between the open door and my face. I wasn't sure whether she'd decide to run back inside, but either way, we needed to get off the sidewalk. People were starting to stare. Next, the camera phones would come out, and I couldn't let that happen. The world didn't need to see this side of her unless she decided to show it to them.

My job now wasn't just helping her through the fear but protecting her from unwanted attention, too. I glanced at Connor, whose body language was on edge. I got the feeling he'd destroy any phone that came out and pointed at us right now, and I exhaled slowly. Of course Kennedy had him under her spell already.

"Kennedy, I can pick you up and put you in this car, but it'd be better to make that choice for yourself. You're strong enough to do this, but you have to choose, and you have to do it now. The longer you wait, the harder it gets. C'mon, baby. You can do this." I coaxed her in a soft voice, not unlike the one I'd use if I was trying to catch a cornered animal. I pleaded with my eyes and tugged gently on her hand.

She glanced at me, her gaze fearful, but something else shone in her eyes, something growing stronger.

Determination.

She didn't say anything, just rushed past me and practically dove into the car. I grinned like a fucking idiot, I was so goddamn proud of her. This was going to work. She'd be okay.

Slipping in the car behind her, I saw that fear had mostly replaced the determination in her eyes.

"We're going to sit here for a few minutes and just breathe again, okay? We have all night." I slid onto the seat beside her and slung my arm around her shoulders, pulling her against my side. I dropped a kiss to the top of her head, and she breathed deeply. There was no hurry tonight. We would take these steps as slowly as she needed.

Connor closed the door behind me and walked around to climb into the driver's seat.

"Want to know what I found out when I was researching how to help you, Sunshine?"

She nodded.

"If you run away when you feel scared, it only makes it worse. You have to stay and wait it out, accept it until you realize there's nothing to be afraid of. The staying and facing are the hardest parts, but they're the most important. We can't run no matter how much you want to, okay?"

Looking up at me, her eyes flared with fear, but she gave a brief nod. "Okay," she whispered.

Finally, I told Connor we were ready, and my Mercedes pulled away from the curb. Kennedy tensed and squeezed my hand.

"My heart is racing, and I feel like I can't breathe. I just want to jump out of this car and run home." She squeezed her eyes closed.

"I know, but it doesn't matter." I pulled her even closer against my side, the seat belt digging into my hip.

Her eyes snapped open. "What do you mean, it doesn't matter? I feel like I'm dying! Of course, it matters!"

"No, it doesn't. It doesn't matter at all because you're not actually dying, and not only that but no matter how you're feeling, you're still doing it. Can't you see how amazing you are? You're doing it even though you feel so scared. I've never seen anyone go through anything like this before. Yet, all I keep thinking about is how goddamn strong you are. You feel all of that and keep taking the steps forward anyway." I tucked that stray lock of hair I loved so much behind her ear, kissing her forehead. I was in awe of her right now, and I hoped she could see it.

"Ugh, why do you have to make so much sense right now?" I chuckled as she squeezed my hand in her white-knuckled grip.

As Connor merged onto the freeway, I turned to Kennedy, tilting her chin up, so she looked into my eyes instead of out the window. "Remember when I told you I had a surprise for you?"

She nodded tightly as she tried to focus on her breathing, but her eyes flashed with curiosity.

I pulled my backpack up onto my lap, unzipping it and pulling out my headphones. "I wrote something for you, and True and I recorded it yesterday. I want you to focus on my voice, focus on the lyrics, and keep breathing," I slipped my headphones over Kennedy's ears.

I took a deep breath, unsure what she'd think of what I'd created for her. I'd never written a song for someone in this way before, and I wanted her to like it, to find comfort in my voice.

Kennedy fluttered her eyes closed, squeezing my hand. I pressed play and sat back, observing her reaction. This song wasn't loud with a pounding beat and screaming guitar. It was slow and soothing. I called it *Brave* because that's how I saw her. She was the bravest person I knew.

The lyrics described how only the strongest people challenged their fears and beat them. It was a song of encouragement and was more uplifting than any of Shadow Phoenix's other music. I'd never felt more inspired than when I wrote it with her in mind.

As she listened, her face relaxed, and her breathing slowed. She leaned over and rested her head on my shoulder, a tear sliding down her cheek. I bent to kiss it away, rubbing the back of her hand with my thumb.

She took the headphones off and stared at me, her blue eyes burning with an intensity I'd never seen before. I hardly ever got nervous, but my heart raced waiting for her reaction. Did I cross a line? Shit, what if she hated it? It wasn't lost on me that those fucking unproductive *what if* thoughts were running rampant through *my* mind now. I ran my hand through my hair as the silence stretched on. She studied my face with an unreadable expression.

"I'm dying over here," I finally said. "Don't keep me in suspense."

She giggled. I hoped that was a good sign.

"Oh, are you dying? Really? Maybe I'll let you sweat it a few more minutes so you can feel how it feels to be me," she teased, her eyes dancing. "That was…" She took a deep breath. "That was the best thing anyone has ever done for me. I didn't say anything because I had no words. I have no words. I just-" She grabbed my face and pulled my lips to hers, her cheeks wet with tears.

I unbuckled her seatbelt and gripped her hips, pulling her onto my lap, holding her close and gently biting her bottom lip. She let me deepen the kiss, and I was in fucking heaven. She whimpered as I placed a soft kiss on her lips, not wanting me to stop.

"That's one way to keep you distracted during this drive," I chuckled. "I don't know why I didn't think of it sooner." She wiggled on my lap with a smile on her kiss-swollen lips. I dug my fingers into her hips, turning her, so she was straddling me.

She pressed her lips to mine again, and I grabbed a handful of her ass, pulling her closer and pushing myself up into her heat. She sucked in a breath, making the sexiest whimpering sounds as her tongue pushed into my mouth. I reached up and teased her tits with my fingers, stopping to pinch her nipples through her dress. She wasn't wearing a bra.

Fuck me.

She began to rock her hips against mine, desperately searching for friction where she needed it most, and I thrust my hips against her again, more than willing to give it.

"Zen, please-" she panted.

"Shh, baby. We don't want to give Connor a show. I'm not sharing this view with anyone else." I kept my voice low so only she could hear me, and I kissed the tip of her nose. "Besides, we're almost there."

She sighed in frustration. "Can't we just stay in the car a little while longer? Let's drive to Oregon."

I laughed. "What happened to my scared Kennedy? Weren't you the one I practically had to throw over my shoulder and drag to the car half an hour ago?"

"She's gone, and in her place is a girl who really wants you to finish what you started."

I let out a low chuckle. If Kennedy had been standing, she'd have her arms crossed and be stomping her foot. She was fucking adorable when she pouted. She was especially cute when she pouted over not getting a chance to take my cock for a ride.

It made my chest, and another place far lower, tighten to know she wanted me as badly as I wanted her. I wasn't going to rush, and our first time sure as fuck wouldn't be in the back of a car with an audience. Not after what that asshole Brock did to her during her first and only time. No, I'd make sure she thoroughly enjoyed herself when the time came. And I'd make sure she was ready, because once I had Kennedy, I wouldn't ever be able to stop.

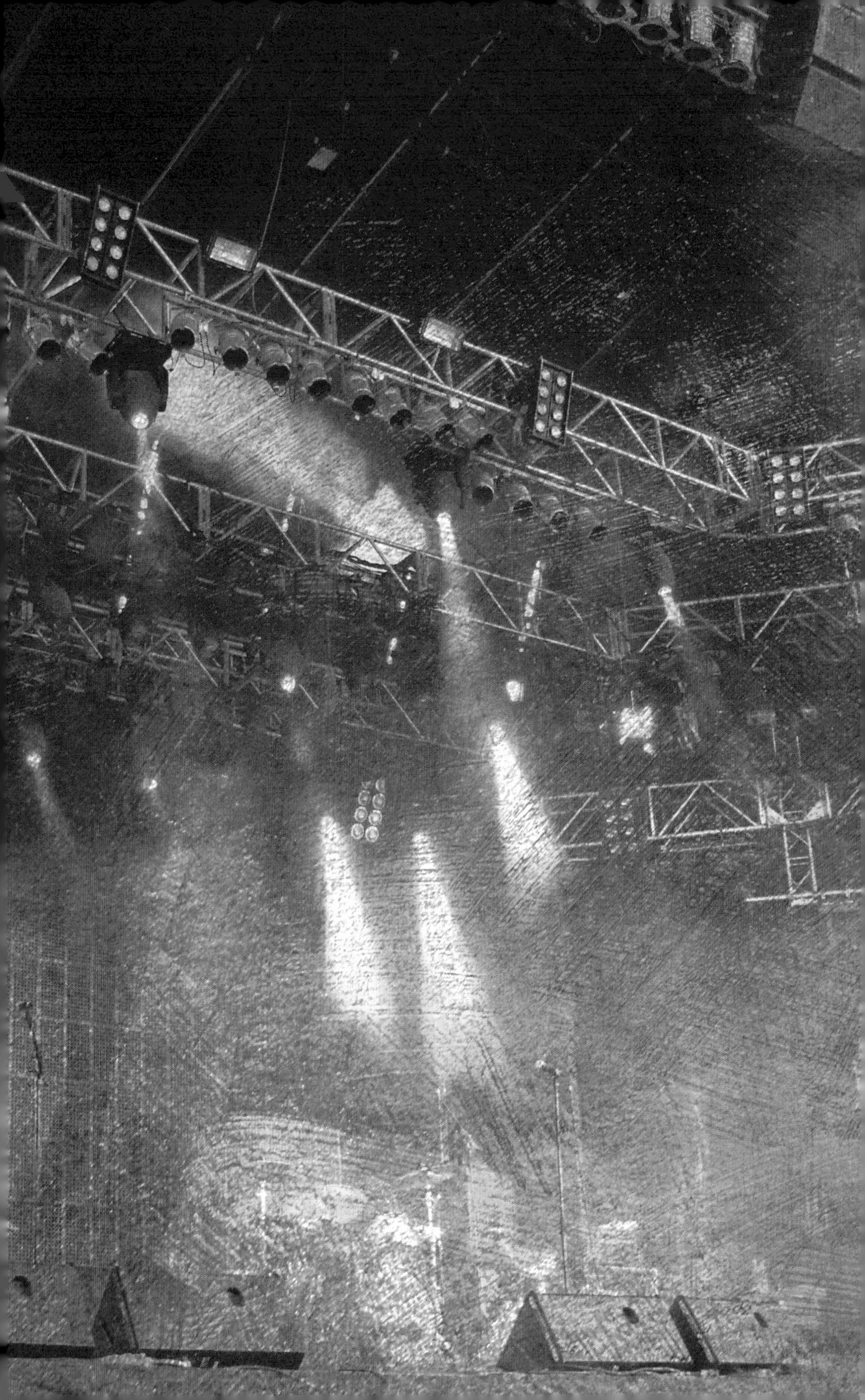

CHAPTER 16

ZEN

I SHIELDED my eyes with my hand as we pulled up in front of the tallest building in downtown Seattle. The low sunlight reflecting off the glass exterior made me squint, despite the tinted glass window. Connor opened the door for Kennedy and me. She climbed off of my lap and onto the seat, molding herself to my side. She started to hyperventilate again.

I looked into her eyes, holding her gaze. "I'm right here, and you're doing so well, baby. You've got this. We're going to go inside to have dinner. I know elevators can be tough for you, but let's keep moving forward, one step at a time like we did this morning."

She nodded tightly, squeezing my hand and taking deep breath after deep breath. Her eyes were almost frantic. I was determined to stay strong for her, even if it killed me to see her suffering. "I really just want to turn around and go home," she breathed.

"I know, but if you do, the panic wins. You won't let it win, will you?" I said, a small smirk tilting the corner of my mouth up with my challenge.

She exhaled loudly. "No, I don't want it to win. Okay, I'll try." Determination and resolve filled her eyes again. I had no idea how long we'd be able to stay, but the fact that she was determined to try made me feel like we could conquer the world. She was incredible.

Whatever progress we'd made vanished when I pulled her out onto the sidewalk, and she froze up. "Talk to me, Sunshine. What's going through your mind right now?"

She gripped my hand as if it were the only thing anchoring her from floating away. "I've got all these worst-case scenarios running through my head. I fucking hate it." Her eyes glistened.

If she cried, I didn't think I could take it. I'd want to wrap her up in my arms and give up on this whole thing, but she needed this. It was getting harder to keep my shit together by the second. It was my job to protect her, but I couldn't protect her from her fear. This she had to face on her own. The best I could do was hold her hand.

"What kinds of scenarios?" I wanted to understand and find a way to make it easier for her.

"You're going to think I'm crazy," she said, hesitating. "But what if my heart beats so fast it just quits? What if we get stuck in the elevator and can't get out? What if something happens to me and I can't get home? What if-"

I pressed my finger to her lips, silencing her mid-thought. "Kennedy, look at me." I waited until her eyes met mine, ignoring the fact that we were standing on a busy sidewalk. "How about we think about all that stuff differently? First, you're healthy. Your heart isn't going to give up if it hasn't already. The fact you're still alive right now shows that it hasn't ever given up during one of these before, right?" I kept my voice soft but firm when I talked to her, not wanting to make the situation worse.

Her shoulders relaxed a fraction. "Yeah, I guess that's true," she sighed, considering my words.

"And as for something happening to you? I already promised you I'd never let anything happen to you, but if you say we go home, we go home. I don't want you to give in to the fear and run away, because I know you're strong enough to make it through this and get better. You've already made it so far today, and I'm so fucking proud of you." I reached out to lightly stroke her cheek.

Out of the corner of my eyes, I saw Connor glancing around at the growing crowd, his jaw tight, and his stance wide. We were exposed out on the sidewalk. With the Mercedes's blacked-out windows and the armed guy standing guard, we were drawing attention, attention Kennedy didn't need right now. I had to convince her to go inside and fast, but I couldn't push her too hard. Like at her store, it had to be her decision.

"Let's think about this a different way," I began. "You keep asking all these 'what if' questions, right? Well, what if we look at the possible positive outcomes instead of the negative? Fuck the negative, Kennedy. There's just as much chance a positive outcome will happen instead. In fact, there's more of a chance that we'll have a positive result. We've taken precautions, and we're doing something fun. So, what if we have fun? What if the food is excellent? What if we get to know each other better? What if this is the best night of your entire fucking life? You'll never know unless you take my hand and follow me inside right now." I stayed quiet, waiting for her decision with my hand held out. In my peripheral vision, more and more people were taking notice of us.

This was her battle, and I could only support her in it. She exhaled, her eyes less stormy. "You're right. Please keep reminding me of the positive what-ifs, it helps. I fucking hate that I'm ruining this right now." Her voice was thick with anger and sadness, her eyes welling up with tears again.

I wrapped my arms around her since she hadn't taken my hand. "You are not ruining anything. This is for you to help you face your fears, and in the process, I get to show you I'll always be here for you, even when you're at one of your lowest moments. And if things go how I think they will, because you're strong and fucking incredible, we'll have dinner and go back to your place, and you'll be so damn proud of yourself when the night is over." I placed a quick kiss on the top of her head and released her, allowing her to make the final decision and holding out my hand again.

Connor shifted on his feet, anxious to get us inside. He looked as if he wanted to grab us and drag us into the building. People started pulling out their phones, their attention sending chills down my spine. Whispers were questioning who we were. Time was up, and as soon as someone recognized me, word would spread on social media like wildfire. There was no fucking way that could happen.

Thank fuck, Kennedy made her decision and grabbed my hand, practically dragging me into the building behind her. A surge of pride welled up inside of me at her bravery.

Once we were in the lobby, we waited for Connor's signal to continue. It took a few minutes, but the small crowd that had gathered outside splintered off, people quickly losing interest in us. I exhaled a breath I hadn't even been aware I was holding, at the sweet relief of knowing Kennedy was safe.

"Connor? Can we go up?" I gestured toward the elevators behind me.

"Yeah, you're good." He strode across the lobby toward us. "I had a team check the top floor before we came, so it's clear. I'll be right behind you."

I turned toward Kennedy. "Ready for the next step?"

Taking a deep breath, she held my hand as if it were her lifeline.

She glanced at the elevator as if a thought suddenly occurred to her. "How many floors up is it?"

Did I tell her the truth? I figured honesty was probably the best in any situation, so I said, "Seventy-six."

She sucked in a deep breath. "Shit." She gripped my hand so

hard that her knuckles were turning white, and my fingers were starting to tingle from lack of blood flow. "Let's get this over with, but I'm warning you, if this elevator gets stuck I'm climbing you to get out the top and rappelling my way down."

I chuckled. "You don't need a reason to climb all over me. My body belongs to you. It's yours to do whatever you want with." I waved my hand around, gesturing at myself.

Her tongue ran along her bottom lip as her eyes traveled down my chest, abs, and lower before snapping back up. Heat blossomed in her eyes, and I found myself suddenly hoping the elevator ride would be slow as fuck. Kennedy would be forced to make good on her threat to climb me like a tree.

Jamming my thumb against the button, we waited until the shiny doors slid open. Kennedy stepped forward, pulling me along with her. Connor nodded at me before the doors closed behind the two of us. He already knew, just from watching, that I wanted the elevator ride with Kennedy to myself. He'd be taking a different set of elevators up. I wanted to have the privacy to distract Kennedy if she needed it. Whatever she needed, I'd provide.

As the elevator began its ascent, she asked through clenched teeth, "Can you please distract me? It's taking everything in me not to stop this thing on the next floor and run down the stairs back to the car."

My girl needed a distraction? Oh, I'd give her a distraction. I turned toward her, wrapping an arm around her waist and pressing my lips gently to hers. I ran my other hand through her hair, softly gripping it and pulling her even closer to deepen the kiss. She threw her arms around me, clinging to me as she trembled, our tongues dancing together. She whimpered, and the sound shot straight to my cock.

She tasted so fucking good. I'd never get enough of her. My thoughts were erratic, but all I could think was *more, more, more*.

I wanted more for the first time in my life. Every time we

kissed, it sank me deeper into a hole I never wanted to find my way out of. The little whimpers she made when I pulled her bottom lip with my teeth, or when I ran my fingers gently down her back as we kissed, would never be enough. I was already so hard that it hurt. I pressed our hips together, wishing the layers between us would magically disappear.

"You're so good at this." Her voice came out low and husky.

I was fucked if she asked me for anything right now because there was no way I could tell her no. I didn't want our first time to be against the wall of an elevator, but at this point I wouldn't be able to deny her if she asked because I'd never been harder, and I was no longer capable of thinking with my upper head.

"You have no fucking idea how good I'm going to make you feel." My control frayed until only a thread remained. Right now, she needed me to be strong enough for both of us. Even if it killed me, even if I had to walk around with blue balls for the rest of the night, I'd do it to prove to her that this was about so much more than sex to me.

Proving to Kennedy that we were the real thing mattered more than giving in to the lust pulsing through my veins. From the moment I laid my eyes on her, she owned me, and she needed to know she could trust that. I reluctantly pulled back, placing a gentle kiss on the tip of her nose.

She looked up at me with longing and confusion. "Come back," she said, reaching for my shirt, wrapping the soft cotton in her fist and tugging gently, trying to pull me back.

I desperately wanted to give in, but I wouldn't. "Sunshine, we're almost at the top. I want to press you against the wall and bury myself inside of you more than anything in this whole fucking world, but right now, you need to do this. Have dinner with me and then we'll go home and finish what we started. Okay?" I pleaded with her, both with my words and my eyes, begging her not to push. I had a thin wall of resolve, and it was already crumbling. If she stuck out her lip in that pouty way she did, I would dive right back in her arms, and we'd never make it to dinner.

The elevator came to an abrupt halt causing Kennedy to fall against my chest.

Fuck me.

Her warm coconut-and-Kennedy scent wrapped around me. My cock ached with the need to be inside her. I reached down to adjust myself, releasing her from my arms and tearing my gaze away from her lips. I exhaled a shaky breath. With my hand on the small of her back, I led her out of the elevator. I barely trusted myself to touch her with how much I wanted to fuck her.

When she stepped into the restaurant, her eyes widened. "Where is everyone?"

I smiled. I wanted to surprise Kennedy because I knew that this day would be hard, and if I could make it easier in some small way, I would. Renting out the entire restaurant just for us seemed like a no-brainer. Once we got through this, we could go home.

Home.

It still caught me off guard how I looked at her as home already. It wasn't the place, it was Kennedy. She had become my home so fast I was surprised I didn't have whiplash. Proving to her how good we could be together, how good I could be for her, had become my new mission in life. I'd never hurt her as long as I lived.

My singular goal had always been to build my career, to make music. I hadn't been looking for Kennedy, but I'd found my whole world the night she'd taken my roofied ass in. Fate stepped in and delivered me this woman who seemed to be made just for me. I wasn't going to fuck it up.

I had two new goals. Show Kennedy how perfect we were for each other and make her see how strong she was. It scared me when I thought about how quickly she had come in and demolished my entire life, but in the best possible way. Music wasn't my number one obsession anymore, Kennedy was. She'd become the most important person in my life in a disturbingly fast amount of time, but I didn't want to step back. I didn't want to think about it. For once, I just wanted to get swept up and feel. I hoped I could be everything Kennedy deserved, and I planned to spend my life trying to earn the privilege of being with her.

"We've got the place to ourselves. I figured if you made it this far, this would be a good reward." I smiled hesitantly, unsure how she'd feel about how much work and money it took to do this for her.

"I can't believe you did this. It's perfect," she whispered, relief and a flash of something I couldn't quite place crossing her eyes, before she threw herself into my arms. I held her for a few seconds, burying my face in her hair before someone cleared their throat nearby.

I hugged her tighter before we turned together and looked at a man standing a few feet away in a uniform, clearly uncomfortable if the blush on his cheeks was any indication. I didn't give a shit. "Your table is ready if you'll just follow me," he said, turning abruptly and striding away.

He led us to a table by the window. As soon as she sat down, Kennedy pressed her face to the glass, gazing down to the city below, bathed in the golden light of a sinking sun. She looked like an angel, haloed with a bright glow. "It's breathtaking," she sighed. I had to agree, but I wasn't looking anywhere but at her. "I've never seen anything like this before. Thank you for sharing this with me." She broke her gaze off the window and locked eyes with mine.

I'd give up everything I had for her to look at me like that again, even once, like I was everything to her. Was I reading too much into that look? Could she possibly feel how I'd been feeling?

The thought made me want to throw her down on the table right here and claim her, to show her and everyone else that I would be the only one that could touch her and give her everything she could possibly want or need.

That she was mine.

My cock hardened and I had to push down the urge to act on the thoughts racing through my mind.

I focused back on Kennedy. "How are you feeling?"

"I'm feeling a lot better, much calmer. It helps that there aren't tons of people here. I can relax a little for the first time since we left. Thank you for being here with me, for pushing me to do this." She reached across the table and grabbed my hand, running her thumb along my knuckles and smiling at me with her bright, innocent eyes locked on mine.

My gaze dropped to her lips, and I began picturing all the things I wanted her to do with her mouth. To have it on me, pressing hot kisses down my chest and lower until she wrapped her soft lips around my cock.

When the waiter dropped off our food, I shifted in my seat, trying to get my raging hard-on under control, but it was hopeless. By some miracle, I managed to get through dinner, letting our conversation distract me. Talking to Kennedy came so easily. I could sit and talk to her forever about everything and nothing at all. She listened to me, didn't judge me for my past, or judge the thoughts I had. For the first time, I could truly be myself, and I didn't have to pretend or put on a show.

When we were getting ready to leave, Kennedy excused herself to the bathroom, and I tried to stay in my seat. I really did. But once I paid the bill, I couldn't take it anymore. I'd been so wound up this entire night my cock felt like it would break through my jeans.

Following her to the bathroom, I slipped in the door as she reapplied her lip gloss in the mirror. She looked at me in her reflection, her eyes widening.

"Zen? What are you doing?" she asked, glancing around.

"We're alone, remember?" I smirked. As I stalked towards her, my footsteps echoed off the marble floor.

"Right." She laughed nervously.

"Now, as for what I'm doing? Well, let's see..." I continued stalking towards her. "I've been trying to be good since that elevator ride, but I've been hard as fuck all night, watching your mouth while you talk and eat, imagining all the things I want to do with it. I couldn't wait until we got home. I'm like an addict with a craving, baby, and you're the only relief." I lowered my lips to hers, ravaging her mouth with my tongue as my fingers stabbed into her hair and twisted around in the strands until they wrapped around my fist and I could tug her head back.

She whimpered as my fingers dug into her thigh, helping her lift it around my waist. Backing her up until she was pressed against the counter, I never stopped kissing her while I let go of her hair and lifted her onto the surface.

Leaning back to stare at the ruined state of her, my tongue dragged along my lower lip as I drank my fill. Her dress was pushed up her thighs so a hint of black lace peeked out that made me crazy. The golden strands of her hair were tangled, her wild eyes stood out against the flush of her skin. Her nipples pressed against the silky fabric of her dress, and I reached my inked fingers out, yanking the top down so her breasts spilled out. When every shred of willpower I possessed had gone up in smoke, I pressed forward, taking my rightful place between her thighs. She wasted no time rolling her hips to press her center against my hard shaft and I groaned.

"I don't want to wait anymore. Please," she begged, and I was done.

So fucking done.

I couldn't hold back anymore.

I pushed her skirt further up and dragged my fingertips up her inner thigh, stroking gently, teasing the smooth skin. Running my tongue down her neck, I dotted her skin with fiery kisses as she shivered beneath me. Smiling against her skin, I slid my finger under the soaked fabric of her panties, stroking my finger lightly along her slit. Jerking at the contact, she bucked against my hand.

"Goddamn, baby. You're so wet for me already."

"Is that okay?" She bit her lip and looked up at me hesitantly. Fuck, her innocence turned me on even more. Kennedy had no idea how hot she was. I'd learn every little thing that made her whimper and writhe. She'd never want another man but me.

"Fuck, yes. You have no idea how hot it is." I kissed her again. My cock strained painfully against my jeans, begging to be let out, but this wasn't about me. I'd give her what she needed. I pulled her panties down her legs and stuck them in my back pocket. Then I slowly ran my finger up and down her slick entrance, each time circling the little bundle of nerves before running my finger back down.

"Oh, fuck," she moaned.

"Do you want my fingers in this pretty little pussy, baby?"

"Yes," she cried out, throwing her head back. "Please," was all she managed to get out, and I smiled. She responded to my touch immediately, lighting a fire under my skin as I slipped a finger deep inside her before sliding it out. She was so responsive. Even the high of standing on stage in front of thousands of people didn't compare to watching Kennedy come apart. She acted as if I held the secret to all her pleasure in the palm of my hand. Maybe I did.

I knelt down between her legs, taking in the sight of her silky, bare pussy as I sucked my finger into my mouth, getting my first taste of her tonight. "Let me taste you."

"Fuck." Her head fell back against the mirror and her eyes fluttered shut.

I'd take that as a yes, and at the first taste, she opened her eyes and leaned back on her elbows against the mirror, watching me from under her lashes.

I had to be the luckiest motherfucker in the whole world. I licked slow and languid, circling and sucking around and around. Her tangy taste exploded on my tongue, making my mouth water.

Her fingers threaded through my hair, tugging at me, trying to get me closer.

"Fuck, your taste on my tongue is pure sin." She rocked her hips against my face, and I never let up, relentlessly pursuing her release. I'd make her come again and again before the night was over. This was just the appetizer. I had a full meal planned for us when we got home.

I sucked gently on her clit and pressed one finger inside of her, hooking it to rub the perfect place inside. She bucked her hips off the counter, and I steadied her with a hand on her stomach.

"Oh, just like that. Keep doing that." I slowly pulled my finger out and pressed it in again before adding a second finger, curling them inside her. Her walls started to contract, milking my fingers and, fuck, I wished they were my cock.

Her legs trembled as she cried out, "I'm going to-"

I sucked on her clit one more time, and she tensed, her nails digging into my scalp as I lapped up every drop of wetness dripping out of her. As she began to come down, I gently removed my fingers and licked them clean before pressing a kiss to her inner thigh. I stood up and tucked her into my arms.

"That was the hottest thing I've ever seen." I kissed her lips, and she opened for me, no doubt tasting herself on my tongue. "I'm going to need a minute before we go downstairs."

She sighed contentedly. "I had no idea it could be like that."

I smirked. "Baby, you haven't seen anything yet."

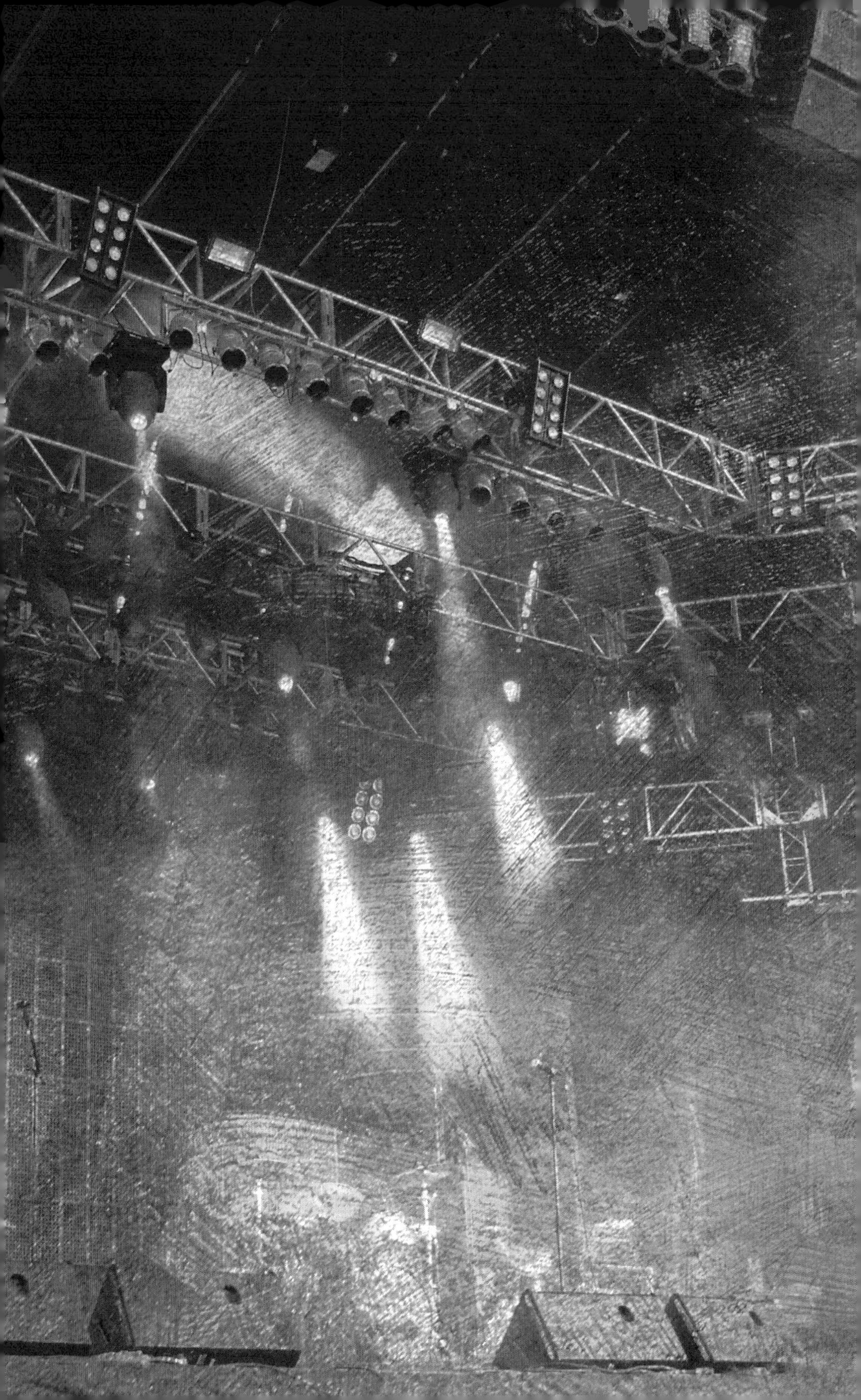

CHAPTER 17

KENNEDY

PULLING UP TO SWEET STORIES, my eyes fluttered open when Zen brushed the hair off my forehead and kissed my temple. I was so worn out I could barely focus.

"Hey, Sunshine, we're home. Wake up." I leaned into him more instead, nuzzling his neck and inhaling. He smelled like the ocean and sandalwood and something uniquely Zen. I could get dizzy from breathing in his scent.

He chuckled, wrapping his arm firmly around me and sliding toward the door Connor held open. I still wasn't quite sure how I even got in the car in the first place, since I'd practically passed out in the bathroom.

He jumped out, and I missed his heat pressed against me. Opening my eyes, I placed my hand in his letting him pull me out of the car. "Wrap your arms around my neck."

I lifted my arms and hugged his neck while he bent down and

slid his arm under my legs, handing his keys to Connor, who unlocked the door. As Connor took the steps to my apartment two at a time, Zen held me against his body, and I took the opportunity to rest my head against his chest.

My eyes were heavy, but a more pressing need than sleep was creeping back up. Zen did otherworldly things with his tongue at the restaurant, and I wanted more. Suddenly, I was wide awake. Heat sparked under my skin, waking up my body. I wanted to feel him inside of me, to be as close to him as I could get. He'd managed to push his way into my heart, crumble my defenses, and now I was ready for more.

Tonight, he stood next to me through all my crazy and held my hand while we walked through it together. I closed my eyes, listening to the steady rhythm of his heart, and let my body relax. My eyes opened slowly when he lowered me onto the bed.

"You're going to stay, right?" I mumbled as he turned to leave. One side of his lips quirked up in a cocky grin.

"Sunshine, there's not a chance in hell I'm leaving this apartment tonight. I need to talk to Connor for a minute. Try not to fall asleep while I'm gone."

I forced myself to stay awake, but it was fucking difficult after the anxiety and events of the day. Panic attacks were exhausting, and despite how turned on I was, my eyelids still grew heavy as I waited for Zen to come to bed.

I must have fallen asleep because the next thing I knew, my eyes fluttered open when warm, soft kisses pressed against my cheeks and then my forehead.

"You're not going to want to sleep through this next part." Zen's lips brushed against my ear as he whispered. "I owe you your prize for making it through tonight." He pressed gentle kisses down my throat, and I shivered as heat flowed through my veins, because I knew the prize would be erotic and I couldn't wait.

Running my hands down his sculpted chest through his t-shirt like I was reading braille, I let my fingers trace over the ridges of his abs and lower. Zen invaded all my senses. He overwhelmed me in the best way. As he crawled on top of me and his body pressed down against mine, the need inside me grew more potent. Desperation to feel him everywhere clawed at me, and I reached for him, trying to draw him closer. My body ached for Zen, but I didn't know if anything would ever be enough. Nothing in my life had ever felt like this before.

Squirming beneath him, I was lost to sensation, heat dripping into my veins like a toxin that gathered between my thighs and poisoned me to any other man. Yanking the top of my dress down, his ink-painted fingers plucked at my nipples as I surrendered to his touch.

"Fuck, fuck, fuck." My mouth seemed capable of only one syllable sounds, whimpers, and moans as he rolled my hardened peaks between his fingers. When I was on the verge of shoving him away, my nipples so sensitive they were nearly painful, his mouth descended, laving away the discomfort and transforming it to bliss.

A flash of fear jolted through me as I realized what was about to happen. The new Kennedy would be strong, would take chances, would go after what she wanted. I was done letting my fears control me. Tonight I'd own my desires.

"Stop holding back." A growl of frustration tore up my throat, and I grabbed his shirt trying to rip it off. This was feral. Animal. Untamed.

He sat back with a devilish curve to his lips, pulling it off slowly as if to remind me he was the one in charge. He stared down at me, his pupils blown so wide with lust his eyes were nearly black. "Before this night is over, you'll have a permanent imprint of my cock deep in this pussy," he promised, his voice dangerously low as his fingers brushed against my slick entrance, his gentle touch at odds with the savagery of his words. "You'll never fucking forget how it feels when I'm inside you."

My dress still sat between us, and as if he were reading my mind, his fingers pulled back, drifting toward the hem where it was bunched up around my thighs. His gaze locked on mine as he reached into his pocket, pulling out a switchblade and flicking it open. How did I miss that when I emptied his pockets? "Hope you weren't attached to this," he murmured before sliding the cool metal under the fabric and slicing the dress off my body. A thrill ran down my spine at the risk, the danger he exudes.

The pieces fell away as he closed the blade, slipping it back into his pocket as he stood and unbuttoned his jeans. My body was laid before him like an offering to this dark god, a sacrifice to his pleasure. Transfixed, I watched as his jeans came off, falling to the floor as if they were undeserving to be against his skin and then he stood before me, cock proudly jutting out, all of his inked skin and ripped body on display.

The mattress dipped as he climbed back onto the bed, tossing a square foil packet onto the sheet beside me. I shivered in anticipation of what he'd do next. My mind whirred with possibilities, each one hotter than the last. "I've been waiting too fucking long for this, and I'm not in the mood to go slow. Grab the headboard, baby."

Reaching above my head, my fingers grasped the slatted wood, barely fitting in the space between boards, but I held on tight. My chest rose and fell, faster and faster with every breath, and I was afraid if Zen touched me again, I'd implode.

A second later I was proven wrong when he ran his finger along the edge of my entrance with the barest of touches, only enough to drive me to insanity. "If I buried my face in this pussy right now, I bet you could drown me."

"Do it and find out," I dared him, and the devious smirk that cut across his gorgeous face was vicious.

"No, I've got a better use for all that sweet wetness." He fisted his monster cock, stroking the full length once before doing it again. Every rumor about Zen Taylor that existed on the internet about what he's packing in his pants was actually under-exaggerated, and my teeth sank into my lip, wondering if I could handle him. He reached down beside me, picking up that packet and tearing into it with his teeth before rolling the condom down his length.

My eyes were wide as my heart pulsed erratically in anticipation and my fingers curled tighter around the headboard.

"Spread those thighs, baby. Let me see my pretty pink pussy all glistening and ready for me to spoil."

Without an ounce of hesitation, I did as he asked, letting my knees fall open and Zen's groan of appreciation buzzed all the way down to my toes. With his fist wrapped around his cock, he hovered over me and slipped the head across my slit, spreading my arousal all over himself. His hips rocked as his shaft slid along my opening, rubbing against my clit with every stroke.

He teased my entrance, letting the tip barely push inside before shifting out again until I couldn't take it anymore. Letting go of the headboard, I reached my hand down between us and started rubbing circles around my clit, needing to come more than I needed my next breath.

Zen slapped my hand away, glaring at me. "Hands on the headboard."

I swallowed hard and wound my trembling fingers back around the wood. Once he's satisfied with my obedience, he finally —*finally*—fills my body. His many, many inches stretched me to full, and I closed my eyes at the overwhelming intensity of it all. I never wanted it to end.

"Still with me, Sunshine?" My eyes blinked open and up into his as I nodded, unable to form words. "I'm gonna move now," he said, groaning as he slid almost fully out of me and then slammed back in. His thrusts were hard and wild, and I wrapped my legs around his waist, holding on for the ride.

At first, the rhythm was unhinged, desperate and brutal, but then…

Then it changed to something deep, a slow grind of his pelvis against mine, keeping me full with tiny shifts of his hips while keeping constant attention on my clit. Dizzy with the lust running hot through my veins, I rolled my body as my pussy spasmed around Zen.

"You're about to come," he announced. "I can feel your pussy trying to drain me. Do it, baby. Make me blow."

His dirty words and pistoning hips were my downfall as pleasure radiated out in waves, tensing every muscle in my body as I came around him. My thighs shook uncontrollably as his cock jerked inside of me and he found his own release.

Zen held himself up so he didn't crush me, but his forehead fell to mine as we both tried to catch our breath.

"Holy shit," I murmured, my thighs quivering and my arms weak and languid. "I think you broke me."

The smug satisfaction on his face was pure alpha-hole. He was an expert with the cock still buried inside me, slowly softening, and he knew it. Still, I put that satisfied look on his face, and something about that made me feel powerful.

He slid out of me and went into the bathroom to deal with the condom while I yawned and enjoyed the show of a very naked Zen on display for my pleasure.

Pulling back the blanket, he crawled back in bed beside me, dragging me against his body where I promptly passed the hell out.

MY EYES slowly opened the next morning, and I smiled at the pleasant achiness between my legs. I leaned into the comforting warmth of Zen. I nestled against his neck, inhaling his unique scent. Heat bloomed inside my belly and worked its way out to my limbs, filling me up. My eyes moved across his sleeping face, taking in the dark lashes fanned across his cheeks and the rough stubble dusting his sharp jawline.

Talk about a hell of a way to wake up. Zen made me feel emboldened and brave. I had the power to bring this rock god to his knees, and it was a heady feeling. Me. Kennedy Adams. The least powerful and brave person I knew.

Determined to have an encore from last night, I slowly slid myself down his body being careful not to wake him up. Not yet. I wanted him halfway down my throat before those hypnotic green eyes opened for the first time. My tongue trailed across the dips and ridges of his abs—all six of them. He moaned quietly but didn't open his eyes. Pausing, I waited to see if he woke up, but when his breathing returned to even and deep, I continued my trail downward.

When I reached my destination, I blew warm breath across his semi-hard dick as goosebumps broke out along his body. I kissed across his thighs, the soft hair on his legs tickling my nose. I'd never done this before, but I was a quick learner and based on the fully erect cock in front of my face, I'd done something right.

My fingers curled around his length, and I took a tentative lick of the tip having no idea what I was doing. Zen lifted his hips in his sleep, gently thrusting himself further into my hand and this time when I licked him, I circled the head of his dick, making sure to taste every part of him I could.

He was salty and sticky, and coated my tongue but I loved every second of it. Tingles rushed under my skin at my exploration, gathering between my thighs. My clit pulsed in time with my heartbeat like an EDM drum beat vibrating through my body.

My lips wrapped around him, testing how deep I could take him as his fingers dug into my hair, fisting it and thrusting deeper into my mouth. With his cock still in my mouth, I looked up at him, his half-lidded stare melting my insides.

Wetness dripped down my thighs as he pumped in and out of my mouth and I tried to keep up. When he went too far and I gagged, he pulled back. Tears ran down my face, but I wanted more.

He popped free but I wasn't done, so I licked his shaft like my favorite ice cream cone. "Jesus fuck. You're going to make me come."

Since that was exactly what I wanted, I sucked him back into my mouth, using my hand to pump his length in time with my mouth. I wasn't experienced enough to take him all the way into my throat, but if the sounds he was making were any indication, I was doing something right.

"I'm going to come down your throat if you don't stop," he warned, but I wanted it. I wanted to know what it was like to swallow every drop of him down, to carry a bit of him inside me.

Instead of pulling back, I increased the suction and speed and he thickened, growing impossibly harder before erupting in my mouth with a grunt. Swallow after swallow, I managed to keep up with his release, and when he was finished, I let him go, sitting back with a naughty little grin. My tongue darted out to lick my lips, making sure I didn't leave a mess behind and his lust-darkened gaze tracked the motion.

"Fuck," he muttered before grabbing my hand and yanking me up, kissing the hell out of me. His pulse raced below the palm I rested against his heart. "That was… I don't even have words."

I laughed. "I've rendered the great Zen Taylor speechless. My life is complete."

His green eyes softened, and I found myself getting lost in their depths.

"Come take a shower with me." He pulled me out of bed. "It's your turn."

After washing each other from head to toe and a couple mind-blowing orgasms thanks to Zen's tongue, I wrapped myself in a fluffy towel feeling warm, cherished, and completely relaxed. Today's Kennedy wasn't the same as the Kennedy that rescued Zen. I felt more powerful and confident and brave. That was the power of Zen. A warm tugging pulled at my insides, and I wanted to fall into it. My heart rate picked up as I glanced at Zen's naked form, and he grinned at me. I could spend every minute with this man, and it wouldn't be enough. Heat pooled in my core, and I had to turn away before we got carried away again.

Getting dressed quickly, we walked hand in hand to the kitchen. I let go and sat down on one of the colorful stools at the island.

Zen dropped a kiss on my lips before walking to the refrigerator. "Omelets okay?"

"You give me two orgasms and cook breakfast? I'm never letting you go." I teased, leaning forward and resting my elbows on the island.

His gaze turned heated. "Is that a promise?"

"Maybe, let's see how your omelets come out first." I laughed, jumping up to go make coffee, and he caught me around the waist, pulling me into his chest and nipping at my neck.

He growled. "First we eat, then I'm taking you back to bed because two orgasms were just the beginning."

"Deal." I couldn't stop the smile from spreading across my face at his delicious promise.

THAT EVENING, as Zen grabbed his phone off my nightstand, he asked, "Do you have your driver's license?"

My brows furrowed as I nodded. "I got it when I was sixteen and kept up the renewals."

"Good, I want to leave my car here with you this week while the guys are here and we're working. Practice with your anxiety, keep pushing boundaries like we did this weekend. I'll be here with you all week by video chat or text or call, whatever you want. I can't physically be here because we get really intense when we're recording. The guys are flying in expecting me to be fully present. But I'll be here in every other way I can."

Thor, this man had come stumbling into my life, but right away he'd stolen bits of my heart, chipping at it piece by piece until now he had the whole thing.

I loved him.

The thought crashed through me, and it felt so right it took my breath away. Taking a steadying breath, I fought the urge to throw myself into Zen's arms and blurt out those three words. Instead, I stood on shaky legs and pulled one of his t-shirts over my head.

He flashed his cocky grin as my legs shook from the countless orgasms he'd given me today. Staying in bed and devouring each other all day because we couldn't get enough had been perfect.

"Okay, I'll work on it. I'm going to miss you." I crossed the room and wrapped my arms around his toned waist.

"I'll miss you, too, baby. So much." He pressed his lips to my forehead.

My thoughts wandered to the week ahead as I listened to Zen's steady heartbeat. Now that I decided my anxiety wouldn't control me anymore, I planned to attack it full force and head-on.

After Connor dropped Zen off at home, he brought back the G500 for me and parked it in the lot behind the building, bringing me a set of keys to both the car and Zen's house. There was a note with the keys:

Sunshine,

This week, you're not alone. When you lay in bed, feel me there

with you. Think of me next to you like I'll be thinking of you. Listen to my voice, singing only to you. Wrap yourself in the shirt I left on your bed and imagine my arms around you until next weekend when I can hold you again.

**Yours for always,
Zen**

His thoughtfulness warmed me down to my soul. No one had ever taken care of me like Zen did. Clutching the note in my fist, I walked into my room and spotted his t-shirt folded up on my bed. I felt achy and empty already, missing his warmth and how safe he made me feel.

But this week I had work to do. I straightened my spine and sank down onto the bed, lifting Zen's shirt to my face and burying my nose inside. I would make progress on my anxiety goals by the time he came back next weekend. It was time to get to work.

The next few days passed quickly as I fell into a new routine. Wake up, bake for the cafe, write for an hour, video chat with Zen, open the store, and when Chloe came in, I'd take Zen's car and drive. Rinse and repeat.

The first day had been the hardest. I hadn't driven anywhere alone in years. I called Amara and asked her to come by on her lunch break and take a quick drive with me.

Amara immediately dropped everything and met me outside of Sweet Stories, hopping into the passenger seat.

She whistled. "Whoa, this thing is insane. I've never even seen anything like it." She ran her hand along the leather seat before pushing every button she could find to see what it did. When she saw the massage feature for the front seat, she sighed happily. "That's it, I officially live in this car now."

I'd have giggled if I wasn't panicking, but my heart raced, and my palms were sweaty. I tried not to think about running up to the safety of my loft. This was why I asked Amara to come. She'd be the perfect distraction. I wanted to take a short drive, driving to Zen's house and back. I missed him like crazy and knew he was inside, even if I couldn't see him today. It made me feel better.

I breathed in and out, almost turning around about a hundred times. Amara held my hand when I needed it, and we made the drive there quickly. He only lived about five miles away, so it was an excellent first boundary to push.

Once we cleared the front security gate, we crept along to the house. I parked in front of the curb, not intending to stay.

"This house is incredible," Amara's face was practically pressed against the glass.

"I know, right? You should see the view from the back."

"Can we? I know we can't stay long, I have to get back to work, but can we just peek?"

I couldn't help but smile at her enthusiasm. "Sorry, the band's in town this week, and they're recording so we can't interrupt the creative process."

"They're all in there? You sure we can't go crash? I still can't believe you're dating a rocker." Amara sighed wistfully.

"No, we can't crash. And you're going to have to get used to it." I tossed my hair behind my shoulder with one last look at the front of Zen's house, where a guard stood on the porch. He eyed us but didn't make a move toward the car.

"Let's go. I'm sure Chloe wants to eat lunch."

Pulling up in front of the store, Amara hopped out of the car and squeezed me in a tight hug, promising to see me later in the week.

Pushing open the front door, I spotted Chloe behind the counter, helping a customer, and she glanced up at me and gave me a small wave.

I crossed the room and moved behind the counter. "Hey, Chloe. How were things while I was gone?"

She edged away from me slightly but glanced up. "Fine. Nothing I couldn't handle. How was your drive?"

"Productive. I wanted to thank you for not only stepping up and helping out so much lately but also not telling anyone about Zen. We both really appreciate it."

She grinned, and it transformed her whole face. "I love it here, and I wouldn't want to mess that up. Besides, your boyfriend is a legend. If he asks me to keep a secret, I'm going to keep it no matter what."

"I'm so lucky to have you," I declared before looking around the shop. "It's slow, and you got the entire shipment restocked. Want to grab a muffin with me? I'll even make your mocha exactly how you like it—extra hot, extra whipped cream."

Chloe brightened, stepping out from behind the counter. "That sounds so good. And you can tell me all about how you hooked Zen Taylor. I've had a crush on him since I was practically in diapers."

Laughing, I followed her to the bakery and stepped behind the counter, working on her mocha. "It's not that interesting of a story, really. I guess I was just in the right place at the right time. I didn't even know who he was when I met him."

Her jaw fell open as she leaned on the counter listening. "No way. How could you not know who Shadow Phoenix is? They're bigger than Metallica and Aerosmith combined!"

"Yeah, and if you asked me to name who's in those bands, I could maybe name one person total." I squirted whipped cream on top of her mocha and handed it across the counter. "Rock isn't really my thing."

I snagged a muffin, following her to one of the tables where we sat down. She sipped her coffee thoughtfully. "It's crazy to me that of all the people he could end up with, it wouldn't be a celebrity or a model or something. It would be a mostly quiet bookstore owner from Kirkland." She laughed, and I couldn't help but join her. She was right, the odds hadn't been in my favor.

I snorted. "If you think I'm mostly quiet, you don't know me very well yet." We finished our little chat, and by the end, I wondered if maybe I'd gained a new friend instead of just an employee. Either way, I had to be careful how much I let Chloe into my life because right now, I wouldn't risk my relationship with Zen for anything.

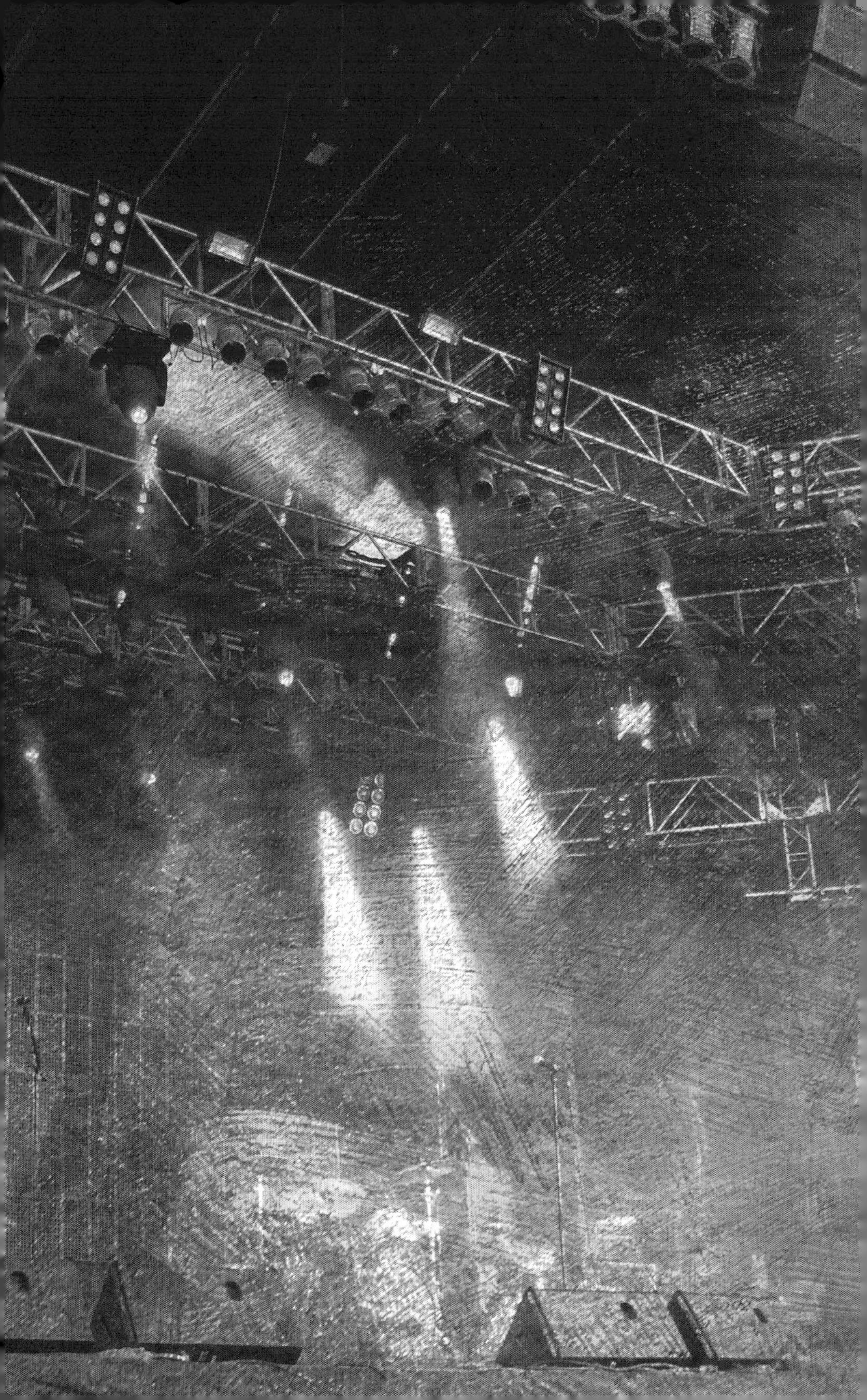

CHAPTER 18

ZEN

THE WEEK DRAGGED BY. My life had become a shit ton more mundane compared to the weekends spent with my girl. It was Thursday, and I'd spent the last few days in the studio with the guys. Any downtime I might have had was split between PR bullshit and Kennedy.

Whenever her name popped up on my phone, I dropped everything. It didn't matter whether I was being interviewed for a magazine or in a recording session. My world revolved around Kennedy, and I was sure I was starting to piss people off.

I didn't give a single fuck.

I suspected this was why the guys asked me to meet up after the last of my phone interviews today. My house was, unfortunately, the one everyone gravitated toward, even when we were in Washington. Hanging up the phone after my last interview, my feet vibrated as loud music shook the floor.

I sighed. All day I'd been looking forward to a video chat with Kennedy and then passing out. Pretending to give a shit about the random assholes in my house wasn't even on my radar. Sleep would bring me one step closer to the weekend with my sexy as fuck girlfriend.

Girlfriend.

A slow smile crossed my face as I thought about how far I'd come when it came to Kennedy. I'd never had a girlfriend before, but fuck if I didn't want everything when it came to her. I wished I could just blow off everything and drive over to see her. My cock twitched at the thought of her body pressed against mine, and a shiver tore down my spine.

As the floor rattled again, I was brought back to reality. Kennedy lived only five miles away, but there might as well have been oceans between us for how far away she felt.

I lifted out of my chair and stretched, steeling myself for whatever bullshit my friends had brought into my house. True and Maddox were getting twitchy the longer the week dragged on. Keeping a low profile wasn't my style, so my lack of drunken antics and sexual escapades this week had Maddox giving me the side-eye more than once. It was only a matter of time before the fucker had enough and decided to let off steam.

Walking down the hall, I spotted Maddox and True shooting a game of pool while half-dressed women lounged around waiting for one of us to take our pick.

I tilted my chin up at my boys before walking to my bedroom, hoping none of them tried to follow. Knowing my friends, they'd send someone my way to shake me out of what they probably felt was my funk.

The thought made me tense. Now that Kennedy was mine, I couldn't be careful enough when it came to other women. No fucking way would I risk losing her over some groupie who got me alone and sold the tabloids a story.

Stepping into my bedroom, I froze. Spread naked in my bed was a woman, her fingers trailing across her skin, apparently waiting for me.

What. The. Fuck.

My blood pounded in my ears as I clenched my teeth together and turned around as quickly as I could. My stomach churned as I realized I'd have to get a new bed. I never brought women here, to this house. It was my sanctuary. I wanted to share it with Kennedy but not like this. I'd spent the last two weeks fantasizing about having her in my bed, and now it had been tainted by a woman who meant nothing to me.

Less than nothing.

Even worse, this girl had the power to take everything from me. My disgust was quickly turning to rage. Her eyes burned into my back. Thankfully, she hadn't spoken. If she said something, I might lose my shit. I needed to get her the fuck out of my bed now. Then I needed to get a new mattress.

Hearing footsteps, I tensed. Her fingers brushed against my back, and they felt like knives stabbing into my skin. I'd never thought much about how people treated me like somehow I belonged to them because I was a celebrity. They touched me whenever and however they wanted regardless of how I felt about it. That shit stopped now. No other woman would touch me like that again.

Stepping away from her, I averted my eyes. "Get. The. Fuck. Out." I didn't wait to see what she did next. Instead, I stalked out to my friends, intending to make someone pay.

"Everyone get the fuck out," I bellowed. "Everyone except you three." I glared at the three of them in turn, daring any one of them to test me. My fists bunched at my sides, and I ached to hit someone. The music stopped as everyone left.

"What the hell, man?" True stood up and set his pool stick down on the table.

"Yeah, what the fuck is wrong with you?" Maddox leaned his

hip against the table and sipped his beer as if he didn't have a care in the world.

"Is your girl not taking care of you or something?" Jericho wondered without even taking his angular eyes off the screen in front of him. He blew out a cloud of smoke before he paused his game and turned to look at me. He had a joint between his fingers and held it out for Maddox, who grabbed it and took a hit.

"Don't talk about her like that," I fumed. "And this isn't about her. This is about the naked girl in my bed. Which one of you did that shit?"

"Again, what the fuck are you talking about?" Maddox passed the joint to True. "We know you met someone. True told us. I heard the song, and it was fucking incredible, by the way. We may be assholes, but we wouldn't fuck you over like that. You should know that by now."

I ran a hand through my hair, frustrated that I was having to deal with this when I should be talking to Kennedy already. "I know."

"Dude, you know we're happy for you, right? Even Maddox," True revealed, passing the joint back to Maddox.

"Debatable," Maddox grumbled.

"I don't understand why you're so upset." Jericho turned back to the screen, unpausing his game.

"He's upset because if the chick in his bed happened to tell anyone about this, his girlfriend could get the wrong idea about what happened," True explained, shooting me a wink. "If she does, we'll tell her what really happened, Z."

"I don't know why you want to tie yourself down to just one woman, but if that shit makes you happy, you know we've got your back," Maddox agreed.

The anger seeped out of me. These guys were my best friends for a reason. They might fuck with me from time to time, but they always had my back just like I had theirs. I should've known they wouldn't sabotage me.

My phone vibrated in my hand as my irritation kicked back up. Talking to Kennedy was the highlight of my day, and I wasn't about to let this little act of sabotage ruin it.

"Who else has been here?" I asked.

Maddox shrugged his shoulders, picking up his beer for another sip. "Ask True, he's been here the longest."

I looked to True, who leaned forward on the pool table, resting his weight on his arms. "I don't know. I didn't keep track of everyone. Maybe some girl took it upon herself to try and bang the famous *Zen Taylor*." He smirked, fluttering his eyelashes and raising his voice to an unnatural octave. "Wouldn't be the first time that's happened."

I rolled my eyes, but my shoulders relaxed. "You're right, I'm just on edge. I fucked up with Kennedy when I didn't tell her who I was, and now I'm fucking terrified of anything coming out that would make her question me." I ran a hand through my hair, tugging on the ends. I probably looked like shit right now, but I didn't care.

"You know something's going to come out at some point. It's the lifestyle, man. You can't stop it," Jericho noted, his attention still on his game.

"I know, but I'm trying to put that shit off as long as I can."

"Look, if this girl, Kennedy, right?"

I nodded.

"If Kennedy cares about you, that shit won't matter. She'll know what's real. Maybe you're not giving her enough credit," True pointed out.

"I just need to know one thing," Maddox chimed in, pushing off the pool table and walking toward me.

"What?"

"How hot is this girl? I know you've got pictures. Let's see." He reached for the phone gripped in my hand, laughing because he knew he was pissing me off.

I bit my cheek to keep from snapping at him. I didn't want to take the bait, and I didn't want Maddox looking at Kennedy. She was mine. It may be my caveman instincts popping up again, but I didn't really give a fuck. If he made a comment, I'd have to fight him, and I'd be later than I already was to talk to her. I couldn't deal with it tonight.

"Forget about how hot she is, which is insanely hot, by the way." Maddox just smirked at me, the fucker. "That doesn't matter. She's not like anyone I've ever met before. She takes my breath away in more ways than one. I don't know how to explain it, I feel like such a chick talking about this." I chuckled. "Let's just leave it at this: I would give up everything to be with her, to keep her out of this life if she asked me to."

True and Maddox wore matching looks of shock on their faces. Jericho even paused his game again and stared at me with a hard look in his eyes. I knew they'd react this way, which was why I'd been trying to avoid this conversation. I braced myself for the ball-busting that was coming.

It took them by surprise how easy it seemed like I'd give up on the band. I knew it would. They'd think I hadn't thought everything through, but I had. The problem was I wasn't just talking about my life when I talked about walking away, I would be fucking with their lives, too. It wasn't a decision I took lightly, but they had a right to know what was on my mind.

Shadow Phoenix was no longer the most meaningful thing in my life.

"You'd walk away from us? Just like that?" True braced his arms on the table again and leaned forward.

"No. I'm not turning my back on you guys. Even if we weren't making music together, you're my brothers. But if it was too much for her, I'd seriously consider it. You know music has been my life forever, and we're family. Nothing will ever change that. But this is different. She's my family, too, and I'm not willing to risk it if it's too much for her."

True blew out a breath, rubbing his forehead. "I didn't know things were so serious."

"So fucking serious that I can't imagine my life without her," I admitted quietly.

Everyone was silent while they processed my words. Finally, True spoke up. "Is that it then? Are you planning on walking away?"

"Fuck, no. That's the last thing I want. I wouldn't know who I was if I wasn't making music with you guys. I'll integrate her into my life in whatever way I can, but she's pretty firmly settled up here. She owns a business. I don't know how it'll work, and it's too soon to worry about it that much. I don't want to scare her off. The thought has been in the back of my mind as an option just in case. You guys have a right to know."

Jericho stood and walked across the room until he stood in front of me. "You know we support you, but if you fucking walk out on us, I'll never forgive you. That's the goddamn nuclear option, the one you never actually take. So, lean on us like we've leaned on you over the years. But don't you dare fucking bail over a girl."

We stood and stared at each other for a couple of seconds before he pulled me in for a hug. "I'm happy for you," he whispered before letting me go and going back to his game.

Maddox finished off his beer and crossed the room to the bar in the corner to get another. "Jericho's right. You're not quitting. I refuse to accept that. *We* refuse to accept that shit. We've worked too fucking hard for this, Z. We'll do what we can to help, but you can't give this up. Remember why we do this, how bad you used to want it."

"I remember." I blew out a breath, a smile tugging at the corner of my lips. "Thanks for the verbal ass-kicking. I guess I needed it."

True nodded, taking a sip of his forgotten beer and lifting his pool stick. "One more thing," he said as I turned to leave.

"What?" I sighed heavily, ready to be done with this conversation.

"We talked it over, and we want to put *Brave* on the new album."

I rubbed the back of my neck. "It's not my song to give, it's Kennedy's. I'll have to ask her."

"Talk to your girl, but I bet she'll agree with me. It needs to be released into the world. People need that song, Zen. I think it could help a lot of people. If you need help convincing her, you could always let us meet her. I bet I could talk her into it." True laughed at my glare.

Having said everything I needed to, I turned and walked back to my room. I eyed my bed as if it were poisonous. The girl left, but her flowery perfume lingered in the air. I stripped the sheets off of my bed before perching on the edge. I pulled my phone out of my pocket, brought up Kennedy's smiling face, and pressed the video chat button. Just like that my world was right again.

WAKING UP FRIDAY, I couldn't stop my grin. I rubbed my hand down my face, my scratchy stubble rough against my palm. I knew no matter what, I'd be seeing Kennedy tonight, and my cock swelled at the prospect of burying myself inside of her. I groaned and sat up, forcing myself to wait until tonight. Picturing her sinking down onto my dick had me wanting to grip my hard-on and get myself off. I knew the sex would be better if I waited until I could be inside Kennedy for real, though.

Yawning, I stood up, shuffling to the shower. This week we'd talked about the progress she made against her anxiety, and I was so fucking proud of her. I needed to go to LA this weekend, and I wanted her to come with me. I knew it might be pushing her harder than she was ready for, but I had to try.

Just like last weekend, I'd have to push her outside of her comfort zone. She'd done a remarkable job pushing her boundaries so far, and my chest swelled with pride when I thought of how far she'd come in such a short time.

With a towel wrapped around my waist, I stepped out of the bathroom. I reached for my phone on the nightstand to send Kennedy a text like I did every morning. Instead, a message from my agent popped up, asking for a video chat. Montana generally left me alone while we recorded a new album. A sense of unease prickled at the back of my neck and slid down my spine.

I threw on a black t-shirt and jeans and padded barefoot down the hall to my office. Pulling up the video calling software, I dialed my agent.

Montana Blackwood was a fucking pitbull in Prada. I met her when Harrison brought her to a concert as his date. It didn't work out, but now they both worked for Shadow Phoenix. In the last five years, she'd stepped up for me time and time again.

I'd always been careful to keep our relationship strictly business. Even though I'd enjoyed more than my fair share of women, I didn't mix business and pleasure. Besides, we treated her like a little sister. Montana was sarcastic as fuck and had a dirty sense of humor. We considered her one of the guys.

As she came into view on the screen, her scowl loomed large in high definition directly in front of me. Montana didn't waste any time tearing into me. "What the fuck, Zen?"

"Good morning to you, too." I frowned, bracing myself for the inevitable shit storm headed my way. I rubbed my forehead. It was too goddamn early for this shit. She narrowed her eyes at me through the screen.

"The fuck it is. I got a disturbing call last night from Maddox. You want to tell me what the fuck is going through your head right now?"

My jaw clenched as I felt my heart rate pick up.

Goddamn Maddox.

That asshole loved stirring shit up. Fucker. "I think I know what this is about. Look, I met someone, and I gave the band a heads up. It's not a big deal."

Montana's voice screeched through the speakers, and I winced. "Not a big deal? You've gotta be fucking kidding me! Listen to yourself."

I picked up a paperclip and started twisting it in my fingers. "Look, if she asked me to, if I felt like my lifestyle would ruin things between us, I'd consider walking away. I don't have any actual plans to do it, but I felt like they should know where my head's at. This call isn't going to change how I feel."

Montana tilted her head back, her eyes rising to the ceiling as if she were praying for strength from a higher power, so I kept talking. "She's the most incredible person I've ever met. I don't think it's going to happen, but it could. And I'd do it in an instant, I don't give a fuck. Right now, there's nothing to worry about, so don't."

Montana dropped her piercing gaze on me, steepling her hands against her mouth while considering my words. "You've got to be out of your goddamn mind. That's the only explanation for this. You're having a mental breakdown. You can't seriously sit here and tell me you'd walk away from everything you've worked so hard—no, we've—worked so hard to build for some pussy, can you?"

"Don't talk about her like that." I seethed, narrowing my eyes into slits as I glared across the screen at her. "I can get all the pussy I want whenever I want it, and you know it."

She rolled her eyes.

"This is different. I'll quit the band if I damn well please, and I don't need a reason. You work for me." I stood up. "We're done." I shut down the call and stalked out of the room. It didn't matter if they all thought I'd lost my mind, maybe I had. But there was no going back now. Kennedy had become my everything. I loved her. In my mind, I'd claimed her as mine, and I'd always protect what's mine.

An hour later, I walked into Sweet Stories. The scent of coffee and blueberry muffins hit me as soon as I walked in the door. My eyes scanned the store before landing on Kennedy. I didn't have time to blink before she'd thrown herself into my arms. She wrapped her legs around my waist and kissed my face over and over. In between kisses, she said, "I. Missed. You. So. Much."

I laughed, holding her tight. "Me, too, Sunshine. Me, too." I glanced around the mostly empty shop, noticing Chloe, who was openly gawking at us. At least with Chloe here, I could have some time alone with my girl. I carried Kennedy over to the cafe, pulled out a chair, and sat down with her in my lap. I didn't want to let her go for a second, and she clung to me just as tightly.

"What do you want to do tonight?" she asked me with a grin, wiggling her ass against my hardening cock.

"Don't worry, we won't be sleeping much this weekend," I assured her, chuckling and sliding my hand down to squeeze her ass. "But, before we get to the naked stuff, I thought we could change things up."

She froze as fear slowly replaced the lust in her eyes. I knew she struggled with spontaneous plans. She just needed a little push. "You trust me, right?"

"You know I do."

"Good, go pack a bag for the weekend."

"Where are we going?" she asked hesitantly.

"LA."

"I don't think I can." She pulled her lower lip between her teeth, a wrinkle formed between her eyebrows, and I reached up to smooth it out with my thumb.

"Yes, you can. You did great last weekend, you've been making progress all week. I'll be with you the whole time, and we'll be in the band's jet so there won't be anyone but the crew and me since the guys flew back late last night. You can do this. We'll put your song on repeat, and you can relax. I'll even hold your hand the whole way."

The guys asked me to talk to her about the song, but I needed to convince her to get on the plane with me more.

She sighed heavily. "I haven't flown before, but you make good points. It's a short flight on a private plane. I need to do this. I will do this."

When she told me about her dreams, at the top of the list was traveling the world. She'd never be able to do that unless she conquered this fear, and this short flight in a private space would be the easiest way for her to take the first step.

With fierce determination in her eyes, she lifted herself off my lap and grabbed my hand, leading me up the stairs. "You're not allowed out of my sight until we're on the ground in LA. If you let me go, I'll probably run back home or open the plane door and jump out at thirty thousand feet."

I laughed at the mental picture of that, but she glared at me. "I'm serious."

I tried to stifle my laugh, but she was so damn adorable. Plus, she'd have to be Godzilla strong to rip a plane door off in mid-flight, but I wouldn't put it past a panicking Kennedy. "I can't live in a world without you, and jumping out of a plane without a parachute will never happen as long as I'm around. I promise I won't let go."

An hour later, we climbed the steps to the jet. I tried not to let my excitement show, but I grinned like an idiot. I couldn't wait to show her what my life in LA was like over this weekend. She gripped my hand tightly as we took our seats. I knew her fear must be off the charts right now, but she was here anyway. Settling into our seats, I looked her over. Her silky golden hair was pulled back in a low ponytail I wanted to wrap around my fist and tug, and she wore a black wrap dress. I lifted our joined hands up to my lips and pressed a kiss to her knuckles.

True to her word, Kennedy hadn't let go since she agreed to the flight. I cracked up as I watched her pack her bag one-handed. She gave me the side-eye when I laughed, which just made me laugh harder.

When she looked up at me now, I saw a mix of fear and excitement swirling in her eyes. She wasn't letting the fear take over as much as she had last weekend. Her hand trembled, her face was pale, and her eyes had a familiar wildness about them. At least it didn't scare the shit out of me anymore when she looked like she was freaking the fuck out.

I felt like I was getting a handle on how to help her, and I'd never felt more needed than when she looked to me for comfort. Still, she hadn't talked about running home once, and she hadn't teared up, which were definite improvements over last weekend. She breathed deeply and wasn't hyperventilating. Yet. I packed a brown paper bag just in case because I couldn't even think about how much it would fuck me up if she passed out.

While we taxied down the runway, I pulled out my phone, handed her my headphones, and pressed play so she could listen to her song. She leaned back into the seat, closing her eyes as she clung tightly to my hand. When the wheels left the ground, I looked over, but she was lost in the song, exactly how I hoped she would be. I smiled softly, something that was so unlike me, but I found myself doing more and more lately. It was my voice comforting her. She needed me.

I'd prove to her that she could fit into my life, all of the parts of my life, and not just stolen weekends away. This would work.

It had to work.

I knew she was strong enough to handle everything that came along with being with me. Soon she'd have the confidence she needed to see it for herself. She didn't see what I saw, but she proved how strong she was to herself more and more every day.

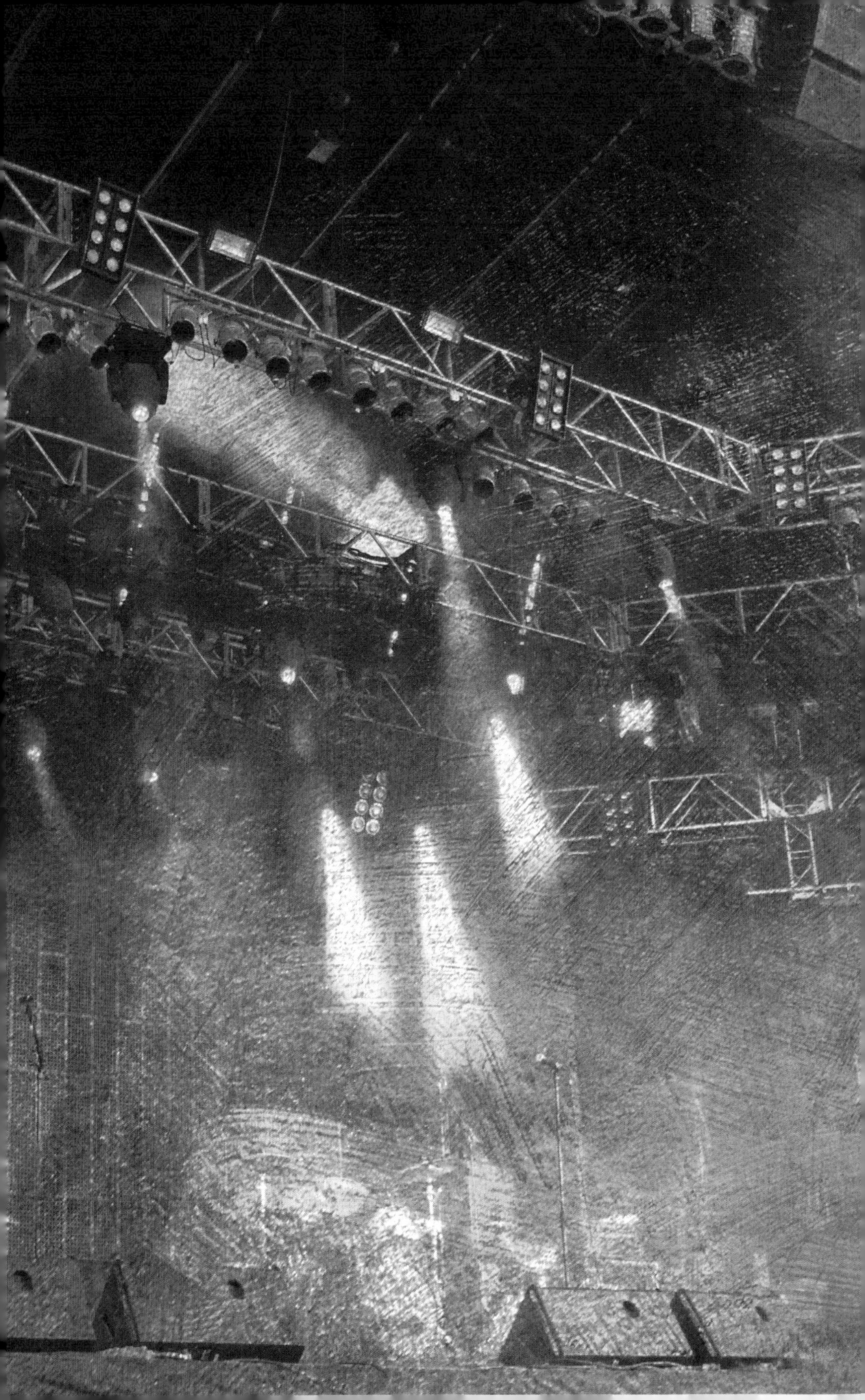

CHAPTER 19

KENNEDY

"I CAN'T BELIEVE I did it," I said with a satisfied smile. "I actually did it!"

Zen grinned back at me. "I never doubted you for a second. About time you're starting to see what I see, that you're strong enough to handle anything that comes your way. Soon maybe you'll believe me about how fucking sexy you are, too."

His blazing gaze had liquid heat pooling in my core, and I shifted in my seat. He smirked knowingly. "I'm so grateful you pushed me and have been here with me every step of the way. I realize I'm the one actually pushing myself, but I don't know if I could have even started without you." I raised my other hand to cup his cheek and pressed a chaste kiss to his full lips.

He squeezed my hand as the plane rolled to a stop, and the door opened.

"Ready to take on LA?" Zen asked with a crooked smile.

His eyes were bright, and I knew he was excited to show me

around. Honestly, I was excited, too, and not just because I'd never been outside of my home state before. Everything would be new, sure, but I'd be seeing it all with Zen, which made this trip even more special. I needed to show both of us I could do this. I would prove to myself I could handle change. I could experience life without breaking down.

Connor loaded our bags into the back of the waiting black SUV. Zen opened the back door, and I climbed in and buckled up for the trip to Malibu.

"Hi, Connor! Did I somehow miss you on the plane with us?" I beamed at him through the rearview mirror. Connor kept Zen safe on a daily basis. I would be forever grateful to him for that.

His stormy gray eyes twinkled back. He really was hot in that clean-cut military sort of way. "I came back with the rest of the band last night for a meeting I couldn't get out of this morning. How was your flight?"

I smiled over at Zen. "It was surprisingly great thanks to this guy and his smooth voice. It could make a girl swoon." I batted my eyelashes teasingly at Zen, but I could tell my words made him happy. He smirked, pulling me close and pressed a kiss to my forehead. I wove our fingers together and turned to look out the window, taking in the Los Angeles skyline.

An hour later, we pulled up to Zen's house. It was bigger than his Kirkland place, but it wasn't as modern. It was gorgeous, though, built right up against the beach. The house stood three stories with palm trees everywhere. Walking up the front steps, I stopped to breathe in the briny salt air. I closed my eyes, enjoying the moment. Arms wrapped around my waist and Zen's familiar masculine scent surrounded me. His firm chest pressed up against my back, and his chin rested on the top of my head. The heat of his body seeped into mine, and I willed him to move his hands either up or down. I didn't care which.

"This place is incredible." I smiled with my eyes still closed.

"You haven't even been inside yet." He chuckled.

"I don't have to, just this, being here with you, the ocean. I don't have words."

Zen held me, and I reveled in the feel of his strong arms wrapped around my body. I could stay like this forever. My stomach betrayed me, the bastard, by choosing that exact moment to growl.

Loudly.

Zen laughed. "Someone's hungry, and we don't want to make it into hangry territory. C'mon, let's put our bags away and then go get some food." He took my hand, leading me into the house.

The inside of his home wasn't anything like the Kirkland house, which surprised me. Where his Kirkland house was all cold marble, concrete floors, and a million windows; this house had reclaimed wood floors, billowy white curtains, and entire walls that were made of windows that rolled open so it felt like you were outside. One side of the house was completely open to the ocean.

This house took my breath away.

"Wow, Zen, this place..." I couldn't find the words to describe how perfect this house was. It felt like him but also felt like home. I'd never been somewhere that made me feel at peace so quickly. The ocean's steady rhythmic waves sounded through the open walls, and I wanted to curl up in his bed and gulp in lungfuls of the salty air until it lulled me to sleep. Later tonight that would definitely be happening.

"Do you like it?" he asked, his hopeful eyes studying my face.

"Like isn't a strong enough word. I love it. The way I can hear the ocean, the open walls making it feel like outside when you're in the house. It's incredible. I never want to go home." For a moment, I forgot about life back home and let myself be here with Zen in the moment.

I never lived in the moment.

He grinned. "You don't know how happy that makes me. Let's

drop off the bags and go get dinner. Then we can come back and really explore." He winked, and I laughed.

"I can't believe you winked at me. Who does that?"

"Apparently me." He laughed.

"Can we seriously just go out and get food? I know you said things are different here, that people will recognize you." I wrung my hands together in front of me, biting my lip. I didn't know if Zen wanted to go public yet, and I refused to embarrass him.

"Yes and no. We can't go just anywhere. There are places you go if you want the paparazzi to see you, and then there are places you go if you want to be more incognito. We'll have to go somewhere more discreet. We can do whatever we want, Sunshine. We just have to take precautions."

I nodded. Precautions I could handle. Besides, having a plan always made me feel more in control.

"Are we going somewhere I should dress up?" I followed him into the bedroom and reached for my bag, trying to remember what I'd packed that might pass for fancy.

"No, I thought we'd go to this tiny little taco restaurant a few blocks away. You could wear jeans and flip flops if you want. You'd look good enough to eat no matter what you wear."

Every time Zen complimented me, my stomach did a little flip. When he looked at me with his piercing emerald heated gaze, I became a quivering pile of desire. That's how attracted to him I was. All it took was one look to make me a mess. This gorgeous man wanted me, flaws and all. I'd started pinching myself every morning as a reminder that this was, in fact, my life.

Digging in my suitcase, I found a printed dress with long bell sleeves and a deep cut V-neck with a skirt that fell at mid-thigh. I changed before throwing on a pair of brown cowboy boots. Since my hair was chaotic from the plane, I did my best to tame it by running my fingers through the wavy strands. Shockingly, my hair only seemed to get better with the effects of the salty ocean air.

I stepped out of the room to find Zen looking down at his phone. When he looked up at me, his jaw dropped, and his eyes widened. "Kennedy, you look—"

"Like I belong at a music festival?" I laughed, twirling around to give him a better view. I'd never been one of those girls who crave attention, yet here I was showing off for my man.

My man.

"Fucking stunning." His gaze raked along my body, his eyes darkening. Closing the distance between us, he grabbed my hips, and our lips collided. Zen pushed me backward until my back hit the wall. I opened my mouth to deepen the kiss, and jumped, wrapping my legs around his waist. Between us there was always this primal chemistry waiting under the surface, and it took almost nothing to ignite it.

His hands slid under my thighs, pushing me against the wall as I rocked my hips against him. I groaned at the enticing friction.

"Feel what you do to me? This is yours." He growled, thrusting his hips forward and making me cry out. He parted my lips with his tongue again, biting and sucking my lower lip.

"And I'm yours."

"You're goddamn right you are."

Leaning back, I took his face between my palms and rested my forehead on his, pressing a final kiss to his lips before I lowered my legs back down to Earth.

"We can eat later—"

I pressed my thighs together. Zen wasn't the only one seriously turned on right now.

"Nope, I'm starving, and this is my first time in LA. I want to get out before you lock me in your bedroom for the rest of the weekend." I smirked before sidestepping his hard body and reaching for the purse I'd dropped onto the floor.

Not that I'd mind spending the entire weekend in bed with Zen.

He groaned, adjusting himself. "Fine, a quick meal out. Then we climb into my bed and don't leave until tomorrow. Deal?"

"Deal." I slung my purse over my shoulder before grabbing his hand and pulling him out of the front door. That had to be the best deal I'd ever made.

The short ride to the restaurant went quickly with my face pressed up against the window, and Zen telling me about the beaches and small businesses we passed. Tiny's Tacos wasn't fancy, but what it lacked in sophistication it more than made up for in location. Sitting a block from the beach, it looked like a hidden gem where you could go relax and eat a delicious meal.

Strung up lights created a romantic and relaxed outside dining area on the deck that overlooked the beach.

"Can we sit outside?" I desperately wanted to not be confined indoors right now. A warm and fresh constant breeze from the water blew my hair away from my face, and I loved it.

"Anything you want." Zen smiled down at me, wrapping his arm around my waist. He pulled me into his side.

Connor's deep voice popped our little bubble. "Zen, this place isn't sec—"

"Make it work." Zen cut him off before opening the door and guiding me inside.

Instantly, I liked this place. It was no secret restaurants weren't really my thing. But this spot was casual. There weren't a lot of diners, and no one appeared to be paying attention to us. Back home, almost nowhere had outdoor seating, so I couldn't wait to try it out.

Zen spoke to the hostess before we followed her outside. She passed us menus and quickly left.

"What's good here?" I scanned the short menu before glancing over at Zen.

"I usually get the grilled fish tacos. They're the best I've had anywhere."

"I'll have what you're having." I set down the menu. Zen stood up and moved to the seat next to mine, taking my hand and kissing the back. When our waiter made his appearance, Zen ordered, and we fell into easy conversation about nothing and everything.

When I finished off the last bite, I patted my full stomach. "You weren't lying. Those were amazing." Lifting my glass, I sipped my beer before setting it back down. "I'm ridiculously full, but it was totally worth it."

"I'm glad you're learning I'll never lead you astray." He chuckled. His phone rang, and he silenced it. "Sorry, I thought I turned it off." His brows furrowed as he looked at the screen. It immediately rang again.

"It's Connor. He wouldn't call if it weren't important."

"Isn't he out front?" I frowned. "You should find out what he has to say." My full stomach churned as anxiety tried to creep in. Something felt off. Some small part of my brain reminded me of the fact that my normal panic reaction had been absent since we landed. It surged back full force now.

"What? How?" Zen pinched the bridge of his nose, squeezing his eyes shut as he listened. "Fine, you have two minutes." He ended the call and stood up, sliding his phone into his pocket. His eyes looked stormy, maybe even angry.

I really started to panic, every worst-case scenario running through my mind at warp speed. The horrific possibilities flew through my mind so fast I couldn't focus. "W-what's going on?" I took a deep breath, trying not to completely lose control.

Zen pulled me up out of the chair and wrapped his arms around me, holding me tight against his body and burying his face in my neck. "Please try not to worry. Connor found someone taking pictures of us. He said the guy must have sent out word to his photographer buddies because they're swarming the restaurant." He sighed.

"I'm so sorry, Kennedy. So fucking sorry. I never thought they'd find us here. I come here all the time by myself, and I've never had a problem before." He sounded anguished, and it broke my heart a little. He was torturing himself, and I wouldn't let him do it. This was an unfortunate reality of being with him, one I needed to learn to deal with if I wanted to be in his life.

I couldn't imagine life without Zen, so it was time I pulled up my big girl pants and handled shit like the badass I wanted to be.

I took a deep, steadying breath. "You have nothing to be sorry for." I hugged him even tighter. "But what do we do?"

"We wait until Connor clears a path for us. Then we run for it, dive into the car, and go home."

I nodded against his chest. Despite everything happening, he smelled like the ocean air, and I bet if I licked his skin, it'd be salty. I was having a hard time focusing on his words while my body reacted with a surge of longing, and I fought off the urge to reach up and run my tongue up his neck.

"It's going to be okay, Kennedy. I promise." I knew he must've been serious because he said my name, something he next to never did. I was always *Sunshine* or *baby*. He tilted my chin up until our eyes met. Right now, I looked into the eyes of a protector who would do anything to keep me safe. I relaxed, knowing I could trust him to get me out of this situation. I rested my forehead against his chest again, closing my eyes and letting him hold me close.

Connor's call came a few minutes later, and Zen adjusted his hold on me to take it. He kept one arm wrapped protectively around me while he talked. Hanging up, he tucked the phone back in his pocket before releasing his hold on me and taking my hand.

He ran his other hand through his hair and exhaled loudly. "Okay, Sunshine. I'm not going to lie to you, there are a lot of those motherfuckers outside." His jaw clenched. "If any of them try to touch you, I can't promise I won't do something I'll regret later, so hold onto me as tight as you can and put your head down. Follow me and don't stop, no matter what they say or do. Okay?" I nodded as my body started to tremble.

Damn anxiety.

"Good girl." His lips brushed my forehead. "Ready?"

"As I'll ever be." I squeezed his hand tighter.

He turned and stalked back inside, moving through the restaurant until we reached the front door. Flashes started going off through the windows. I kept my eyes on the floor like Zen said and held my breath.

"Coast is clear. Hold on, baby. It's about to get crazy." He threw open the door to the restaurant and pushed his way through the crowd of photographers as they shouted questions.

"Who are you?!" someone yelled. More followed, all of them super uncomfortable.

"Are you after Zen's money?"

"Zen, is this your new flavor of the week?"

"How's the new album coming along?"

The shouted questions blended together, and while the walk to the car was only about fifty feet, it felt like an eternity. I tried my best to block out the noise and focus on Zen's feet moving in front of me, and the feel of his hand gripping mine so tight it hurt a little.

Zen stopped, helping me jump into the car and climbing in behind me. I said a silent thank you to the sky because he hadn't hit anyone, but once Connor slammed the door, I looked over at Zen. A muscle in his jaw ticked. His eyes burned with pure rage, and his fists were clenched.

"Zen, look at me." I reached up to gently guide his face toward mine. "Please."

As we started to move, he turned toward me, and the anger melted away into anguish and fear. "God, Kennedy. I'm so fucking sorry. I never thought that would happen, at least not yet. Not until we were ready."

My stomach twisted. I didn't embarrass him, did I? My mind

raced, playing into all of my fear scenarios, the ones where I told myself I wasn't good enough. I slid across the seat, putting distance between us.

His eyebrows squished together as he closed the gap until our thighs were touching again. "What did I say? What made you close off from me?" He took my hand and folded it into his. "Please talk to me."

"I'm sorry if I embarrassed you. I didn't think about the fact that you wouldn't want people to know about me." Great. Now my eyes were welling up with tears. I stared down at our joined hands.

"What the fuck are you talking about? Are you serious right now? What would make you think for one second that I'm embarrassed by you?"

"I don't know." I shifted uncomfortably. "I guess I figured you were upset because now it could get out that we're..." I paused. He'd called himself my boyfriend once, but we'd never really talked about it.

"Together, Kennedy." He finished for me. He took my face between his hands, staring into my eyes. "I'm yours, remember? You're mine. Whatever you want to call it, boyfriend and girlfriend, partners, I don't care. You're mine, and I don't care if the whole world knows. Fuck, I want the whole world to know."

He twirled a lock of my hair around his finger before continuing. "The reason I wanted to keep them at bay was for you. I know how relentless and cruel those motherfuckers can be. They don't write the truth, Sunshine. They make up shit to get clicks. I don't know what them finding out about us means yet, but I do know this is just the beginning."

Pulling up to the house, we walked around back to the deck overlooking the ocean. "We need to talk about something important." He sat down on the outdoor sofa and pulled me down into his lap. Neither of us wanted to let go of the other right now.

Zen ran his fingers up and down my arm, leaving goosebumps

in their wake. "I've thought about it and already talked to True, Mad, and Jericho. I want you to know, if this is too much for you, the attention from the media or the fans or the whole damn lifestyle, I'm willing to walk away from Shadow Phoenix for you. For us."

My breath caught in my throat.

How could he think I'd ever want that?

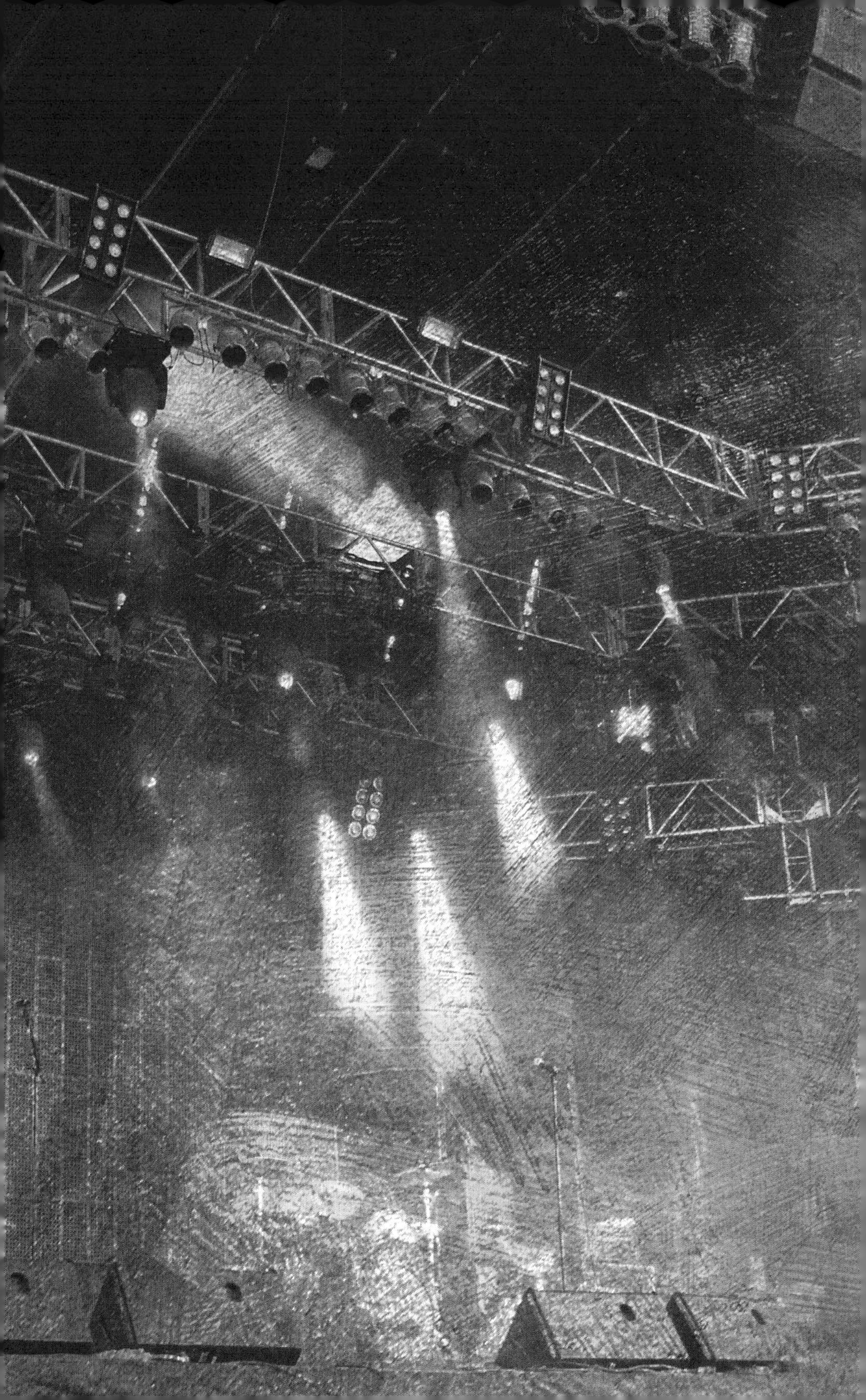

CHAPTER 20

KENNEDY

MY MOUTH FELL OPEN, and a heaviness settled in my stomach. When I looked into Zen's eyes, I saw nothing but sincerity and affection. But he wouldn't seriously walk away from Shadow Phoenix for me, would he? No way could I let that happen.

"I don't even know what to say." I leaned into him, closing my eyes and letting the warmth of his body sink into my skin.

"I know what just happened was intense, but it's not like that all the time. I'm going to go talk to Connor about what happened and give you some space to think. I'll be back in a few minutes." Zen got up, his lips brushing my forehead, and made his way into the house.

I sank further into the sofa cushion, letting my brain run wild. The fact Zen was willing to give up everything told me where we stood. It told me everything I needed to know about his feelings.

Actions speak the loudest, after all.

For the last two weeks, Zen had consumed almost all of my

waking thoughts. I knew our relationship was moving fast, but I couldn't find the will to care. For once, I let myself be spontaneous and free. Going with the flow.

Sure, the idea of completely giving my heart away to someone scared the shit out of me, especially someone with a reputation like Zen's. I was learning to run towards the things that scared me. Falling in love with Zen meant risking the greatest pain I'd ever known. But he'd shown me through everything he'd ever said, everything he'd ever done, that I could trust him and he'd do everything he could not to hurt me.

His reputation for being a bad boy and a player didn't matter. He'd never shown me that side of himself, and if he had been that guy at some point, he didn't seem to be anymore. I hadn't read up on him online because I decided to let him show me who he was. Headlines could be deceiving. Tabloids made up stories. I loved fiction—it was why I owned a bookstore—but I didn't want make-believe for my life. I craved something real and having something real meant taking risks.

While I learned to run toward fear, I also needed to learn to trust my instincts. My gut told me what I needed to do, but I wanted an outside opinion from someone who knew me and our situation. Amara hadn't met Zen yet, so I couldn't call her. With a sigh, I pulled my phone out of my purse and called my brother.

"Ken! How's Hollywood?" Grayson's familiar voice made me smile.

"Hey, Gray. It's been pretty great so far, at least until about half an hour ago."

"What do you mean, what happened?" His tone turned serious.

I picked a stray thread from the couch cushion. "Zen took me out to a little hole in the wall restaurant, and we got completely swarmed by paparazzi. It was awful. We had to have security escort us out. They were shouting all these really personal and frankly shitty questions at us the entire time, the douche nozzles. I don't know what the fallout is going to be, and Zen's pissed that it happened." I paused, giving Grayson a chance to absorb what I'd told him.

His voice softened. "Kennedy, you knew this was a possibility in being with him, and you told me it was worth it. Remember?"

"I remember. That's actually why I called. Zen just dropped sort of a bombshell on me, and I think I know how I feel, but I want to make sure I'm not making the wrong decision, so I want your opinion before I talk to him."

"Okaaay... I don't really have any experience with this type of situation, but I'll do my best."

"I don't either," I laughed. "When we got home, he told me he'd already talked to the band about quitting if it was too much for me. He said he'd give up everything, Gray." I whispered, afraid if I said the words out loud, they'd come true. Not only that, but I was still shocked this gorgeous, talented man wanted me that much.

Grayson whistled. "Wow, Ken. That's fucking crazy. You're his Yoko." He chuckled. "What decision did you make?"

"I refuse to break up the band, Gray. No way will I be responsible for that no matter how bad shit gets with the public. I care about him way too much to let him walk away." I chewed on my lip. "You haven't seen me much this week, but I've made a ton of progress battling my monster. I mean, look at me, Gray. I'm in LA for fuck's sake. I flew here on a plane."

Grayson laughed. "How else would you fly there? Flapping your arms really hard?"

I rolled my eyes. "Shut up. You know what I mean." I exhaled. "What you've been telling me for years finally sunk in, that I'm strong enough to handle anything. I just have to believe in myself. My confidence is getting better every day, and I'm believing in myself more and more. I really care about Zen. It would kill me if he gave everything up, and I'm not willing to let him go. So, that means this is going to become my life, dealing with these situations. I can handle it if I have a plan, if I know what to expect, and now I do, sort of. But am I being naive? Am I making the wrong decision here? Am I letting lo... Strong feelings blind me? Help, Gray." My words were coming faster as the weight of them washed over me.

"This is pretty serious, huh?" he asked softly.

"I know it's really soon—"

"That doesn't mean it's wrong."

I smiled as my chest constricted. I loved my twin. He understood me on a level not many people did. Maybe it was a freaky twin bond thing. "That's what I think, too. Do you think I'm making the right decision?"

"Let me ask you this, do you think you'll be happy in a life with Zen if you have to face those photographers every day?"

Letting my mind wander with possibilities, I pictured what our life would be like out in the open in LA. Butterflies filled my stomach, but not because of fear. A hum of excitement coursed through my body as I thought of us not having to hide, of being able to wake up next to Zen every morning, of eating breakfast on this very deck overlooking the water.

"Yes, I do. I think the paps part will suck a whole bag of dicks, but overall I think I'd be ridiculously happy."

"Then there's your answer. It's not that hard. You know me and Amara will support you no matter what you decide, but for what it's worth, I don't think you're making the wrong decision. Follow your heart, take chances. That's what life is all about, right?"

"Right. Thanks. I'll text you when I get home Sunday."

"You better, munchkin."

I hoped he could hear the eye roll in my voice. "Would you knock that shit off? You're only older by a few minutes!"

"And don't you forget it. Bye!" He laughed as he hung up.

A slow smile spread across my face as I leaned back against the soft cushions. A peace settled over me, and I knew choosing Zen could never be a wrong decision, even if it ended in heartbreak. I had to take the leap.

SATURDAY MORNING, I woke up to a gentle breeze blowing my hair and Zen's strong, tattooed arm lying across my naked body. We hadn't talked any more about what happened the night before or the decision I'd come to. Zen had walked outside, wordlessly picked me up and carried me to bed, making love to me until we both passed out from exhaustion in the early hours of the morning.

Lifting my gaze, I studied his face. Stubble that wasn't quite a beard dotted his jawline, and long, dark eyelashes laid against his cheeks. He looked so peaceful. My mind wandered back to last night and the decision I'd made after talking to Grayson. A plan began to form as a slow smile crept across my face.

Showing Zen I could handle his life, and all its complications would be my goal today. I knew what I was signing up for.

His phone buzzed on the nightstand, but he didn't stir. I snuggled deeper into his arms, relishing the quiet before the day intruded on us. His phone vibrated again, and this time he groaned, batting at it until he finally picked it up, answering without bothering to look at the screen. "What?"

He sat up and rubbed a hand down his face. "Okay, thanks." He ended the call and tossed his phone back on the nightstand. That had to be the shortest phone conversation I'd ever seen. Zen turned and flashed me a sleepy, lopsided grin.

"Good morning, Sunshine." He pulled me up into his lap. "True just updated me about some band stuff." He kissed my lips softly. "Did you have sweet dreams?" I hummed. Being this close to Zen made all coherent thought fly out of my brain.

"What do you want to do today?" He leaned back against the headboard, studying my face. "I wouldn't mind staying right here." He ran his hand down my body, making me shiver despite the warm air.

I giggled. "You're pretty irresistible, you know that?" I wiggled in his lap, and he groaned. "But this is my first time in LA. I really want to go out and do something fun first. Then we can come back and spend the rest of the day in bed."

He raised his eyebrows. I figured he'd be surprised that I wanted to go out considering what happened last night.

"Are you sure you want to go out? We could order takeout and stay here. Tonight the guys are coming by to hang out and meet you." Zen pressed an open-mouthed kiss to my bare shoulder, and I whimpered as a tingle started between my legs.

"You're so tempting, but I need to do this. We can dress up incognito and blend into the crowd. So, are you up for an adventure with me today?"

He laughed. "An adventure? Who are you, and what have you done with my scared girl?"

"That doesn't answer the question, Taylor." I narrowed my eyes, shifting in his lap.

"Oh, it's gonna be like that? Well, challenge accepted Sunshine. Where are we going on this adventure of ours?" I felt a little giddy at his use of the word *ours*.

"The beach, specifically the Venice Boardwalk. Have you ever been?"

His brow furrowed. "I've heard of it, but I can't say I've been there before. Let me send Connor a text so he can plan, and then you and I have a date with the shower." He waggled his eyebrows suggestively.

"Is that so?" I slowly ran my hand down his sculpted chest, the smoothness of his skin contrasted with the hard ridges of defined muscle under my palm. My center clenched as the need to have him inside me grew by the second.

Zen tossed his phone aside, hopping out of bed with me still on top of him as if I weighed nothing. He threw me easily over his shoulder, and I yelped when he smacked me on the ass.

"Yep." I squealed as he carried me into the bathroom, excitement coursing through me.

AFTER WE SHOWERED, and Zen gave me two good morning orgasms, we found ourselves in the car with Connor driving toward the boardwalk. I'd never been to a boardwalk before. They didn't have them where I grew up, so I was doubly excited. I could show Zen if we got swarmed by fans or photographers again, I could handle it. I had the opportunity to experience something completely outside of my comfort zone with him by my side. This new me was both exciting and terrifying. I actually looked forward to doing something new and different today, and I was still getting used to having the confidence to try out new things. Surprisingly, I enjoyed the challenge.

Pulling up to the boardwalk, I pressed my face up against the glass, taking in the bright colors of all the stalls, shops, and crowds of people. The three of us did our best to look casual and inconspicuous. After last night's fiasco with the paparazzi, none of us were eager for a repeat. I watched as Zen climbed out of the car, taking in his black baseball hat, mirrored Ray-Ban sunglasses, and black V-neck t-shirt. The ink on his arms was on display, and I licked my lips, wanting to trace every inch with my tongue. I felt sort of like an imposter in my hat and sunglasses. Who really gave a crap about who I was anyway? But Zen insisted.

Connor usually dressed casually, and this was no exception, but he had a pair of dark sunglasses shielding his grey eyes. I'd be willing to bet those same eyes were scanning the crowd behind his shades, but a casual observer would never know. Hopefully, anyone looking at us wouldn't bother with a second glance.

Zen linked our fingers together and started walking down the boardwalk with Connor following closely behind us. "Was there anything, in particular, you wanted to see or do?"

Just getting this far had been my only plan, so I let my eyes drift over the busy pier. Crowds of colorful people and storefronts, street performers, and food stalls lined the boardwalk. There was so much to see, so much life, it was hard to take it all in. "Let's go with the flow and see what happens."

He laughed. "Go with the flow? I've gotta say I'm enjoying this new Kennedy, but it's a little unsettling."

I grinned. "I know, right?" I wanted to be fun, but until now I'd never been that girl. Being left behind and left out of experiences because of fear sucked. I was so very done with it all.

Fuck fear.

As we walked, I took in everything, ignoring the pull of anxiety in the pit of my stomach. The smell of fried food wafted through the air, the sound of cheers and bells ringing from the carnival-style games, and the brightly colored storefronts with their signs beckoning us to come inside. There was so much happening; it was hard to focus on anything in particular.

We walked halfway down the pier, and so far, no one recognized Zen. Connor walked behind us a few paces. My eyes went wide when I saw the sign that read *Psychic Readings*. I always thought it'd be fun to have my future predicted, but I was too scared of what I might hear.

"Yes! We are so doing this!" I squealed, clapping my hands and bouncing on the balls of my feet.

Zen lowered his sunglasses, reading the sign. "Are you serious with this shit?"

"What's the worst thing that could happen? We're out twenty bucks, but at least it'll be entertaining." I tightened my grip on his hand, dragging him into the booth with me. We walked into a beaded curtain that rattled as we passed through. Connor cut in front of us, holding out his arm so we'd wait while he searched the small area. When he finished, he stepped to the side, and I glanced around the dark stall.

A table covered in a dark velvet cloth with a giant crystal in the middle sat in the center of the room, and a woman stood just behind it. She had long, gray hair pulled back off her face with a wide headband. Her hazel eyes were kind and wrinkled at the corners when she smiled, like right now, as she welcomed us in. Her wrists jingled as stacks of bracelets clanged together. My first thought?

Stereotypical.

It was perfect.

"Welcome! Sit, please." The woman gestured her arm toward the seats on the other side of her table and smiled warmly. "I'm Nora."

"Kennedy, and this is Zen." I introduced us as Zen pulled down his sunglasses.

"Hey." He tilted his chin in greeting before dragging out a chair for me and taking the other one for himself, moving it right next to mine.

"Nice to meet you both." She smiled. "What would you like to know?" Her eyes were intense as if they saw right into your soul. I wondered how many of these so-called fortune-tellers were the real thing, if any. Even if they were all fakes, it could be fun hearing what she might say. Stepping into Nora's booth had been my way of facing another fear head-on and trying to just have fun with it.

"I don't have anything specific. How about you?" I glanced over my shoulder at Zen, raising my eyebrow.

He shrugged. "This was your idea. I'm just along for the ride." Scooting his even chair closer, he draped his arm across the back of my chair.

I turned back to Nora. "How about just whatever comes to you?"

Nora nodded and held out her hand palm up. "Can I have your hand?"

Leaning forward, I reached out and took her warm hand. Nora closed her eyes and breathed deeply for several awkward seconds. I exchanged a glance with Zen, who shrugged again. Trying to stay still, I held my breath. She hadn't said to hold still, but it felt like the right thing to do.

Nora suddenly gasped, dropping my hand like it burned her. Her eyes flew open, and they filled with concern. Zen sat up straighter, his arm tightening around my back protectively.

"What?" Zen snapped, his patience at this situation clearly gone. His muscles tensed, and the look in his eye had me worried he might literally throw me over his shoulder and run for the car. I hoped he wouldn't do something drastic over nothing.

Still, the familiar jolt of adrenaline twisted in my stomach as my body prepared to fight or flee. My heart fluttered against my ribcage as the air thickened with tension. Even Connor looked to be on edge. The energy felt charged, and I dreaded the words that might come out of her mouth. Suddenly, all I wanted to do was leave. I didn't want to hear what she had to say. This idea had been stupid, and now I needed to get out.

Nora looked shaken and unsure whether she should share what she'd seen. She cleared her throat, pressing her palm to her chest. "Promise me you'll be careful, Kennedy."

"You're scaring me. What do you mean, 'be careful'? What's going to happen?" I reached for Zen's hand and gripped it in mine.

"Promise me. The picture wasn't clear. All I know is something is coming, and it's not going to end well." Nora's eyes met mine sympathetically.

"That's all you're going to tell us? This is bullshit." Zen jumped up, pulling me up with him. He threw a couple of bills down on the table and stalked out of the booth without a backward glance.

Stepping into the warm sunlight, I tugged his hand as the crowd continued to move around us. "Hey, slow down for a second. You don't actually believe her, right?" My heart raced as I started to freak out. I needed reassurance that he thought Nora was a fake.

What if she could actually see the future?

Clenching his jaw, he turned to face me, and his eyes softened. "It may be nothing, but I'm not taking any fucking chances when it comes to keeping you safe. I made you a promise, and I'll keep it if it's the last thing I do. We've had enough fun. We're going home. Now." His tone didn't leave room for argument, and truthfully I was glad.

Zen made me feel like nothing could touch me. Taking care of myself for so long had been exhausting. It was nice to have someone to share my fears with, someone to lean on.

I glanced around. "Where's Connor?"

"He went to get the car. Come on." He turned, and we hurried back to the entrance. Just as we stepped out, Connor pulled up. Zen yanked the door open, and I quickly slipped into the back seat.

"What the hell was that?" Connor's gravelly voice cut through the sound of me trying to catch my breath. Zen made me feel protected, but Connor was a part of that, too. I trusted they wouldn't let anything happen to me. That thought made dealing with the chaos of Zen's life more bearable.

Zen sighed, running his hands through his hair and over his face. "I may have slightly overreacted. After what went down yesterday, the psychic freaking out today scared the shit out of me. Did you hear what she said, Connor?"

Connor nodded.

"What the fuck did any of that even mean? Do you think we need to take her seriously? You know I'm not willing to take chances when it comes to Kennedy." Zen turned to look at me and cupped my face with his rough palm. He hadn't said those three words yet, but right now, the look in his eyes told me how he felt.

"Hey." I moved closer to him, so our bodies touched, and I tried to ignore the fire his skin ignited in me. I wrapped my fingers around his wrist and leaned into his touch. "Nothing's going to happen to me. Know how I know?"

He didn't say anything, but the corner of his mouth quirked up. "No, how?"

"Because I know you, Zen Taylor, would never let anything happen to me as long as you're breathing. I trust you, and you won't let me down. You've promised me, and I know you'll keep your promise."

The fierceness in his eyes left me a little breathless as he brought his forehead down to rest on mine. "I'll never betray that trust, Kennedy. I'll do anything I have to do, and I mean anything, to keep my promises to you." His eyes searched mine as if he wanted to say more, but then he turned back forward, and I rested my head on his shoulder, closing my eyes.

"We're home." Zen kissed the top of my head a while later, and I smiled.

Home.

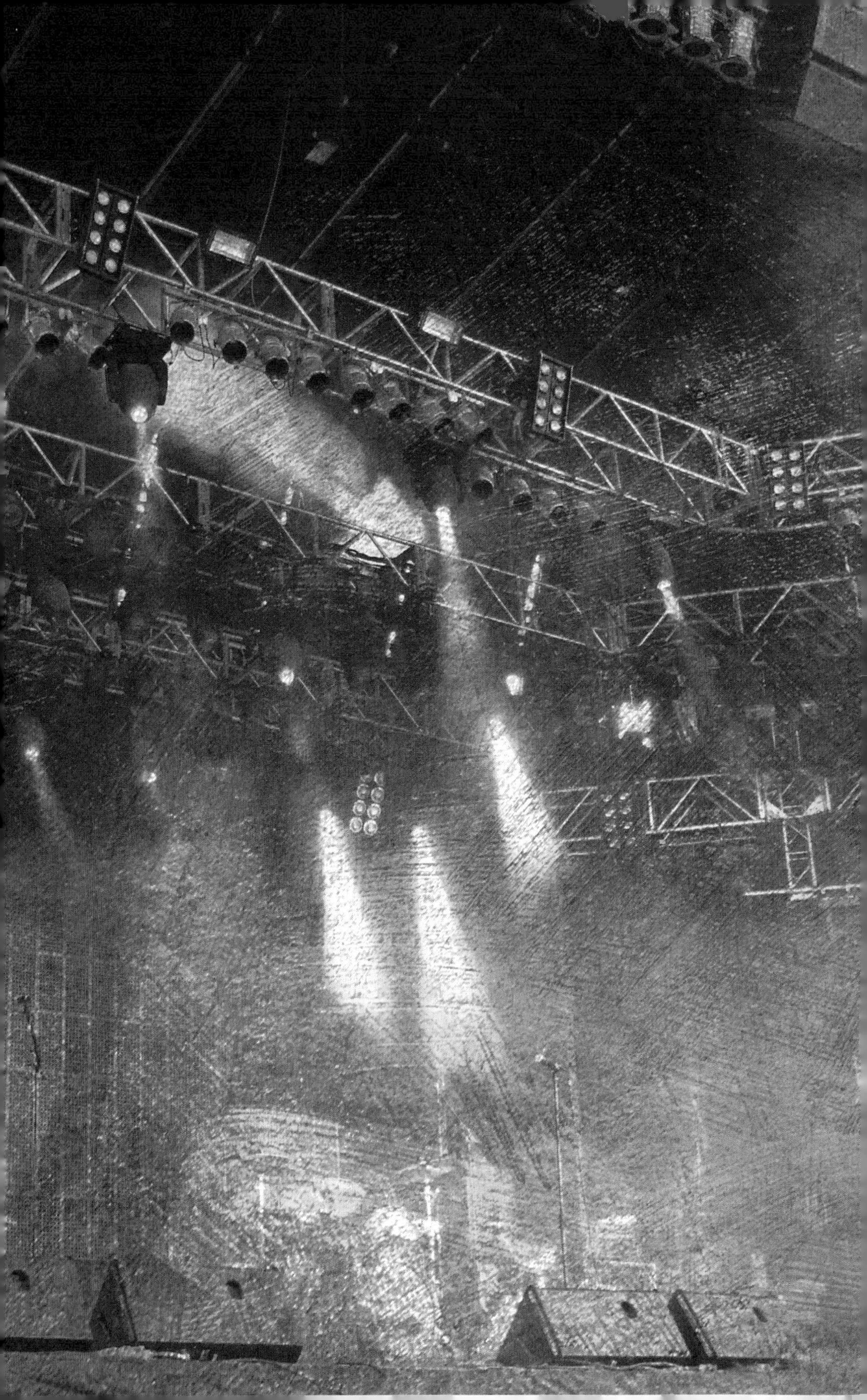

CHAPTER 21

ZEN

RUNNING my hands through my hair, I yanked on the ends. My blood boiled, and I paced the room like a caged lion. Connor calmly sat in the chair in front of my desk, waiting for me to get over myself. His calm demeanor pissed me off more.

"Fuck!" I slammed my fist down on the desk, but I didn't feel it. "How can I protect Kennedy when I don't even know what's coming? What else can I do? I refuse to let anything touch her because of what I do."

"You don't think you're taking this psychic shit a little far?" Connor folded his arms across his broad chest patiently.

"What the fuck do you expect me to do? It's probably a complete joke, but if I don't take it seriously and something happens, I'll never forgive myself." I sighed, sinking down into the chair behind my desk. The anger leaving my body only left exhaustion in its place.

"We keep our eyes open, keep security tight, and go on with

business as usual. I'm good at what I do, or you wouldn't keep me around." He smirked.

I leaned back in my chair. "I wouldn't trust anyone else to watch my back or keep her safe."

He chuckled. "I know."

A thought occurred to me. "What's going on with the stalker situation?"

Connor sat forward and leaned his elbows on his knees. "I've got security staffing the house around the clock, even when you're not there. If something happens, I'll know." He shifted in the chair. "Have you seen the headlines today?"

I could tell he was just as concerned about Kennedy as I was. I almost wanted to smile at the thought that my bodyguard felt protective toward her, too. People couldn't help but love her. She was a bright spot in our dark world. Seeing life through her eyes was like experiencing everything for the first time all over again. She was kind, full of empathy, hope, and wonder. It was a relief that I wasn't dealing with this situation alone, and Connor had my back.

I rubbed my temples, trying to fight off the pounding in my head. "No, but True called me this morning to let me know Kennedy and I were all over them. Right now, they don't know who she is, but they're digging. It's only a matter of time."

"Have you told her?"

"Not yet. I'm going to before we go home, but I wanted to give her this weekend. I don't want to ruin this trip for her." I lowered my head into my hands. "Fuck, I thought I was so careful."

Connor stood up, walking around the desk and placing his hand on my shoulder. "You were, but when you're famous as fuck and in LA, there's no such thing as careful enough."

"Thanks."

Connor chuckled as he walked across the room and turned before exiting through the open door. "Hey, it keeps me in a job, so I'm not going to complain too much."

I smirked. "Get out of here and go do your job."

I'd need all the help I could get.

LATER THAT NIGHT, while Kennedy and I were finishing up the dinner I'd made, the front door opened, and Maddox called out, "Hey, asshole! Where's your hot as fuck girlfriend?"

My three bandmates strolled into my house like they owned the fucking place. True walked out to the deck where we ate while Maddox grabbed a beer out of the fridge. Jericho flopped down onto the couch just inside.

"Damn, man. You weren't kidding." True's eyes wandered up and down Kennedy's body before he reached his hand for her. "I'm True, and you're fucking stunning." He winked at her.

What the fuck did he think he was doing? True was *not* the kind of guy who used cheesy pickup lines to hit on girls. I was pretty sure he was fucking testing me.

I tensed up, my hand clenched into a fist until Kennedy's voice broke through the blood pounding in my ears. "My eyes are up here, dick face." She slapped his hand away, and I couldn't help but laugh at the stunned look on True's face. He had no idea my girl had been fending off unwanted attention for so long that she didn't take bullshit from anyone. I thought that would be a fun surprise for my boys when they met her, so I'd kept it to myself.

I still wasn't sure how the fuck I'd managed to get her to pay attention to me, but I had no intention of letting her go now. She was mine.

True held up his hands in surrender. "Whoa, I was just playing around. I'm the sweet one, you know. I respect women and shit."

She giggled at that, but I decided to step in. "Back off, True.

You could have just said 'hi' like a normal person instead of being an asshole about it."

"You're right, I was kind of an asshole." True smirked. "Sorry about that. Hi, I'm True." He again extended his hand, and she took it.

"Kennedy."

"I can see why you like her," True said to me with a smile. "I'm gonna play pool. You coming?"

I nodded. "I'll be there in a minute. Let me make sure Maddox doesn't behave like you did, and then we can play."

True turned and walked inside, leaving Kennedy and me alone. I took her hand and brushed my lips against her wrist. "I'm sorry about that, Sunshine. To be fair, True isn't normally such a bastard. Maddox and Jericho are the assholes of the group, but I used to be right there with them until I met you." I ran my thumb across the back of her hand, and she shivered. Fuck, I loved how she reacted to my touch. "They're harmless, though."

"I get it, the rockstar life, and all that." She waved the hand I wasn't holding around in the air. "I don't mind sticking up for myself or putting them in their place if I have to. It's actually pretty fun. Did you see the look on his face when I smacked his hand?" She giggled again, and her eyes sparkled.

God, I loved her. When she really let herself be free and relaxed, there was nothing quite like it.

I stood up, tugging her up out of her chair along with me. "Sadly, True is the best of us. The worst? That award goes to Maddox. If I know you as well as I think I do, you'll probably like Jericho the best since he's the most chill, as long as no one fucks with him. If that happens, he turns into the asshole I told you he can be."

Linking our fingers together, we turned and walked inside to face Maddox.

When we crossed the threshold, I called out. "Mad, come meet my girl."

Maddox stepped out of the game room, sauntering down the hall toward us. "Well, well, well. If it isn't the hottest piece of—"

"Finish that sentence, and I'll rip out your tongue," I growled. My possessive side roared. Not for the first time tonight, I found myself struggling not to put my fist in one of my best friends' faces.

Maddox flashed me a cocky grin before chuckling. "Touchy, are we?"

The bastard knew exactly what he was doing. Riling me up was his favorite pastime. Well, the second favorite after being a manwhore. I couldn't blame him, he and I used to fuck anything that walked, sometimes at the same time. Way back when we were making our first album, we even made out once or twice. But that was ancient history. There wasn't anything but brotherhood between us now and the love-hate relationship that came along with it.

He stepped in front of Kennedy, reaching to take her free hand into his and bending down to drop a kiss on the back of it. She snatched her hand away before he made contact with his lips and reached for me instead. I was only too happy to move closer to her and wrap my arm around her waist protectively.

"No touching," she snapped, and Maddox tucked his hands into the pockets of his jeans.

"I like a challenge." Maddox grinned.

Kennedy rolled her eyes, but my grip tightened. She was exactly Maddox's type—blonde with blue eyes. But he wouldn't touch what was mine. "It'll never happen. Anyway, I'm Kennedy. We'll get along just fine if you keep your hands to yourself and your eyes at neck level and above." She gestured with her hands to her neck and head.

Maddox smiled widely at her. "I can tell I'm going to like you." He glanced over at me. "Nicely done, Z."

I chuckled, ready to change the subject to something that made me want to kill my friend less. "Thanks. Are we playing?"

Now that I'd introduced her to Maddox and she put him in his place, I could relax a little. I didn't need to protect her from him, but I would if I had to.

I turned my head toward her, burying my face in her hair. "Want me to introduce you to Jericho?"

She put her hand on my chest and pushed lightly. I tilted my head in the direction of the living room, where Jericho was on the couch, playing a game on the Xbox.

"Nah, I've got this. Go have fun." Kennedy leaned up to press a kiss to my lips, which I quickly deepened, weaving my fingers into her hair and pulling her body flush against mine. I didn't give a fuck who was watching, I could get lost in Kennedy anytime and anywhere.

Maddox whistled obnoxiously, and I let her go, stepping back. It was easy for the world to melt away when I held her in my arms, but no fucking way would I give my friends a show. At least not much of one.

No one got to see her like that but me.

A shy smile crossed her face, and her eyes danced. "I'll just be in there." She let go of my hand and pointed in the direction of Jericho.

Of all my friends, I thought Kennedy would get along with Jericho the best. He could be quite the asshole, but for the most part, he was quiet and had a calm energy about him. He was controlled and organized and not at all chaotic. He slayed that particular dragon years ago, and now nothing got to him. His relaxed vibe would fit in well with her more high strung one.

When I walked back into the living room to check on Kennedy a while later, she had a controller in her hand. She sat next to Jericho, both of them animated and calling out commands back and forth as if they were on a real battlefield.

"I've got your six!" She jumped up and mashed the buttons before pumping her fist in the air.

"I'm almost at the checkpoint, toss me a grenade," Jericho commanded.

I stood back, watching them go back and forth with a huge smile on my face. I had a feeling they'd get along. Jericho wasn't the kind of guy who partied it up like my past self and the other guys. He didn't chase women. In fact, I couldn't remember the last time I'd seen Jericho with someone since the incident with Kayla years ago. He kept his shit on lockdown, not even sharing it with the guys or me. He was particular about sex, and I wasn't about to touch that conversation.

Breaking the spell, I moved to stand behind where she sat on the couch. "Hey, Sunshine." I pressed a kiss to the top of her head.

She turned and grinned up at me, her eyes bright. "Hi! Why didn't you tell me Jericho was the fun one?" She punched Jericho on the shoulder lightly, turning her full smile on him.

He leaned back, and his lips tilted up on one side. "Your girl just helped me kick ass. I like her."

Huh.

That was the most positive I'd ever heard Jericho talk about one of our flings or girlfriends.

"Mind if I borrow your gaming buddy for a little bit? We have some band stuff to talk about."

"Yeah, of course." She waved her hand, already back into her game. "I'm just gonna keep building up my arsenal. Rematch when you're done, Jer?"

Jericho smiled at the nickname, one he punched Maddox in the face for using once. "Wouldn't fucking miss it. Make sure you collect some more plasma grenades. We'll need them."

"Done!" She turned her focus back to the screen.

I'd be filled with jealousy right now if Kennedy were already so comfortable with True or Maddox. But with Jericho, Kennedy wasn't his type. I knew he wouldn't go there, but if she became his friend? He'd be protective as hell, and another set of eyes looking out for my girl was nothing but a good thing.

Jericho got up and followed me back to the pool room. "About time you found someone worth a damn to bring around. I can see why you fell for her."

I faltered in my steps. Was I that obvious? I never wanted to be away from her, and when we weren't together, I spent all my time thinking about her. I was quickly becoming obsessed with keeping her safe even though I knew she could handle herself. I spent more and more time picturing our future, a future that involved calling her my wife and seeing her bring our babies into the world.

The conversation I was about to have was the biggest clue about how far I'd fallen in love with Kennedy. I was willing to give up everything that'd been important to me up until now for her.

It was too soon to tell her that I loved her, though. Instead, I tucked the words away for the right time. Smiling, I clapped him on the back. "Thanks, man." What else could I say?

Stepping into the game room, we found True and Maddox shooting a game of pool. True glanced over at Jericho and me before leaning down to sink a solid red ball into the corner pocket. "Finally, you're back. Took you long enough."

"Can you guys stop for a minute? I want to talk to you about something." All three of them turned their attention to me. I ran my hand through my hair. "True called me this morning, and I'm sure you've all seen the headlines."

"Harrison called me and warned me about it. I told him to lock it down, but he said it was too late. I asked him for a list of names so I could start hunting them down, but he said there were too many to stop it." True shrugged. "Sorry, man. I tried."

Harrison did Shadow Phoenix's PR. That British bastard gave us all a run for our money on how easy it was for him to pick up women. His fucking accent was no joke. Women threw themselves at him.

Harrison set up all our interviews and handled the band's image in the press along with our individual images since that's a thing when you're famous.

The rockstar persona.

It was a fucking joke but a necessary evil in my line of work. He also gave us a heads up whenever bad news would hit the tabloids. Usually, he called me first, but since I had my phone off, he went to True.

"Shit." I blew out a breath. "There wasn't anything he could do to stop it from getting out?"

"Dude. I tried. I was ready to hunt down every single fucking photographer that shopped pictures of the two of you if that's what it took, but by the time he reached any of us, it was too late. Sorry, Z."

I shrugged. "Fuck it. It doesn't matter now, what's done is done. But that's not the only problem. You guys said you'd help me protect Kennedy, and as much as it kills me to say it, I need you. She doesn't know about the headlines or the pictures yet. She has no fucking clue how bad shit is about to get for her."

Maddox lifted the beer in his hand and took a long sip before breaking the silence. "You know we've got your back, Z. I don't think you're giving your girl enough credit, though. She seems pretty fucking tough to me. She had no problem handling shit on her own earlier tonight. For what it's worth, I don't think she'd want you to quit."

I folded my arms across my chest. "If it means protecting her, I'll make whatever decision I have to. But the headlines aren't the only thing."

Jericho pulled a joint out of his pocket and stuffed it between his lips, lighting it and taking a deep pull before blowing out a cloud of smoke and passing it to Maddox. "I like Kennedy. She busts my balls."

"I knew you were into some fucked up shit, but damn. That sounds painful," Maddox goaded, but Jericho didn't take the bait, rolling his eyes and snatching the joint back from him.

"I already told you you're not leaving the band. If shit gets complicated, we handle it like we always have. Together. Now tell us what the fuck else there is."

"You know the paps cornered us the other day? It was fucked up and really freaked her out. She doesn't know about the headlines or the photos actually hitting the internet yet. They're going to dig into her past. There's some shit that doesn't need to come out." I paced back and forth in front of my three friends, who all had their eyes locked on me but silently waited for me to finish.

"What is it?" Maddox asked.

I sighed, raking my fingers through my hair. Shit, I should've told him about this when I first heard about it. Maddox would've made Brock pay by now. "She gave it up to a guy in high school. He told everyone, taunted her, mocked her. Called her crazy. Made up a bunch of shit to make it look like she really was crazy. And the entire school joined in. She was attacked by a group of girls and left bleeding and naked on the bathroom floor. And it traumatized the fuck out of her. She ended up in inpatient therapy for a while until she got better."

"Fuck," Jericho bit out, his jaw clenched in agitation. I knew him. He'd already taken a liking to Kennedy. I bet he was envisioning all the ways to murder that Brock asshole, which was why I couldn't ever tell him who the guy was.

"She didn't deserve that shit. What should we do?" True wondered.

"I can go out and do some stupid shit tonight. Give them something else to talk about for a few days," Maddox suggested, but I shook my head.

"It's only a matter of time before they find it. They're relentless. I need to talk to Harrison to see if we can stop it, but if we can't, it's going to be bad for her. She's strong, you're right, Mad, but when it comes to this, it's her kryptonite. On top of all of that," I rubbed my temples, "It looks more and more like I've got another stalker up north. Near her. Connor told me someone's been in my house and left letters. That's way too fucking close to Kennedy. Now with us showing up all over the fucking media, whoever this threat is will find out about her. I'm really close to losing my shit because I don't know how to fix it."

My body trembled, the anger starting to manifest itself on the outside since I couldn't contain it inside anymore. I wasn't just angry. I also felt helpless, which was a fucked up feeling that I wasn't used to. I couldn't remember the last time I felt afraid if ever. In fact, I wasn't used to feeling much of anything at all until recently. Sometimes I wanted to punch something, which was why I put a punching bag in my garage.

Lately, I'd been finding myself in the gym more, beating my body into submission, hitting the punching bag repeatedly until I could barely lift my arms. It helped me process—sort of.

"I'll call Harrison in the morning and warn him. When we have more information, we can make a plan from there. We've got your back when you need us, but Mad is right. Your girl is stronger than you're giving her credit for. She can handle it." True clapped his hand on my back a little harder than necessary before picking up his stick and aiming his next shot.

I hoped they were right.

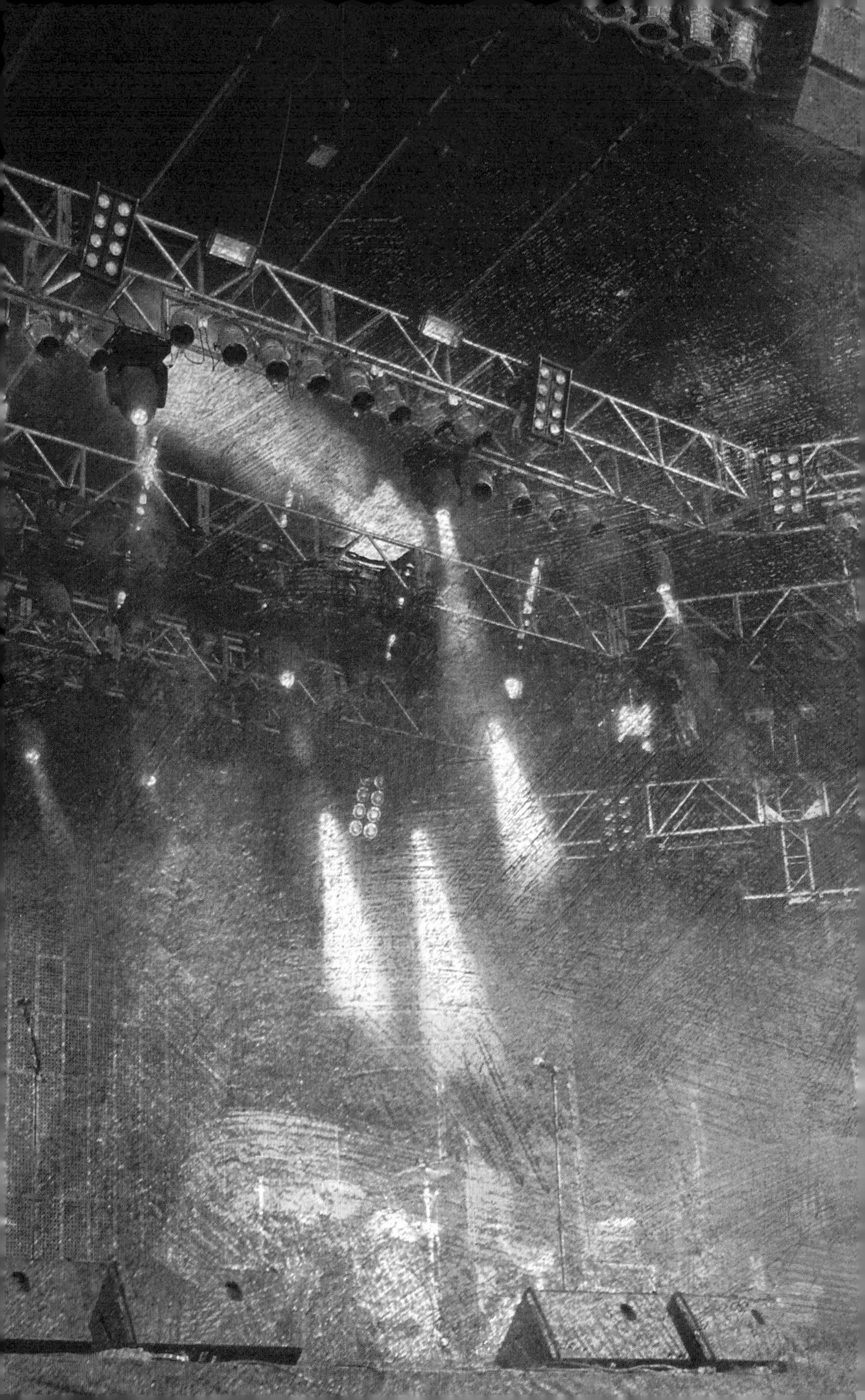

CHAPTER 22

ZEN

JERICHO and I walked back into the living room half an hour later and found Kennedy's game paused as she paced the living room with her phone pressed to her ear. Her eyes were squeezed shut as she spoke through clenched teeth. "What do you mean? What does it say?"

I crossed the room, reaching out to grab her hand, but she held it up to stop me, and I froze. Who the hell was she talking to? She'd never stopped me from touching her before, and I fucking hated it. A chill ran down my spine. Jericho lowered himself onto the couch, but his narrowed eyes never left Kennedy, watching closely.

"Tell me, Amara! Spit it out already. You can't call me with this and leave parts out."

There was one mystery solved, her best friend was on the phone. What happened to make her so upset? I really wanted to touch her right now. I took a step closer, and her eyes flew open and narrowed at me.

What. The. Fuck.

Could there be something wrong with her brother or the store? Then it hit me like a goddamn fist to the face. I swore the ground shifted underneath my feet. How had I not expected this? I'd been so caught up in the ramifications of yesterday's run-in with the paparazzi that I hadn't considered the fact someone she knew might call and tell her. I planned to tell her everything tomorrow, but the outside world got there first. She knew about the photos of us, the headlines calling her a gold digger and worse.

Fuck.

The tabloids had labeled her my fling of the week. They didn't know her name yet, but it was only a matter of time. When that happened, her identity would be spread on every gossip site on the internet. I fell back onto the couch, burying my face in my hands. I knew a shitty conversation was coming, and I just hoped she didn't walk away from me. The thought of losing Kennedy sucked the air from my lungs. Jericho leaned over and patted my back, and I steeled myself for the conversation coming my way.

I looked up at her as she hung up the phone, crossing her arms over her chest as if she were protecting herself. From me. My heart felt like it was shredding into tiny pieces.

She pressed her lips into a thin line. "You and I need to talk outside. Now." Her tone suggested she wasn't fucking around. I got up and followed her outside, where she started pacing again.

"Why didn't you tell me?" Kennedy crossed her arms, stopping to glare at me. I'd never seen her angry before. Not really. If I wasn't so terrified of her ending our relationship, I'd tell her how cute she was and kiss her all over her perfect face until she forgave me.

I didn't fucking dare, though. I also didn't try to pretend I had no idea what she was talking about.

I ran my hand across the scruff on my jaw, the rough scrape on my palm somehow soothing. "I was going to tell you tomorrow. I didn't want to ruin your first trip here."

She sighed, her eyes softening. "Did you not think I could handle it?"

"It wasn't that. I know you're strong, Sunshine. I know you can handle anything that life throws at you, but it'll be worse than the pictures and headlines out now. They're going to start digging. You know what that means, right?" I leaned against the deck railing and shoved my hands into my front pockets. I wanted to touch her so badly, but I had to respect the distance she wanted.

She blinked as she considered my words, fear creeping into her eyes. She started to walk back before falling into the patio chair. "They're going to find out my name, my store…"

I nodded, pushing off the railing and walking over to her, unable to give her any more space. I'd reached my limit. I pulled her out of the chair before taking her place and dragging her down onto my lap. The need to touch her overwhelmed me. She leaned back against my chest, and I exhaled as she didn't push me away. I breathed her in. The knot inside my chest loosened at her touch.

Kennedy rested her head on my shoulder, and I ran my fingers through the silky strands of her hair while I finished my thought. "Yes, but not just that. They won't stop until they dig up everything, Kennedy. Everything."

She tensed before sucking in a breath. "You mean—"

"Yes, high school and everything that happened there and after. It's all probably going to come out. I don't know when but you should prepare yourself for it. I'll do everything I can to keep it from coming out, but honestly, I don't think there's a lot I can do."

She trembled in my arms. Her body curled closer into mine, and I swept a piece of hair off her forehead, tucking it behind her ear. "Kennedy?"

She pushed herself up off me and stood up, fists clenched by her sides, and her cheeks flushed pink. Her chest rose and fell with shallow breaths. "Let it come out. I don't care. I know what my life is, what my truth is, and so do you. I know what I want and what I don't. Nothing they can say will change that."

She leveled her intense blue eyes on me. "What will change what's between us is if you hide something from me again. That's twice, and there won't be a third time. I'm strong enough to handle it. I don't want you to think you have to fix things on your own. I told you before, and I'll tell you again. I want us to be a partnership. We're in this together. No secrets, no lies, and no hiding things from each other."

I stood up and wrapped my arms around her, pulling her tight against my body. "No more secrets, I promise."

She relaxed into me, wrapping her arms around my waist. We stood with the ocean at our backs and a warm, salty breeze blowing her hair against my face. I took a deep breath. I wouldn't be losing her over this. Kennedy continued to surprise me with her strength and perseverance, and I kept letting her down.

That stopped here and now.

I'd stand here and hold her all night if she'd let me. I turned my face into her hair, breathing in the familiar warm scent of her before she stepped back out of my arms. I missed the heat of her body pressed against mine immediately.

"One more thing." She took my hand in hers. "About what you told me last night. There's no way you're quitting this band. I know what you said, but I will never be happy knowing you gave up your dream for me. No matter what, we'll get through whatever happens together. That includes those guys and your music. I can't be with you if you give up everything for me. I couldn't live with myself."

I coughed to hide the fact that my eyes were stinging, and emotion clogged my throat. What the fuck could I have possibly done to deserve her? "I'd give it up in a second."

"I know, and you have no idea what that means to me, but Zen, you can't. I don't want that."

Don't say it, don't say it, don't say it.

I chanted those three words in my head instead of the other three words I was in danger of blurting out right now. I didn't want to scare Kennedy off with the intensity of my feelings for her.

Plus, I was terrified she didn't feel the same way.

"You're unreal, you know that?" I said instead, gazing down at her, running my finger down her cheek.

She looked up at me through lowered lashes. "I don't know, I feel pretty real." She slid her hand down my chest and stomach, over the front of my jeans, which were tightening by the second.

"I'll be the judge of how real you feel." I grinned wickedly, reaching down and picking her up, tossing her over my shoulder caveman-style.

"Put me down!" She squealed and smacked me on the ass.

"Not a chance in hell. We're going upstairs." I turned and strode back into the house and toward the stairs. I didn't give a fuck about my friends right now.

"We're starting the private party now and won't be back down tonight. Let yourselves out," I called out, climbing the stairs.

"Nice to meet you all!" Kennedy shouted between giggles. "Rematch next time, Jericho!" He shook his head and laughed. The dude actually laughed. My steps almost faltered at the sound of it echoing through my house. Fuck. Jericho never laughed.

In my bedroom, I kicked the door closed before throwing her on the bed. She bounced once, her musical laughter filling the room before I climbed on top of her and silenced her with my lips. My skin hummed with anticipation while I stared down at her. With her lips parted and her cheeks flushed, she was the most beautiful creature I'd ever laid eyes on. Gazing into her eyes, I connected with her on a soul-deep level. Underneath it all, she was pure and good. Everything I wasn't.

She never gave men a second glance. I'd seen it for myself. Yet by some fucking miracle she'd chosen me. *Me.* She let me inside her heart and her body. It was an intoxicating feeling, being drunk on Kennedy.

I leaned down to press a soft kiss to her lips and trailed kisses down her throat and collarbone, sucking and biting every inch of smooth skin. She smelled like heaven and tasted even better as I licked along the curve of her neck. Her body shivered at the feel of my tongue on her flesh. She tilted her chin up, exposing more of her throat to me, and I smiled against her skin.

"Mmm," she moaned, running her hands along my shoulders and back, trying to pull my shirt off. I leaned back to let her, and she lightly scraped her fingernails along the ridges of my chest and down across my abs once it was gone, leaving a burning heat in their wake.

Kennedy pulled her shirt over her head, and I groaned. "Fuck, you weren't wearing a bra?"

She shook her head, biting her lip as her eyes filled with lust. "If I didn't know any better, I'd say you were trying to get me to murder one of my friends, Sunshine."

She blinked at me innocently before that impish grin that meant nothing but trouble made an appearance. "I would never."

"Mm-hmm."

Leaning back down, I swirled my tongue against her tightening peak. "You're my favorite flavor." I swiped my tongue across her chest until I found the other nipple, pulling it into my mouth and releasing it with a pop.

She wiggled her hips underneath me, reaching between us to unbutton her jeans. I slowly moved down her body, pulling her pants and panties down while placing open-mouthed kisses along all the newly exposed skin of her stomach, hips, and legs. When her body was free of her clothes, I leaned back to admire her stripped and ready before me, my eyes raking over every inch of her angel-like perfection.

My hard-as-steel cock pressed uncomfortably against the zipper of my jeans. I pushed myself against her, and her moans had me desperate to bury myself inside her. I'd be lucky to last thirty seconds in her tight pussy.

"Zen." She breathed my name, and need spiked through me. Hearing my name on her lips turned me the fuck on. She gripped my face between her hands and forced my eyes to meet hers. "Get inside me."

I fucking loved it when she told me exactly what she wanted. My girl knew what she needed, and I'd make damn sure she got it. She rubbed her palm against my denim-covered length, rubbing me up and down at a tantalizingly slow pace. I bit out a curse before running the flat part of my tongue down her stomach.

"Stop." The word was like a bucket of cold water to the face, and I froze. I lifted my eyes to meet hers, which were sparkling, a mischievous smile on her lips. "It's my turn."

Kennedy sat up, pushing me backward with a hand on my chest until I was lying flat on my back. She reached down to unzip my jeans and yanked them down my legs as my cock sprung free.

Her eyes widened, and she licked her lips. I couldn't help the cocky smirk that spread across my face. "Like what you see, baby?" I wrapped my fist around myself and stroked up and down.

She groaned and began placing slow, warm kisses down my stomach until she took my cock into her hand, wrapping her soft fingers around me. She grinned before licking me from base to tip and swirling her tongue around the head. My head fell back onto the pillow as I focused on not coming.

She sucked me into her mouth, bobbing her head up and down, sucking and licking. I threaded my fingers into her hair, thrusting up into her mouth. The sounds she made vibrated up her throat and along my cock, and I pushed deeper. She struggled to take me all in but never stopped, instead reaching down to touch herself.

"Fuck, baby. You need to stop or this is going to be over in about two…" my voice caught as I fought for control, "seconds." When it came to Kennedy, I found myself walking around in a constant state of arousal. All it took was one look from her, the sound of her voice, a light touch, and I was instantly hard. Having her mouth on me like this was almost too much. If I wasn't careful, I'd explode before I got the chance to satisfy her, and that was fucking unacceptable.

I pulled her up gently, settling her hips over mine. She looked down at me through her dark eyelashes, desire swimming in her eyes. She settled her hands on my chest and lowered herself onto me. She cried out, and I clenched my jaw. She felt too fucking good, all tight and wet and warm.

I froze, giving her time to adjust to my size. Her eyes fluttered closed, and she wiggled on top of me.

"That's it, baby. Use me, take what you need." Rotating her hips, she rocked on top of me. Being inside Kennedy must be what heaven felt like, surrounded by her warmth and light. I swear I could see stars behind her eyes.

She moved faster as she trembled above me. My body screamed out, begging me to take control, to drive harder, to go deeper. Her body sucked me back in as if even her pussy couldn't stand to let me go when she rose too high.

As we found our rhythm, I adjusted my hips so I hit just the right spot, and the little noises she made drove me insane. "Come for me," I demanded, not trusting myself to hold on much longer. My fingers found her clit and rubbed small circles that matched the driving rhythm I set. In just a few more thrusts, she cried out my name, pulsing around me, and I followed her over the edge, emptying myself inside her. We clung to each other as we breathed hard and I rolled over, pulling her on top of me.

My cock softened and slid out of her, and I realized I'd made a mistake. A potentially huge fucking mistake.

"Sunshine?"

"Mmhmm?" she mumbled sleepily.

"Are you on the pill?"

This was what Kennedy did to me. I'd never fucked anyone without protection, not once. I couldn't believe I'd been so stupid. I wanted Kennedy to have my baby someday. Fuck, I did. But not like this. My job was to protect her, and I'd hate myself if I failed and got her pregnant before she was ready.

She laughed, and her hair tickled my chest. "How are we just now having this discussion?"

"Fuck, I should have asked sooner. I'm sorry." I ran my fingers down her back, and she shivered.

"It's not like I volunteered the info, and it's not all on you. Is it weird to say I'm not concerned about consequences right now?" She leaned up and pressed a kiss to my chin before snuggling back against my chest. "Whatever happens, I know we'll handle it together because it's you and me, right?"

"You and me forever," I corrected.

I felt her smile against my skin. "Having said that, yeah, I am." She laughed. "I started it years ago and never stopped even though I didn't need it. I guess I just got in the habit of taking it."

I breathed out a sigh of relief. Then a thought occurred to me. "Wait, what if I'd knocked you up?"

She shrugged. "Would that be such a bad thing? We'd get through it together, and how can something that we made be anything but perfect?"

She had a point. "No more barriers between us from now on."

"Agreed," she said, sighing contentedly.

She snuggled into my chest as I wrapped my arms around her, drifting off to sleep.

SUNDAY WENT BY IN A BLUR, but spending the day in bed together tended to do that. Neither one of us wanted to get up, knowing it would be another week before seeing each other again. We'd only be a couple of miles apart, but I had interviews and recording sessions scheduled all week. The band was doing me a favor and working out of Kirkland, so I had to be present.

The last thing I wanted was to go, but I had responsibilities to Shadow Phoenix, and she had her business depending on her. It was crystal fucking clear to me that I needed her by my side every day. I'd long ago surpassed wanting her by my side and had entered needing her territory.

Seeing Kennedy only on the weekend wasn't working for me, and I could tell she felt the same. I wanted her to wake up in my bed every morning. Right now, people were counting on both of us, though, and as much as I wanted to, we couldn't let them down.

As Sunday passed, the later in the day it got, the more quiet Kennedy became. She climbed out of bed and crossed the room while I took in her naked body. Her perfect ass, long legs, and smooth skin. We'd had so much sex, I was surprised I could still get hard, yet my cock perked up watching her lithe body move across my bedroom.

I stood and moved to where she packed her bag, pulling her hips back against my growing erection. "Think we have time for one more round?"

She groaned. "I wish. The guys are meeting us on the plane in an hour. We're already going to be late as it is."

I spun her around and pressed my lips to hers. "I wish we didn't have to go."

She cupped my cheek with her palm. "Me, too." Turning, she pulled a shirt over her head.

Fuck me. No bra again.

I swear this woman loved to torture me. She turned and flashed me a smirk that told me she knew exactly what the fuck she was doing.

Three hours later, the plane touched down in Washington. Connor moved out of the plane first, making his way to the G500 we'd left parked in the hangar.

Taking Kennedy's hand, we carefully stepped down the stairs and hopped in the car. The rest of the guys had their own rides, so we took off without waiting for them. We planned to drop by my house first to make sure security was set up and running smoothly. There'd been way too many fuck ups lately when it came to security, and, just like with Kennedy's safety, I needed to oversee this myself.

I ran up the steps, unlocking the front door with Kennedy right behind me. When we stepped into the house, I shut the door and locked it. "I need to grab a change of clothes and talk to Connor. Will you grab us a couple of waters from the kitchen while I pack?" She nodded, squeezing my hand before venturing off toward the kitchen.

Walking to my bedroom, I grabbed a duffel bag from my closet and tossed it down on the bed. I didn't technically have anything scheduled until tomorrow, so sleeping over at Kennedy's was a no-brainer. I'd take every minute with her I could get.

I shoved clothes inside the bag before going into the bathroom to grab my toothbrush. Then I glanced up at the mirror.

"Oh, fuck." I gripped the edge of the sink and took a steadying breath to try and calm my suddenly racing heart.

In red lipstick, someone had scrawled a message across the glass.

End it, or I end her.

If there'd been any doubt that I had a stalker before, that doubt had just been erased, wiped away with one blood-red message smeared across my bathroom mirror. I ripped the phone out of my pocket, trying to stay calm enough not to smash the glass in. Snapping a picture, I sent it to Connor as adrenaline coursed through my veins. My fingers shook as I dialed his number.

Logically, I knew Connor had been with me all weekend in LA, but that didn't stop me from being irrationally angry at him for this slip-up. Why the fuck was security having such a hard time keeping this house secure? Normally nothing got past them. I only hired the best, and Connor personally vetted everyone on the team.

It fucking unsettled me. Whoever had me in their sights got around all my security, and now they were threatening the woman I loved more than life itself. A jolt of fear ripped through me like I'd never felt before.

The call connected, but before Connor could say anything, I growled into the phone. "Master bathroom. Now." Ending the call, I waited impatiently, tapping my foot on the floor. With my fists clenched. I'd forgotten Kennedy was here and had a momentary spark of panic at the thought that this person might still be in the house. I grabbed my phone and redialed Connor.

"I'm almost there."

"First, I need you to get to Kennedy right fucking now and make sure she's safe and get her out of here. Have one of the other guys stay with her." I exhaled a shaky breath and closed my eyes. I couldn't look at that goddamn mirror for another second, or I might smash it.

"Done." He ended the call, and I exhaled, knowing he'd make sure she was okay.

Kennedy didn't need to see this, and I hadn't been sure before about the stalker, so I hadn't mentioned it yet. Christ, the last thing I needed was for her to think I was hiding something. I made a mental note to tell Kennedy everything in the future, even if it was just a rumor or suspicion. I didn't want her to question her trust in me. Ever.

Connor's heavy footsteps sounded outside the door a couple minutes later. I glanced over at him as his eyes roamed over the mirror. "Shit."

"Yeah, you think? What the fuck, Connor? How does this psycho keep getting around you guys? You're the goddamn best. Nothing will happen to her, Connor. Not one fucking hair on her head will be hurt." My eyes narrowed to slits, and I lowered my voice into a threatening tone. I wasn't fucking around.

His jaw clenched. "I'll take care of it."

"I know." I spun and stalked out of the room, stopping to grab my bag off the bed and going to find Kennedy. I paused before leaving the bedroom, turning back to Connor. "I want someone to stay with her this week since you and I can't. Set it up now. You have until tomorrow morning when I leave."

I walked out of the room to find my girl, my favorite person, the one thing I was most afraid to lose. I refused to let that happen. I'd do whatever it took.

I fucking hated the idea of leaving Kennedy this week. I hoped the fact that the paparazzi hadn't figured out her name yet would buy us a little time to get security set up. My stomach dropped when we pulled up to Sweet Stories. There was a shit ton of paparazzi outside camped out waiting for us. Our time had run out. They'd figured out who she was.

Fuck.

Connor's deadly calm voice from the driver's seat cracked through the tense silence in the car. "Kennedy, is there a back entrance to the store?"

She had her face turned toward the glass, staring out at the waiting crowd with wide eyes. "Yes, but there's no way to access it by car. We have to get out here either way." She sighed, and I could tell by the slump of her shoulders that she'd resigned herself to face this even though she wasn't necessarily ready. I was so damn proud of her for going through this for me.

I reached out and took her hand. "It's going to be okay, Sunshine. Fuck them. They don't get to ruin today."

She nodded, straightening her spine. "You're right. We just have to get inside. No big deal, right?" She lifted her lips in a half-smile that I wanted to kiss off her face until we were both breathless. Instead, I let my gaze wander over her, taking in the bravery in her eyes when she set her mind to do something. She was such an incredible person. I still couldn't believe she was mine.

"Ready?" Connor scanned the crowd before turning to look back at us.

I looked at Kennedy, who nodded. "Yeah, we're ready. Just hold onto my hand, baby. Don't let go."

I brushed my lips against hers before the door opened and I stepped out. Kennedy followed right behind me, our hands linked together. The crowd immediately lunged toward us, lights flashing, questions being shouted. I wanted to take out the rage and frustration I'd been holding in on every one of these fuckers, but Kennedy was my first priority.

I kept my eyes forward, and my jaw locked closed. My hand wrapped around hers protectively. We made our way up the sidewalk, and I used my key to unlock the door. When we got inside, Connor lowered the blinds, and I locked the door behind us.

Kennedy dropped into one of her cafe chairs, exhaling slowly. She trembled slightly but seemed better than the last time this happened. "Are you okay?" I searched her eyes for signs of distress.

"I'm okay." She offered me a small smile that warmed my insides better than tequila ever had.

"Let's go upstairs, crawl in bed, and binge Netflix. We can order takeout, and Connor or one of his guys can get it for us." Truthfully, it sounded like fucking heaven to me, just the two of us buried in a pile of blankets and existing in our own little world.

"Sounds perfect." Kennedy stood and lifted onto her toes, pressing a kiss to my lips.

All I wanted to do was bury myself inside her and show her that her safe place was with me. I would prove it to both of us.

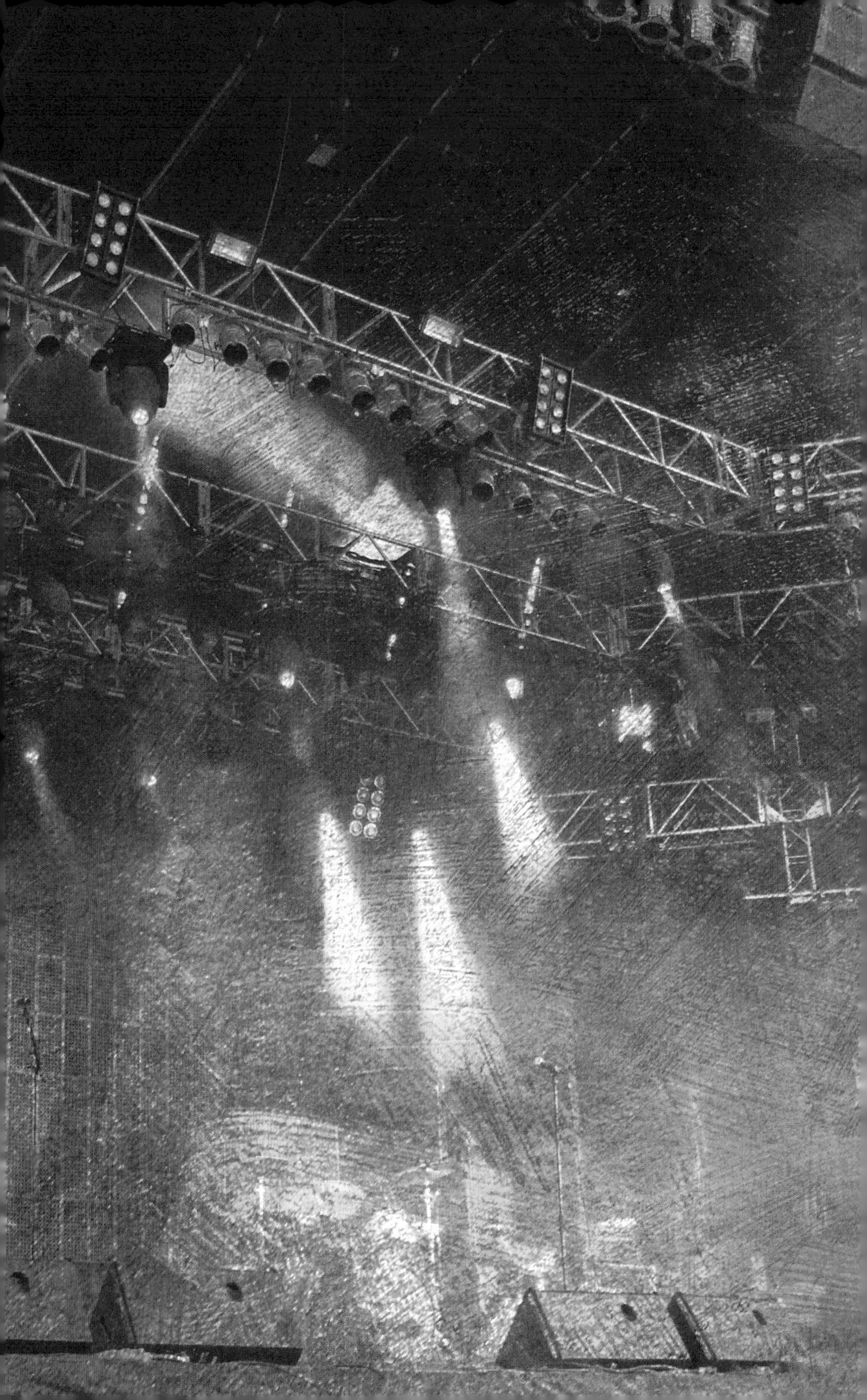

CHAPTER 23

ZEN

WAKING BEFORE SUNRISE, I glanced out the window. The inky black sky had the beginnings of bright, colorful streaks shining across it. Warmth wrapped around me as Kennedy's head rested on my chest, and her naked body curled around mine. Her slow, even breaths were calm and peaceful. More than anything, I wanted to hold her a little closer and drift back to sleep in this perfect moment.

Instead, I had to go home and handle my business, not just for the band but also for Kennedy. Now that the paparazzi knew her name, it was only a matter of time before they found out about her past. There had to be a way to protect her from it getting out, and I would find it.

After Kennedy fell asleep last night, I stayed up thinking about what the fuck I was going to do about this whole stalker situation. I needed to tell her and soon. I couldn't risk her finding out about it from anyone else, especially after the way she'd found out about our relationship going public. If she found out before I could tell her I'd be fucked. She might never trust me again or decide being with me wasn't worth all of this. My stomach rolled with that thought.

I couldn't let that happen. I promised her I wouldn't hide anything from her, and I meant it. I had to tell her everything this morning before I went home.

I reluctantly slid out from underneath her, immediately missing the warmth of her body wrapped around mine. I slipped out of bed, intending to take a quick shower. I waited by the bed to make sure she didn't wake up, and she sighed, reaching her arm across the bed as if reaching for me.

"Kennedy?" I whispered. No answer. She was back to breathing evenly, asleep.

I slowly crept to the bathroom, taking a quick shower. I needed to talk to Connor and straighten shit out before I woke Kennedy and drove home to meet the guys. After getting dressed, I walked down the hall to the living room where Connor stood guard for the night. His forehead was creased, and he had dark circles under his eyes, but still, he stood watch.

Sinking down onto the couch, I watched as Connor sat in the chair across from me. "We need to talk about what's going to happen this week."

Leaning forward, I rested my forearms on my thighs and clasped my hands together. "I know I asked you to figure out security for Kennedy during the times I'm not here, but I had an idea." I hesitated because I knew Connor wouldn't like this next part.

"The more I thought about the situation last night, the more I realized this person has been able to counter every attempt to keep them out except when you're around. I don't trust anyone else with this. Assign someone else to stay with me this week. I want you here with Kennedy."

Connor surprised me by nodding his head, as if he'd been thinking the same thing and was more than ready to protect my girl. That was why I trusted him with this more than anyone else.

"Do you see any problem with this plan?"

Connor shook his head before folding his arms across his chest. "You know I'd protect her with my life just like I would you, and any one of my guys is more than capable of handling your security." Connor's steely gray eyes hardened.

"I know." I nodded before pushing up off the couch. "I'm going to wake up Kennedy and fill her in. Then I'm going home. You work out the logistics." I stepped past Connor and walked back into the bedroom. I found myself both looking forward to this moment and dreading it. I wanted to spend as much time with my girl as I could, but I wasn't thrilled about the conversation I was about to have with her.

Climbing back into bed, I pulled Kennedy into my arms, grazing my fingers down her back and brushing the hair off her forehead. First, I pressed my lips to the tip of her nose, then her forehead, then her cheeks before finally her lips. "Sunshine, wake up. We need to talk before I go."

I kept dropping soft kisses on her face as a lazy smile stretched across her plump, kissable lips. "If you keep that up, I'm never going to let you leave. I'll lock you up and keep you here forever."

I smiled against her skin. "That's not much of a threat, Sunshine, when I already don't want to leave." I let out a low chuckle. "Open your eyes for a minute, please. I have something serious to talk to you about before I go."

Her eyes fluttered open and settled on my face as her brows furrowed. "What's wrong?"

I made my voice as soothing as possible because I knew her well enough to know she was already panicking. "Baby, calm down. I just want to go over security with you." The tension in her face relaxed a little, and I looked away. "There is one thing. You want me to share everything so we can be a team and handle it together, right?" I needed to be sure she really wanted that before I burdened her with what was coming.

She sat up a little, her eyes suddenly more alert as she nodded. "Yes, definitely. Whatever we go through, we do it together. Tell me."

I blew out a breath, reaching my hand down to stroke her velvety skin with my thumb. "I've been having some weird stuff happen at my house for a couple of weeks now. Do you remember last night when we were there, and Connor took you outside?"

She nodded.

"Right, well, someone wrote a message on my bathroom mirror in red lipstick. It was... threatening. Toward you."

Kennedy inhaled sharply, her eyes going wide. "I thought you had security there."

"I did, I do, which is what made it even more fucked up." I ran my hand through my hair. "The note threatened you if I don't end our relationship."

Her bright blue eyes widened even more. "Are you going to?"

I frowned. "Going to what?"

"End our relationship?" Her chin started to quiver.

"What? Fuck, no! Why would you even ask me that? Baby, I will *never* end us. The only way you're getting rid of me is if you walk away."

She sniffed, and I reached for her hand, pressing her palm over my heart because I needed to feel that she was here with me.

"What it means is I've got a stalker, someone with a really fucking unhealthy obsession and probably some kind of mental illness. I've had them before, and usually, it's not a huge deal. I hire security to find them, I have my lawyer deal with a restraining order in court, and that's the end of it. This time it's different, though."

I scrubbed my hands over my face. "I've never had anyone in my life I cared about, and no one that's been threatened besides me. I've also never had a stalker so goddamn crafty and persistent. Because I can't be physically with you this week, security is extra important. Last night Connor hired a new guy to stay with you, but the more I thought about it, the more I didn't want to leave you with a stranger."

She looked up at me with a tear running down her cheek. "But what about you? What if this person comes after you?" Leave it to my girl to be more worried about me than herself. I reached out and wiped the tear off her cheek with my thumb.

"They haven't threatened me so far, only you. Honestly, I sort of wish they'd come after me so I could do some fucking damage to them. But I'm not going to be alone, either. I'm taking a couple of Connor's team with me and leaving Connor and the new guy, Julian, here with you."

Kennedy visibly relaxed, exhaling loudly. "You're leaving Connor here?"

"Yep and Julian will be here later today. Is that okay?"

"Yeah, that actually makes me feel a lot better. At least I won't be here with a stranger. I trust Connor."

"Me, too." I rubbed circles on her bare shoulder with my thumb. "And I'll be checking in with you and Connor both constantly, so it'll be like I'm here."

"Except it won't be the same, but I get it. I'll see you Friday, right?" Kennedy moved closer.

I held her tightly. "Or sooner if I can manage it, but probably Friday. It's going to be okay, baby. I promise." I kissed her gently before leaning back.

"You know the last thing I want to do right now is leave, but I have to. The guys are waiting at my house. I fucking hate leaving you here."

She nodded solemnly. "I know, me too."

"I'll text you as soon as I can, okay? Try to get some more sleep, baby." *I love you.* I wouldn't say it yet, though. I hoped my gaze said the words for me as her eyes lifted to mine.

"I know, and I will. I'll miss you." She stuck out her bottom lip, pouting up at me. I leaned down, biting her lip gently and sucking it into my mouth before kissing her, swallowing her gasp.

"I'll miss you more than you know." I stood up, grabbing my bag and glancing back at her, trying to memorize the sight of her adorably rumpled from sleep with her messy blonde hair framing her bright blue eyes, the sheet pulled around her naked body as she stared at me. Her eyes clouded with worry and something deeper. *Love?* I could only hope. Tearing my eyes away, I left the room and started toward my house.

TUESDAY, I had to make a quick trip back to LA for a meeting. Before the plane even rolled to a stop, I'd already sent Kennedy a text checking in. The entire flight I worried about leaving her, about what might happen without me there. I had a responsibility to the band, and I knew Kennedy didn't want me to give up on Shadow Phoenix, but I had a feeling it would be pretty fucking difficult to concentrate this week. I had to remind myself that the more I focused, the faster this would go, and the faster I could get back to her.

I'd be meeting with Harrison. He was basically our fifth band member who didn't know shit about making music. He was one of the guys, and while I didn't consider him a brother like True, Maddox, and Jericho, he was pretty damn close.

Striding into Harrison's office, I plopped down in the plush chair in front of him. We were about the same age and of similar build, but Harrison was clean-cut and British, which apparently was a golden ticket to all the pussy he could ever want. All he had to do was open his mouth and say some bullshit about how *smashing* a woman looked, and he was in. Where I was inked up and preferred jeans and t-shirts, Harrison was clean-cut and wore suits to work every day.

"Z, what the fuck, mate? You couldn't give me a heads up?" Harrison started in on me as soon as I walked through the door.

I leaned back in the chair. "I would have if I was a goddamn psychic." I rubbed the back of my neck. "It's a good thing you're the best at what you do."

Harrison flashed me a cocky smirk, sitting down behind his desk. "You're not wrong. What is it you want from me with this whole thing? Who's the girl?"

I stiffened a little, reminding myself that I needed to calm the fuck down. Harrison was a total player, but he was on my team, and I could trust him not to fuck me over. Besides, I needed his expertise. Relaxing my shoulders, I blew out a breath. "I met her a few weeks ago. Her name is Kennedy."

Harrison grinned, flashing me the charming smile that, combined with his accent, was a potent combination to unlimited no-strings hookups. "Do you fancy her? Is this one going to stick? I'd imagine the reason the vultures started stalking you is that they hadn't gotten any good dirt on you in weeks. No shots of you pissed, leaving the club snogging some random as per usual."

"Yeah, well, I don't know how the fuck I did that shit for so long, but I'm over it. Kennedy isn't just anyone, and she, without a doubt, is staying in my life." Rubbing my hand along the stubble on my jaw, I leaned back in my chair. "I've got a couple of problems, though."

"Let's hear 'em." Harrison held up his hand, motioning for me to bring it on.

"First, Kennedy has something from her past that's sensitive. The media will eventually dig it up." I waited for Harrison to ask the question I knew was coming.

"You know I have to ask." He picked up a pen and tapped it against the polished surface of his desk.

"I know."

"Okay then, out with it."

Pressing my lips together, I hesitated. Talking about anything, Kennedy told me in confidence felt like a betrayal. But I needed help, and I had to be completely honest with Harrison. He'd helped the band out of more publicity messes than I could even count, and I knew we could trust him.

Leaning forward, I planted my elbows on my knees. I couldn't seem to hold still. "The TL;DR version? Her high school boyfriend slept with her and then spread rumors she was crazy because she had panic attacks. A group of vicious girls attacked her. The assholes she went to school with taunted her about it relentlessly until the depression got so bad that she had to go to inpatient therapy. It's a huge trauma in her life, and the fact it's going to come up now scares the shit out of me because it's going to hurt her, and I can't stop it."

Harrison's shoulders relaxed. "That's it? The way you were acting, I thought you were going to tell me something like she hunted humans for sport." He rubbed his chin. "We can actually work with this. I haven't heard anything about it yet, which means the press hasn't discovered it either, or they'd be calling me to comment. But you're right. It's only a matter of time before those wankers find out."

He stood and started pacing behind his desk. "We need to put it out there first, so we're in control. It should be a tiny blurb in a bigger interview about the band's new album and your new relationship. People will gloss over that small detail, but it'll be out there, which means the story won't hold any headline weight. They won't have a reason to dig into it further."

I sat back, considering the plan. It made sense. Was I missing anything? This seemed too simple.

As if reading my mind, Harrison stopped his pacing and sank

back down into his chair, chuckling. "Sometimes, the easiest solution is the best one."

"When would we do this? I still have to talk it over with Kennedy."

Harrison pulled out his phone and began tapping and scrolling. "It needs to happen soon before they have too much time to dig. I can get you an interview with *Pulse* on Friday. You'd have to fly back down here, though. They won't come to you. Does that work?"

I nodded. "I'll make it work. Set it up."

Harrison nodded, typing into his phone before setting it down and turning his attention back to me. "You said there was more than one thing."

I nodded.

"Out with it, mate."

"It looks like I have another fucking stalker. I don't need you for anything yet, but I wanted you to know because you may have to do some cleanup later. This way, you can at least start planning the narrative now if things get ugly."

"Thanks for the warning." Harrison grinned. "It's better than I usually get. How the fuck does this keep happening to you anyway? You've got like a stalker collection by now."

"Don't remind me. You try living with this face." I cracked a smile and stood up. "Text me about Friday. We'll be ready."

He stood, buttoning the top button of his jacket as he walked around the desk. "I'll meet you there to make sure everything goes smoothly."

I turned and walked out. That seemed almost too easy.

AFTER THE MEETING WITH HARRISON, I'd flown back to Washington, where the guys and I spent the afternoon in the studio. When we finished for the day, they all left, and I found myself cooking dinner in my kitchen. The music I had playing cut out as my phone vibrated on the counter.

Glancing down, my stomach dropped at the name flashing across my screen.

Grayson.

Trying not to overreact and think the worst, I hit the green button and lifted my phone to my ear. "Hey, Gray, what's going on?"

"You tell me. Have you talked to Kennedy?" He bit out through clenched teeth.

My heart rate picked up. "Not since this morning. Why? What happened?" I gripped the counter until my knuckles turned white, closing my eyes and bracing myself for the worst.

"Nothing happened except this whole situation. Has she told you how bad it's been for her the past couple of days?" I heard a door slam on his end.

My shoulders relaxed only slightly. "Not really, just that she's been keeping a low profile, and Connor or Julian has been with her constantly."

Grayson laughed, but it was humorless. "You really have no idea. I just came from seeing her, which was an entire process, by the way. There are so many photographers outside of her store, she had to close it down. She doesn't know when she'll be able to reopen. She can't leave the house, and she looked tired and stressed the fuck out when I saw her. Amara stayed with her last night to try and cheer her up. They had some sort of girl's night or some shit."

I felt like an asshole for putting her through this, and I felt even worse that I didn't know it was that bad for her. She hadn't said anything. I should be there with her, and even worse, I should've known. "Look, Gray—"

"I know you don't want this for her, and you didn't ask for it to happen. I trust you to take care of my sister, and I know you'll fix it. But do it now before I take her and hide her away from all this bullshit. That includes you." I didn't miss the threatening tone in his voice.

"I have a plan. We just need to get to Friday, and everything will get better."

"Have you told her this yet? Because when I just talked to her, it seemed like she had no idea when this might end."

"I'm talking to her about it on our call tonight."

Grayson sighed. "Fine, but I'm close by, and if anything else happens or this doesn't get better soon, I'm going to step in."

"Good, I'd expect nothing less." And I meant it. Grayson was a good guy and an even better brother and protector for Kennedy. "I'll text you when we've talked. I just want to talk it out with her first."

Saying our goodbyes, we ended the call. After hanging up, my shoulders slumped. Suddenly I felt drained. All I wanted to do was leave all this bullshit behind me, crawl into bed wrapped up with Kennedy, and fall asleep in our own little world. Unfortunately, tonight I wouldn't get what I wanted.

THE NEXT MORNING, I waited in the hall outside the studio for Maddox. True and Jericho were already here, all of us feeling the stress of producing another album. None of us were sleeping well, and I paced back and forth because standing still felt wrong. We all worried about what the fans would think of our new music. This wasn't our first rodeo, being our seventh album, but it never seemed to get easier. If anything, the pressure got worse every time.

When Maddox strolled in, sunglasses on, coffee in hand, and

looking like he didn't have a fucking care in the world, I snapped at him. "Nice of you to join us this morning."

He smirked. "Just be glad I crawled out of bed and made it at all. My head is pounding, and the two chicks I left naked in my hotel room were a fuck of a lot warmer than this reception."

True walked out into the hall and looked Maddox up and down. "Jesus, Mad."

Maddox shrugged, lifting his coffee to his mouth and wincing as he took a sip.

True's eyes shifted to me. "What's up with you? Something happen with Kennedy?"

Jericho stepped into the hall and leaned his shoulder against the wall, shoving his hands into the front pockets of his jeans, but he didn't say anything.

My shoulders slumped. "It's been a helluva week."

Jericho and True both nodded. Jericho's eyes narrowed into a full-on glare. "You better fucking not tell us you're about to quit."

"Yeah, I heard you last time." I rolled my eyes at Jericho, who flipped me off. Turning back to True, I ran a hand through my hair before continuing. "I told you about my goddamn stalker. There have been threats against Kennedy. I'm handling it the best I can, but between that and the paparazzi and the new album, I'm starting to feel like I'm fucking drowning."

I felt a fucking boulder lift off my shoulders, admitting everything out loud.

True flashed his trademark dimpled smile at me, punching my shoulder lightly. "Dude, we've got this. Your girl is basically our girl, too." I narrowed my eyes, and he held up his hands in surrender, laughing. "You know it's not like that, Z. I just meant whatever you need we're there."

The corner of my mouth lifted in a half-smile. It was the best I could do right now, but a wave of relief crashed over me. I knew they'd have my back because that's how our relationship worked.

We could be fighting, and if someone from the outside threatened any one of us, the others had our back immediately and without question.

"Enough with the feelings shit. Let's make some fucking music," Maddox grumbled before turning and walking into the studio, and we all followed. For the first time in a week, my steps were lighter, my shoulders more relaxed like I wasn't carrying the whole goddamn world on them.

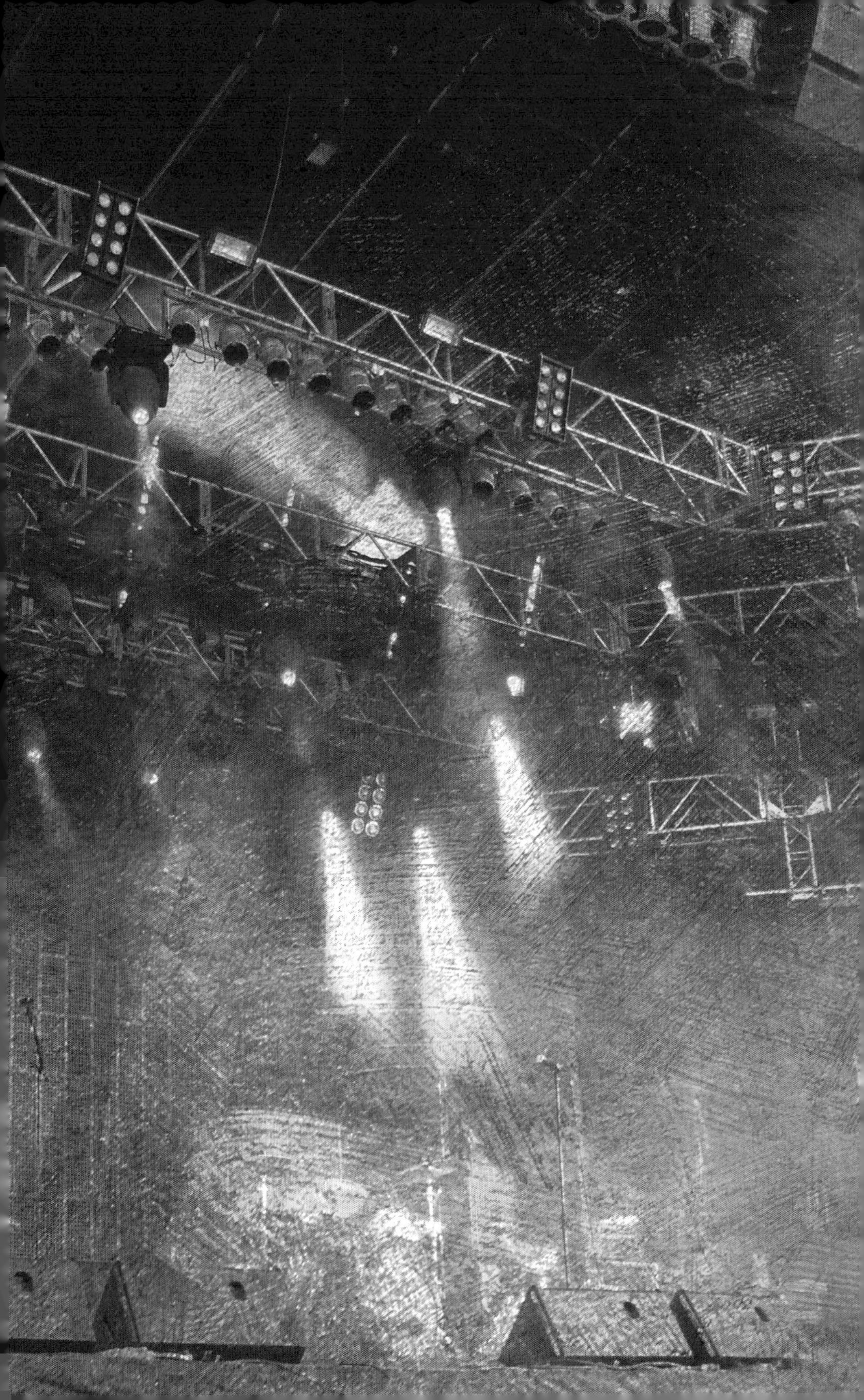

CHAPTER 24

KENNEDY

I WOKE to my heart pounding and that spiders running across your skin feeling that someone was watching me. I held still, barely cracking one eye open and tried to keep my breathing even despite my racing pulse. The darkness of the room made seeing anything, or anyone, nearly impossible. Moonlight poured through the open window, casting long shadows across the floor.

Moving my one open eye slowly upward, I nearly gasped when I saw a dark figure standing next to my bed, but I clenched my teeth together to keep from making a sound. If I thought my heart was racing before, it was damn near breaking out of my chest now. A cold sweat broke out across my brow, and I was sure my chest rose and fell quickly with my shallow breaths. Still, I didn't dare move a muscle.

I didn't have any experience with this type of situation, but instinct told me pretending to be asleep was the right move. Thankfully, I had a lot of experience with my overactive fight or flight response. I dealt with these feelings all the time, and I was getting better at ignoring them in favor of logic every day. I just needed to think.

I needed to gather information. Who was in my room? What did they want? If I could be convincing, I might be able to figure it out.

Refocusing my attention on the figure looming over my bed, I took in their appearance. They wore dark clothing and had a black hood over their head. Suddenly, they moved, and moonlight reflected off of metal in one of their hands. In the blink of an eye, my plan flew out the window.

Jolting upright in bed, I screamed as loud as I could for Connor. "Connor! There's someone in my room!"

Less than a second later, his thundering footsteps slammed down the hallway as the figure turned and dove for the open window and fire escape outside. My bedroom door bounced off the wall as Connor burst into my room. His hair was disheveled, his gray sweats and white t-shirt so different from his usual outfit of dark clothes or suits. He'd obviously been asleep, but he glanced at me before whipping his head around to catch a glimpse of movement outside the window.

He ran to the window, sticking his head out and holding up his gun before he shouted into the night, his deep voice booming, "Stop right fucking now." Without looking my way, Connor held out his hand. "Give me your phone."

I slipped it into his waiting hand, and he clicked it a few times before holding it outside and snapping a few pictures.

"D-Did you g-get anything?" My teeth chattered uncontrollably, and my whole body shook as adrenaline flooded my bloodstream.

He turned his attention back to me, his eyes softening for a moment. "I don't know yet." Then he yelled for backup. "Julian!"

Julian stormed into the room from where he'd been standing watch at the front door, gun drawn, with his eyes laser-focused on Connor.

"We had a breach. Secure the perimeter. Check the back alley. I bet they're gone, but do it anyway. Call the police on your way down. I'm staying here just in case."

As Julian nodded once and then left my room, Connor's large frame dropped onto the mattress beside me. He probed me with his soft grey gaze as if looking for any injuries. "Are you okay?"

My heart still raced, and tears ran down my face. I tried sucking oxygen into my lungs, but the effort was futile. No matter how hard I tried, I couldn't get enough air. My body shook uncontrollably as a realization washed over me. They could have killed me right here, even with security in the other room.

Nowhere was safe.

I rocked back and forth, trying to get some damn air into my lungs as my mind spiraled with all sorts of unhelpful thoughts about the fact I could have just been murdered while I slept in my own bed.

"I'm going to call Zen and sit here with you until the police come. Then I'll have to go talk to them." Connor spoke softly as if I were a frightened child. I guess that's probably what I looked like.

All I could do was nod as tears continued streaming down my cheeks. My shallow breaths in and out weren't helping me calm down, and my fingers had gone numb. My vision started to go black around the edges, and I hoped I wouldn't pass out from a lack of oxygen.

Connor moved closer, holding up my phone and pressing buttons until the video chat option popped up and began to ring. It was nearly two a.m., so I doubted he'd be awake or answer quickly. I hoped his phone wasn't on silent because I needed him.

After about six rings, Zen's sleepy voice came through the speaker, but the screen stayed black. "Kennedy? Are you okay?"

I tried to speak, but nothing came out since I couldn't catch my breath. I looked helplessly up at Connor.

"Sunshine? What's wrong?" Zen's sounded more alert, his voice on edge.

Connor cleared his throat. "We just had an incident."

"What the fuck does that mean, Connor? Where's Kennedy? Is she okay?" Zen clicked on a lamp and sat up in bed, his bare chest and tattoos on full display, his hair messy from sleep. His eyes were narrowed at Connor on the screen before they swung over to me.

"She wasn't hurt, but she sure as fuck doesn't seem okay." He moved the phone closer to me, but kept himself in the frame. "That's why I took her phone and called you. I'm waiting for the police, and I'm sitting with her, but I thought maybe you could calm her down. I'm not really sure how," Connor admitted, turning the phone fully on me, highlighting my red-rimmed eyes, tear-stained face, and messy hair. I looked *spectacular*, but I also couldn't find the will to care. Zen's face on the screen was like a lifeline right now, and I held on tight.

"Baby, look at me. Whatever happened, you're okay. Connor's there, the police are on their way, and I'll be there in ten minutes. Take a deep breath for me. Breathe with me, Kennedy. Please breathe in for four, okay?" His tone was soothing as he inhaled deeply and exhaled. I watched him closely.

His deep voice soothed me like a balm to my soul. The tremors wracking my body slowed, and for the first time in what felt like hours, oxygen inflated my lungs. I focused on his face, his voice, and his counting as I breathed along with him.

"Zen, I'm so scared." My voice trembled as I took the phone from Connor's large hand.

"I know, baby, I know. Just keep breathing with me. I'm going to send a quick text, but I'm not letting you go, okay? Just keep breathing." I watched as he typed, but I just tried to focus on keeping the precious air flowing into my body in a steady rhythm. "Are you breathing, Sunshine?"

I nodded. "I'm f-feeling a l-little bit b-better." I let out a shaky exhale, wiping my cheek with the back of my hand. I glanced at Connor, who watched me, his eyes filled with concern. We both looked up as Julian stepped into the room.

"The police are here. They want to talk to you."

Connor nodded before turning back to me. "Are you going to be okay if I go to the living room?"

My heart took off again, and in seconds all the progress I'd made disappeared. I was on the verge of full-blown panic again. He wanted to leave me here alone?

Oh, hell, no.

Zen finished his texting and filled the screen again as I tried to focus on every detail of his gorgeous face to distract myself from this new wave of panic. "Connor, are you still there?"

Connor shifted the phone in my hand so Zen could see him. "Yes."

"Don't you dare leave her alone in that room. If you have to talk to the police, they either come to you or have Julian stay with her. Or they can fucking wait for ten minutes. I don't want her alone for one fucking second. Clear?" Zen's voice came out low and threatening, and as Connor turned the phone back toward me, I saw Zen moving around his room, throwing on clothes.

"Crystal." Connor nodded to Julian to stay in the room and then looked down at me one last time, remorse filling his eyes for just a second before he walked out. I knew he must feel horrible someone got in on his watch, but I couldn't worry about it now.

Zen's voice cut through my inner turmoil. "Baby, are you breathing?"

I nodded, exhaling a shaky breath.

"I don't know what happened, but I'll be there in just a couple of minutes. Keep breathing. I texted Grayson, and he's on his way, too, okay?" My eyes filled with tears again, and all I could do was nod. I could tell Zen was trying to be brave for me, but his voice shook slightly, and his eyes were wide and unblinking.

"I'm so sorry, Kennedy." His voice was sad as he walked through his house. "I'll be there soon, but until I get there, you'll have Grayson, Connor, and Julian there with you."

"It's not the same. Someone got in even with Connor and Julian, Zen. Someone got in." It came out a whisper because that was all I could manage before my throat closed up and I choked back a sob.

"Jesus Christ, someone was in there? Fuck, baby. I'm not letting you out of my sight again. I'm getting in the car now. Just stay on the phone with me."

"It helps to hear your voice, you're good at calming me down." I gave him a small smile. "At least I get to see you sooner than Friday."

"If you wanted to see me, there were definitely easier ways to do it, Sunshine." He let out a low chuckle before his voice turned serious again. "I promise I'm not going to let anyone hurt you."

"What if we can't stop—"

"Kennedy, no more what-ifs. We'll stop them no matter what it takes. I promise. Have I ever let you down?"

"No." I exhaled. "Okay, no more what-ifs."

"Not unless they're good what-ifs, like our song." He flashed me his full smile, and despite everything, warmth flooded my system that had nothing to do with anxiety.

I feigned ignorance. "Oh, is that our song? I thought our song was *Brave*."

"No, that's your song. Our song is definitely *What Ifs*. It fits us perfectly. If you need something to occupy your mind, think about those kinds of what-ifs instead."

The longer I listened to his voice, the more I relaxed. Unlike anyone else in my life, he could calm me down with the most delicious distractions. My mind wandered to the song he claimed was ours.

What if we really were made for each other?

I could get behind that being our song. He'd become such an

important part of my life over the past few weeks that I didn't even know how I'd lived without him for so long. For a while, I'd suspected, but at this moment, this imperfect and crazy moment of trauma and fear, it hit me just how hard I'd fallen for this perfectly imperfect man.

I sat up straight as realization washed over me. Zen was mine. Just like he'd protect me, I'd fight a million battles to protect him. No longer would I be weak. I refused to be the reason he had to walk away from everything else he loved. Our future wouldn't be dictated by people who wanted to take us down piece by piece. We made our own destiny. There wasn't any other option because I was wholly and hopelessly in love with him.

Snapping myself out of my thoughts, I shook my body and straightened my spine. "I feel so violated, Zen. I'm so glad you're almost here. I won't feel safe until you wrap your arms around me."

I heard a knock on the door and low voices before my brother pushed his way into my room. "Grayson's here." I turned the phone around for Zen.

"I'll be there in five minutes, baby. I'll let you go talk to your brother."

I nodded. "Okay." *I love you.* I turned and locked eyes with my twin. A fresh wave of tears threatened to fall, but I refused to let them. I would be stronger than that.

"Jesus, Ken. Are you okay?" Grayson sank down next to me and pulled me into his arms, crushing me against his body. I crumpled in my brother's familiar embrace, nodding. "God, you're shaking. Is that Zen?" Grayson gestured to my phone.

"Yeah, he's been talking to me on his way here." I held my phone up so Zen could see us.

"Gray," he said tightly. "Thanks for getting there so fast."

Grayson sighed. "Of course I'd get here fast. Thanks for the text, Z."

"You'll stay with her until I get there?"

"I'm not going anywhere." Grayson put his arm around my shoulders and hauled me up against him. We may be twins, but he'd always been a lot taller and stronger than me.

"Good. Be there soon." Zen hung up.

"Want to tell me what the fuck is going on? Zen sent me a text that I needed to get my ass over here because something happened, but he didn't know what. No one is telling me anything." Grayson tightened his grip on me.

I noticed Julian slip out of the room when my brother came in, and I was glad. I didn't really know him, and it made me uncomfortable having another stranger in here after what happened. But then a police officer stepped inside behind my brother and I knew I couldn't avoid reliving this nightmare any longer.

My shoulders slumped, and I wasn't sure there'd ever be a time from now on that I wasn't at least a little shaky.

Shit. I could've died.

I bit my lip before locking eyes with my brother, staring up into a pair identical to mine. "I woke up because it felt like someone was staring at me. You know that weird feeling of being watched?"

He nodded.

"I somehow managed to not freak the fuck out when I noticed them standing by my bed because I wanted to see if I could figure out who it might be. Then I saw they were holding something shiny in their hand. Something metal that lit up when the moonlight hit it. That's when I started screaming." I shuddered, and my stomach rolled.

"Goddamnit it, Kennedy. I had a feeling something like this would happen. It's why I told Zen to protect you from this shit." Grayson rubbed his forehead.

"He did his best, Gray. He hired security to be here with me twenty-four hours a day. He had to go home. It's not his fault some crazy person is doing this." I'd defend Zen to my brother until my last breath, but I was exhausted and hoped I didn't have to. "Please don't blame him."

Some of the tension relaxed out of his body. "Fine. I'll stay in here until he gets here, but then I'm going to talk to Connor." He sighed. I yawned, suddenly exhausted. The officer had listened quietly and made notes while I spoke, then slipped out.

Moving out of my brother's grasp, I laid down but saw movement out of the corner of my eye. A new round of adrenaline flooded my system as I tensed up. When I realized it was just the curtain, I exhaled loudly. "Gray, can you please close the window?"

He nodded and stood, crossing the room and slamming the window shut before securing the lock. He paced back and forth, his fists clenched at his sides, but I couldn't worry about his anger right now. I was too exhausted.

I closed my eyes for just a second before I heard voices whispering nearby. I shot upright, my heart racing all over again. "Gray?"

My brother's bulky frame came into view and relaxed. "Yeah, I'm here. Zen just got here. You're okay. I'm going to crash on the living room floor. Yell if you need me."

A new kind of butterflies filled my stomach, and I sagged against my pillows, knowing I could relax. Everything would be okay.

"Baby, I'll be right back. I'm just going to go talk to Grayson, okay? Connor's right outside the open door." Zen's soft voice sounded tired.

I nodded, closing my eyes while I waited for him to come back.

A minute later, Zen was back, tossing his clothes off and climbing into bed, pulling me tight against his body. "I was so scared tonight." He whispered against my hair.

"Me, too." My eyes stung, but I refused to shed another tear.

"No more time apart, at least not until we catch whoever's doing this." He ran his hands across my flat stomach before tightening his grip around me. "I can't handle it."

"Neither can I."

"Sleep, baby. I've got you. We can talk about everything tomorrow. While you were sleeping, Connor secured your window, so we're safe here tonight."

"Zen?"

"Yeah, Sunshine?"

"I'm glad you're here. I really needed you."

"I should have been here in the first place. I'm sorry you had to go through that alone. I won't make that mistake again." Anger radiated off of him as he held me, his muscles tense. I knew he'd beat himself up over this just like Connor, but I was too exhausted to talk about it now. Keeping my eyes open any longer was an impossible task. Before I knew what happened, I was asleep in the safety of Zen's arms.

THE NEXT MORNING, movement in my apartment woke me up. I stretched before turning around and pressing my lips against Zen's chest. The world seemed so right when we were together. What seemed hopeless and terrifying the night before now seemed like a problem we'd tackle together. A lazy smile spread across his face as he pulled me even closer and tucked my head under his chin.

"We should get out there and figure out what our next steps are." My voice came out muffled since my lips were pressed against the ridges of his chest.

He groaned. "Fuck that. I say we just stay here forever and never leave." I flipped over, and he shifted his hips until the hard ridge of his cock pressed against my ass, and his lips burned a white-hot trail of kisses down my neck. Goosebumps broke out across my skin as heat flooded my core.

I pressed myself back against him and a low rumble that sounded suspiciously like a growl vibrated against my back as he snaked his hand around to cup my breast. "You make an enticing case, but now that I've had a taste for adventure, I'm not willing to shut myself in anymore. Just a quick meeting and you can carry me back here and do whatever you want."

His eyebrow raised, and a wicked smile spread across his face. "Whatever I want? You should be careful what you offer."

Pushing Zen's buttons was becoming one of my favorite things to do. "Why? You don't think you're up to it?"

"Oh, Sunshine. You haven't even seen half of what I'm capable of." He rolled his body so I was pinned underneath his delicious weight. It became obvious we weren't getting out of bed anytime soon, and I couldn't be happier.

HOURS LATER, we dragged ourselves out of the bedroom with messy hair and matching satisfied smiles. I threw on clothes and wandered into the kitchen for coffee and brunch. Zen never let go of me, and I couldn't say I was mad about it. His touch kept me calm. Whether he held my hand, sat next to me with our legs touching, or swept loose strands of hair off of my face, it was like he was afraid to be too far away.

I grabbed the piece of paper lying on the counter. "Gray had to go into work early this morning, but he'll check in with both of us later," I recounted after scanning the message.

"Okay, baby. I'll keep him updated." He let go of me for the first time today, but only moved a few feet away to make breakfast. He kept his eyes on me the whole time.

Watching Zen make scrambled eggs in my kitchen had my mouth watering but not for food. I let my eyes wander his body appreciatively, feeling my nipples tighten under my shirt. The muscles rippled across his back while he stirred, and I found myself wishing his shirt would disappear.

He grinned at me. "I like it when you stare at me."

I bit my lip. "I just wished your shirt would disappear so I can appreciate all of your assets more fully."

He set the bowl down and stalked across the kitchen until he stood in front of where I was perched on a barstool. He pushed my legs apart and stepped between them until our chests pressed together, my hardened nipples pressing into his firm body. I fought back a moan.

He reached down to the hem of his shirt and dragged it slowly upwards, teasing me with every inch of smooth skin he revealed. I looked up through my lashes and met his fiery gaze.

I dropped my eyes to his broad chest and licked my lips before tracing the black phoenix tattoo on his side with my tongue. He shuddered and tossed his shirt on the floor before gripping my thighs and pulling me to the edge of the stool. His hard-on pressed against my center, and my eyes rolled back.

He leaned down and licked down the curve of my neck, and it felt like sparks ignited under my skin. I moaned and reached up to bring his face to mine.

Just as our mouths collided, the front door closed. I sighed and pulled back, frowning. I couldn't help it. Whenever we got interrupted, I pouted like a kid whose favorite toy was just taken away.

Connor stepped into the room as Zen reluctantly went back to the eggs, shooting a glare at his bodyguard. "Can we talk about last night?"

I gestured to the stool next to me, and Connor slid it out before sitting on the edge. Zen stirred the eggs, his narrowed eyes on Connor. I knew Zen wasn't going to forgive the fact that someone got in on his watch easily.

Zen set the bowl down and folded his arms across his bare chest. I tried to ignore the way his forearms and biceps flexed. His voice was eerily calm, like the eye of a storm. "I want to know how it happened and what we're doing moving forward."

Connor cleared his throat. "We think Kennedy's window had been locked, but it has an old lock mechanism, so it was easy to manipulate to get the window open. The individual climbed up the fire escape ladder, got the window open, and climbed in."

I knew the windows were old because they were original to the building, which had been built about a hundred years ago, but I had no idea the locks could be undone so easily.

"Okay, so new windows. What else are we going to do?" I twisted a stray piece of hair around my finger.

"We're going back to LA this afternoon. This isn't going to be a fun trip like last time. We have shit to handle, but it'll fix a lot of these issues." Zen poured the eggs into a pan before leaning his hip against the counter. "It's going to be hard on you, so I want to bring Gray and Amara, too, if she can get the time off. Gray already said he'd come and that he'd talk to her."

I swallowed hard, my appetite going up in a puff of smoke. "What do you mean it's going to be hard? What are we doing?"

His shoulders slumped a little as he turned to stir the eggs. "I talked to Harrison Tuesday, and we came up with a plan to deal with the stuff in your past. I know how important it is to you that it doesn't come out, but too many people know what happened. We can't just bury it."

My heart sank as I twisted my fingers in my lap. Zen crossed the room and grabbed my hand, closing it in his warm grip. "What do you think about doing an interview together about our relationship, the new album, and then just slipping in a tiny blurb about your time in high school? Harrison thinks if we do it this way, the information would be out there, but it'll get lost in an article with tons of other interesting stuff in it like how we met and how irresistible I am." He flashed me a bright grin, wiggling his eyebrows.

Chewing on my lip, I considered the idea. On the one hand, it seemed easy enough. With enough better material, odds were no one would latch onto something that happened almost a decade ago. On the other hand, what if they did? "I can see how that might work, but what if—"

Zen pressed his finger to my lips. "No, baby. No what-ifs. This is the best plan. I know it's going to be hard for you to talk about it, and I know you're not used to doing interviews, but that's why I want everyone to come with us. Let's surround ourselves with the people we love and take control of this situation."

Maybe Zen was right. Maybe just getting in front of this shitshow would be better than waiting for it to come out, every day wondering if today would be the day everyone found out. I didn't know if I could handle the humiliation all over again, and this time it would be on a huge scale. Enormous. Frighteningly far-reaching.

I shuddered as my skin got a little clammy. Controlling the way this all came out had to be the best way, right? Not only that, but I'd been working so hard to face my fears, and this was one of the biggest ones I still had. People finding out about my past scared me so much it'd kept me from any meaningful connection with anyone for almost ten years.

No more.

I was done.

I sat up straighter and smiled up at him brightly, and he blinked, momentarily caught off guard by my cheerful expression. He reached up and ran his thumb along my cheek. "What's that smile for?"

"This is a genius plan, I actually love it. You're right, it's not going to be easy, but I'm strong and can handle this."

"That's my girl." Zen wrapped me up in his strong arms and peppered my face with kisses, making me giggle.

"Hey!" I pushed against his hard chest, but it was no use. He was like a wall. Through my laughter, I said, "I have a question."

He stopped with the sweet, teasing kisses on my face and leaned back. "What?"

"That only fixes one problem. What do we do about this stalker situation?"

Zen's smile faltered as he rubbed the stubble on his chin. "Yeah, that one's not as easy. We're taking Connor back to LA with us, but Julian's staying here to work with the police. Whoever they are, they seem to be Washington-based, so I think Connor can handle our security by himself in LA."

Connor stood up and nodded before leaving the room.

Zen sighed. "Despite what happened, I still trust him. As much as I want to put the blame on him for what happened, I can't. He's only human."

I rested my cheek against his chest and closed my eyes, listening to the steady beat of his heart. "No, he did everything he could. He was there in less than five seconds, and he looked like he wanted to kill someone."

"I'm sure he did, and if he caught the person he might have. I know I wanted to." He stepped back, dropping a kiss to the top of my head before walking to the stove and taking the pan off the burner. "Hopefully, by the time we're back, we won't have to worry about it anymore, and the fucking psycho will be in jail."

I set my elbow on the counter, resting my chin on my hand. "What about my store? And Chloe? I've been closed most of the week because customers don't want to walk through a crowd of photographers to buy a book or a coffee. Chloe hasn't worked for the last three days, actually the last four days if you count today."

"This interview should get the paparazzi off your back for at least a little while, and you can reopen. If we have to, we'll get a restraining order against them for interfering in your business. But for now, let's just take this one step at a time. We'll do the interview and then figure out where to go next. I really believe it's the first step to life getting back to normal or better than normal even."

I looked up at Zen, this beautiful man who consumed my thoughts, who'd become my whole world in a matter of weeks and felt myself relax. I was ready to be strong, but strength didn't mean being alone. I'd discovered that strength meant asking for help when you needed it. I didn't have to depend on myself alone anymore, and for that, I'd be forever grateful. It was time to show the world what Kennedy Adams was made of.

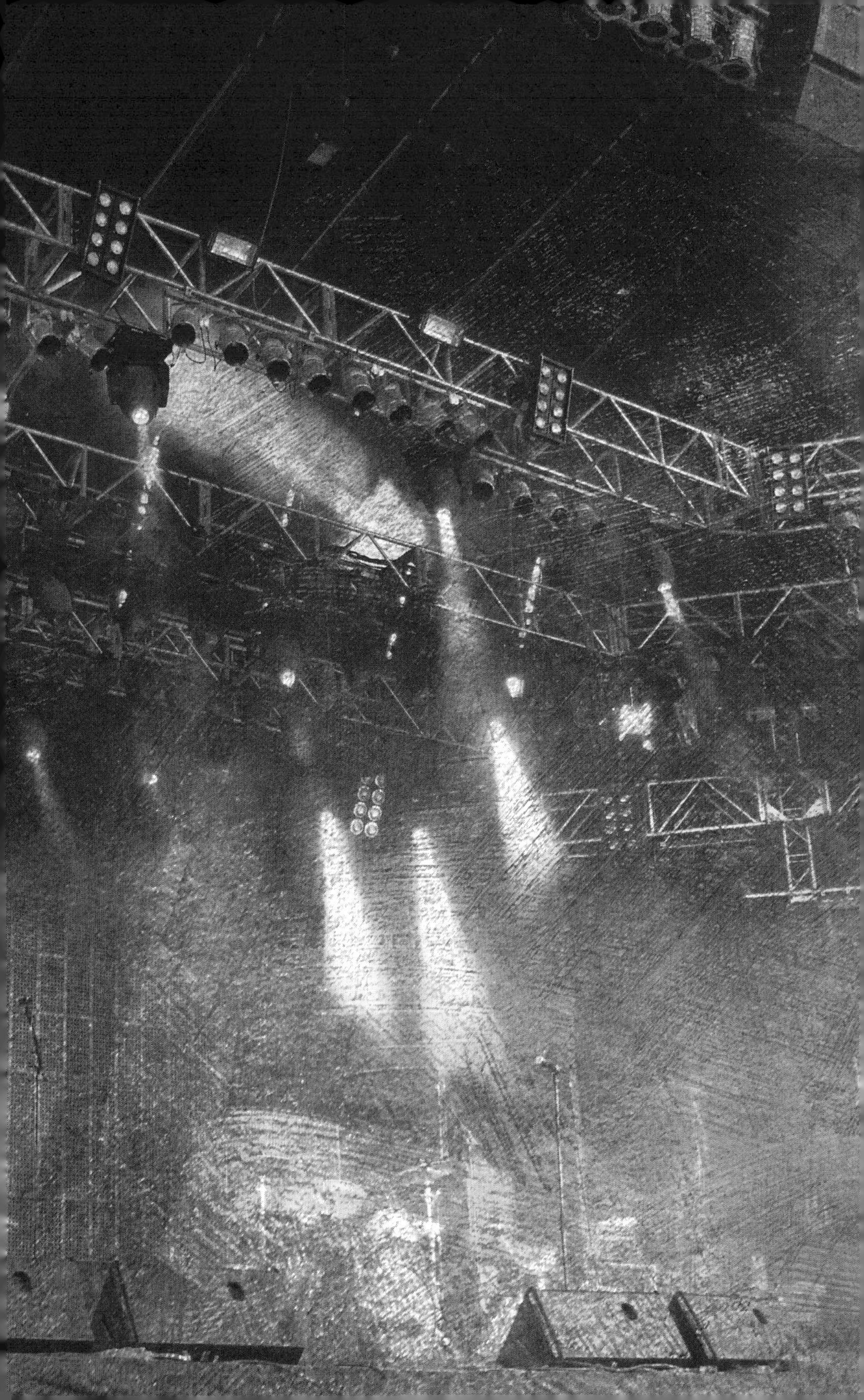

CHAPTER 25

ZEN

AFTER SPENDING yesterday in Kennedy's bed, I was ready to get back to LA to do this interview so we could have some semblance of a normal life. Spending the day wrapped up in each other had been my version of heaven, but I could tell by the way her forehead wrinkled, and her eyebrows furrowed every time she got lost in her head, everything was weighing on Kennedy. The guys had flown home yesterday, and now it was our turn.

I'd be fucking ecstatic to get home and get all this shit behind us. So much had happened with Kennedy, I'd almost completely forgotten about the reason I was exiled to Washington to begin with. Hopefully, the interviewer wouldn't bring up the video of me fucking some random chick. Kennedy didn't need to think about that on top of everything else. It was probably too much to hope for, though. At least if she did, we had Harrison to spin that shit into a good thing. The dude's a magician.

When we'd been in LA, Kennedy was carefree and relaxed. I think it was because the beach brought her peace. She could close her eyes, breathe in the fresh air, and hopefully relax a little bit. I had another reason for wanting this trip to go well. It'd be a test to see how the people most important to both of us got along.

Our friends and family would be meeting for the first time, and it felt like a huge step. Kennedy needed her people to fit into her life with me. Honestly, I was more nervous about everyone meeting than I was about the interview. Then again, I'd done thousands of interviews before, but I'd never done the whole meet the family thing. I had no intention of letting Kennedy go, so today would be an important step for the future I'd been starting to plan in my mind. Hopefully, my friends didn't fuck it up.

Pulling onto the tarmac, I spotted Grayson's Jeep already parked. He, and who I assumed was Amara, stood next to it, luggage at their feet. The tension melted out of my body as my chest expanded. The two of them making time to come with us this weekend would make Kennedy feel more relaxed, and I'd do anything to make her happy.

I squeezed Kennedy's hand and leaned over to press a kiss to her soft cheek, breathing in her scent. A huge smile stretched across her face, and her blue eyes sparkled up at me. When she was happy, everything felt right in my world, and this week had been really fucking wrong. I'd take as many of these small happy moments as I could get.

"They came." She laughed a little. "I can't believe they came!"

When the car came to a stop, I jumped out, not bothering to wait for Connor to open the door, and held out my hand for Kennedy. She took it, beaming at me as if I was her favorite person in the world. My pulse sped up, and I wondered if I really was her favorite person in the world.

Fuck, I hoped so.

When my girl looked at me like I was her everything, it stole the breath from my lungs. "I could get used to that smile on your face," I told her, pulling her close for a quick kiss. She stepped back, dragging me along with her as she practically skipped over to her brother and best friend.

"You guys made it!" She threw herself against Amara, who laughed and pulled her into a hug.

I refused to let go of her hand, so it was awkward as fuck. I didn't give a shit. Ever since Wednesday night, I found myself terrified to be away from her even for short periods. Physically touching her, feeling her skin pressed up against mine, reassured me that she was okay. I knew I couldn't keep this up forever, it wasn't normal. I was acting like a goddamn possessive asshole. But while there was a serious threat against the woman I loved, I'd sure as shit be keeping her as close as I could get away with. My most important job had become keeping Kennedy safe.

Grayson lifted his chin in greeting, his lips quirking up on one side like he knew how fucking gone I was over his sister and planned to give me shit about it later guy-to-guy. I didn't mind. It meant he was warming up to me. I gave him a cocky smirk back to show him I'd happily take whatever he had coming my way because I gave zero fucks as long as I had Kennedy by my side.

I'd wondered if there were any romantic feelings between Kennedy's brother and her best friend, but based on what I'd seen between them, there was zero sexual chemistry there. They looked and acted more like brother and sister than anything else. Kennedy stepped out of her best friend's embrace and gave her brother a quick hug before introducing Amara to me.

"Amara, this is Zen," Kennedy said, wrapping her arm around my waist and giving me a bright smile.

Amara whistled. "Wow, girl. You did good."

Kennedy chuckled, and Amara grinned at me, reaching out her hand to shake mine. She had caramel skin, amber colored light brown eyes that were almost golden, framed with dark lashes, and long, wavy brown hair. Her full lips curved into a friendly smile.

"I'm not a piece of meat, you know," I teased, briefly shaking her hand. I'd have to warn her about my friends. Maddox was going to have a goddamn field day. Even though she wasn't his type, he'd still be a flirtatious asshole.

"Nice plane," Grayson smirked.

I chuckled. "Yeah, it's pretty fucking nice to be me sometimes."

I laced my fingers with Kennedy's and led her up the steps.

The regular flight crew that staffed the plane met us at the top of the stairs. Hilda, the head flight attendant, greeted us. "Welcome aboard, Mr. Taylor, Miss Adams. We'll be taking off shortly. Let me show you to your seats."

"Thanks, Hilda." I flashed her a grin.

The flight crew was always professional, and, as a general rule, the guys and I had all agreed we didn't mix business and pleasure. The plane we shared was a grey area, so we made sure not to hire young flight attendants as a precaution because Maddox couldn't resist temptation. Fuck, who was I kidding? Until recently, I'd have been right there with him if for no other reason than to entertain myself on a long flight.

She maneuvered down the body of the plane, taking our luggage and storing it for us.

"Can I get you anything before takeoff?" Hilda offered.

I glanced at Kennedy, who shook her head. "No, thanks."

All of us strapped in for the flight. Before long, we were up in the air.

Kennedy sat next to me with her headphones on, and her eyes squeezed shut. I knew she was still awake by the death grip she had on my hand. Her fear of flying was still something she was working through. I'd gladly let her break all of my fingers if it made her feel better.

I leaned down, placing a soft kiss on her lips. Her eyes snapped open, and she put her hands on either side of my face, pulling me back toward her mouth as if she'd just been waiting to pounce on me. I groaned as she deepened the kiss. I pulled back, and she stuck her soft bottom lip out, tempting me to bite it.

"Baby, we aren't alone, and I don't think you want your brother to see me fuck you, although that might be funny." I pretended to be considering taking things further, but in reality, I'd never put her in that position. I didn't give a shit about what Gray thought, but I knew it'd make Kennedy uncomfortable.

Her eyes filled with desire, and the last thing I ever wanted was to tell Kennedy no when she looked at me like she wanted to jump on my cock and go for a ride. I didn't give a shit about her brother or her friend, but I was trying to be respectful for her sake. If she pushed me much harder, though, I would drag her to the bathroom and lock us in for the rest of the flight.

I wasn't a goddamn saint.

"I need to go over the plan for today with Grayson and Amara. Want to come with me?" I asked instead, needing to change the subject.

She pouted, sticking out her delicious bottom lip again. "Fine, you're right, I guess. I can't help it; I just lose all sense of reason when you kiss me. It's like everything else disappears."

I knew exactly how she felt because I felt the same way. I could easily get lost in Kennedy.

I traced my thumb along her soft bottom lip, desperately wanting to taste her again, but I knew if I gave in now, I wouldn't be able to stop.

"Fuck, baby. It's taking every ounce of self-control I have to not lay you down across this seat and give us both what we want. Let's go before I change my mind." I stood and adjusted as my dick hardened. I tried to think of anything else, but Kennedy's nipples were poking through her shirt, and I had to avert my eyes. I couldn't look at her for another second and not kiss her.

I moved out of the way to allow her to stand up, and she slid in front of me, her body moving against mine, making me groan. We made our way toward the back of the plane where Grayson and Amara were. The last thing I needed was to show up to a chat with her brother sporting wood, so I sang one of our new songs backward in my head and tried not to stare at Kennedy's perfect ass in front of me.

Taking the empty seat in front of Grayson, I pulled Kennedy down on my lap before she could sit in the chair next to me. I'd just barely gotten my hard-on under control and her wiggling her gorgeous ass on my dick wouldn't help matters, but I couldn't help it. I needed to have her close, and she seemed to need the same thing. She pressed against me, tossing me a playful glance over her shoulder because she knew exactly what the fuck she was doing to me.

Oh, she wanted to play? I gripped her hips to hold her still, rocking so my dick pressed against her. A small whimper escaped her lips, and her body trembled. I felt her squeeze her legs together, and I chuckled.

God, she was hot as hell.

Grayson cleared his throat, and I narrowed my eyes, shooting him a glare for interrupting.

He took out his headphones, and Amara closed the magazine she'd been flipping through. "You need something, or were you just planning on providing me some nightmare fuel?" Grayson wrinkled his nose.

Kennedy blushed. "Sorry."

She flashed me a shy smile, so I knew she wasn't really sorry at all. I ran my hand across her thigh, and she squirmed again, which made me chuckle. She wanted me just as bad as I wanted her.

"I'm not sorry. I can't help it if your sister's hard to resist."

"I didn't need to hear that."

Kennedy leaned back against my chest as I wrapped my arm

around her waist. "There are a few things we need to talk about before we land."

"You couldn't just text me? I really could have gone my whole life without seeing you guys get all handsy with each other."

"Grayson."

He rolled his eyes. "Fine."

"First, we're doing the interview today. It's going to be stressful on Kennedy, but she can handle it. Right, Sunshine?" She nodded.

"It'll only take about an hour. After that, my friends are coming over. Since you're staying with us, you'll be meeting them today, which brings me to my second point." I turned my gaze to Amara, who raised her eyebrows. "Amara, you should know, my bandmates can be…" I wasn't really sure what to say that wouldn't scare her or make my friends sound horrible because they all could be assholes.

"A bit much," Kennedy finished for me, a huge smile on her face. "They're used to having women throw themselves at them, and they can come on strong. Well, actually, that's only accurate for Maddox. Jericho's quiet but don't piss him off. He's my favorite." She giggled.

I placed my hand over my heart, pretending she'd wounded me. "I thought I was your favorite."

She laughed, running her hand along my cheek and pressed a quick kiss to my mouth. "He's my second favorite," she corrected.

I knew I had a stupid grin on my face, but I didn't give a shit. She made me ridiculously happy.

"Anyway…" Grayson said, rolling his eyes.

"You'll like Jericho, Am, and maybe True, too. He's sweet and flirty, so try not to fall for his charm. Maddox, on the other hand…" Kennedy scowled. "Just no."

I refocused my attention, tearing my eyes away from her but rubbing small circles on her hip with my fingertips. "When we do the interview, we're doing it at my publicist's office downtown. Then we'll come home and eat and have drinks, and everyone can meet each other. Just be prepared for my friends, like Kennedy said. They're really harmless, they just act like assholes sometimes."

Kennedy burst out laughing, giving me a look that said *right, sometimes*.

I chuckled. "Okay, most of the time. After the meeting, I'm sure we're just going to want to relax and enjoy the afternoon. It'll be a nice break from the week we've had."

Grayson nodded. "I'll whip something up for us for dinner. I'll call a Lyft when we get to your house and hit the grocery store. When you guys get back, you'll have a hot meal waiting."

I shook my head. "Don't take a Lyft. Take one of the cars in the garage."

"I hope you have something expensive," Grayson smirked and rubbed his hands together.

"I'm sure you can find something you'll like, Gray." Kennedy shifted on my lap, and all logical thought drained out of my brain faster than the blood rushing south. What had he been saying? Something about food?

"It's been way too long since I've eaten your food. I figured having a world-class chef for a brother I'd be eating amazing meals all the time," Kennedy teased, smiling playfully at him before sliding her hand down my stomach. I blew out a breath. Keeping my raging hard-on under control was fucking impossible.

I grabbed her wrist, stopping its downward path, and pressed my lips to it before letting her go. Glancing at her brother, I asked, "You're a chef?"

Grayson laughed. "Is that hard to believe?"

"No, I guess I just pictured you in an office job or something."

"No way, man. I'd die of boredom if I had to work in an office. I'm the head chef at Avo in Kirkland."

Head chef? That was pretty impressive, considering Grayson was only twenty-four. "When things settle down, we'll have to come to check it out."

"Sure, but I'm not going to be there much longer."

"Why not?"

"I've been taking every shitty job I could find, working under asshole chef after asshole chef, gaining experience and saving money for years to open my own restaurant. I'm almost there. I probably have another six months or so before I'm ready to take the leap."

I looked up at Kennedy, who was smiling proudly at her brother. She leaned back against my chest, laying her head on my shoulder while I wrapped my arms around her. "Gray has worked his ass off, making his dream come true. Amara and I are super proud of him, right Am?"

"Right. Gray's had to do some really awful jobs to get to where he is, but look at him now." Amara laughed, reaching over to pinch Grayson's cheek and shaking it slightly. "Our little Grayson's all grown up."

Grayson laughed, swatting her hand away. "First of all, I'm older than both of you."

"Oh, here we go." Kennedy waved her hand at her brother and rolled her eyes.

"This again? Come up with a new argument, Gray." Amara picked her magazine back up and effectively dismissed us all.

I watched their interactions curiously. I didn't have any brothers or sisters, so I had no idea what that relationship dynamic was like. The closest I got were True, Maddox, and Jericho. I found myself again hoping we'd all get along this weekend.

"Are we all clear on the plan?" I needed this to go smoothly for us, even if I was restating the obvious. I felt powerless and out of control, and it was making me restless.

"Yeah, we've got it." Grayson smirked before putting his headphones back in.

Kennedy slid off my lap, pulling me up flush against her body. I felt every soft curve, the warmth of her skin lighting me up through my clothes. My pants strained uncomfortably as my dick tried to escape their confines. As much as I wanted to stay pressed against her, I couldn't. I was in real danger of losing the battle I'd been waging all day not to fuck her here in front of her brother, and right now, my dick was winning.

Her hooded eyes were locked on mine and filled with lust. With just a look, she told me she'd be down for me to bend her over right here, pull her soaked panties to the side, and push myself inside her.

"Fuck it." It came out as a growl, but I didn't give a fuck. I grabbed her hand and practically dragged her behind me until we got to the front of the plane. I may have given up on trying to stop the inevitable, but I wouldn't do it in front of her brother. Apparently, there were some lines I wasn't willing to cross.

Who knew?

Slamming the tiny bathroom door open, I pushed Kennedy inside and followed her in. I heard Amara laugh but ignored her. There was just enough room for the two of us, and I closed and locked the door behind me.

Turning, I backed her against the counter and gathered her hair into my fingers. I leaned down and kissed her, our lips moving frantically together, teeth clashing and tongues exploring.

The longer we made out, the more frenzied we both got. Kennedy made these little whimpers that drove me insane and made my cock impossibly harder. I ran my hands down the silky skin of her body, and the heat of touching her burned up my fingertips, spreading through my arms and straight to my dick.

While I fucked her mouth with my tongue, my hands met the bare skin of her thighs where her skirt ended. I grabbed her legs and lifted her onto the counter, positioning myself between her thighs, my body fucking begging to be inside her.

Kennedy ran her fingernails over my chest, down my stomach and lower, frantically working at the button on my jeans. I lifted her skirt, running my hand up her inner thigh until my fingers brushed her already soaking core and ripples of need tore through me.

"Fuck, baby. You're so wet for me already," I bit her lower lip gently before pressing open-mouthed kisses along her neck and down to her collarbone.

"I need you inside me," she pleaded, her voice husky, her eyes meeting mine and begging me to give her what we both needed. I shoved my pants down, stepping out of them and returned to devouring her mouth. My hand reached underneath her shirt, moving upwards until I felt the soft curve of her breast.

"Fuck. You're not wearing a bra again? What the hell are you trying to do to me?" My breath caught at the sight of her flushed with arousal for me. I'd never get tired of seeing her like this. She was like a drug, and I couldn't get my next hit fast enough.

She clawed at me, trying to get me closer, to pull me inside of her. She'd wrapped her legs around my waist, and my rock-hard cock pressed against her still clothed entrance. I chuckled before reaching down between us, tearing the thin material covering her slit away from her body before sinking myself balls deep in one thrust.

"Oh, fuck, I needed this." She closed her eyes and clung to my body as I drove into her, her tight walls enveloping me, sucking me back in every time I pulled out. We fell into a rhythm, both of us climbing higher. She whimpered and clenched around me, her fingernails digging into my back, trying to get me deeper inside her as if she couldn't get me close enough.

I thrust, pulling almost entirely out before slamming back into her over and over again. I could feel her starting to shake around me, and I reached my hand down between us to rub circles on her clit. I wouldn't be able to hold out much longer. I started to lose control.

"Come for me, baby," I commanded, swiveling my hips to hit

the spot I knew would make her explode. I'd been learning her body and knew just the right angle that would make her come.

She arched her back, constricting around me, milking my cock with her tight, convulsing pussy. After a few more erratic strokes, I finally let go, exploding inside her, pulsing again and again until my knees almost buckled.

We stayed connected, both of us clinging to each other and catching our breath.

She laughed. "Guess I can say I've joined the Mile High Club now."

I smiled lazily, planting a kiss on her lips. "Give me a minute, and we can go again."

She lightly pinched my nipple and wiggled her hips as I started to grow hard again inside her. "I'll be generous and give you two."

LATER THAT DAY, we pulled up in front of our house. To me, the beach house was already ours. I hadn't told Kennedy yet, but this was where I saw us building our future. I was all in with her.

The four of us piled out of the Model X, grabbing our bags and making our way inside. I took Kennedy's and my bags into our room, quickly going back downstairs to show Grayson and Amara their bedrooms down the hall. Once that was done, I sent a group text to my friends, letting them know what time to show up this afternoon.

Kennedy disappeared into our room to freshen up from the flight, and I followed her in, hoping to catch a glimpse of her changing. I couldn't get enough of her. I'd sit and watch Kennedy get undressed, or fuck, who was I kidding, do literally anything, happily all day every day for the rest of my life.

"How're you doing right now?" I sank down onto the bed and watched her dig through her bag, my eyes exploring every delicious curve. "With the interview," I clarified.

She pulled out a new thong and began sliding it up her legs.

"Hey, what are you doing?" I jumped up and closed the distance between us in just a couple of long strides.

She put her hand on her hip and glared at me. "I'm not going to this interview without underwear on, and you ruined the ones I was wearing." I smirked, giving her a look that said I'd happily ruin these, too.

"I'm already freaked out enough about having to do this." She finished sliding them up her legs and sighed.

I pulled her into my arms, and she melted into me. "I could keep you distracted easier if you take them off." My lowered voice was full of promise.

She buried her head in my chest, breathing deeply. I smiled to myself because I knew I could calm her down like no one else could. I was more proud of that accomplishment than anything else I'd done so far in my life.

"How long do we have?" she mumbled against my chest.

I let out a low chuckle. I loved that she wanted me at least as much as I wanted her. "Not long enough, unfortunately. We've got about five minutes before we have to leave. Hold that thought for when we get home, though."

She leaned back and smiled ruefully up at me. "We'll have a house full of people when we get home."

"Do you think I give a fuck?" Leaning down, I kissed her.

"Zen…"

"You threw down the gauntlet, and I'm picking it up. Challenge accepted."

She stepped back, placing her palms against my chest. I'd let her win this round.

"Fine, I'll behave. But you say the word, and I'll have you in bed before you know what's happening."

It was her turn to laugh. "I'll keep that in mind."

I tightened my arms around her briefly before letting her go to get ready for the interview. As I sat on the bed watching her, I couldn't help but hope that this would be the first step towards gaining back our freedom.

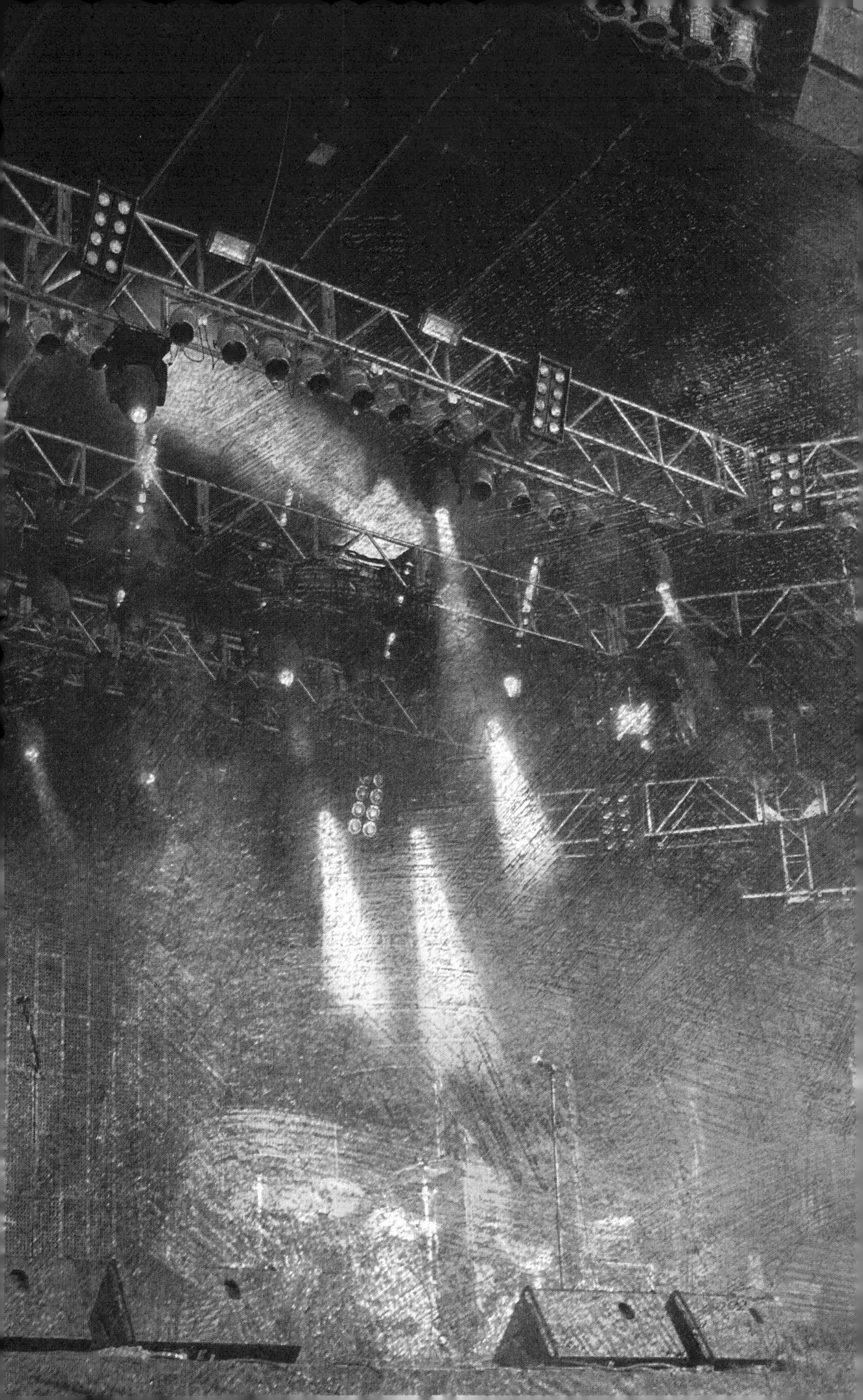

CHAPTER 26

ZEN

GOD, LA traffic sucked. On the plus side, I got to spend the hour it took us to get downtown distracting Kennedy with my hands and mouth. Connor pulled up in front of Harrison's tall, mirrored high rise building, avoiding our eyes and pretending he hadn't seen or heard anything over the last hour.

I really needed to install a privacy barrier in this car.

Harrison's office was sleek and modern with glass walls, white accents, and dark wood floors. The plan was to meet him in his office so we could go over strategy to make sure we wouldn't fuck this up. We only had a few minutes before the reporter showed up.

Kennedy and I stepped off the elevator on the twenty-eighth floor. We were immediately escorted into the glass-walled conference room.

Kennedy was starting to freak out even though she was trying her best to hold it together. I knew her. My body was attuned to hers. Anyone else wouldn't have picked up on the fact she was nervous, but I saw the truth. Her eyes were slightly wide, and she was absently chewing on a non-existent hangnail, staring off into space. The hand I held felt like it had mine in a death grip, and it was cold. She trembled slightly, too.

"Sunshine, look at me." I tilted her chin up until we locked eyes. "We've got this. They'll mostly want to talk to me, and we'll be together the whole time. If you get too uncomfortable, you can leave at any time. If you go, I'll go with you, no questions asked. Whatever we do, we do it together. I don't give a fuck what anyone thinks or says. It's you and me. Okay?"

She nodded, her shoulders relaxing slightly. She exhaled loudly, giving me a small smile. "Thank you."

Harrison swept into the room with a flourish, carrying a stack of notebooks and magazines. "Hey, Z, Kennedy. Nice to meet you. I've been reading past interviews and just trying to do the prep work, so you're not caught off guard by this bloke. His name is Blane Hoffman, and he has a reputation for being a bit of a—"

He paused, his eyes darting between Kennedy and me, clearly trying to figure out a more politically correct version of what was on his mind. I rolled my eyes. "Just say what you're thinking, Harrison. Kennedy cusses almost as much as I do, you're not going to offend her."

Kennedy let out a musical laugh at that moment, breaking the tension. "Damn, you're making me sound like some sort of heathen." For just a second, her eyes sparkled, and I was glad I'd been able to make her forget about her stress even for a second.

Harrison chuckled. "Great, well, in that case, the guy's a complete wanker. I've heard some stories, and I just hope that most of them aren't true. Also," he paused to dig through his paperwork. "I'm hoping that meeting here with me present will keep him on his best behavior, but we have to prepare for the worst."

Kennedy tightened her grip on my hand, and I traced comforting circles on her wrist with my thumb. "What's this guy's deal?"

Harrison shuffled a few more papers around. "From what I've been able to find, he wants to rile you up and get as much drama out of you as possible. The editor at *Pulse* assured me they'd print the article no matter what, so I'm going to suggest you try to stick to the music and even your relationship but really play down the stuff from your past." He said that last part with a glance up at Kennedy.

"Just do your best to keep as calm and on message as you possibly can. The less you give him to work with, the better."

I nodded. "Do you have any questions, Sunshine?"

Kennedy shook her head, taking a breath. "We've got this." I glanced down at her, and she had a look of steely determination in her eyes, and I was so fucking proud of her. A slow smile spread across my face. If there was one thing I was sure of, it was that my girl knew how to handle douchebags. She'd had years of practice. Hell, this might even be fun.

WITH PERFECT TIMING, the guy doing the interview strolled into the office with a cocky grin. I hated him immediately. He had a messenger bag slung over his shoulder and was dressed in a distressed band t-shirt (not my band) and too-tight skinny jeans. His hair was tied up in a bun on top of his head, and he wore dark-rimmed glasses that I doubted he actually needed to see. In fact, I bet if I stuck my finger through, there wouldn't even be glass. He had one of those faces Maddox referred to as punchable. What a tool.

He stepped into the conference room, taking his time pulling shit out of his bag.

His man-purse? Maybe this guy took fashion advice from *Friends*.

Without so much as a glance in my direction, he muttered, "I'm Blane Hoffman. I'll be set up in a sec, and then we can get this over with."

Kennedy glanced over at me, silently asking if I knew what the fuck this guy's deal was. I lifted one shoulder in a shrug. I had no idea. He seemed like not only could he not care less about doing the interview but that we were inconveniencing him. I already couldn't stand the arrogant fucker, and he hadn't said more than a handful of words. Keeping my temper under control was going to be a challenge.

When Blane was done setting up, he strode over to the other side of the table, holding out his fist for a fist bump. It took everything in me to hold back the massive eye roll at the douche vibe he was putting off. His gaze settled on Kennedy, and I saw the interest spark in his eyes.

Clenching my fists, I watched his eyes lingering on her body longer than they should, running up and down her curves and leering over what was mine. I'd never felt more violent in my life, like an animal waiting to be unleashed. I wanted to rip his eyes out of his head and shove them down his throat.

Somehow I didn't think that'd make the best impression, and the whole point of this was to protect Kennedy, so I managed to hold back but barely. His eyes were calculating, trying to figure out his next move. I could see it. He acted as if I weren't even there. It was as if he'd already forgotten I was also in the room despite the fact Kennedy was sitting so close to me she was practically in my lap. I wrapped my arm firmly around her and pulled her even closer.

Blane held out his hand for Kennedy to shake, and she glanced down at it, hesitating as if unsure if she should touch him. I knew she wanted to smack his hand away more than anything. My eyes met hers, and I read her thoughts loud and clear. Her look said *don't worry, I'll rip his balls off and make him eat them in front of us if he tries anything*. Then she flashed me a wicked smile before turning her attention back on super douche. My body relaxed, and I grinned.

That's my girl.

I knew she could sense his bullshit a mile away.

She finally reached her hand out and placed it in his as lightly as she could before trying to snatch it back like his hand was on fire, but Blane must have had other plans. He wrapped his other hand around hers and held on tight, trapping her fingers between his palms. She gave him an over-bright smile before he winced in pain, dropping her hand immediately. We shared a quick glance, and her eyes danced. I knew she'd probably dug her fingernails into his skin to make him pay for touching her without her permission.

He inspected his hand before shaking it and then winking like a total sleaze. "That's some grip you've got there. I bet that comes in handy."

I was going to fucking kill this guy.

Shaking with rage, I found it harder and harder to keep from acting out the violent fantasies currently running through my head. Harrison stepped in before I could completely lose my shit.

"Blane, we only have a short window for the interview. If we could get started, that would be ideal."

Blane tore his eyes off of Kennedy long enough to glance at Harrison before rolling his eyes and whining like the little bitch he was. "Yeah, fine. Let's get this over with."

He made his way back to his computer, sitting down in front of it before his eyes settled back on Kennedy. "Remind me to get your number later, though." The fucker winked at her again, and the muscles in my jaw protested how hard I was clenching my teeth together. I'd be lucky to not crack a molar by the end of this.

Placing her hand on my thigh, Kennedy rubbed soothing circles. When I looked at her, she was glaring at Blane with fire in her eyes. Blane, the douche, had pissed her off even more than he'd pissed me off. Exhaling, some of the tension left my body. She wouldn't stand for this guy treating her like a plaything any more than I would. "I'd rather give my number straight to the paparazzi or post it on the internet than give it to you." Kennedy narrowed her eyes even more until they were little slits, and I swear I could see smoke coming out of her ears.

Blane smirked as if he hadn't heard her. "Yeah, we'll see. Anyway, I have a few questions I've prepared. Feel free to jump in with anything else you want to have on the record once I'm done with the questions. Your team already gave us some photos to go along with the article so we can avoid having to do a photoshoot."

"Fine."

Blane kept smirking, and I wanted to punch it off his face, but I somehow refrained. "Let's just jump in then." He leaned toward me, an evil smile plastered on his smug face. "You've been in hiding since your infamous sex tape hit the internet. Who's the girl in the tape? An ex-girlfriend? And how did it get out?"

My fist twitched as I fought off the urge to smash his face into the table. I swallowed and tried to keep my cool. "She was no one, just a random person I met. She recorded me without my knowledge or permission and released it. I had no idea it existed or would be coming out."

Blane's eyes flicked to Kennedy, waiting for her reaction. I shifted my eyes to the side just as she leaned up and pressed her lips softly against my cheek. I closed my eyes for a second, thanking whatever fucking god existed yet again for bringing me Kennedy. She deserved better than me, but I'd do anything to prove myself worthy of her.

Blane's lips pressed into a thin line, and he tapped his foot. "Is that all you have to say about it?"

"Yep. Next question."

He rolled his eyes and crossed his arms. "Let's talk about Shadow Phoenix's upcoming album. Then we'll dig into more personal stuff," he said, letting his gaze travel up and down Kennedy's body again.

God, this fucker was testing me.

"Then we'll talk about whatever else you feel is important. Sound good?" Finally, he looked up at me, and I put every ounce of possessive caveman asshole into the death glare I gave him in return.

I squeezed Kennedy's hand so hard I felt her tense next to me and loosened my grip, shooting her an apologetic look. She gave me a small smile. She understood.

"Yep," I said through clenched teeth.

Blane looked down at his laptop as if I hadn't just threatened his life with my glare. "You guys have been in the studio working on your seventh album. Do you have an official release date for it yet? Or a title?"

I'd done these types of interviews a thousand times before and felt myself slipping into professional artist mode. "We've been recording for about a month now. We've been writing all new songs and finding inspiration in some unexpected places, which means we're going deeper into our music than we ever have before. It's been an interesting process, but so far, the music is coming out incredible. I'm really excited to share the new stuff with our fans, and I know the guys are, too."

While Blane took notes and checked the phone he'd placed in the center of the table, I flicked my eyes over to Harrison, who gave me a slight nod.

The clicking of Blane's keyboard snapped my attention back to him. "Mmhmm, and when you say you've been going deeper into your music, does that mean you're exploring themes and situations you hadn't previously?"

He seemed bored with this line of questioning, so I knew at some point I'd need to feed this guy something more interesting than Kennedy's story. No time like the present.

"Right, we're older now than we were when we started Shadow Phoenix, and we've grown a lot. We've all been through a lot, and our life experiences are starting to be reflected in our work."

Blane perked up. "Life experiences like relationships?"

I pressed my lips together. The last thing I wanted to do was talk to this asshole about my relationship with Kennedy. I glanced at Harrison, who gave me a pleading look. I exhaled. "Right, like relationships."

Blane looked like a kid on Christmas morning. "We've all seen the tabloids. I didn't take you for a relationships kind of guy. In fact, I don't think I've ever seen you with the same girl more than once. Ever." He emphasized the last word, smiling with glee as if he thought he was sharing this fact with Kennedy for the first time, and maybe he'd have a chance to come between us. "Does that mean you're writing about hookups and one night stands?"

I took a deep, steadying breath. Blane knew how to push all my buttons, and I caught Harrison's worried glance. We'd worked together long enough that Harrison could tell when I was close to blowing up. He shook his head almost imperceptibly.

Fuck.

Kennedy gently squeezed my hand, giving me the reassurance I needed. She never judged me for my past, never worried about the things I'd done before her. It was one of many reasons why I was utterly in love with her.

"I'm not going to sit here and deny any of that, but it's all in the past. Do I wish I could take it all back? Honestly, no, I don't. It's a part of me, what made me into who I am today. That being said, I'm done with all that shit and have been for a while because I've met someone who makes me feel alive in a way I never felt before, someone who has shown me what true strength and determination looks like…" I wasn't sure how much I wanted to reveal. "Someone who I can't imagine my life without. When I met her, it was like my eyes were opening for the first time. I know that sounds really cliché, but it's true."

"That's because you were insanely hungover, and it was a really bright morning," Kennedy's amused voice chimed in, teasing me.

I laughed. "Fair enough, but it was more than that. From the first moment I saw her, I knew I was in trouble."

She beamed at me, her eyes were bright, and her hand gripped mine tightly. She leaned against me, resting her head on my shoulder while we answered questions.

The rest of the interview didn't take long. We made a very brief mention of the time Kennedy spent in "rehab" in high school. The phrasing was Harrison's idea, and Blane seemed to want to linger more on our relationship than on that little fact, which worked out perfectly. He tried to put a wedge between Kennedy and me at every opportunity, but we were rock solid. There was nothing Blane could say or do that she didn't already know. He got more and more frustrated as the interview went on, especially as he realized his shitty tactics weren't working.

Despite Blane's attempts at sabotaging our relationship, the interview went as well as it could have. Kennedy held her own, was her usual charming self, and immediately shut down any and all advances by the jackass.

Blane's face reddened as he turned off his recorder and shoved his computer and notes into his bag. He didn't seem like he was used to being turned down by women, and Kennedy didn't give him an inch, busting his balls every chance she got. I'd never been more impressed with anyone.

Harrison walked him out, tossing a smirk over his shoulder at me. Kennedy and I were alone in the conference room for the first time since we'd gotten there, and I finally felt like I could breathe. "That was like the fucking eighth circle of hell," I noted, brushing hair off her face and tucking it behind her ear. My fingers lingered on her cheek, and she leaned into my touch.

"It was," she agreed, sighing.

"You did so well, baby. I'm proud of you. These interviews are never easy. They're like vultures looking for a scrap of meat. Not to mention that fucker was completely out of line." My blood heated all over again at the reminder of how Blane looked at Kennedy as if he planned on eating her for dinner.

"He was a creep, but nothing I couldn't handle." She smiled, and for the first time since we got off the plane, she looked relaxed.

"I wanted to kill him."

"I know, but he's not worth the jail time."

She made me feel like we could conquer the world together. She'd stood toe to toe with one of Hollywood's most scummy reporters and came out unscathed. I grinned.

"What's that smile for?" she asked, smiling back at me. "Not that I don't love it, because I do. That smile does things to me." Her eyes lowered to my lips.

"Things? What kind of things?" My voice went husky as I lowered my mouth to hers and pressed a soft kiss there.

"For starters, it makes me want you to throw me on this table right here." She gestured to the conference table in front of us.

"Baby, keep talking like that and you're going to get your wish." My dick instantly hardened.

Her breathing hitched, and she licked her lips. "Promises, promises."

Fuck, I needed to get us out of here and fast. When it came to Kennedy wanting me, I couldn't help but give her everything she asked for and more. Telling her no wasn't an option. The best thing I could hope was to postpone the inevitable until we were somewhere more private, even if that meant the back seat of my car.

Connor was in for an exciting drive home.

I stood up, pulling her with me. "Let's go. I need to be inside you, and I don't think I can wait until we get home."

She laughed, almost having to jog to keep up with my long strides.

"Harrison, text me about the article," I yelled out in passing, jamming my thumb into the elevator call button. I glanced at the sign for the stairs, considering whether to run down twenty-eight flights instead of waiting.

I may not be ready to tell her yet, but I planned on spending a good part of the afternoon showing Kennedy just how much I loved her.

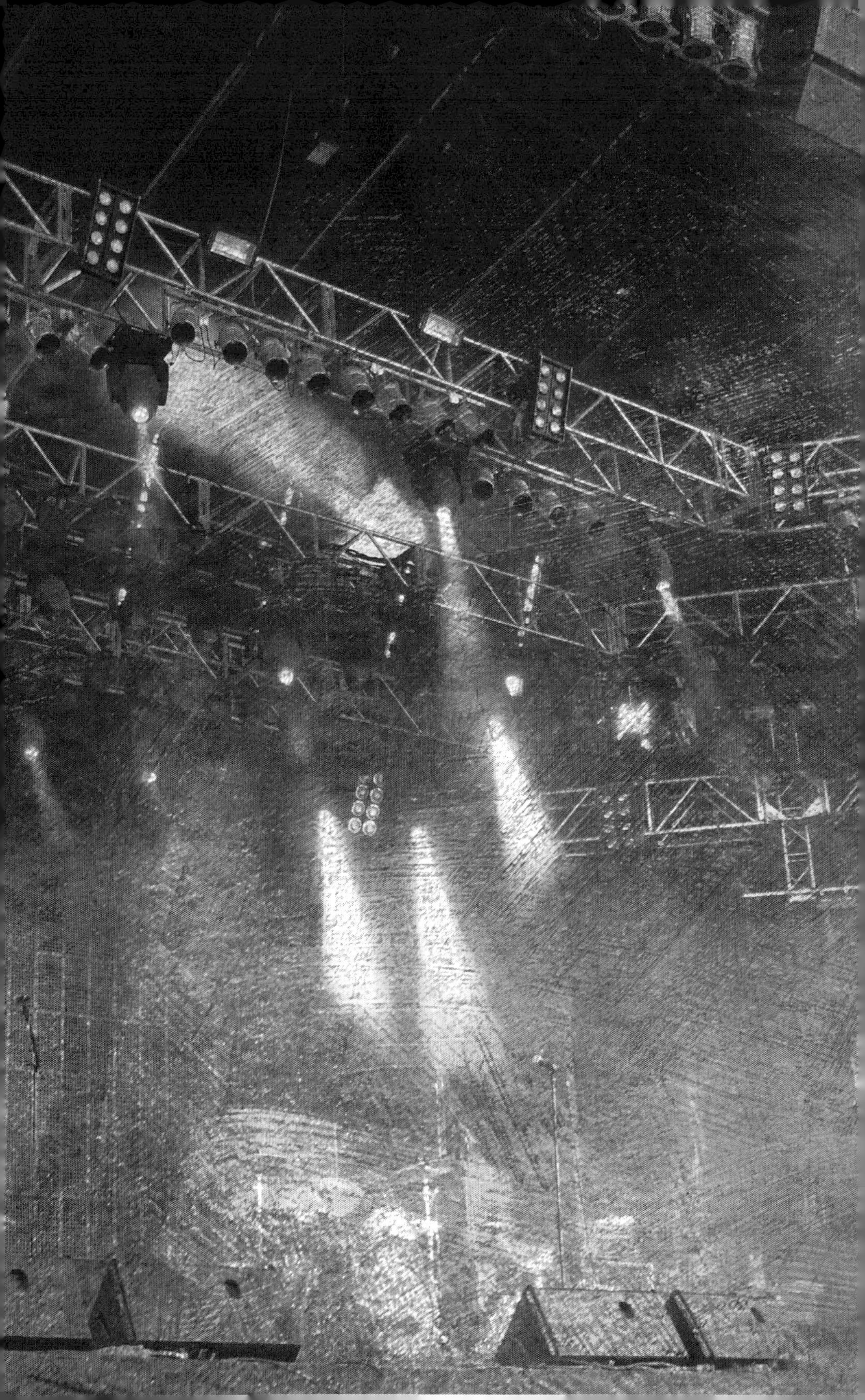

CHAPTER 27

ZEN

WALKING INTO THE HOUSE, I heard voices and laughter echoing down the hall. In the past, when I came home, my house was either silent, or my friends were throwing a party. These sounds were different, but I found myself smiling. My house felt warm, like a home. It was filled with our friends and family. I hadn't known how much I needed it until just this moment. Kennedy brought warmth into my life. It was why I called her my sunshine.

Kennedy smiled brightly at me, her eyes shining. "Let's go see what kinds of trouble they've gotten into while we were gone." I chuckled, letting her pull me towards the kitchen.

"Hey, they're back!" Grayson called out to Amara from behind the island, looking up from the vegetables he was chopping.

"Ken!" Amara squealed, running over and throwing her arms around Kennedy's neck. "How was it? Tell me everything." Amara pulled Kennedy from my grasp toward the deck outside. Kennedy threw an apologetic smile over her shoulder before turning and following. I watched her go, completely consumed with the swaying of her hips and the way the sunlight shone off her golden hair.

"Damn, man. You've really got it bad." Grayson gave me a knowing smile before walking to the fridge. "Beer?"

I reluctantly tore my gaze away, taking the beer Grayson held out for me and twisting off the top. "What's for dinner?"

"I thought we'd do Mexican. Enchiladas, tacos, quesadillas. Even with everyone that's coming, I don't think we'll be able to eat all the food." He laughed. "I was worried about Kennedy, though, and when I stress, I cook."

I sipped my beer. "I get that. When I stress, I write. Whatever works."

"When are your buddies showing up?"

"Anytime. I texted them on our way home to let them know they should come over. Who knows what they're up to, though." Pulling out a bar stool, I sat down. "Can I help with anything?"

"Nah, I've got it. Thanks." Grayson pulled a bunch of cilantro onto the cutting board and began chopping.

The front door burst open, and Maddox called out, "Time to get this party started!"

I rolled my eyes but grinned, hopping off the stool and turning until I spotted Kennedy. I breathed a sigh of relief when I saw her outside on the deck, still talking to Amara. My three best friends strolled into the kitchen.

"What's up, asshole?" Maddox asked.

True rolled his eyes. "Maddox is so classy."

Jericho's lips twitched in an almost smile before his almond eyes scanned the room for what I could only assume was Kennedy. "Where's your girl, Z? I want to say hi."

"She's outside." I jerked my head in the direction of the patio.

True and Maddox turned their heads, too, both of their eyes going slightly wide before they looked at each other, grinning.

"Just calm the fuck down." Before they could even say anything, I had to cut this shit off. "That's Kennedy's best friend, Amara. She's off-limits to you two."

True placed a hand over his heart. "You wound me. Maybe she's my soulmate. You don't know. Are you going to stand in the way of destiny?"

Maddox laughed, throwing his head back. "I wish you could hear yourself. You sound like a chick." He turned his attention to me. "She's not my type."

"Good but I mean it. She's going to be around a lot, so don't go fucking it up," I warned.

"Yeah, yeah. We get it, dad," Maddox mocked.

"Before you two go out there and make fools of yourselves, come meet Grayson." They followed me into the kitchen, and Grayson stopped mixing whatever was in the bowl he was holding. He walked out from behind the counter.

"Hey, I'm Grayson, Kennedy's brother. Good to meet you." He nodded at each of them in greeting.

"Kennedy has a brother? You never told us that, Z," True said, smiling at Grayson. "It's nice to meet you, too. I'm True. Sorry you've had to put up with this asshole," he said, pointing at me.

"Ha-ha." I picked up my beer, taking a long pull.

"Maddox."

"I'm Jericho," he said coolly, as he looked past Grayson to the meal in progress spread throughout the kitchen. He turned and went out to the patio to greet the girls without another word.

I watched as Kennedy hopped up and gave him a hug, smiling up at him before dragging him to the empty chair at the table. I chuckled. Jericho was the last guy on earth who would typically participate in a gossip session with a couple of girls. Yet, there he was with a grin on his face indulging Kennedy and her friend enthusiastically. It was just what she did. She had this irresistibility about her, people couldn't tell her no. It was probably a good thing she didn't realize she had this power, but that just made her all the more attractive.

I turned back to my friends and Grayson. "Gray, how long until dinner's ready?"

"Fifteen minutes or so. You can start taking stuff to the table."

I grabbed plates from the cupboard, motioning for Maddox and True to follow. We made quick work of setting the table and bringing what Grayson had already finished out. A knock sounded on the door, but before I could see who it was, the door opened and slammed shut.

Whoever it was had to pass security, so I wasn't concerned.

"Hey! Anybody home?" Montana called out a few seconds before she popped into the kitchen, followed by Harrison.

"Oh yeah, I invited Montana and Harrison." True rubbed the back of his neck. My agent and our publicist hung out with us a lot as our unofficial fifth and sixth members.

"I brought beer!" Montana held up a case of an expensive imported beer. We treated her like a little sister even though she was the same age as all of us. It was a good thing she didn't date and focused on her job because I doubt anyone she'd bring around would stand up to all of our standards for treating her.

"That'll go great with the food." Grayson grinned, lifting the box out of her hands.

"Who are you?" Montana leveled her curious gaze on Grayson.

"Grayson, Kennedy's brother." He gave her a little wave as he pulled bottles out of the box and stuck them in the fridge.

Montana looked around before noticing the table outside where Kennedy, Amara, and Jericho sat. "I take it one of them is her?"

I nodded. "The gorgeous blonde."

"I'd better go get in on that action, then." Montana smoothed down her fiery hair. "It's about time you assholes brought some other women around for me to hang out with, instead of the usual skanks."

She made her way outside, and I watched as Kennedy and Amara both stood up and hugged her as if they were old friends. Jericho took that as his signal to leave and headed back inside with all the guys.

True glanced at Jericho with a smirk. "You one of the girls now? Going to braid each other's hair?"

"Ha-ha. You go out there, and they'll eat you alive. Fair warning." Jericho flashed me a knowing look before chuckling.

"Yeah, we'll see. Girls love me and my sweet as fuck charm." True grinned before turning and walking outside.

I cracked a smile as I looked outside, watching the girl I couldn't seem to tear my eyes away from. For the first time in as long as I could remember I was relaxed and happy, and it was all because of Kennedy and the people she brought into my life. She made everything seem lighter and more fun.

I picked up a plate and scooped guacamole onto it. I looked up as True followed behind Amara with a dazed look in his eye. He didn't even look my way because his attention was focused entirely on the exotic beauty in front of him. That fucker was going to piss me off if he made things awkward between my girl and our friends. I could only hope he wouldn't fuck things up by falling in love.

I glanced at Kennedy, and she lifted one of her shoulders, her eyes filled with amusement. My body relaxed. If Kennedy didn't seem concerned, I'd trust her to know her friend better than I did. She walked over to me, stopping to place her palm on my chest and push up on her toes, stealing a soft kiss.

I set down my plate and wrapped my arms around her waist, lowered my voice, and whispered in her ear, "Let's have dinner in bed."

Kennedy's pupils dilated, and she pressed a little closer. "You know I can't. My brother cooked this for everyone." She looked away before biting her lip. "How about dessert in bed, though?"

My eyes immediately dropped to her mouth, and every muscle

in my body tightened, begging for her. "I don't know if I can wait until dessert, Sunshine."

She pressed her perfect tits against my chest, and her skin flushed. Her mouth parted and drifted toward mine until her warm breath brushed across my lips. It took every ounce of will I had to tear myself away from her, pressing a soft kiss to her forehead before I grabbed her hand, curled my fingers around hers, and kissed her knuckles.

Picking up my plate, I filled it with food I no longer had an appetite for. My body craved only one thing: Kennedy.

She blew out a breath, and I leaned over and whispered in her ear. "How fast can you eat, baby?"

Excitement lit her eyes. "Pretty fast, but wouldn't it'd be rude? We can contain ourselves until after dinner, right? We're adults. We can do this."

I was pretty sure she was trying to convince herself more than she was saying it for my benefit, which was fucking adorable.

We took our seats and dug in. Everyone got along better than I even thought possible, considering my friends could be complete jackasses. Jericho even joined the conversation, talking animatedly with Kennedy and Montana about his latest video game find. I stared at him with my jaw slack for a minute while I wondered what the hell he'd done with my friend and who this guy was in his place.

I watched as True tried (and failed) to get Amara to give him any attention. She seemed to enjoy talking to him, but if he tried to flirt, she immediately shut him down. I'd been laughing my ass off most of the night. Amara and Kennedy made quite the ballbusting pair.

Harrison, Grayson, and Maddox got into a discussion about organic food. It was boring as fuck, so I mostly tuned out, instead alternating between watching True fail epically and staring at Kennedy.

Her hand traced slow circles up and down my thigh, inching

higher and higher. She teased me all through dinner, keeping me at least semi-hard the entire time. I leaned close to her, placing a kiss just below her ear and watched her shiver. The way her body reacted to mine sent heat spiraling to my groin.

The tension from earlier hadn't gone away. If anything, it'd grown into a fucking monster, and we were both on the verge of giving in and devouring each other.

My arm rested across the back of Kennedy's chair while my thumb lightly stroked her shoulder. The heat of her body ran down my side like she really was my own personal sun. She turned her huge blue eyes on me, her silent plea to give her relief coming across loud and clear.

Her desire radiated around her like a storm cloud ready to burst, electricity pulsing, and snapping between us. My heart started to pound.

My girl needed me, and I'd make sure I took care of her, but I wouldn't do anything here at the table with all our friends and family as witnesses. We needed to get away.

Now.

Standing, my chair scraped across the floor as everyone's eyes were on me. I tugged Kennedy up out of her chair, moving her in front of me so she hid my hard-on. "Thanks for dinner, Gray. I'm ready for dessert, though, so we'll see you later."

Kennedy gasped before smacking me lightly on the chest. I let out a low chuckle before grabbing her hand and practically dragging her behind me. She called out, "Don't leave, we'll be back!"

"No, we won't, baby." It came out like a growl, and right now, I felt more animal than man. The need to get inside her overwhelmed me.

"We can't just leave our own dinner, can we? Isn't that rude?"

"I don't give a fuck. They're in our house eating our food. We stayed for the entire dinner, which is longer than I thought we'd make it. I'm done waiting."

"Me, too." She launched herself at me as I stepped into our bedroom and kicked the door shut behind us. If I could, I'd lock us in this room forever to keep her safe, but she'd never let me. I didn't know what would happen next, but I knew we had tonight and I planned to make the most of it.

I WOKE up with Kennedy's naked body wrapped around mine. The entire wall in our bedroom was open to the ocean, and the moonlight reflected off the waves. A breeze off the water filtered into the room and rustled the gauzy curtains that hung around our bed.

My eyes drifted down her sleeping form, taking in her golden hair, her glowing skin, and the light dusting of freckles that covered her shoulders. I pressed my nose into her hair, inhaling her scent. I could live in this moment forever.

Kennedy had become my biggest passion; my thoughts were filled with her. I found myself never wanting to be away from her. The moments like this where I got to hold her in my arms and just be, the calm and peaceful moments where we could get lost in each other were suddenly what made life worth living.

My fingertips lazily ran up and down the silky skin of her back. My eyes drifted closed as my other senses became heightened. Her warm vanilla scent, the heat of her body pressed against mine, her taste on my tongue, the sound of the breath leaving her swollen lips.

After dinner, we ravaged each other again and again until we passed out from exhaustion. Neither one of us could get enough of the other, but it was always like that with Kennedy. We were explosive together. I'd never met anyone like her. She made me want to give her the world, to be a better person.

She nuzzled her head into the crook of my neck, her fingers

dancing along the lines of my abs. "Sunshine?" I whispered, not wanting to wake her if she wasn't already up.

"Hmm?"

"I need to tell you something."

She tilted her head up until her sleepy gaze met mine. My heart hammered in my chest, and I was sure she could feel it under the hand she had resting on my chest. I'd wanted to tell her for a while but hadn't felt the time was right. This moment right here felt perfect.

Fuck it.

Despite how ready I was to tell her, I was fucking terrified I'd scare her off. There were questions in her eyes, but she stayed silent, giving me space to speak when I felt ready. Time didn't exist in this paradise of ours, the darkness of night blanketing us in quiet. The nearly full moon outside was our only light.

"Baby, you're the bravest person I know. When I wake up in the morning, and you're not in my arms, I know that day is going to suck because that means you're not here."

She watched me as her hand drifted across my chest. "I'm so proud of you, and even though we only met a few weeks ago, I can't imagine my life without you. You're what makes my life worth anything. When we're not together, all I do is think about you, and when we are together, I can't get enough of you. I never want to let you go."

I sucked in a breath trying to will my heart to calm the fuck down. "My whole life, I never knew I needed anyone else. I've always been so independent, and I fucking hate leaning on people, but you came along and broke down every single wall I'd thrown up. I know you don't see it, but you light up every room you walk into. I still can't believe I'm the lucky bastard you decided you want."

I slightly shook my head, running my thumb along her cheek before pressing my palm against her face. "Kennedy, I love you.

I've loved you since the first sober moment I met you, maybe even the first drugged moment." I chuckled. "If I could remember it."

She giggled, the tinkling notes of her musical laugh echoing around the quiet room. I had no idea what to expect from her, but my greatest wish would be for her to feel the same way.

She pushed her body up against mine, throwing her leg over my hips and straddling me. She gazed down into my eyes, hers dark with intent and burning with something else.

Love?

I was afraid to hope.

She placed both her hands against my jaw, leaning down to press her forehead to mine. "I love you, too, Zen. You're everything to me."

Warmth flooded my chest as I surged up and captured her lips in a heated kiss that quickly deepened, our tongues tangling together. She loved me. I needed to hear her repeat it because I almost couldn't believe my own ears.

"Say it again," I demanded.

"I love you, Zen Taylor. I love you," she laughed softly as I rolled her over and covered her body with mine.

STEPPING OFF THE PLANE, we said our goodbyes to Grayson and Amara before driving back to Sweet Stories. The store was closed on Sundays, so we'd be spending the day at Kennedy's so she could prep for the upcoming week.

On the flight, Kennedy told me she planned to reopen the store this week. I didn't want her to because it left her vulnerable while the stalker situation was still up in the air, but there wasn't anything I could do. I refused to be as overbearing as my heart was demanding. The possessive asshole inside was getting harder to shove down when it came to Kennedy's safety, but thankfully the logical side of my brain was still in control.

During dinner Friday, Harrison let us know the article would be coming out tomorrow, so I'd bet the paparazzi presence would get a fuck ton worse this week before it got better.

I told the guys not to bother coming up this week. They weren't happy about postponing again, but I hadn't left them much fucking choice. I wasn't going to leave her alone no matter what, and I didn't give a shit how pissed off they got. They told me they'd help, so I expected them to stick to their word and get over it.

We pulled up to Sweet Stories, and I glanced out the window. A crowd of about twenty paparazzi camped outside despite the fact the store was closed. I let out a heavy sigh. "You ready for this, Sunshine?"

With a determined gleam in her eye, she jerked her head in a nod.

Connor hopped out of the driver's seat, coming around to open the door for us and clear a path. The photographers jumped up as expected, crowding around us as if we were the next coming of Jesus or some shit. My jaw tightened as we pushed our way through. When we reached the front of the store, I took out my key and unlocked the door.

Kennedy practically knocked me over to get inside. I slammed the door shut as Connor went to the windows to lower the blinds. I had no idea how we'd keep the cameras out tomorrow when the store opened.

Kennedy wrinkled her nose as she glanced outside through a crack in the blinds. "Those guys are such snakes, selling personal pictures for a quick buck. It's fucking disgusting."

I brushed her hair off her face and tucked a strand behind her ear before leaning down to place a firm kiss on her mouth. "Yeah, they suck." I smiled against her lips.

She giggled. "Fuck those cunt nuggets."

I threw my head back and laughed. "I love you so much."

She beamed up at me. "I love you, too."

WE CLIMBED the stairs to the apartment side by side, the apartment where we'd spent so many nights getting to know each other and where Kennedy no longer felt safe. I wanted to whisk her away from this place and move her to LA right now, but she needed her own space until she decided she was ready. It wasn't my decision to make for her.

She unlocked the door, and it swung open. She walked ahead of me as I turned to close the door. Kennedy's keys hit the floor with a loud metallic thud, and I spun around to figure out what happened.

Frozen in place, her wide eyes were locked onto the wall in front of her living room. Closing the gap between us, I wrapped her in my arms. I needed to make sure she was okay before I could think about anything else.

"What's wrong, baby?" My stomach rolled, and weight crushed down on my chest as adrenaline made my heart rate spike.

Kennedy didn't speak, instead pointing with a shaky finger at the wall in front of us. My eyes followed her trembling finger, and my breath caught. "Oh, fuck."

Drips hung from each red spray-painted letter spanning the length of the wall.

I warned you. Now everyone you love dies.

Kennedy shook in my arms, and I broke the skin of my palms, digging my nails into them to keep from smashing through the wall with my fists. The edges of my vision were turning black as the tunnel vision of rage started to consume me.

Scooping up her keys from the floor, I led her back down the stairs. Her hand shook, and her eyes overflowed with tears that traced tracks down her cheeks.

Leaving Kennedy in the cafe, I stormed over to Connor as my rage swirled. Connor sensed me coming and turned, his phone still pressed to his ear. When he took in the look on my face, he immediately hung up the call without a word.

I got in his face and jabbed my finger into his chest. "I don't know how the fuck this keeps happening, but I'm done. Whatever the fuck you have to do, do it. I'm done letting the woman I love be threatened. Do. You. Understand?"

"I understand. You can back the fuck up. I don't want to see anything happen to Kennedy and would lay down my fucking life if I had to for her. So you can keep your fucking anger pointed where it belongs, at the person doing this shit." Connor's face was inches from mine, and his jaw clenched. His fists tightened at his sides. He looked just as pissed off as I felt, and I almost wished he'd hit me so I could fight out my fury.

But I liked Connor for a reason. He took this shit personally. Kennedy was under his protection, and I knew it wouldn't sit well with the ex-Marine that someone got through his team. Again.

"Go look upstairs. We're leaving in five minutes."

Turning to Kennedy, I softened my tone. "Baby, you're okay, we're okay. Connor will handle this. We won't let anything happen to you." I leaned down and pressed a kiss to her forehead before standing back up and moving in front of her protectively. I dared any motherfuckers to come out of the empty shelves and test me.

She looked up at me as tears continued to stream down her face. "What about Grayson and Amara? This person's not only threatening me anymore."

"I'll text Gray from the car and ask him to talk to Amara. We'll set them up with security, too, although I doubt your brother's going to be very happy." All I could do was laugh. Grayson would be *pissed.*

Kennedy nodded, sniffling quietly. If Connor were down here, I'd pull her into my arms, but I needed to keep watch. The paint on the wall was still wet. What if they were still here?

The need to keep her safe welled up inside me. It was up to me to be the barrier between my rock star persona and my real life, and I intended to keep the two separated for her sake. It fucking killed me that so far I was doing a shitty job.

After getting into the car, Kennedy curled up against me like a kitten, her legs stretched across my lap. My fingers sifted through her hair soothingly. I sent a text to Grayson, letting him know what happened, and he responded exactly how I thought he would. He said he could take care of himself, but no fucking way was her brother's pride going to cause her any pain. If Grayson got hurt, Kennedy would be devastated.

Security was not fucking optional, and I let him know it.

Kennedy slid the phone out of her pocket and texted Chloe. My girl was so steadfast. She wouldn't let this stop her from reopening. I tried to talk her out of it, but she said that meant they won. The fire in her eyes told me I wouldn't win this argument, so I met Connor's gaze in the rearview mirror instead, a silent agreement passing between us. Both of us would be sticking to Kennedy like glue until we caught the person responsible.

We pulled up to my house, and I took Kennedy inside. She flopped down onto the couch, pulling out her phone and sending a text. She grabbed the Xbox controller and turned on the console, reaching for the headset.

I cracked a smile. "What are you going to play?"

She looked down at her buzzing phone, tapping at the screen. "Not sure. I texted Jericho to see if he'd play with me." A warm feeling washed over me, and I briefly felt overwhelmed with everything that had happened in such a short time. Most of all, I was grateful Jericho could be there to distract Kennedy now while I handled shit with Connor.

She looked up at me with puffy eyes and messy hair, but I'd still never seen anyone more beautiful. She made my chest ache. "He's getting on right now."

"Have fun, Sunshine. I'll be in the office with Connor. Julian will be out here if you need anything." I shot Julian a warning glare that said *nothing better fucking happen to one hair on her beautiful head* before leaning down to drop a kiss on the tip of her nose.

I turned and walked into my office. Connor already sat in front of my desk, waiting. "Tell me we've got a fucking lead or a plan or anything," I began, my voice hard and unyielding. I only hired the best, so I knew if I fired Connor over this, I wouldn't find better to replace him. Despite recent events, I fucking trusted him, and that didn't come easy for me.

I had to have faith that he was doing everything he could, but I found it difficult when a mistake meant jeopardizing Kennedy's safety.

"We don't know how they keep getting around our safety protocols, but the way they move around Kennedy's building makes us believe it's someone familiar with her or someone she interacts with regularly. They have access already. She's friendly with essentially everyone on her block, so we've started canvassing, talking to neighbors, and running background checks on everyone we can. We're waiting on results now, but we should have them by tomorrow. Until then, the two of you are safest here where we have front gate security and Julian and me to monitor the house, plus cameras covering every inch of the exterior." Connor folded his arms across his chest.

I blew out an irritated breath. "That's all we can do right now? Hole up and wait?"

He nodded. "Yes. It's not for long. Hopefully, tomorrow we'll have some answers."

"Hopefully? Get me some fucking answers, Connor. No matter what it takes, I want this over by the end of the week. Do whatever you have to. I mean it, whatever you have to." I didn't care if he had to break the law, lie, cheat, steal, kill. I didn't fucking care at this point. I had no limits where Kennedy was concerned.

"Understood."

If they hadn't caught this asshole by the end of the week, I'd take drastic measures. I hoped I didn't have to, but I'd do anything to keep Kennedy safe, even if it meant giving everything up.

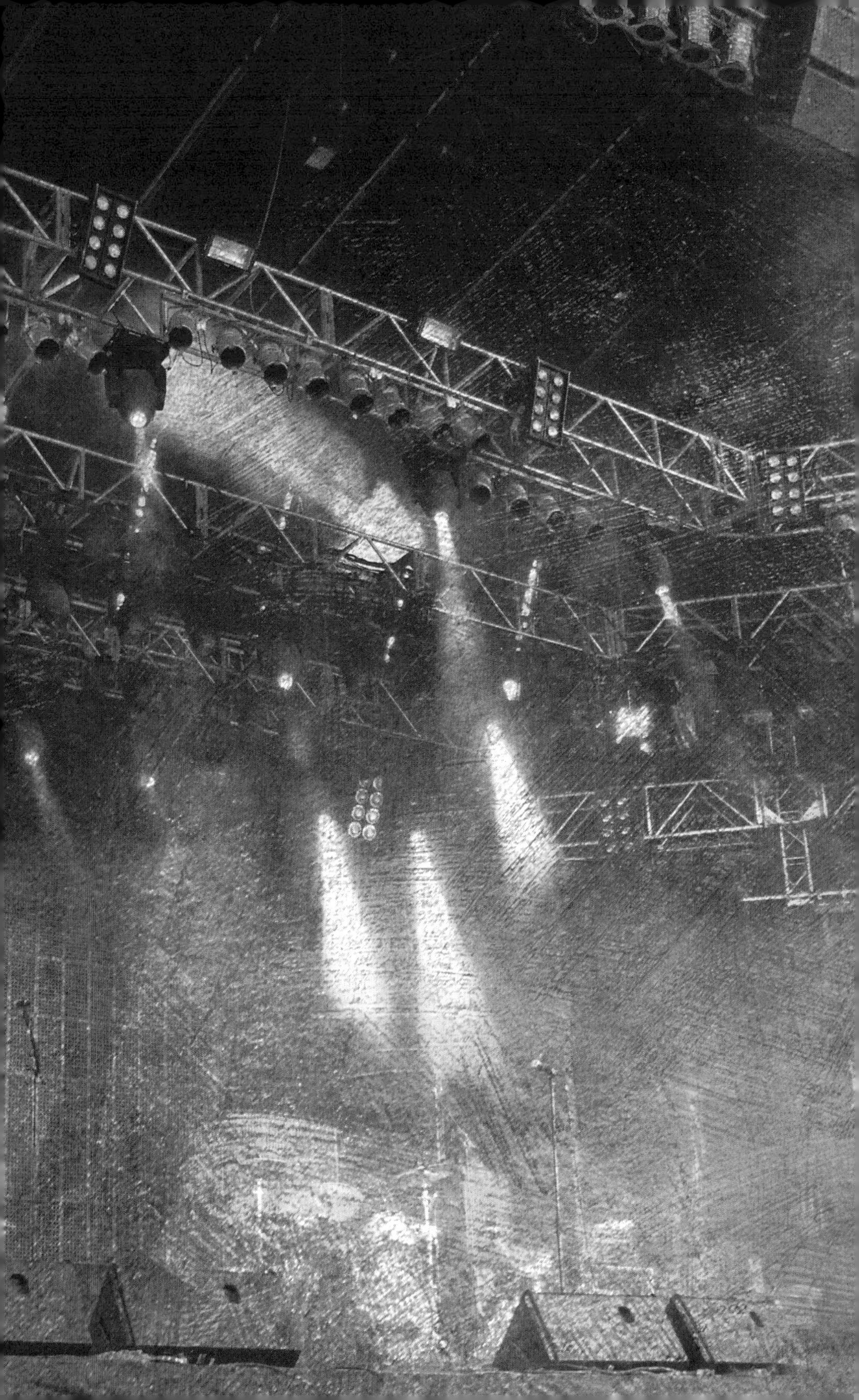

CHAPTER 28

KENNEDY

TANGLED up in soft cotton sheets, I woke up with the bed next to me cold. It took a second before I realized that I wasn't in my own bed, and a lazy smile spread across my face when I remembered last night.

Stretching, I sat up, pulling the sheet up around my naked body. Zen hadn't let me out of his sight for more than a few minutes at a time in days. I knew he'd be close by. My body was so attuned to him I could feel his presence without seeing him. Sure enough, a few minutes later, he came through the door holding two cups of coffee.

He smiled, holding out one of the cups of deliciousness for me. "Good morning, Sunshine. I thought you'd want to start your day with some coffee, so I had Julian grab some. How'd you sleep?"

I took a small sip of the burning liquid as I watched him sit down on the bed. "I slept great until I woke up and you weren't here. I was a little disoriented."

He frowned slightly. "I'm sorry, baby. I should've thought about that. You're not used to traveling and waking up in a different bed or a different room all the time like we do. It won't happen again." He leaned over and kissed me softly.

"It really wasn't a big deal. I'll get used to it, I'm sure."

"You won't have to because it won't happen again."

I blew out a breath. "Thanks."

"You don't have to thank me. I want you to feel safe. Making that happen is just part of my job as your boyfriend. A job I love, by the way." He grinned before lifting his own cup to his mouth. "What's your plan this morning?" He set his coffee down on the nightstand.

I pulled my lip between my teeth as I thought about what I wanted to do today. Reaching for my phone on the nightstand, the sheet slipped down to my waist, exposing my chest to the cool air in the room. I shivered as cold air breezed against my skin, causing my nipples to harden.

I left the sheet where it was. The way Zen worshipped my body made me want to show it off to him. I brought my phone up to check the time and glanced over the top at Zen. His steamy gaze was locked on my chest, and I shimmied my shoulders a little, shaking my boobs playfully. "See something you like?"

A wicked smile crossed his face before his gaze traveled slowly back to mine. I swear the heat in it made me feel like I could combust. "I could stare at you all day and never get tired of it," he said, his voice husky. "Are you planning on starting your day with a shower?"

Tossing my phone aside, I leaned forward and crawled toward him, throwing my legs over his lap until I straddled him. Then, I ran my thumb over his bottom lip. "Yep, want to come in me?"

He coughed. "What?"

I giggled. "I meant want to come in with me?"

He growled, gripping my thighs and standing up, and I grabbed his shoulders to steady myself. "Hey! Watch where you're going!" His eyes were locked on my boobs again as he carried me toward the bathroom.

I don't know how he did it, but he managed to get us into the bathroom before he set me down. He quickly turned on the water and pushed me against the wall.

AN HOUR LATER, I'd showered, dressed, and found myself in the back of an SUV with Connor at the wheel. Zen sat next to me, the left side of his body pressed along the right side of mine. His fingers intertwined with mine, and I gave him a small smile as he squeezed my hand.

Despite Zen and Connor's protests, I planned on reopening Sweet Stories today. Having to close down last week blew. Not only did my regular customers depend on me, but so did Chloe. On top of that, I loved my store and refused to let anyone destroy what I worked so hard to build.

I hadn't worked out how it would all go yet, particularly with the crowd of vulturous jackasses, also known as paparazzi, still hanging around. There were at least twenty-five of them when we pulled up in front of my store, the crowd even bigger than last week.

Zen prepared me for this. He knew it'd be coming even though he hoped the interview would tone the interest in me down. I was ready for whatever came. It didn't make getting through right now much easier, though.

Today was the first step. I texted Chloe yesterday, letting her know I'd need her at work today. I'd be reclaiming my life. I refused to let this stalker win.

Still, it bothered me. How had someone gotten such unrestricted access to the places that were most private to me? The people I cared about the most? I worried that whoever this was clearly knew how to get to me and made threats against not only my safety but Grayson's and Amara's, too. At least they weren't threatening Zen. I didn't think I could handle that.

We exited the car as Connor led the way into the store. Zen gripped my hand, and I put my head down and stared at the sidewalk while questions were shouted, and lights flashed all around us.

Having Connor and Zen here made me feel safe. There had been a few instances over the past few days where I'd feel a freak out coming on, but I slipped earbuds in my ears and listened to my song, getting lost in Zen's haunting, smoky voice. I'd developed a coping mechanism where I almost went into a meditative state using the music as something to focus on. I breathed deeply to the mellow beat of the music to calm myself down.

Stepping into the store, I ran for the stairs, taking them two at a time with Zen on my heels. He swung the door open and asked me to wait outside while he checked to be sure it was safe. I had to admit, protective Zen was hot as fuck. Connor stayed downstairs and checked the store for anything out of place.

Zen stepped into the doorway and motioned for me to come inside. He pressed me into his side, shielding my eyes from the destroyed living room wall and taking me to the bedroom. A chill ran through me when the window next to my bed came into view, and I thought about the figure standing over me. He felt me shiver next to him and pulled me even closer.

"It's weird being here now. It doesn't feel safe, it doesn't feel like home anymore. I don't know how to get that feeling of security back that this place used to bring me." I turned my head into his chest as my eyes welled up with tears.

"I know, I'm sorry, baby. You have no idea how sorry I am, but we're going to catch the bastard who did this. I can promise you that, and when we do, I think that will go a long way towards making you feel safe again." Zen ran his fingers through my hair.

"It's not your fault. I don't blame you. I want to be in your life, and I know this is what I'm signing up for. I guess I just wasn't expecting to be thrown in the deep end like this so quickly. I thought I'd have some time to adjust." I gave him a watery smile before stepping out of his arms and walking into the closet.

I grabbed a bag and started throwing in clothes. I had no intention of staying in this apartment until the stalker had been caught. Even if I wanted to, I doubted either Zen or Connor would let me. I finished stuffing clothes into the bag before throwing on some skinny jeans and a lightweight cardigan over a tank top and slipping on some flats.

Connor's deep voice carried through the loft. "Zen? Kennedy?"

"We're in here, Connor," Zen called back.

Connor's heavy footsteps echoed down the hall before he strode into the room. "Julian just called, and both new security guards were no-shows today. We don't know what happened, but he saw suspicious activity on the cameras at your house. I've checked the entire perimeter here, and everything is clear. He needs backup."

He hesitated, his eyes trained on Zen. "Either you go, or I go, and I'd rather not go. This person hasn't made threats against you, but they have against Kennedy. No offense, but I'm trained to disarm and protect. I can take someone down if necessary, and I wouldn't hesitate to do it to protect her."

Connor glanced at me, tilting his head in a slight nod before turning back to Zen. I was grateful for his loyalty. I'd always liked Connor. His eyes were friendly, and he had a big heart, even if he hid it underneath a gruff exterior. I didn't know much about him other than he was an ex-Marine who protected my boyfriend. I made a mental note to get to know him better when all this was over.

If he'd be with us long-term, I wanted to be on friendly terms. I couldn't see a scenario, unless Zen quit the band, where we wouldn't need at least some form of security. Zen had already mentioned this wasn't the first time he'd dealt with this type of stalker situation. With my fucked up imagination, I only saw it getting worse with our relationship out in the open.

Up until now, Zen had always been available. Now that he'd claimed me as his publicly, I bet his female fans probably weren't taking the news so well.

Zen let out a frustrated breath. "Goddamnit. Of course, this had to happen today of all days. How the fuck does this keep happening?" He rubbed his hand over his scruff. "You're right, Connor. Fuck, you're right. I just—" His eyes darkened, and his tone was lethal. "Nothing will happen while I'm gone. Not a single thing, Connor, or I'll go fucking scorched earth."

"I won't leave her side until you get back," Connor promised.

Zen sighed heavily. "Fuck. I really don't think I should go."

I stepped towards him, wrapping my arms around his waist. "It's only going to be, what? Half an hour? Maybe an hour? I'll be fine. Connor is well-trained, and I trust him, and I know deep down you do, too. So go and come back quickly." I rested my hand against his cheek, pressing my lips to his lightly.

He stepped out of my arms, leaning down to kiss me again before reaching down for the bag I'd packed. "Is this ready to go? I'll take it with me."

I nodded. "Yep, thanks. I hope you don't mind that I basically invited myself to stay with you indefinitely. I just don't feel safe here right now."

Zen stopped and dropped my bag before lifting my chin until I stared into his intense green eyes. "Never apologize for that. If it were up to me, you'd move in with me right now for good, so please don't feel like you're unwanted in any way. We could pack up everything you own right now and move it to my house if you'd let me."

Thor, I loved this man. He made me feel so cherished and

desired. I still couldn't believe this gorgeous and amazing guy wanted me despite all my many flaws. He loved me just as I was.

"I'm not ready to give this place up just yet, but I appreciate that more than you know."

"I love you." He pressed a soft kiss to my lips.

"I love you, too."

He stepped back, leaving a chill across my skin where the heat of his body had been. I wanted nothing more than to curl up in his arms for the day and ignore the outside world, but I knew I couldn't. We both had responsibilities, and I'd always been the responsible one. I wouldn't just abandon everything I'd worked so hard for because of a little challenge. No, the new Kennedy was strong and would rise to the threat. I'd prove to myself that I could do this.

He bent down and picked up my bag, slinging it over his shoulder before making his way out of the room. He glanced back over his shoulder, his eyes stormy, before leaving the apartment.

A thought occurred to me. "Connor! Don't leave him to deal with that crowd of paparazzi on his own. Can you please escort him out to the car and then come back in? Hurry, or you're going to miss him!" I felt the panic rising up and tried to take deep, steadying breaths. I was barely holding myself together as it was. I couldn't handle it if something happened to Zen.

Uncertainty crossed Connor's face for a split second before he turned and rushed out of the room, calling out for Zen to wait for him. I wanted to stay near them, so I followed, shutting and locking the apartment door before heading down to Sweet Stories.

Zen waited at the door, and Connor strode across the room towards him. "Let me get you to the car. The building has been checked, and I'll lock the door behind me so she'll be safe inside."

"Please, Zen. Let him go with you. I'll sit here and wait for him to come back." I pleaded with him because I knew he'd give me whatever I wanted within reason, and I didn't ask him for much. I saw the moment he relented. His eyes softened, and his shoulders relaxed.

"Fine, I'll do this for you," he said before turning to face Connor. "But you've got one minute, and then I want you back in this store."

Connor nodded once.

"Stay safe, Sunshine. I'll be back before you know it." Zen blew me a kiss and waited for Connor to open the door.

I lowered myself into one of the mismatched chairs in the cafe, breathing deeply and closing my eyes, trying to imagine myself back in Zen's bedroom in Malibu. I could hear the waves, feel the sea breeze on my face, gently teasing my hair so it tickled my cheeks. It was almost as if I was there.

The sound of the bell jingling above the door pulled me out of my relaxing daydream. My eyes snapped open to find Connor had stepped back inside. "He's gone."

"Thanks, Connor. Guess I should get to work, huh?" I flashed him a small smile.

"I'll just sit here and keep an eye out." He pulled out the chair across from me as I stood up.

I moved to start prepping the store to open. I turned on all the lights and filled the display case in the bakery with pre-packaged snacks I'd ordered from a local supply company. There was no way I could be in my apartment long enough to bake anything from scratch.

Just as I started pulling up the blinds, the front door unlocked, and the bell above the door jingled. I spun around at the same time I heard Connor jump to his feet.

Chloe popped into my line of sight, and I relaxed. She looked more disheveled than usual, but then again, I bet I did, too. She had dark bags under her eyes, her clothes were wrinkled, and her hair was messy as if she had rolled out of bed and stumbled into work.

"Chloe! I didn't know if you were coming in. You never texted me back." I clicked on the open sign.

"Yeah, I was busy," she grumbled. I flinched at her tone, but she sort of had a right to be upset about the past week and being out of work without notice. It had to be hard on her to be without pay. It was why I'd suggested Chloe come in today even though I doubted we'd be very busy with a crowd of photographers outside.

"I'm really sorry about last week. With all those photographers outside I had to shut down the store. I didn't really have a choice," I explained.

Chloe rolled her eyes. "I bet you're really sorry about it all, aren't you? Doesn't change what's happening, though." Her tone was bitter, and I had no fucking clue where all this hostility was coming from.

"Look, Chloe, I'm sorry if my shutting down the store put you in a hard position but—"

"Save it. You have everything, and it's easy for you to just do whatever you want without worrying about anyone else. No need to explain yourself to me, your lowly employee."

Connor stood there with a scowl on his face. I could tell he didn't like her talking to me this way. He was just as protective as Zen. I shrugged, not sure what to make of Chloe's attitude, either. I understood being frustrated at the situation. Hell, I was disappointed about everything that was going on, but I'd made the decisions I had to protect myself and my store. Chloe needed to get the hell over it.

Chloe walked over to the register and threw her purse down, irritation coursing off of her in waves. I was starting to feel uncomfortable at the level of anger she was displaying. Sure, Chloe had a right to be upset, but she wasn't acting anything like the employee I'd gotten to know over the past weeks. Maybe it'd been a mistake asking her to come in, and I should ask her to go home.

The more I tossed that thought around in my mind, the less it made sense. Chloe was upset because she lost out on her pay from the week before. If I sent her home today, that'd be another day with lost wages. Unfortunately, I'd have to face this sooner or later. Hopefully, Chloe would cool off as the day wore on, and we could get back to normal.

After an hour had passed, Chloe was still ignoring me, slamming books around, and she'd yelled at the only two customers that dared come into the shop so far today. I needed to do something to get her to snap out of it.

I barely had time to register the fact that an hour had passed, and Zen hadn't come back yet. I was too busy trying to keep an eye on Chloe. If her attitude didn't improve by the end of the day, I'd have to fire her. I couldn't have my employee chasing off every customer that came into the store. Frankly, I didn't deserve her shitty treatment, and it was starting to piss me off.

I glanced at Connor, who'd been keeping an eye on me since the moment Chloe walked into the store. His eyes shifted between her and me, and something in his gaze put me on edge. He looked uneasy. I crossed the room to the table he was sitting at before plopping down next to him, wincing as Chloe slammed a box down onto the floor across the store.

"Have you heard from Zen yet?" I bounced my knee, trying to dissipate the nervous energy.

"Not yet. Sounds like you really pissed that one off," he observed, jerking his thumb toward Chloe.

I pinched the bridge of my nose and squeezed my eyes shut. "I guess. She won't talk to me or let me talk other than when she snapped at me when she came in." I lowered my voice. "I may have to fire her if she keeps it up."

Connor shifted his eyes to the side, watching Chloe out of the corner of his eye. "If you want me to step in, say the word. I won't hesitate to handle it."

"Thanks, Connor, but I think I can deal with my employee. Plus, she's what? Five feet tall, maybe? I could take her if I had to." I tossed a playful wink at him as a teasing smile broke out across my face.

He grinned back. "I can't say I'd hate to watch that." He chuckled.

Another box slammed down on the floor. I sighed. "I'm going to have her go out and pick up cafe supplies. Maybe getting her out of here will be the break she needs to snap the fuck out of it."

I pressed my hands onto the table and pushed myself up, turning to walk over to Chloe. "Chloe? I need you to run to the restaurant supply store and grab this list of supplies for me." She stood up, her eyes narrowed into a glare before she ripped the paper I held out of my hands.

"Whatever."

"Don't come back until you've calmed down. I know you're mad, but treating me the way you are right now is unacceptable. Fix your attitude, or I'm going to ask you to leave."

She huffed and glared at me, and I watched Connor stand up and move toward me out of the corner of my eye. "My credit card is on file, so just give them our business license number."

"Whatever you want, boss." Chloe murmured irritably before turning and storming off, leaving the box she was working on half unpacked at my feet.

I took my phone out of my back pocket and dialed Zen. His voicemail picked up, so I left a quick message. "Hey, it's me. I'm worried about you. It's been more than an hour, and Connor hasn't heard from you, so I hope everything is okay." I sighed. "Chloe came in, and she's making me a little uncomfortable, but hopefully her attitude will get better by the time you get here. Call me when you get this and let me know you're okay. I love you." My stomach dipped as I ended the call.

Bending down, I started unpacking the box of books Chloe abandoned, trying to push down the worry that gnawed at me. My brain felt like it was going to explode with everything swirling around in it. Just as I'd shove my concerns about why Zen hadn't come back out of my mind, thoughts about Chloe and her shitty attitude would take over.

Lost in my thoughts, another hour passed. Between organizing my store and the customers beginning to trickle in, the time flew by. I flicked my eyes up at the front window, and the crowd of paparazzi had thinned. Covering the front of my book store had to be boring as fuck for them.

My phone vibrated, and I pulled it out to see Chloe's number pop up.

"Hi, Chloe. What's going on? Did you get everything?"

"Yep!" Chloe's cheerful voice caught me off guard considering her demeanor before she left, but I could use a break today, and it seemed like she'd gotten rid of her shitty mood. "I do need some help carrying all this stuff in, though. Do you think you can meet me out front? I'm pulling up now." I looked out the front window just as Chloe's car pulled up.

"Sure, I'll be right there." I hung up and slid my phone back into my pocket. I stepped out from behind the counter and glanced at Connor, who had his phone pressed up to his ear, and his back turned, speaking in a low voice so I couldn't make out what he was saying.

I didn't know if I should tap him on the shoulder and let him know I was stepping out or just pop out for a few seconds. I thought about Zen and knew I had to tell Connor what I was doing. I reached up and tapped him lightly on the shoulder. He spun around quickly, looking down at me with a question in his eyes.

I whispered, "I'm helping Chloe outside for two minutes, tops." I didn't know if he'd heard me since he was listening intently to whoever was on the phone, but I'd let him know and felt satisfied with that.

Stepping outside the front door, I walked in Chloe's direction. My phone vibrated, so I grabbed it out of my pocket and looked down at the screen. Zen's face flashed across my phone, and my whole body relaxed. I smiled as I swiped to answer, relief flooding through me. "Hey, stranger."

"Hi, Sunshine." He sighed and sounded worn out. "I'm so fucking sorry for how long this has taken. Everything's okay, outside of security being a total shit show. I'll probably be here a couple more hours."

I looked up as Zen spoke, spotting Chloe behind the wheel of her car. She waited as I walked down the sidewalk, listening to Zen's voice as he told me what was happening at his house. Just before I got to the front of her car, my eyes locked on hers. The hatred in them made a chill run down my spine. Something wasn't right.

The car engine revved, and my stomach dropped. My eyes widened as the tires squealed and the car barreled towards me. Chloe steered up onto the sidewalk. I dropped my phone and screamed, trying to dive out of the way, but I knew it wouldn't be enough. I should've waited for Connor, but it was too late now. Zen's face flashed across my mind before everything went black.

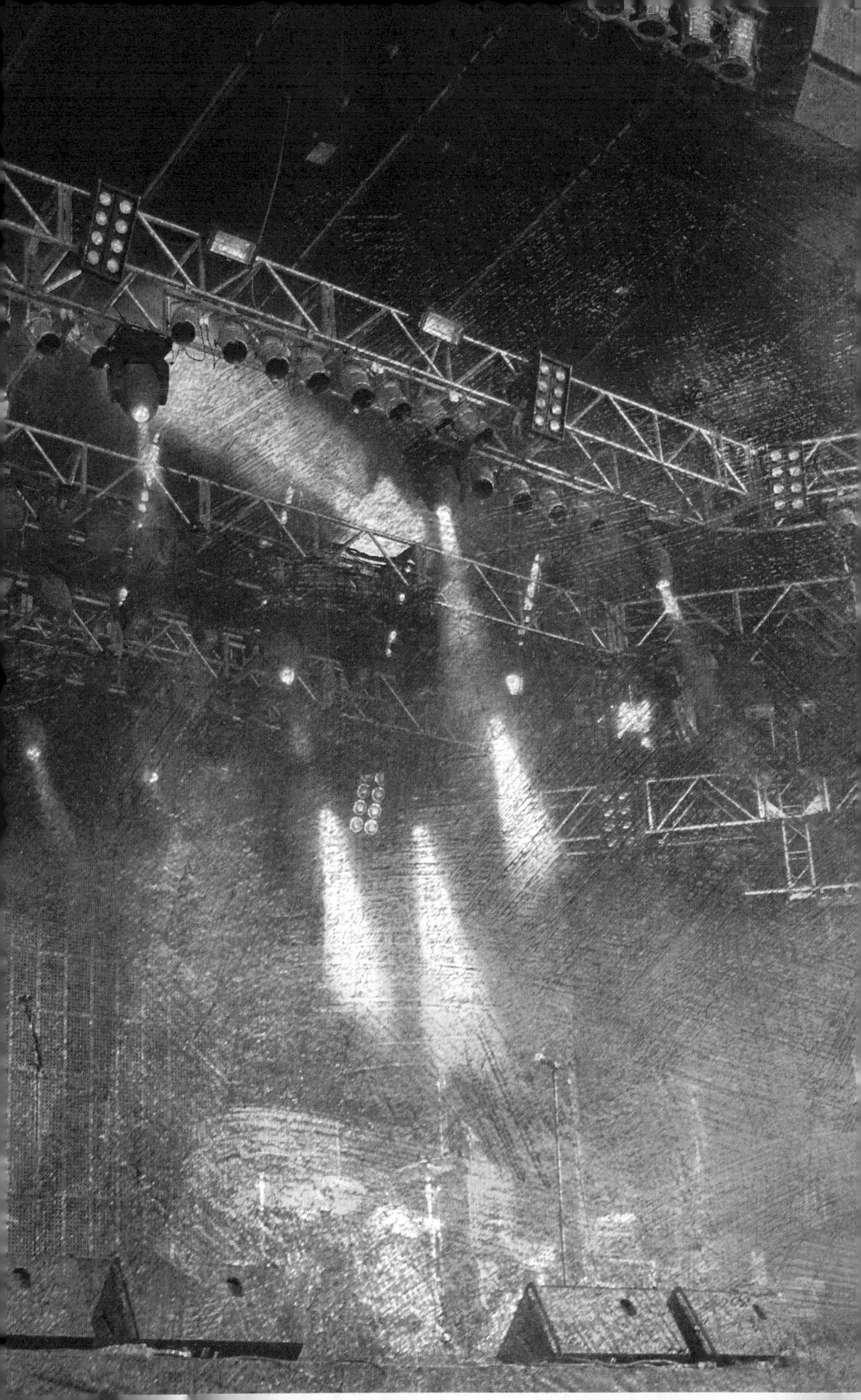

CHAPTER 29

ZEN

"KENNEDY? KENNEDY!" I screamed into the phone, feeling like my heart was climbing up my raw throat. What the fuck was happening? I needed to get to Kennedy, and I needed to figure out what was going on right the fuck now. I kept my phone pressed to my ear, continuing to call out for Kennedy until I heard a fast beeping tone signaling the call had dropped.

I cursed loudly, sprinting across my house to find Julian while dialing Connor. It was a miracle I hadn't tripped over anything on my way to the garage. His voicemail picked up. Connor wasn't answering either. This was really fucking bad. My gut this morning told me I shouldn't have left her, and I couldn't help but feel like whatever was happening now was my fault for not fucking listening. I should have trusted my instincts.

I needed to get to Kennedy and fast. My heart raced, and all I could do was hope that she'd dropped her phone and that everything was okay, that this was all just some massive overreaction on my part.

I figured Julian would reassure me when I found him, but instead, he was already jumping into the Mercedes and starting the engine. "Get in," he commanded, and I didn't question him. I lunged into the passenger seat. The garage door was barely open before he stepped on the gas. The tires squealed in protest at the sudden acceleration. I wouldn't have given a shit if he just plowed the door down if it got us to Kennedy faster.

"What the fuck happened, Julian?" I yelled, my fear threatening to completely consume me. I felt like I couldn't breathe and wanted to crawl out of my skin.

"I was talking to Connor, and the next thing I know, I heard an engine rev, tires squealing, and a scream. Then I heard Connor curse and the phone went dead. That's all I know." His jaw was set, and his movements were tense and controlled as we tore down the road.

I spaced out, wondering if the pure terror threatening to overtake me was similar to how Kennedy felt during one of her panic attacks. I'd never felt such a strong reaction before because I'd never cared enough about someone to fear losing them.

Just the thought of Kennedy almost paralyzed me as her bright smile flashed across my mind. I felt like I couldn't breathe, couldn't get enough air into my lungs. I gripped the door, my knuckles turning white. The car moved around me, and I saw the streets passing by in a blur, yet felt I like I was standing still. It took what felt like an eternity before we turned onto her road, but when we did, everything moved in slow motion.

I scanned the street, and Julian slowed the car. My stomach dropped, and my heart skipped when I saw the flashing red and blue lights surrounding Sweet Stories.

"Julian—"

"I know, but we don't know anything yet. Let me park, and we'll see what's going on." Julian's voice was tight, but he was trying to keep it even for my sake. I was sure he could tell I was on the verge of completely losing my shit.

"I don't care if you have to park in the middle of the street, I'm getting out of this car right the fuck now," I growled, starting to open the door before the car jolted to a stop.

"Jesus, Zen. You trying to get yourself hurt?"

But I didn't give a fuck. All I could think about was getting to Kennedy. She had to be okay. I refused to accept any other outcome. I turned and sprinted towards the store, trying to avoid running into the people who'd formed a crowd. I hadn't even pulled on a hat before I left the house, and the crowd was big and no doubt full of photographers.

I stopped abruptly when I reached the storefront, my eyes frantically scanning the chaotic sidewalk in front of me before landing on Kennedy. She sat on the ground behind the bus bench in front of her store, which was mangled and virtually unrecognizable.

A blanket was tucked around her shoulders, and her hair was messy like she'd been in a wind tunnel or something. Her eyes were red-rimmed and dazed, and tears slid down her cheeks. Connor stood beside her talking to a paramedic. She glanced up, and our eyes locked. Closing the distance between us, I dropped to my knees and pulled her into my arms, and her body melted against mine.

She trembled, and warm tears soaked into my shirt. She held onto me tightly as if she was afraid if she let me go, I'd disappear. I ignored the clicking cameras around us as her body shook with sobs, and my own eyes started to sting. "I'm so sorry, baby. I'm sorry I wasn't here. I'm sorry," I repeated into her hair again and again until her cries eventually stopped.

I heard a throat clear next to me, but I didn't bother moving. "What?"

The paramedic stepped into my line of sight. "She's got some cuts and scrapes but otherwise seems fine. You were fortunate today, miss."

"Thank you, we'll keep an eye on her," I heard Connor reply coolly before walking the man back to the ambulance and returning to where I stood holding Kennedy. I had a feeling he wouldn't be very far from either one of us until this shit got resolved.

"Let's get you into the car with Julian, Sunshine." I needed to get her away from the paparazzi lingering around, so I pulled her against my side and led her to the SUV as people called out our names and tried to push toward us. Connor held them back, barking threats into the crowd. Julian sat behind the wheel, and I crawled in the back seat behind her, not willing to let her out of my sight.

"Go talk to Connor and find out what the fuck just happened," I demanded through gritted teeth, trying not to lose my cool as my fear gave way to anger at the situation. "And call Harrison about media control." I didn't want to scare Kennedy with her frayed nerves, but I glared at Julian in the rearview mirror. I fucking hated how powerless I felt.

He wordlessly left the car, leaving Kennedy and me alone in the back seat. I leaned up and locked the doors before returning to the back seat and pulling Kennedy into my lap. I wrapped my arms around her, and she buried her head into the crook of my neck. She was still shaking, but her tears had stopped.

I took out my phone, shooting off a text to True.

Zen: Something happened with Kennedy, still getting details. Can you come up? I need you.

A few seconds later, my phone buzzed.

True: Give us a couple hours, and we're there.

I let myself take a deep breath. I'd been trying to handle this situation by myself and look where it got me. For some reason, this stalker appeared to always be one step ahead of whatever measures I put into place.

I also knew I'd have to call Grayson, and I sure as fuck was not looking forward to that conversation. He was going to be pissed.

I sighed, running my free hand through my hair before wrapping it tightly around Kennedy again. "Sunshine, I'm not trying to rush you, but what the fuck happened out there?"

She shifted on my lap before she sat back slightly, and her eyes searched mine. "I... I thought I was going to die. I thought I'd never see you again." She shuddered, her eyes brimming with fresh tears. One tear escaped and rolled down her cheek. I reached up and gently wiped it away, cupping her cheek in my palm and staring deeply into her eyes.

"But you didn't, and you're safe now. I'm here. I'm not going anywhere, baby. Please tell me," I pleaded.

"It... It was Chloe. Chloe did this. She tried to run me over with her car. I'm pretty sure she's the one stalking you. She was so angry and cold today, and I couldn't figure it out. I thought we were starting to become friends. Fuck, I thought it was just because the store had been closed."

My muscles tightened, and my jaw clenched as I thought about Chloe having free access to Kennedy this entire time. I thought about all the times I'd seen her and interacted with her, how she'd made me feel uneasy, how she'd looked vaguely familiar the first time I saw her.

"Oh, shit. She's the girl from the lake," I whispered, my eyes widening with realization. Kennedy lifted her brow waiting for me to explain.

"That day we went to the lake the first weekend when we met. Do you remember? There was a girl who came up to me and asked me for a selfie. I told her no because I didn't want our time interrupted—"

"And you didn't want me to know who you were," Kennedy cut in, her tone a little lighter like she was teasing me a bit.

I chuckled. "That, too. But when I told her no, she called me an asshole and stormed off. I figured she was just another entitled fan, but it was a while later when she showed up in your store, so I didn't make the connection. I meet so many people every day that the fact she looked familiar the first time I saw her in your store wasn't really surprising. I didn't place it until just now."

"Great, so the first time I put myself out there and hire an employee, she comes after everyone and everything I love." Kennedy's eyes filled with tears again. I could feel her heart pounding and hear her breathing getting faster as she started to panic.

I rubbed her back and started singing her song to her, cradling her against my chest. Her breathing began to slow, and before long, it was even and steady. Just as I wondered if she had fallen asleep, she said, "Who knew a bus stop could have such an impact on my life?" Then she let out that musical laugh of hers.

I joined her, chuckling softly. "Yeah, we're going to have to rebuild it and dedicate it or something. It saved my life, too. If something had happened to you today, fuck, Kennedy. I'd have died right there with you. My life is nothing without you."

"I'm not going anywhere, I promise. I love you," she said, before settling back into my lap and closing her eyes. I tightened my arms around her, taking a deep breath. Now that I had a minute to think, I couldn't believe how close I'd come to losing the love of my life today. I did everything I could to not leave her alone for any extended time since this all started, but still, Chloe slipped through.

Fucking Chloe. We underestimated her at every turn, and I was sure as shit done with that now. I wouldn't be taking a single chance from here on out. There was only one place we could go now that I felt we'd be safe for the night, where we could regroup with our security team and our friends and formulate a plan. I took out my phone, sending a text to the one person I knew without a fucking doubt could keep my girl safe tonight. Connor had already let me down a couple of times, but I needed help. I couldn't do this alone anymore, and it was time to call in reinforcements.

AN HOUR LATER, we pulled up in front of a split level house in a beautiful but quiet neighborhood a few miles away from the store. Kennedy was still in my lap, but she'd fallen asleep. Julian and Connor were up front. No one was talking, so we didn't disturb Kennedy.

When we left Sweet Stories, we all exchanged glances, an unspoken agreement we'd discuss everything when we got to our safe house.

The front door swung open, and Grayson stood there, arms folded across his chest, a scowl on his face. Julian stepped out of the car, closing the door quietly behind him. He walked towards Grayson and exchanged a few words before making his way around the perimeter of the property.

I assumed he was checking to be sure the house was safe for us. Grayson rolled his eyes and turned his back before stalking back into the house, leaving the door open. Julian made his way back to the car, nodding at Connor, who hopped out of the driver's seat.

He opened my door, waiting for me to exit. I didn't want to wake Kennedy, but we needed to get in the house to figure out what the fuck we were going to do next. I stroked her hair gently. "Baby, I need you to wake up. We're at Gray's. Let's go inside so you can lay down." I couldn't maneuver her out of the car without her help, so I had no choice but to wake her up.

She sat up slowly, disentangling herself from me clumsily, and I couldn't help but smile. She reminded me of a tiny kitten. Where her body had been pressed against mine was now cold as she moved out of the car. I missed her already. Was it possible to want to live inside someone? To crawl into their body and curl up just to be closer to them?

When did I become such a sappy motherfucker?

I had to push that thought away to analyze later. She waited for me to join her, reaching for my hand the second I stepped outside. Connor closed the door and followed us into the house.

Once I got Kennedy settled in the guest room we'd be staying in, I went downstairs. Grayson glared at me. "How the fuck did you let this happen to my sister?" He stood from his chair with his hands balled into fists, looking like he wanted to take a swing at me.

I couldn't blame him. I was angrier at myself than I'd ever been. It was my job to keep Kennedy safe. How many times had I promised her I'd never let anything happen to her? And yet today, I failed. I fucked up.

Today I almost lost her.

My stomach twisted, and I had the sudden urge to throw up when I thought about how close Chloe had been to taking Kennedy from me. I was glad I hadn't eaten since breakfast.

"I messed up, Gray. I let her down, but I promise you it won't happen again. The guys are on their way, I've hired more security, and now the police are working with us, too." I ran my hand through my hair again.

"I'm tired of your fucking promises. The police should've been working on this from the beginning," Grayson yelled, stalking closer to me. "You shouldn't have tried to handle everything on your own." I was standing only inches away from Grayson now. I could see the rage storming in his navy eyes, his jaw clenched. I wouldn't stop him if he tried to hit me. I deserved everything Grayson could throw at me and more.

"I know. I fucked up."

Grayson sighed heavily, stepping back. "Yeah, you did. But you're trying to make it right, and you came to me, which is a good start," he gave me a half smile. "At least we can still fix this. She's okay. She may have some emotional scars, but we both know she's strong enough to overcome those."

Grayson walked over to the couch and dropped down. I followed. "What's the game plan?"

I motioned for Julian and Connor to take the seats across from Grayson and me. "We need to put together all the information that we have. Kennedy told me that Chloe is the one who…" I couldn't say the words, and my hands curled into fists in my lap. "Chloe fucking did this. It makes sense when I think about it."

"Wait, Chloe? That tiny little girl that works at the store?" Grayson sounded just as surprised as I was.

I nodded. "Yeah. When Kennedy told me she'd been driving the car today, everything sort of clicked into place. Kennedy and I had our first date at the lake, and that day this girl came up and asked me for a selfie. When I told her no, she cussed at me, but it happens, so I moved on with my day and didn't think about it again. Today everything fucking clicked, and I realized it was Chloe that day at the lake."

Grayson blew out a breath. "Damn. Talk about going off the deep end when you don't get something you want."

Julian and Connor were listening, but neither said anything.

"It makes sense if you think about everything that happened, especially the shit at Kennedy's apartment. Chloe had keys to everything. She had access and knew Kennedy's schedule. If we hadn't been fucking blinded by the fact that she seemed friendly, we probably would've seen it sooner. That's a mistake we won't make again." I narrowed my eyes at my security detail.

"There were warning signs today, and that shit is on me for not stepping in and watching closer." Connor's eyes met mine, and they were filled with remorse.

"Look, Z. I know I was hard on you about all this, but I also know that you've done the best you could. This shit is new to you like it is to us. Don't beat yourself up too bad. I mean, definitely beat yourself up some because my little sister did get hurt on your watch." Grayson's mouth tilted up on one side again. "But, what's done is done. We need to figure out how to catch this chick before she does any more damage."

Leaning back against the couch, I rubbed my hand down my face. I must've aged at least ten years today. "Thanks, Gray. I'll never forgive myself for this, but thanks." I turned my tired gaze on my security team. "I've called the guys, and they're flying up as we speak. I think we can lay some sort of trap for Chloe. Up until now, she's been able to evade us. We've underestimated her every step of the way, and that stops right the fuck now."

"What did you have in mind?" Connor asked.

"At this point, we don't have any evidence that it was Chloe. Kennedy saw her drive the car, but she could just claim that she lost control or some bullshit, so it's not solid. We need to be able to pin her down with all the threatening shit she's been doing plus trying to kill my girl." I felt a wave of nausea pass over me again as I said the words aloud. I'd almost fucking lost her.

There wasn't a harsh enough punishment for Chloe as far as I was concerned, but I'd settle for a lifetime behind bars to start.

"That's true," Connor mused. "We don't exactly have anything on her that would stick."

"I want to wait until the guys get here, but it's me she wants. I think I can use myself to entice her and get her to confess."

Grayson raised his eyebrows. "Dude, my sister will never go for that. Offering yourself up as bait? Imagine if she wanted to use herself that way. You'd freak the fuck out."

Grayson had a point. I'd never allow it to happen if the roles were reversed. On the other hand, I couldn't see another way to get enough evidence to have Chloe arrested without her doing more harm to the woman I loved. Who knew what the fuck she would do next?

Letting out a heavy sigh, I glanced at her brother. "I know she's not going to like the idea, Gray, but what else am I supposed to do here? If you have a better idea, I'm all ears." I waited, but after a couple awkward-as-fuck minutes, no one spoke up.

"That's what I thought. I don't have an official plan yet. I want to wait until the guys get here, and we have a little time to think, so let's figure it out tomorrow."

Grayson nodded in agreement before blowing out a breath. "Yeah, that's a good idea. I'll go start dinner. Are your friends coming here, too?"

"They're on the jet now and coming here when they land if that's okay."

Grayson nodded. "Yeah, it's probably best we have everyone stay together, so no one else gets hurt, but it'll be tight. I only have two open bedrooms, so we're gonna have to squeeze in."

"We'll make it work. Thanks again, Gray."

"Don't mention it. You know I'd do anything for my sister, and now that she's with you, you're family, too. Just don't fuck it up again," he warned.

"I won't."

AFTER THE TENSE conversation I just had, I wanted nothing more than to curl up in bed and pull Kennedy close. I found myself needing the reminder that she was real, that she was still here with me, that she was okay. I was also ridiculously exhausted.

I walked into the room, closing the door softly behind me before turning and walking to the bed. Kennedy was curled up in the middle, her golden hair spread out on the pillow. I crawled on the bed and pulled her tightly against my body, wrapping myself around her. I closed my eyes and drifted off to sleep, relaxing with the heat of her body and listening to the sound of her steady breathing.

I WOKE to my phone buzzing in my pocket. I didn't know how many hours had passed, but Kennedy was still asleep with her body tucked against mine. It was dark outside, and I blinked at the bright screen of my phone when I pulled it out. It was a text from Grayson.

Gray: Come downstairs. We have a serious problem.

Shit.

My heart started to race as I quickly untangled myself from Kennedy, being careful not to wake her up. I bent down to place a soft kiss on her forehead. I moved off of the bed and quietly made my way out of the room.

I jogged downstairs, meeting Grayson in the living room. His face was pale, a dazed look in his eyes. I felt a sudden urge to shake him or slap him to snap him out of it. "What the fuck happened, Gray?"

Grayson slowly moved his eyes to meet mine. "I..." He cleared his throat and shook his head slightly. "I just got a call from the police," he began shakily.

My heart rate skyrocketed at the words that just left his mouth, and my stomach churned. "Spit it out, Gray," I demanded impatiently.

"They tried Kennedy first, but her phone was smashed in the accident so they couldn't get to her. I was the emergency contact she had on file with the city," he explained. I had no idea what the fuck that had to do with anything. I was quickly running out of patience.

"Yeah, and? Why would they be calling you? She's safe upstairs."

"Because there was a fire," Grayson whispered.

I felt like all the air was sucked out of my lungs, and I collapsed onto the couch.

"Shit." My head fell into my hands.

"They said because it was an old building, it collapsed. Everything is gone, Z. Everything."

I had no idea how I was going to tell Kennedy the place she felt safest in the world, the place she'd worked so hard to build, had been so proud to call her own, was now gone. Everything she'd built had gone up in flames. Because of me.

I looked up at her brother, and our eyes locked. "Did they say what started the fire?"

"They aren't sure yet, but they think it might have been intentionally set."

Fuck.

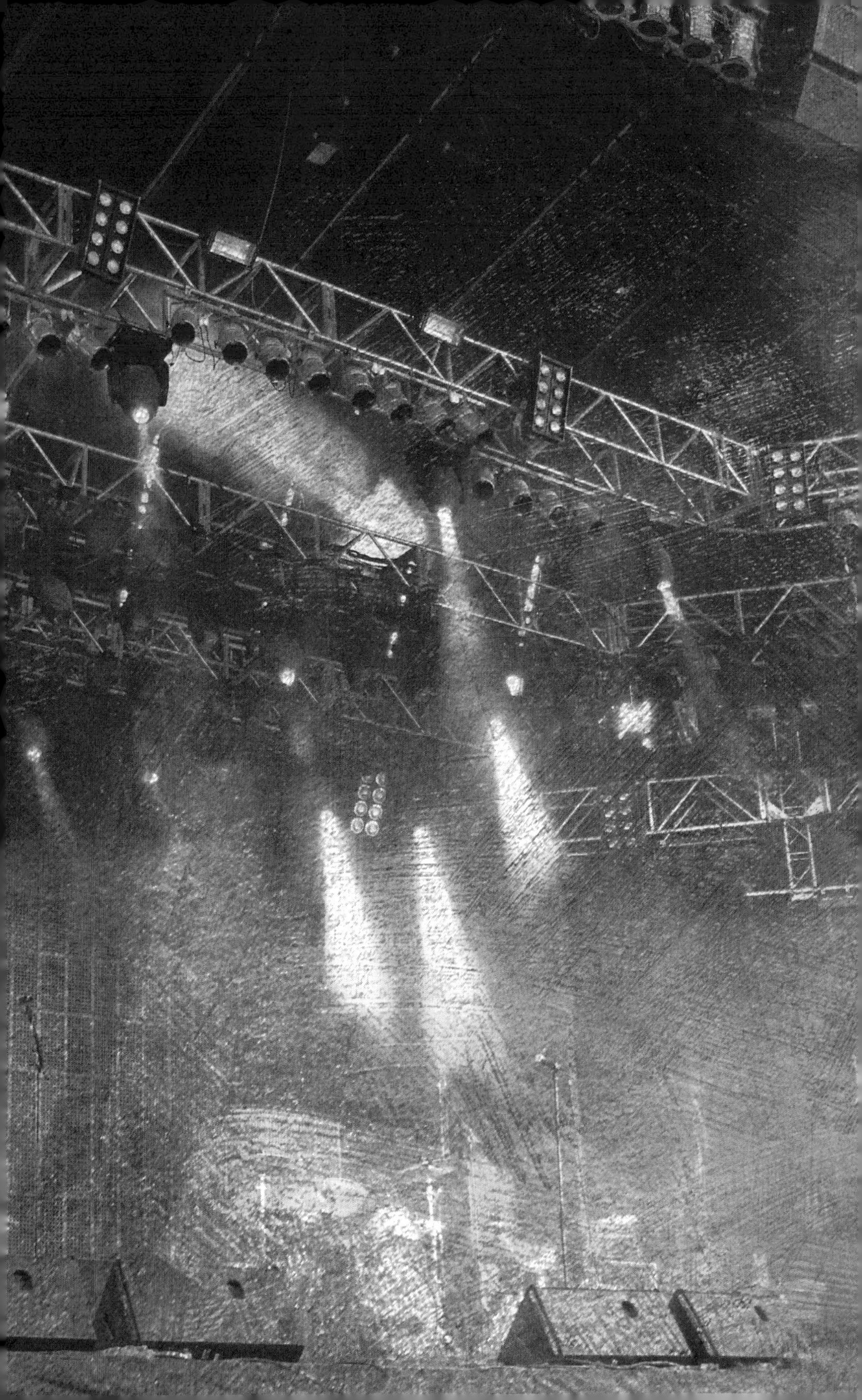

CHAPTER 30

KENNEDY

"IT'S GONE." Zen's quiet voice barely cut through the buzzing in my ears. I hadn't registered the words the first time he'd taken my hands in his and told me that my dreams had just gone up in literal flames.

Blinking my eyes, I tried to make sense of the words I was hearing. An inferno began to build inside me, bubbling rage replacing the overwhelming sense of loss. "Chloe did this."

"We don't know that yet, Sunshine."

Zen had been trying to keep me calm, but I was devastated and pissed the fuck off. I wanted to make Chloe suffer just like she had done to me. I should probably be grateful that Chloe hadn't hurt anyone I loved, and they were all safe, but all I could manage was the white-hot fury that continued to build.

"Who the fuck does this psycho think she is? That crazy bitch thinks she can take everything from me, and I won't fight back?

Well, she is sorely mistaken. She's fucked with me for the last time. I want her to pay, Zen. She will not get away with this." My whole body vibrated.

"I promise you, Sunshine, she'll pay for what she's done," he reassured me.

I took a calming breath before blowing it out slowly. My logical mind was starting to regain control. I'd lost everything, but I had insurance. I could come back from this. It'd be a speed bump in the grand scheme of things. A tragedy, sure, but nothing I couldn't overcome.

Besides, the city council vote hadn't gone my way, and there was a more than strong possibility the man who owned my building was going to sell to a developer, and I'd have to move anyway. This could've been so much worse.

What really mattered now were the people in this house. We were all together and safe, at least for now.

"Does Chloe know about this place?" Fear spiked through my body, threatening to throw my emotional state into chaos again.

Zen shook his head. "I don't think so. If she does, we haven't seen any sign of her. Gray has a security system since I forced it on him a couple weeks ago, and we have our team here. Plus, True, Mad, and Jericho are here, too. We've got the place covered."

He looked exhausted. The stubble on his jaw had grown out, and he had dark circles underneath his eyes. He ran a hand down his handsome face. "We're working on a plan to get her to confess to everything. Gray and I talked to Connor and Julian, and we all agree there's not enough evidence to get her put away yet. We don't have any proof Chloe did any of this shit except the accident, and even then, she could just say she lost control. We need evidence to give to the police. Come downstairs, and we'll eat dinner and talk. Amara just got here, too."

He smiled softly down at me. "She almost beat me up here. I had to convince her to let me come talk to you about this, just the two of us first. I thought you'd want to know in private so you could process it before having to be around everyone," he explained. He ran his fingers along my jawline, the light touch causing goosebumps to pop up all along my neck. He leaned forward and pressed a soft kiss to my lips, nipping at my bottom lip, before sitting up and sighing deeply. I tried to pull him back down, and he chuckled, standing up from the bed.

"Ready to get this shit show over with?"

"Don't make spending time with our friends sound appealing or anything," I teased, feeling the heavy weight that'd lodged itself in my chest ease just a bit. That earlier inkling of gratitude I felt had spread and grown. Zen, Gray, and Amara were all okay. My resolve hardened into place. I'd make sure they all stayed safe. I was strong enough now to do it.

I stood up and laced our fingers together as he led me out the door. By the time I was done, Chloe would never hurt another person I loved.

Walking into the kitchen, I noticed Grayson finishing up dinner and Zen's bandmates seated around the table. They all had drinks in front of them, and True was attempting to get Amara's attention and had a bright smile on his face. Maddox stood by Gray in the kitchen, looking over his shoulder at what he was making. Connor was near the doorway with his arms folded across his chest, keeping watch.

"Ohmygod," Amara practically screamed when she noticed me, making it sound like it was all one word. She jumped up and pulled me into a choking hug. "I can't believe you almost died today. Who is this crazy psycho, and what does she want with you? Grayson hardly told me anything." She pouted, glaring at Gray over my shoulder.

I leaned into her, squeezing her back just as hard. "You remember my employee Chloe?"

Amara nodded, pulling back from our hug but not letting me go.

"She has an unhealthy attachment to my boyfriend. She sees me as an obstacle to her being with Zen, so she wants to get rid of me. She's been stalking him for a couple of months, before we even met."

"Jesus. That's terrifying and so disgusting. You know we're all in this together now. You guys don't have to deal with her alone anymore. We're going to get through this." Amara squeezed my arms gently.

"I know, thank you." My eyes stung, but I refused to let the tears fall. At this point, I didn't know how many more tears I had left to cry. I was wrung out and exhausted despite having slept most of the afternoon away.

Amara let me go, squeezing my hand one last time before walking back to the table and sitting down next to True. He smiled wide at her before draping his arm around her neck. She laughed and leaned into him, and I wondered if there might be something there. She glanced over at me and winked before rejoining her conversation.

I didn't have time to dwell on my friends' love lives right now. I was both starving and anxious to deal with Chloe. I needed a plan of action. I always felt better when I knew what the next steps were and what to expect.

I moved towards my brother, who was putting the finishing touches on dinner. I leaned on the island, lowering my elbows to the countertop. "Thanks for having us, Gray. I know this is a full house for you." My brother didn't like people invading his personal space. Grayson was a private person through and through.

In his restaurant, he was always on, having to entertain people, manage an entire kitchen staff, and be generally extroverted. I knew my brother better than that. We shared a twin bond. He was more like me than he let on. He was good at faking it, but his house, just like mine had been, was his safe place. The fact he'd let us into his space was a huge deal.

Grayson waved his hand around nonchalantly. "It's fine, I'm happy to do it. It's just for one night anyway, right?" His lips quirked up in a knowing smirk.

"Right," Zen confirmed, coming up from behind me and wrapping his arm around my waist. He pulled me tight against his body, and heat exploded from every point our bodies touched. "No matter what, this ends tomorrow. We need to figure out what we're going to do."

"Let's eat. I'm always more productive when I'm not hangry anymore." Grayson loaded his arms up with platters full of food.

"Is hangry an Adams twin thing?" Zen looked amused as he grabbed our drinks.

I grabbed a bowl and followed my brother to the table. "No, lots of people say hangry."

"Damn, man. After last weekend and this meal, you're spoiling us. You need to come cater our next tour," True said appreciatively, eyes wide at the spread in front of him.

We slid into our seats, and Zen chuckled, reaching under the table for my hand. "I doubt Gray wants to go on tour with us."

Gray passed me a platter of quesadillas while shaking his head. "No fucking way. I don't know how you guys handle being on the road for months at a time."

"Pussy, man. Lots and lots of pussy." Maddox's gravelly voice carried across the table, and Zen stiffened next to me.

"At the dinner table, Mad? Really?" True rolled his eyes.

Maddox shrugged. "What? It's true. Well, I guess not so much for this one anymore." He pointed at Zen. "Still, it's easier to make it through when you don't give yourself time to dwell on the fact that you don't know where the fuck you are day after day. That shit blends together."

We ate in relative silence after that, letting the events of the day wash over us. I thought about what would come next. Connor sat with us, but his eyes were trained between me and the living spaces around us. His eyes never strayed from me for long. I knew he felt guilty about everything that happened, but he couldn't keep this up. He was on high alert even as he ate. He had to be exhausted.

Zen cleared his throat. "You all know what happened today, right? What's been happening up to this point? I just want to make sure we're all on the same page before we figure out how to take this psycho down."

Everyone nodded their agreement. "Good, so we know Chloe's the one who's been harassing us, and we know she's the one who tried to…" He trailed off, not wanting to say the words out loud. I squeezed his hand in encouragement as our eyes locked.

He cleared his throat again, and when he spoke, his voice was gruff. "Anyway, we need to get her to confess to every fucked up thing she's done." He nodded to Connor, who started to explain in more detail.

"We'll be recording her on an audio recorder. We'll also need to get a video of her from multiple angles, just in case she tries anything or tries to take out one of the cameras. We need to set up cameras inside the house that record audio and video in real-time to back up the audio recorder. We're going to need everyone to make this work. Yes, she's just one person, but she's managed to slip through every defense we've put up until now, so we can't underestimate her."

The muscle in his jaw ticked. "We need to be clever, and I'm fresh out of ideas. Does anybody have any thoughts?"

True leaned forward with a cocky smirk on his lips. "It's fine, Z. I can bail you out. I've got an idea. It's pretty bat shit crazy, but I think it'll work. We'll see what your security boy thinks." True shifted his eyes to Connor, who'd been staring into the living room over my head. His eyes snapped over to True, giving him his full attention.

"What's the one thing this chick wants but hasn't been able to get yet no matter how hard she's tried?" he asked, that cocky smirk still on his face.

My stomach dropped as I realized what he was getting at. "Zen."

Zen turned his concerned gaze on me before turning to face True. "I had the same idea, but I hoped one of you would come up with something different." He sighed heavily. "What did you have in mind?"

"We use you as bait. It's risky, though, like I said. We already know this chick is capable of pretty much anything. But you've got all of us, plus security, plus the cops. I think it'll be fine," he finished, leaning back and lacing his fingers together behind his head, looking pleased with himself.

"Are you fucking insane?" Maddox asked, glaring between True and Zen. "You're crazier than this bitch. We have no idea what she'll do if she thinks she has Z alone. I'm all for handling this shit ourselves, but physically taking a woman down feels fucking wrong, even if she's insane."

A bubble of hysterical laughter made its way up my throat, and I couldn't hold it in. Everyone turned to stare at me as I laughed so hard tears ran down my face. My emotions were so raw from the past several hours, I couldn't even process them anymore. Everything was erupting out of me at once like some sort of deranged volcano of emotion.

Zen rubbed my back in slow circles as I caught my breath. My cheeks burned, and I wanted to crawl under the table.

"I think you're underestimating us," Jericho countered, staring at Maddox. "You know what we've been through, and we've all handled hard shit. I have no problem getting physical if I need to, and I know you guys don't either."

"That's True. Jericho's fucking terrifying with a blade," Zen admitted. "And Mad, I've seen you beat someone to unconsciousness more than once. And you go shooting with Connor at least once a week."

Our attention all turned to True, who shifted uncomfortably. "Don't look at me. I can hold my own in a fight, but I'm not good with a gun or a knife like any of them. If someone comes at me, I can throw down and handle business. Don't worry."

I stared at them each in turn, taking in the mixture of cocky, resolute, and solemn expressions they wore.

Connor's deep voice cut through the tension, and I turned my head slightly to search his face as he spoke. "I'll bring my computer guy, Sebastian, in on this. He can get the cameras set up and deal with the security system and notifying the police. This isn't the worst idea. I don't have one better. We'd have to take precautions, prepare for every scenario we can think of, but…" He sighed, his eyes drifting to the ceiling as he considered his next words. "I think it could work."

Zen's body went rigid. I knew he respected Connor's opinion. If Connor thought this idea was worth exploring, Zen would go along with it. My heart sank. I'd just been thanking my lucky stars that no one had gotten hurt, and they were about to throw Zen into harm's way. In the blink of an eye, any sense of calm I'd managed to hold onto disappeared.

My heart started to race as I tried to hold onto control. I couldn't lose Zen. I'd just found him, just allowed myself to lower all my defenses and let him in. I'd found a once-in-a-lifetime kind of love. What would happen if I lost him? I'd never recover.

I felt like I might pass out. I couldn't breathe, my lungs weren't working. Somewhere in the distant recesses of my mind, I remembered something about how to calm down, but I couldn't latch onto the thought. I was too far lost to the panic now.

Zen's attention snapped to me as if he could feel the shift in my energy. He'd become so in tune with my feelings, I had no doubt he could sense the panic swirling within me, pulling me under.

As if they were speaking through water, I heard everyone continuing to hash out the details of the plan, but I couldn't make out their words. Somehow this insane idea had solidified into place despite my terror at the thought. I needed to run, but I was afraid to get up. If I stood, I might pass out right there on the hardwood floor of the dining room.

Zen stood abruptly, pulling me up against his body on my shaky legs and bent down, scooping me up into his arms. "We'll be back." He didn't wait for anyone to respond before carrying me out of the room and up the stairs.

Once we were in the quiet, dark room, he laid me down on the bed and curled himself around me protectively, stroking my hair, and holding me tightly.

I trembled as every possible scenario of what could go wrong played through my head like some twisted movie where I had a front-row seat. I couldn't seem to stop my thoughts. I felt like I was falling into a hole of panic that I didn't know how to come back from. I was losing control in a way I never had before.

"Baby," he whispered against the top of my head, which was tucked under his chin and against his chest. "We don't have to do it this way. We can figure something else out. It's going to be okay. Nothing's going to happen to me. I just found you, I'm not going to leave you no matter what."

The fierceness in his tone helped my head clear some. I latched onto his words like they were a life preserver ring thrown out to a drowning woman. I finally felt like I could take a couple of shaky, deep breaths, feeling relief as my lungs filled with much-needed oxygen.

"I love you, Kennedy. I'm not going anywhere," he repeated, sensing his words and his voice were calming me down. When he used my name, I knew he meant business.

I nuzzled my face even closer to his chest because I couldn't seem to get close enough. I inhaled his scent, the smell of fresh air on his skin. I relaxed even more as my heartbeat slowed down.

"Thank you for getting me out of there before I embarrassed myself even more," I whispered as my lips moved against his firm chest. I was amazed how in tune with me he seemed to be. He'd known exactly what I needed and didn't care what anyone else thought. He'd just taken care of me when I hadn't been able to take care of myself.

It hit me then how strong I'd grown fighting my demons for so long. I'd finally come out on the other side. I understood now that I'd probably never be one hundred percent okay, but when I wasn't, when I needed someone to help me through those times, I could lean on the people I loved. It was okay to let people in. I didn't have to pretend to be stronger than I was.

Zen showed me I could lean on him, and now I needed to show him how strong I could be. Even though I'd never been more afraid of anything in my life, this was my chance to prove that I was stronger than my fear. With Zen at my side, I could face anything life threw at me. I wouldn't let the panic stop me from doing what needed to be done.

"I'll always pick you up when you need me to," he vowed, pressing a kiss to the top of my head before stroking my hair.

"That means more to me than you could possibly know. It's strange, but going through everything we have today made me freak out, but when I stepped back just now and thought about it all, I realized how strong I've become. I feel like I can get through anything, and if I can't, if I slip or fall, you're there to catch me, to make sure I'm able to stand on my own two feet again." Hot tears ran down my cheeks, but they weren't sad tears. They were tears of gratitude and love.

"No matter what happens tomorrow," I looked up into his intense green eyes, my voice gaining strength as I spoke. "You will come back to me."

"Sunshine, nothing will ever keep me away from you again. That's a promise." His fingers tangled in my hair. He brought his lips down to mine. "I love you," he whispered against my lips.

"I love you, too." I burrowed back into his chest.

He squeezed me tightly, holding me against his body until I drifted off into a dreamless sleep.

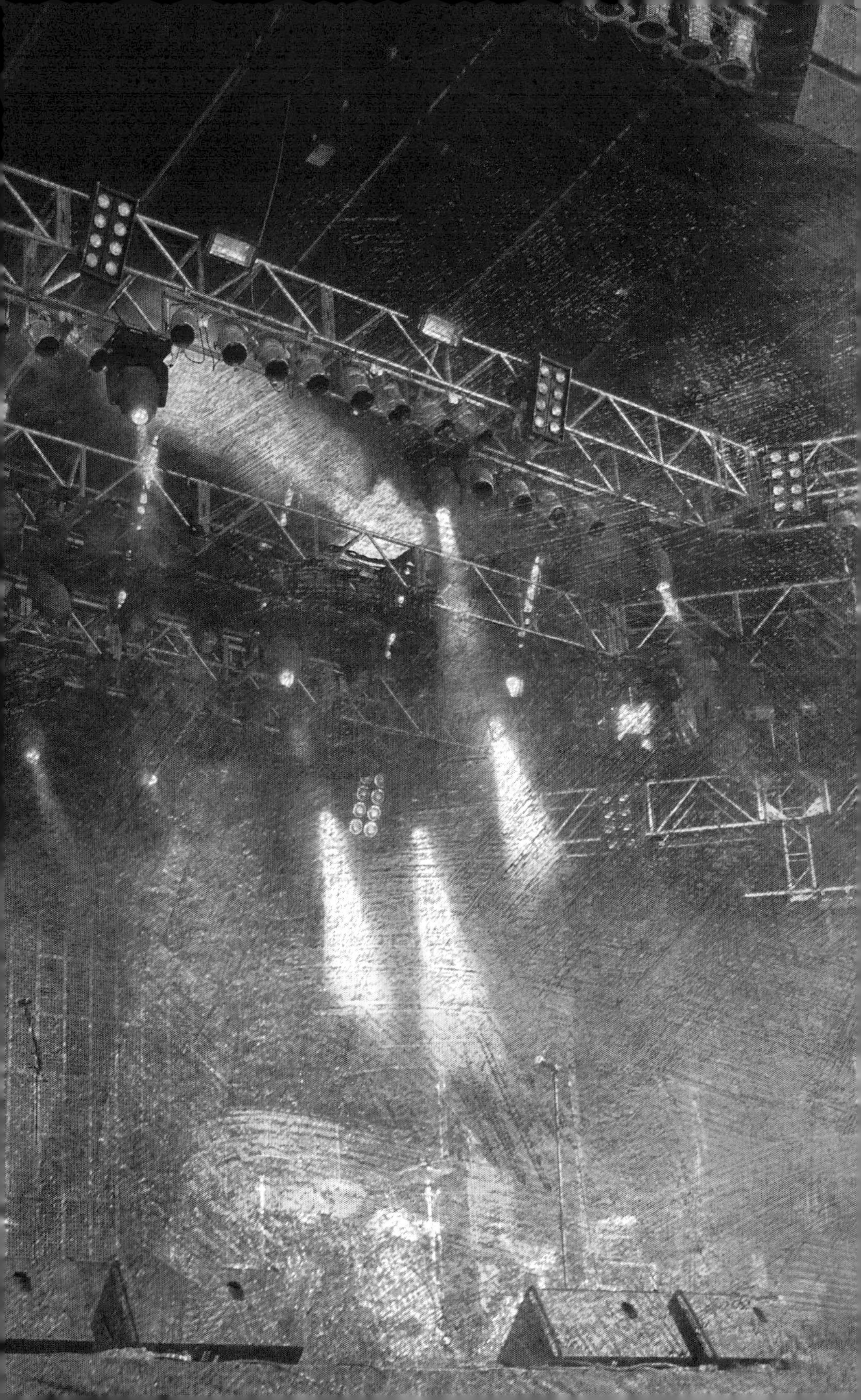

CHAPTER 31

Zen

EVERYONE GATHERED DOWNSTAIRS EARLY the next morning. We needed to go over the plan to make sure we'd accounted for every possible scenario we could think of.

"Zen, True, Maddox, and Jericho will be at Zen's. Sebastian will be in a van outside monitoring the cameras and audio, making sure we capture everything Chloe says from multiple sources. You will also be the ones to notify the police when the time is right," Connor said, making eye contact with each of us as he listed off our tasks.

"Grayson, Kennedy, Amara, Julian, and I will be here. Julian, Grayson, and I will be keeping watch, making sure no threats come near this house." Connor nodded at Julian, then Grayson, who nodded back.

As far as I could tell, we'd accounted for every possibility I could think of and some I hadn't. Everyone appeared to be focused and ready for this to be over today.

I'd always taken everything on my own shoulders and tried to handle it myself, but this situation taught me a valuable lesson. There were people who loved me and were willing to have my back in impossible situations. The feeling was mutual.

Instead of making me feel weak, I felt powerful. My only fear about today was for Kennedy. Carrying out this plan would be hard on her. She'd worry herself sick today, but this was the only way to end this nightmare, and we both knew it. I turned my head, meeting her eyes, and tilting my lips up in a confident smile.

With her small hand tucked in mine, I brought her knuckles to my lips and placed a light kiss there. "Everything's going to be okay, Sunshine."

Connor cleared his throat, and I looked up. Everyone was watching us. I sighed. "What's the plan after we're all in position?"

"Then we call Chloe," Connor confirmed.

AN HOUR LATER, after going over everything in detail again and again, True, Maddox, Jericho, and I were inside my house waiting for the signal to call Chloe. Sebastian had to wire all the cameras and get the audio set up. He'd also be hacking into my security system and using it to notify the police when the time was right.

"Are you sure you want to go through with this, Z?" True wondered, his brow furrowed with concern. "It's not too late to back out of this disaster waiting to happen and let the cops handle it."

I crossed my arms. "No fucking way am I backing out. For the cops to collect evidence, we'd have to wait for Chloe to do something else. No offense, True, but you've never had anyone threaten someone you love like this before. I'd do anything, and I mean any-fucking-thing, to protect Kennedy. She's my reason for living. I need her like I need air in my lungs. If something happened to her, it would shatter me. I'd never be the same. No, we're ending this today."

I didn't want to have to hurt Chloe, but I'd do whatever I had to do to stop her. She'd never so much as look at Kennedy again as long as I was breathing.

"Back off, man." Maddox clapped his hand on True's shoulder. "He's good. If you want to back out, though..." he trailed off, his lips lifting in a mocking smile.

"Fuck off, Maddox," True grumbled. "Let's get this done."

"You can always go sit on the couch and let us deal with her," Jericho added, pulling a knife out of seemingly thin air and inspecting the blade.

"You can fuck off, too," True snapped before folding his arms and leveling a glare at both of them.

I understood his hesitation, but it didn't matter. He'd understand someday what it felt like to be in love, care about someone else more than you cared about yourself, and have someone who made you feel whole, like you found a piece of yourself that you never knew was missing.

When my friends found the piece that completed each of them, no one would be happier for them than I would.

I TOOK Chloe's number from Kennedy before I left her this morning. I gave her a kiss I never wanted to end before promising again that I'd come back to her. The worry in her eyes had been haunting me ever since. I'd do everything in my power to make sure I never saw that fucking look again.

I sucked in a deep breath before blowing it out. "Ready?" I asked the room, looking first at True, who nodded and then at

Maddox and Jericho.

"Oh, we're more than fucking ready," Jericho confirmed.

Maddox moved over toward the garage door and nodded at me.

I typed out a quick message and hit send before I could start to overthink it. My stomach churned because what I typed to Chloe? Those words weren't meant for anyone but Kennedy. Every fiber of my being screamed at how wrong this was. I was disgusted that anyone but Kennedy would read words like that from me, even if they were meant as a trap, and I didn't mean one damn syllable.

Zen: I need to see you. Can you come to me?

I shuddered, the sudden desire to scrub all of my skin off was overwhelming. A mixture of rage and disgust rolled through my body. "Sent."

Every second seemed like it took hours as we waited for a reply. None of us knew what to say. True, Maddox, and Jericho would be hiding out of sight as soon as we knew she was on her way.

My phone vibrated in my hand. I glanced down at the screen and saw the message.

Chloe: I'll be there soon.

"She's on her way."

True and Jericho both turned and stalked from the room, positioning themselves just out of sight but close enough to step in if necessary. We didn't know how far away she was or how long it'd take her to get to us. The fact she didn't bother asking for my address or where I was also didn't slip past me. Her knowing exactly where to find me just further confirmed our suspicions that she was, in fact, the stalker.

I absently tapped my fingers on the counter, perched on the edge of a metal barstool with my phone beside me. My thoughts churned, and I reminded myself I needed to stay focused. I refused to let some deranged woman take any more from me. She'd already taken Kennedy's safety and caused me more stress than anything else in a long time, maybe ever. Thinking back over the past fucking month, I was incredibly proud of Kennedy and how she'd dealt with everything thrown her way. My girl was a lot tougher than she thought. I could tell from the beginning, but she was starting to see it for herself.

My attention crashed back to reality when the front door slammed open. I'd locked it myself when we came in, so I wasn't expecting her to just walk right in like she belonged in my fucking house. My muscles tensed at the loud bang, but I held back my flinch. My heart raced, but outwardly I tucked my hands into my pockets and stood up from the stool, leaning against the counter as if she hadn't just stormed into my house like she owned the fucking place. I plastered on the cocky smile I used when I was performing or doing a photoshoot. I pushed myself off the counter and, as casually as I could make it appear, began taking slow, steady steps towards Chloe.

I hadn't seen her in a while, but the way she looked scared the shit out of me. Her short hair was sticking up in every direction, her wild eyes had dark circles underneath them, and her clothes were huge on her tiny frame and dirty. Mascara ran down her cheeks as if she'd been crying, but her eyes were dry.

"I knew you'd see the truth if I just showed you how good things could be without that insignificant bitch," she babbled, pulling her lips back into a toothy grin that looked unnaturally wide for her face and eerily cheerful. The hair on the back of my neck stood up at how fucking unsettling her behavior and words were.

I'd normally never let anyone talk about Kennedy like that, not a fucking chance. The need to protect and defend my girlfriend bubbled under the surface like lava, and it took everything in me to push it down. I needed to keep a cool head if this was going to work.

I had to keep her talking.

"That's right, I did, because you showed me I was wrong. I see it now. We're meant to be together," I agreed in a soft voice, speaking to her as if she were a cornered wild animal I was trying to get to come out so I could throw a leash around her neck.

The words tasted bitter in my mouth. I wanted to snatch them back and shove them deep down inside where they'd never see the light of day. I kept reminding myself all of this was for the greater good. For Kennedy.

Chloe began to laugh, at first chuckling before her laughter turned hysterical. She doubled over, bending at the waist and clutching her stomach. Her laugh sounded harsh, high pitched, and grated on my already frayed nerves.

I cleared my throat, attempting to put her attention back on me. She stopped abruptly, standing up and gazing over at me as if she'd forgotten I was there. She stared at me, blinking slowly and waiting for me to make the first move. I hadn't really considered what I'd do once she was here other than getting her talking. I'd say whatever it took even if it killed me inside.

"So," I began. "Thanks for helping me see that I needed to get Kennedy out of my life. You were the only one who told me the truth." I felt like a knife was twisting in my gut, and I wanted to throw up, but on the outside, I was calm as fuck.

She smiled at me, but her eyes darted around the room. "I only pushed a little," she said, taking a step toward me. I had no intention of letting her touch me in any way. I might be willing to say whatever it took, but I belonged to Kennedy. Even in this fucked up situation, I wasn't going to let another woman lay a single finger on me.

I quickly wracked my brain. What could I say to get her to confess? I decided to try something direct. "I only know about part of what you did to help, but I'd like to hear the rest so I can properly thank you." I held my breath while my heartbeat pounded in my ears. I wasn't a good actor, and I hoped she'd buy it. Maybe she'd want to brag about everything she did to gain my favor. It was fifty-fifty. She was so unstable, she might not care what the real version of me thought because the fake one in her mind was cheering her on. Who the fuck could tell?

She cocked her head to the side like a dog. She took another couple of steps toward me and was now within an arms' length of my body. "Let's see..." she said, a gleeful smile filling up her face as if she enjoyed the memory of how she'd tortured the woman that I loved. I'd never hit a woman before, but the look on her face right now made my fingers curl into a fist. I took a deep, steadying breath, trying to suppress the adrenaline running through my body. She'd get what was coming to her. I'd make sure of it.

"I saw you at the lake, but *she* distracted you. I could see you needed my help. So I followed you back to the store. I planned on watching from a distance to find out when I could get her out of your life, but then that Help Wanted sign was put up the next morning, and I knew that was my sign. I went home and made up a fake resume and then came back and got the job."

"At first, I thought I'd become her friend, and then when she trusted me, I could get close enough to get rid of her for good. But I wanted to be subtle about it because I didn't want anything I did to look bad on you." She gave me a twisted smile that made me cringe.

"I tried to warn you off of her first because if you could find a way to push her away, it'd be easier. But she wouldn't let you go that easy, so I had to step in. That was when I snuck in to scare her at night. I hoped she'd get the message through the note I left here, but obviously, she didn't. Stupid bitch. Sneaking in didn't do it either. I got so mad because she was keeping us from being together. You had to go to her that night instead of being there with me like you should've. How could she do that to me? It was obvious that we should be together, everyone told me so."

What the fuck was she talking about? Everyone? I wondered who everyone was. Probably the voices in her head. She was on a roll. I needed to encourage her. "You snuck in? I don't know if I heard about that. What happened? How'd you get past security?"

Chloe began to absently pull on the short locks of her hair, yanking it in what looked to be a painful way, yet she didn't so much as flinch. Christ.

"Security was easy. There were a couple new guys, and all I had to do was flirt and let them fuck me, and they were putty in my hands. They let me in your house whenever I wanted so I could leave gifts behind for you. Don't worry, those guys didn't mean anything, though. I did it for us," she explained.

"Oh, right. I understand." I didn't fucking understand *at all*.

She continued this time without me prompting her. "At Kennedy's, I didn't need any help. When she wasn't there during the day, I went upstairs with my key and unlocked the window. That night, I climbed up the fire escape and got inside. If she woke up, I'd stab her so she'd be out of the picture for good. I couldn't risk her coming in and trying to steal you away once I had you to myself," she said, a satisfied smirk on her face.

Jesus. I knew I'd come close to losing her that night, but I had no idea how close.

I widened my eyes, trying to convey surprise. "What happened when you were in her room?"

"I stood there watching, trying to decide how I wanted to do it. Right when I decided to pierce her heart in the best form of poetic justice I could think of, she started screaming, and I had to run away. I was so angry." She yelled that last part and stomped her feet. "Every step of the way, she ruined everything!"

"After that, I knew I had to finish her. She was never going to step aside and just let us be together. You needed my help. She thought she had you, but she was wrong because you were mine from the day I saw you when we were in LA. Long before I met you at the lake and she kept you from me," she spat, continually ripping at her hair until clumps of it were starting to fall around her.

"I had to do something, but I wasn't sure what until she called me back into work. I had that whole week to think, and when she asked me to go get supplies, I knew what I had to do. She'd come out to help me, and I could just let my car 'accidentally,'" she paused her yanking to make air quotes, "go over the curb and take out the problem for me. Easy-peasy." She spoke in a sing-song voice as if she wasn't describing the murder of the woman who completely owned me.

It was disturbing as fuck.

She swayed a little, hugging herself with her arms around her middle, closing her eyes, and humming a Shadow Phoenix song. I shivered, and my stomach turned.

"I could sing that for you, if you want," I offered, wanting to buy time for Sebastian to call the cops.

"You could?" Her dark eyes widened, focusing on mine for maybe the first time since she walked in the door.

I nodded. "Sure, but first finish telling me about everything you did for us."

She jutted out her bottom lip then sighed heavily. "Fine, I don't know why you want to keep talking about that bitch. She's out of the picture now, and I'd rather focus on showing you how good we are together." I could tell she was close to losing her temper, but I almost had her. I only had a little further to go. I most likely had enough information already for the attempted murder, but I wanted to get her for Kennedy's store as well.

Kennedy needed to feel safe, to feel justice had been served for everything. I'd make sure to give that to her. No matter what it took.

"Because it makes me feel good to know you've done so much for me. It makes me feel closer to you," I finished, feeling the acid rise up in my throat.

She giggled. "Fine, but just this once. Then we're done with her." Her mood swings were giving me whiplash.

"Deal."

"When that stupid bus bench got in my way, I couldn't find her. I had no idea where she went since she wasn't here or at her place, but I knew what would hurt her most. Losing her store and her apartment. I figured it'd finally convince her I was serious and to let go of you. So, I let myself into the store and made a pile of all the books I could find. They make great kindling, by the way," she said, throwing her head back and cackling at her own joke.

I had chills running down my spine. She acted like ruining Kennedy's life was nothing, like it was her goddamn entertainment.

"I poured on some gas, and I threw a match and got the hell out of there. It was as simple as that. And obviously, it worked because here you are," she said, gleefully clapping her hands together and taking another step toward me.

I maneuvered myself backward a step, trying to put distance between us. She frowned.

"I told you everything. Why're you moving away from me? You said we'd be together." Her eyes hardened, and she stomped her foot on the ground.

I couldn't know if Sebastian had called the police, so until they busted through the door, I'd keep playing along. "Oh, I'm…" I hesitated, wracking my brain for something. "I'm thirsty, thought I'd get something to drink. Do you want anything?"

I stepped around the island but walked backward so I could keep facing her. I didn't trust her at all and wasn't about to turn my back. Fuck that. She seemed unstable as fuck.

"No." She narrowed her eyes. I turned for a second to grab a bottle of water out of the refrigerator, taking my eyes off her for no more than a fraction of a second despite knowing I shouldn't. Her clothes rustled. When I turned back around, she'd pulled a handgun out of thin fucking air and pointed it directly at my head.

I held up my hands, releasing the bottle of water. It slammed into the ground, splashing everywhere and making her jump. "What are you doing?" I growled, pissed the fuck off that she dared pull this shit with me. She didn't get to threaten me. Not after everything.

"We're going to be together. No more moving away from me." Her eyes narrowed into thin slits as Maddox sneezed.

Chloe whipped around, the gun in her hand shifting to point at Maddox's hiding spot by the garage door. She couldn't see him yet, but her weapon was aimed inches from where he stood. As deranged as she was, she might fire randomly, and I couldn't risk that.

I didn't even think, I just reacted. I launched myself over the island counter and jumped on Chloe, tackling her to the ground. Her grip on the gun was surprisingly tight. She twisted when she fell, ending up face down on the ground, but she managed to pull the trigger once, firing into the wall near Maddox.

"What the fuck?" His yell made its way through the ringing in my ears. "This bitch has a death wish, Z!"

I slammed my knee down onto Chloe's arm, pressing my forearm into her upper back to keep her on the ground. "Hold still!" I shouted, trying to keep her writhing body pressed underneath me. She hadn't let go of the gun yet, and her small size and quick, jerky movements made her surprisingly hard to pin down. I was doing all I could to not get any of us shot.

"Someone get me a goddamn zip tie!" I shouted to the room, trusting someone would jump into action. Footsteps pounded up behind me, and drawers were flung open before finally True stood over me, leaning down to hold her wrist while I ripped the gun from her other hand. I passed it off to Jericho, who stood behind me.

He took it gingerly between two fingers before grabbing a plastic bag and sealing it inside. Maddox appeared by my side, taking the gun out of Jericho's hands.

Jericho kneeled down in front of Chloe's face, unsheathing his knife and pressing the blade against her throat. "Listen up, little girl. You're going to calm the fuck down and stop moving, or I'm going to push my knife into your throat. Understand?"

Her eyes widened, and she stilled underneath me. I moved my knee to bring her wrists together. True wrapped the tie around her and tightened it. I was breathing heavily as I moved off of her completely, and True and I both stepped back. Jericho stayed where he was, his eyes narrowed and trained on Chloe.

She started screaming profanities at us, her speech muffled by the way her mouth was lying on the floor. "You love me! You told me! I know you do! We'll be together! I'll kill her! I'll kill everyone! I'll burn the goddamn world to the ground until all that's left is you and me!" she shrieked, every proclamation louder than the last.

A couple of minutes later, the police showed up, rushing into the house and taking the cursing Chloe into custody. Sebastian brought in copies of the recordings to hand off. Maddox turned over the gun, and then it was quiet.

The police wanted to take statements from everyone, so they took their time making sure they were thorough and detailed before they finally left. I hadn't had a chance to let Kennedy know what was happening, and I figured no one else had either. I cursed under my breath when it hit me that this whole time she'd probably been jumping to all sorts of conclusions about what was going on and whether or not I was okay. I knew how her brain worked.

I took out my phone to call her, but it went straight to voicemail. Shit. I forgot her phone was smashed yesterday in the attack.

"I'm going to Gray's," I called out, already run-walking to the garage to get in my Mercedes. Sebastian followed me, hopping in the passenger seat, followed by Jericho, True, and Maddox. They climbed in as the wheels were already starting to roll, slamming the doors as the tires squealed on the concrete floor. I wasn't waiting for anyone. My singular focus was Kennedy.

I could finally start to breathe again after this fucking nightmare, knowing that we were all safe for now, and Chloe was no longer a threat. It was only a matter of time until this happened again, mainly because my relationship was now public knowledge. If some other over-excited fan took things too far, we could have repeat after repeat of what just happened.

The thought of that potential future was enough to make me want to spend the rest of my life off the grid at some secluded cabin in the woods. I couldn't risk endangering Kennedy or our future family with my career. I refused to put us through it again.

"Listen, guys..." I searched for the words to express what I needed to. "Thanks for what you did back there, for Kennedy and for me. I couldn't have done it without you all."

"You know we've got your back, Z," True said with a grin.

"I almost got shot for you, asshole," Maddox grumbled, but I could tell by his tone he wasn't mad.

"I'll take your PRS McCartney 594 for having to deal with that bullshit," Jericho asserted. "And don't even think about swapping it for one of your low rent fucking acoustic guitars. That was some fucked up shit."

"Fine," I agreed begrudgingly. "But since when do you collect vintage guitars?"

"Since now. That's your favorite, right?"

"Yes," I confirmed.

He nodded. "Perfect."

"Asshole," I bit out, but there wasn't any heat behind my words. I'd gladly give up my favorite guitar if it meant having Jericho there for me when I needed him. Besides, the guitar was his way of keeping shit even. He'd always have any of our backs, but he didn't like to feel like people owed him or he owed them.

"Now that this shit show is behind me, I don't think I can keep doing this. I can't risk Kennedy and our future together. I'm not walking away from her or giving her up. I refuse to put her in danger again. I won't fucking do it. After we're done recording this album, I'm done," I declared, gripping the steering wheel hard until my knuckles turned white.

I didn't want to give up making music with my three best friends, playing for sold-out crowds. It was less important to me than it once was, but having that creative outlet and getting to do what I loved with my friends was everything I'd ever dreamed of. At least it had been until I crossed paths with a certain leggy blonde-haired, blue-eyed beauty who'd stolen my heart from the first moment I laid eyes on her. She was my future, my forever, and I wouldn't do anything to jeopardize that.

"I get it, Z. I think we all get it at least a little bit," True began. Maddox nodded in agreement, but Jericho just glared at me in the rearview mirror. "But a whole bunch of shit just went down. How about we take a minute to catch our breath? Talk to Kennedy and finish recording the album. Then we can talk again, and you can make a decision. Sound good?"

True was trying to be the voice of reason, and he made sense. His words were cracking through the wall I'd built up around my decision. I exhaled loudly. "Yeah, I can do that."

"You're not fucking quitting, Zen. We already told you." Jericho glowered at me, and I shifted my gaze away. I couldn't make that promise.

"Good, now let's go tell your girl what a hero you were today." True punched the back of my seat and flashed me a grin.

"Shut up, dick."

I couldn't wait to tell Kennedy that she was safe, and she didn't have to worry about this anymore. I'd always protect her no matter what.

She was mine, and I planned on never letting her go.

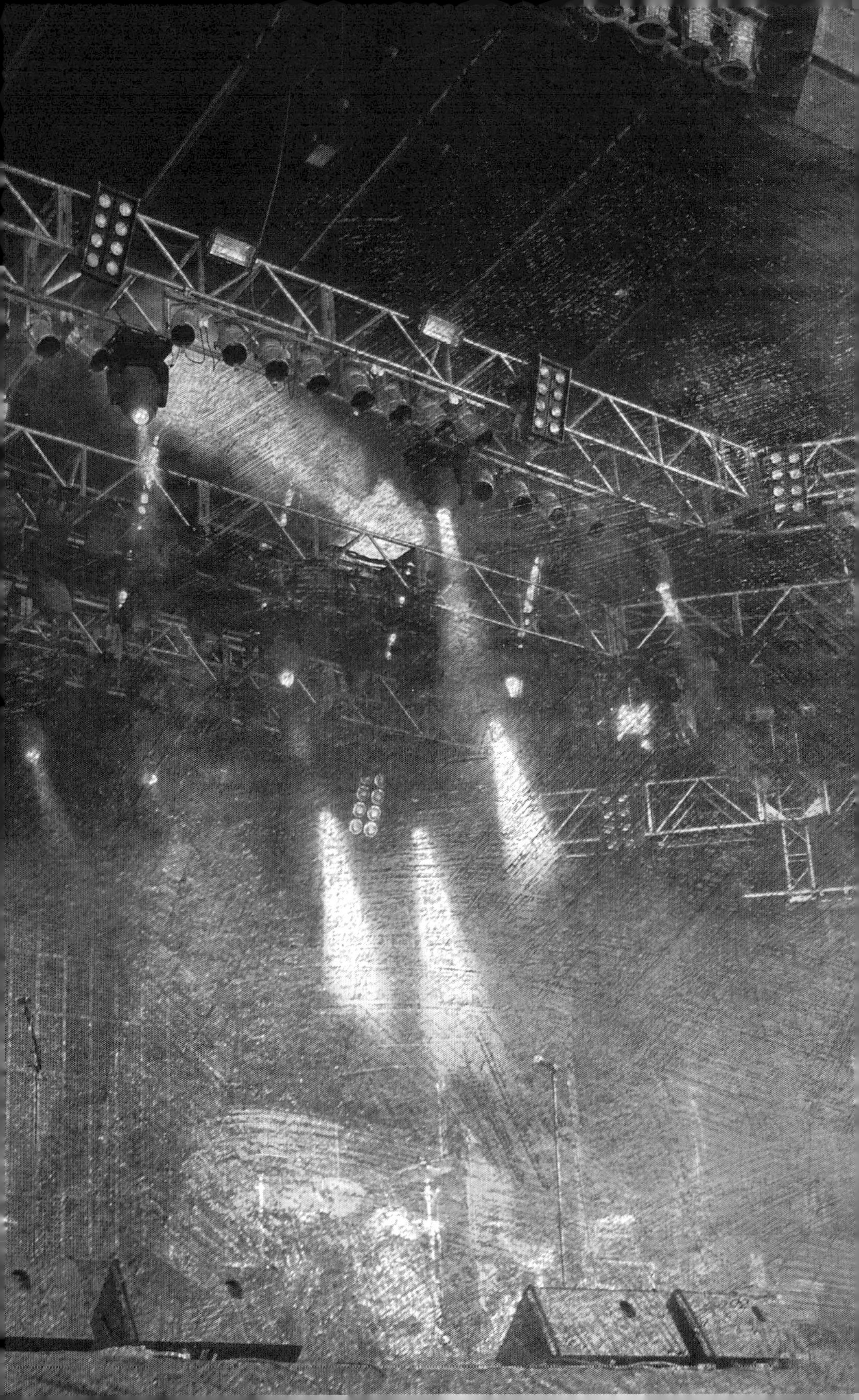

CHAPTER 32

KENNEDY

I'D BEEN PACING back and forth on the floor for what felt like days. I had to keep my body in constant motion to prevent the adrenaline of my nervous energy from turning into full-blown panic. For a while, Amara paced beside me, but she gave up a long time ago, and now it was just me. I was determined to keep my wits about me today and not lose control. If anything went wrong, I had to be prepared to think clearly.

I didn't have my phone with me, which really sucked. Just another thing Chloe took away. I lost it somewhere in the attack and hadn't had time to get a new one. I turned to where my brother sat in the living room.

"Have you heard anything yet?" I asked, for what must have been the hundredth time today.

He sighed and pinched the bridge of his nose. "No, Ken. You know I'll let you know as soon as I do."

I whipped around to face Connor, who stood by the front door, his eyes tracking my movement. "How about you?"

"Nothing yet."

I raised my eyebrow at Amara, and she shrugged. "I'm not exactly top of the phone tree for getting updates."

I sighed heavily and continued my pacing. I watched out the window for any sign of movement and noticed a black SUV making its way down the road. My heart leaped in my chest. Could it be them? I hadn't expected them back before we heard from anyone, so I was afraid to get my hopes up. My heart slammed against my rib cage. I launched myself towards the window, ripping open the curtains to get a better look.

"Kennedy! Stay away from the damn window," Connor barked, jumping in front of me and physically holding me back.

"Move, Connor! I need to see if it's them." I struggled against the hold he had on me but failed to move him even an inch. He was like a goddamn mountain.

"No, I'm not risking your safety. We'll know in a minute," he said, pulling me into the living room and motioning with a jerk of his chin for me to sit on the couch with Gray. I glared at him, and he crossed his bulky arms across his hard chest, raising an eyebrow as if daring me to challenge him.

"Fine," I huffed, plopping down next to my brother, and Amara dropped down beside me. The second Connor moved or looked away, I intended to run for the window, but before I had a chance to plan my escape, the front door swung open.

"Kennedy?" Zen called, his voice the most soothing sound I'd ever heard. It was like a balm to my frayed nerves.

"Zen!" I leaped up off the couch and ran straight at him, launching myself into his arms and wrapping my legs around his waist. He caught me easily, chuckling at my enthusiasm. "Miss me, Sunshine?" he teased, pressing a heated kiss to my lips.

I pulled back to look at him and, out of the corner of my eyes, spotted Amara throwing her arms around True. "I'm so glad you're okay," she rasped against his chest, the words a little muffled. His eyes widened, and he slowly brought his arms around her, hugging her close.

Turning back to Zen, I kissed him again. I didn't give a shit that we had an audience or even what happened with Chloe. The only thing that mattered to me right now was that he came back, and he was safe. We'd both made it through this relatively unharmed and stronger than ever. He pulled back and dotted my jawline with kisses before returning to my mouth. I opened for him, our tongues twisting together in a heated dance as a soft moan escaped my lips. I felt his hardness pressed against me, and rolled my hips. He groaned, and it just made me hotter.

A throat cleared somewhere behind us, but I didn't care. He pulled back, smiling against my lips. "I should put myself in danger more often," he teased, kissing me one more time before setting me down on my feet. He pulled my body flush against him, and I could feel every rock hard muscle and bulge pressing into me. My panties were completely soaked, and I found it difficult not to climb back up on him and beg him to take me upstairs.

"Don't you dare."

"Okay," he said simply, smiling at me before grabbing my hand and leading me into the living room. Everyone had gathered there and were talking about what happened. Zen stood behind me and wrapped his arms around my waist.

Grayson looked up at us. "I could have gone my whole life without seeing my sister like that, man." He glared at Zen.

Zen threw his head back and laughed. "Sorry, not sorry. Be thankful I had enough restraint to stop."

"Gross," Grayson replied, rolling his eyes.

"So, what happened?" Now that the overwhelming need to make sure Zen was here and really okay, I wanted to know.

"Z sent the text, and Chloe showed up, just like we thought she would. When she got there, he had to say a bunch of shit to get her to talk, but she sang like a fucking canary. We got everything on video and audio from multiple angles, so the plan worked perfectly. Well, right up until she pulled out a gun and almost shot Z and then me," Maddox rehashed.

"What?!" My head snapped around to look up at Zen.

Zen glared at his friend. "Thanks, Mad. Next time think before you open your goddamn mouth."

He spun me in his arms. "Baby, everything turned out fine. She pulled out a gun, but we handled it. I took her down, and we got the gun out of her hands. Jericho kept her still, and True restrained her. I promised you I'd come back safe, and I did, right?" His eyes were full of sincerity, but knowing he almost got hurt? It killed me.

I held out while I considered his words. It was true. He had promised me that, and he was here. What had happened really didn't matter that much, I guess. I exhaled slowly. "Right, you did."

"The police have her and her gun now."

"Plus all the evidence," True chimed in.

Zen nodded. "Right. She can't hurt you or me or anyone else we love, okay?"

"That bitch isn't going to see the outside of a padded jail cell for a long fucking time," Jericho added.

"Okay," I whispered, burying my face in his chest and grabbing a fistful of his shirt. I breathed deeply. My eyes burned with unshed tears, but I refused to cry. Everything was going to be okay now. I kept breathing Zen in while he stroked my back in slow circles.

Everyone else in the room resumed talking about what happened, but suddenly I needed some alone time with my man. The heat I'd been feeling earlier flared to life, and I shifted myself closer until my hips were pushed against his.

Zen reached down and swept me up into his arms bridal-style, sensing what I needed like he always did. He turned and walked up the stairs to the room where we were staying. He didn't even bother saying anything to anyone. It was hot as hell, like I was the center of his attention, and nothing else mattered.

He laid me down on the bed and walked back to close the door behind him, then he crawled in behind me, pulling my body to his. Neither of us said anything. I knew how he must have felt yesterday. I could've lost him today. Zen Taylor. The man who held my soul in the palm of his hand. What would I have done if Chloe had taken him, too?

"I love you," I whispered.

He pressed a kiss to my forehead. "I love you, too. More than you'll ever know." He brushed a piece of hair off of my forehead and tucked it behind my ear.

He sat up, leaning on his elbow as his emerald eyes met mine. "I want to talk to you about something. We've had this discussion before, but after everything we just went through, I feel like I should be done with Shadow Phoenix. We got Chloe this time, but who knows how many more Chloes are out there? You're the woman I'm going to spend my life with, have babies with, grow old with. You're the piece of my soul that lives outside of me. I'm not willing to put you at risk again." His voice was gravelly.

Warmth blossomed in my chest. I loved this man with everything I had, and it still took my breath away how fiercely he loved me back. His vision of the future sounded perfect to me, with one exception.

I placed my hand on his cheek, feeling the soft stubble of his jaw brush against my palm. "Do you remember the first time you took me out to work on my anxiety?"

He nodded.

"Do you remember when I started to give in to the panic outside of the high rise, and you told me not to think about the what-ifs unless they were the ones from our song?"

He nodded again, a smile spreading across his face as he figured out where I was going with this.

"How many stalkers have you had before Chloe?"

He thought for a moment. "I'm not sure, four? Maybe five?"

"Okay, so in ten years of being the mega-famous Zen Taylor, this has happened four or five times. How bad were the others?"

He played with my hair absently now with his free hand. "Not bad. I didn't even really notice because security handled everything pretty easily."

"So, what you're saying is that in ten years, the worst thing you've been through danger-wise was Chloe?" I was willing him to see the truth of the situation.

"Yeah, I guess so. When you put it like that, it doesn't sound that bad."

"That's because it's not. People go through hard and horrible shit every single day. If we just went through this together and came out stronger on the other side, I think we can handle anything else life throws at us. Don't you?" I flashed him my grin.

He leaned down and pressed his lips against mine. "What are you saying?"

"I'm saying I've been doing a lot of thinking today. I was sitting here wondering if I'd ever get to see you again, wondering what our life might look like or what my life might look like without you in it if something happened to you, and I had to try to pick up the pieces and move on. This whole thing made me realize how strong I've gotten, and you were the one that pushed me to grow, to shed my insecurities and the boundaries I'd built around myself. You helped me find myself, and I don't want to spend time apart anymore. I don't want to have to wait to see you on the weekends. I told myself that if you came back to me today, I'd go all in, and that's what I intend to do."

"Good—" he started, but I placed my finger across his soft lips.

"Shh, I'm not done yet. The fact that my store and my home are gone is actually a blessing in disguise. Not only do I not want you to quit the band, but I'm free from anything tying me here outside of Gray and Amara. You're not quitting the band no matter what, Zen. It's your life's work, and I'm not about to let you give up on it. But I'm not giving up on mine either. I can write from anywhere and as for Sweet Stories? I'm going to reopen but better than ever, in LA with you."

His eyes widened. "Are you sure? I mean, your family—"

"Is wherever you are." I leaned up and kissed him long and lazily, enjoying the luxury of unlimited time right now.

He pulled away gently, sitting up and wrapping his arms around me, burying his face in my neck. I wove my fingers through his hair, holding him close.

"You're incredible, Kennedy. I never pictured sharing my life with anyone until I ran into the most amazing woman I've ever met. You're compassionate, kind, caring, fucking gorgeous, honest, refreshing... There aren't enough words in my vocabulary to describe the level of love I have for you. As long as I'm alive, there will never be anyone else for me. I'm yours," he said, running his fingers along my cheek.

"And I'm yours." I'd found my other half, the person who my heart would belong to forever. I'd never love again like I loved this man. He possessed my heart, and I'd never been happier than in this moment, safely tucked into the arms of the man who made me feel whole. He showed me the strength I had inside myself.

Heat flared up in my veins as a wave of goosebumps rushed down my spine. Even the lightest touch of his fingertips had me desperate for him. I pushed myself towards him, rolling him onto his back and throwing my leg across his hips until I straddled him. His body flattened beneath me, his eyes burning up into mine.

I bent down and covered his mouth with mine, nipping at his bottom lip. One of his hands gripped my hip while his other hand wove through my hair. He pulled my mouth even closer and plunged his tongue deep inside as if he wanted to explore every corner. My body tingled, and I shivered as his hands danced across my skin. I couldn't imagine anyone ever coming close to making me feel how Zen could.

I rocked my hips against him, feeling the thick ridge of his growing erection through the layers of clothing keeping us apart. A pleasure-filled groan escaped his lips. I moved my body down his, first peppering his jaw with kisses before sliding my tongue back up his throat.

His fingers pulled at the hem of my shirt, and I leaned back, letting him yank it off and toss it aside. He quickly unhooked my bra, and his fingers slowly trailed up my body, sending shivers down my spine.

"You're so fucking beautiful." His tone was reverent. He sat up, wrapped his arms around me, and flipped me over so he was on top. Feeling the weight of his body pressed down into mine made me even more hot and achy. He lowered his mouth to my pebbled nipple before circling his tongue around it, lightly pulling it into his mouth before releasing it with a soft kiss.

I writhed underneath him, pulling him closer. I couldn't seem to get him close enough.

"Tell me what you need, baby," Zen said, his voice husky.

"You, Zen. I need you inside of me."

He leaned up, pressing a kiss to my lips before pulling off what was left of our clothes. I watched him, my need making me impatient. "Are you almost done?" I sounded a little breathless.

He let out a low chuckle. "Is someone tired of waiting?"

Instead of wasting time answering, I reached for him and pulled him back down on top of me. I couldn't hide what he did to me. My mind was hazy as I wrapped my hand around his hard length. I stroked him slowly a few times before guiding him to my entrance. I was needy as fuck, slick and hot and ready.

Our eyes locked as he pushed inside in one slow thrust. I arched my back as I let out a moan, the feeling of fullness and possession exactly what I'd been missing. He stilled, letting me adjust before he started to move.

"Oh, fuck! That feels so good." I'd never get tired of having him fully inside of me, owning my body like he did my heart.

My fist clenched the sheet as I tried to hold on while he took me to new heights. The pleasure was building inside of me, making me feel like I was soaring. As our hips rocked together, he teased the flesh of my neck with his tongue, biting and sucking while he thrust in and out of me.

"You're so fucking tight." He growled in my ear.

I trembled and tightened, my legs beginning to quake. I could feel myself barreling toward release. I was along for the ride, helpless to stop it.

"Don't stop, don't—" I moaned before losing the ability to form words. The waves of pleasure crashed over me as my walls pulsed. He fell over the edge with me, cursing and calling out my name.

It made me hot all over again, and he hadn't even pulled out of me.

He rolled over, pulling me on top of him. Our bodies were still connected as we came down from the high we'd just brought each other to. He gently stroked my back and played with my hair as I caught my breath. My cheek rested on his chest, and my arms fell against his sides as I straddled his hips and listened to his heart beating.

"Tell me again you're mine," he whispered.

"I'm yours, Zen. Forever."

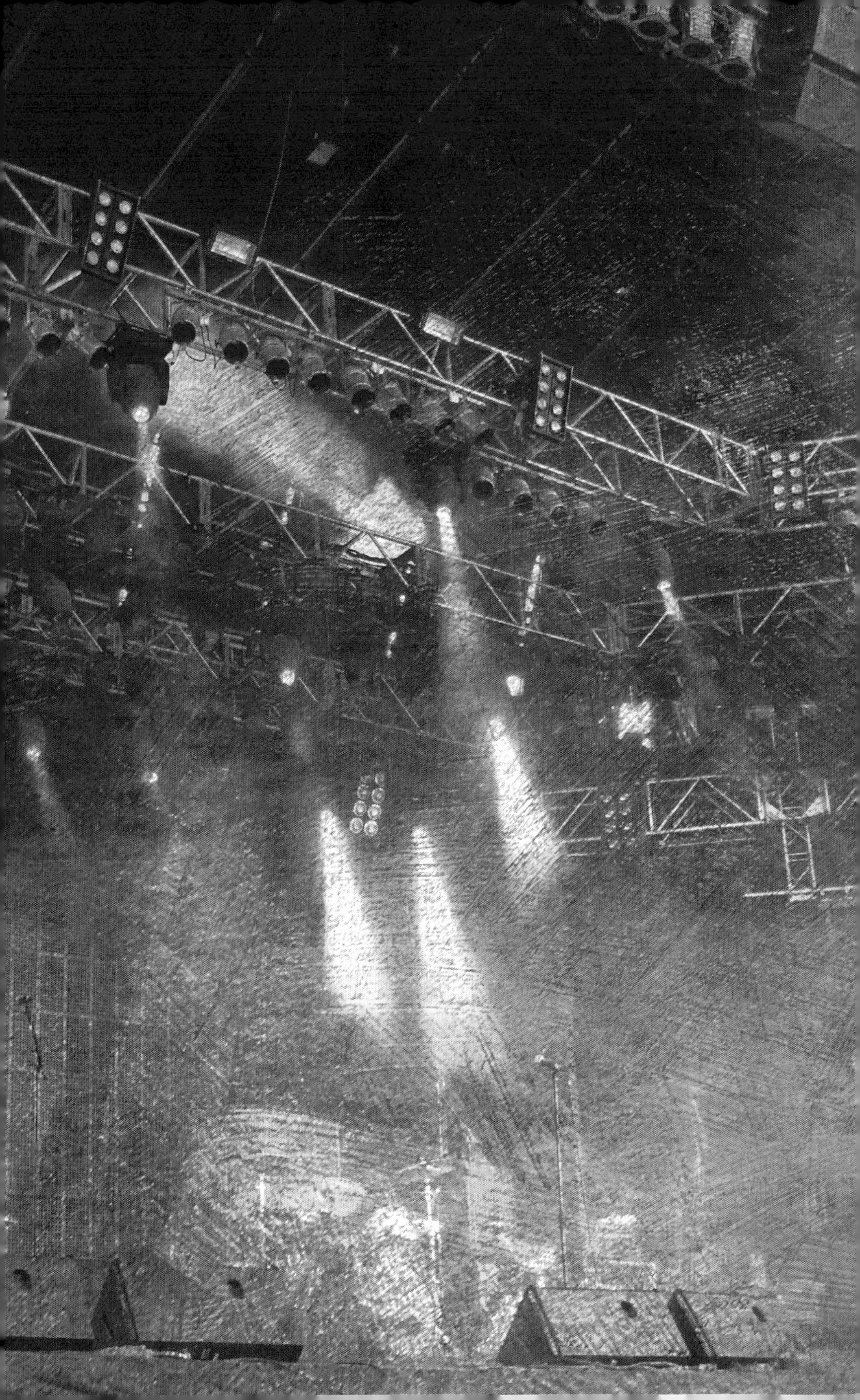

EPILOGUE

ZEN

Six months later...

I KNEW from pretty much the moment I laid eyes on her that Kennedy was it for me. Not only did she take care of me like no one else before, but she allowed me to take care of her when she needed it. We were a true partnership, and I loved her more than anyone else in my life. There was no comparison. Love didn't feel like an adequate word to describe all the things I felt for her.

Six months ago, when her store burned down, my girl showed just how resilient she could be. I always believed in her inner strength, but she went above and beyond even my expectations when it came to how well she handled her entire life changing. It was as if she'd been bottling up all the experiences she'd dreamed about having for years, and my stumbling into her life by chance that summer night had been the catalyst to let it all out.

I was more than happy to go on that journey with her. I still couldn't believe that she chose me and stuck by me through everything all those months ago. She reopened Sweet Stories in Malibu near where we lived, but she'd insisted on hiring employees to run it. She loved owning a bookstore, but she told me she had a new dream now. She wanted to travel with me and see everything she hadn't until this point in her life. I loved her ambition and that she had goals and was focused on them. I'd do whatever I could to make every single one of her dreams come true.

Once the investigation wrapped up in Kirkland, we flew back to LA together and never looked back. We sold the house up north. It held too many shitty memories and didn't feel safe anymore.

I got word from my lawyers when Chloe's trial was, but Kennedy didn't want to go. My lawyers took care of everything, and with the evidence we collected, Chloe wasn't getting out of jail anytime soon.

While all that was going on, Shadow Phoenix finished recording our album and released it to the world. Shockingly, the critics and our fans loved it. I'd talked with Kennedy about putting *Brave* on the album, and she loved the idea. She told me that it helped her through more times than she could count, and she wouldn't feel right about depriving any of our fans of the same comfort it gave her when she was struggling. Just thinking about how much she cared about all our fans, most she had never met and never would meet, made warmth flood my chest. I wasn't a very emotional guy, but when it came to Kennedy, she was my weakness. I felt everything, and I fucking loved it.

We toured for our new album release, but I only agreed to go if Kennedy would come with us. I made her a promise once that I wouldn't leave her alone, and I meant to keep it no matter what. Even though Chloe was no longer a threat, I had no idea when the next issue might come up, and it terrified me to think that all it would take was one time for me to be gone, and something could happen to her. Instead, she toured with Shadow Phoenix, and I watched as her eyes lit up when we drove into every new city.

I'd developed an insanely overprotective side when it came to Kennedy, but neither one of us minded. She'd just smile sweetly at me and rise up on her toes to press a kiss to my lips, her eyes sparkling while she reassured me she understood. She told me she loved how protective of her I was, and it made me want to pound on my chest like a goddamn Neanderthal.

Last night was the last stop on our U.S. tour. We'd be touring Europe and Asia over the next three months, but we had two weeks free. I had a surprise in store for Kennedy, one my stomach was in knots over. I hoped she'd go for it.

As was tradition, we finished in LA last night, and today I found myself standing in a private hangar at LAX waiting for Kennedy. The black Tesla pulled up, and Connor stepped out of the driver's seat, walking around to open the back door. My breath caught like it did every time I saw her.

Her blonde hair was loose in waves hanging down her back, and she was in a white lace floor-length dress with sandals. She smiled at me before throwing herself into my arms and wrapping her legs around my waist like she always did. Kennedy didn't just hug me, she always tackled me like she couldn't get close enough.

"Hi, baby," I said, my arms wrapped tightly around her.

"Hey, I missed you," she sighed, smiling.

I let out a chuckle. "I just saw you this morning."

She shrugged. "Does that mean I can't miss you?"

I laughed. "Considering I missed you like crazy, too, I'd say no."

I leaned down, pressing a soft kiss to her lips before letting her slide down my body, stepping back and taking her hand in mine.

"Where are we going?" she asked, gazing behind me at the Shadow Phoenix jet waiting. Hilda was standing at the top of the stairs, in the entrance doorway to the plane, with a soft smile on her face.

"It's a surprise, but first," I said, using one finger to nudge her chin back in my direction, so I looked into her eyes. "I've got something to tell you."

"I'm listening."

I took a deep breath, blowing it out slowly. "When I first met you, I was out of my mind messed up, roofied and on the verge of being kidnapped, and yet you took pity on my pathetic ass and took me in. You brought me, a total stranger—"

"A crazy hot stranger." She laughed.

I grinned. "A crazy hot stranger into your home and watched over me. Every day since then, I've been enchanted by you. By your beauty, by your heart, by your passion, by your determination, and by your bravery. Right there at that moment, I was terrified because I realized you would become my world, and I was right. You're the bright, warm light that drove out my demons. You showed me that life can be fucking incredible with the right person by my side."

I reached into my pocket, pulling out the velvet box I'd been carrying around all day and dropping to one knee. I knew six months ago when I bought the ring that I wouldn't spend another day without her.

She gasped, her hand flew up to her mouth, and her eyes filled with tears.

"Kennedy, I made you a promise that we wouldn't spend another day apart, and this is me making good on that promise. I don't want to spend even one single day of my life without you. I love you with everything that I am. There aren't strong enough words to express my love for you. Will you get on that plane and marry me right now?"

The tears were running down her face freely. "Right now?" she squeaked. "As in, marry you today?"

I nodded, my breath stuck in my lungs while I waited for her to answer. "You're killing me, baby. What do you say?"

"Yes! Took you long enough," she said with a chuckle. "Like I'd ever say anything but yes. I love you so much, I can't wait to marry you. Let's go." She pulled me up and began tugging me by the hand toward the plane.

I laughed, pulling back and scooping her up in my arms,

twirling her around before setting her back down and kissing her deeply. "I know it'll be the shortest fucking engagement ever, but I don't want to go on one more stop of this tour without being able to call you my wife."

I slid the ring onto her finger, and she glanced down at it, wiggling her fingers and watching it sparkle. "I like the sound of that. I'd go down to the courthouse and marry you right now. I don't even care as long as I get to call you my husband."

I found myself wondering for what could easily be the millionth time how I got so lucky. "C'mon, we've got a plane to catch." I wove my fingers with hers and led her to the staircase.

"Congratulations," Hilda said with a soft smile before stepping aside to let us board.

"Thanks, Hilda," Kennedy grinned, and her eyes sparkled.

I smiled when I followed her through the door, knowing this was only the first of many surprises in store for my future bride today. I wanted to make sure this day was perfect for her, and I'd been working on it for months in secret. We buckled in, and before I knew it, we were on our way.

SIX HOURS LATER, the wheels of the plane touched down on the tarmac of Oahu. The jolt of the aircraft coming to a stop stirred Kennedy from the nap she'd been taking. I spent the flight writing. The emotion of today wasn't lost on me. Feelings always fueled great songs, and this milestone in my life was no exception.

We didn't talk about it because guys just didn't do that type of bullshit, but I was pretty sure none of my friends had ever been in love before, so the intensity happening in my life was entirely new for our brand of music. There was a vast well of inspiration inside of me for our next album. It was going to be hard not to go all love ballad on it, but I'm sure Maddox or Jericho would be there to kick my ass if I tried. Still, I kept a journal with me at all times now, so I wouldn't miss out on any love-fueled thought that popped into my head.

"I'm going to go fix my hair, back in a sec," Kennedy told me, grabbing her bag and making her way to the bathroom. Connor hopped up and stepped through the open cabin door. I stood up, reaching for my bag and heading to the other bathroom at the front of the plane to change my clothes. I quickly slipped into a pair of gray linen pants and a white button-down shirt. I checked my hair and added some cologne before brushing my teeth and stepping out into the plane. My eyes locked on Kennedy. She was striking in her long dress, her blue eyes bright, standing out against the tan skin she'd gotten from doing yoga outside every morning. I never missed a chance to watch her bend and twist. It became my favorite part of the morning.

She smiled at me before I closed the distance between us and took her hand in mine. "Are you ready for what comes next?" I asked.

"As long as it's with you, I'm ready for anything," she said, grinning.

I led her out of the plane and down the stairs into the waiting Tahoe. Connor waited with the door open for us, nodding at me with a small, knowing smile. He knew what I had planned because he'd been in on it. He had a big role to play in our important day.

A short ride later, we pulled up to Waimanalo Beach. I stepped out of the car, holding out my hand for Kennedy. When she slid out of the back seat, she gasped at the sight before her. She'd always wanted to go to Hawaii, and I vowed to make all her dreams come true. This was just one of many I planned to fulfill throughout our life together.

The sun was sinking toward the horizon casting the white sand

and turquoise waters with a golden glow. Behind the shoreline was a dense green forest backdrop, which served as a private barrier. I watched her take everything in as her eyes welled up with tears. Finally, her gaze settled on a spot several feet down the beach.

Candles lined the pathway for us to follow, their light flickering in the gentle breeze coming off the water. At the end of the path was a crowd of people, most of them lounging on blankets on the sugary sand. At the very end was a driftwood archway strung with white gauze and twinkling fairy lights. Kennedy looked at me, her eyes filled with happiness.

"I can't believe you did all this," she said. "What did I do to deserve you?"

"I ask myself the same thing every damn day about you, Sunshine," I said, placing a gentle kiss on her lips.

I looked up then, and a figure was walking up the aisle toward us.

"Gray." I nodded at him.

Grayson wrapped Kennedy in a tight hug. "My little sister's getting married!"

"Gray, knock it off with that 'little sister' shit," Kennedy said, but she had a huge smile on her face.

"Get out of here so we can get this done already," Grayson said, turning to me.

"Fine, I give you two minutes to get down the aisle before I come back up here and throw you over my shoulder and carry you down there," I threatened, narrowing my eyes at them. I wasn't fucking around. I'd waited long enough.

"We should probably do what he says," Kennedy laughed. "I wouldn't test him on his threat, I have no doubt he'll actually do it."

Grayson laughed, too. "He's crazy enough about you that it wouldn't surprise me either. Are you sure you're ready for this? Just say the word, and I'll hijack a boat, and we'll get out of here."

I turned back around, glaring at Grayson. "Gray," I said, my tone laced with warning.

Grayson laughed and threw his hands up. "You know I had to say it, my loyalty is to her first."

"I know, that's the thing I like best about you." I switched my glare to a grin. "One minute." I held up one finger to make my point.

I turned my back and made my way down the aisle. Connor stood underneath the middle of the archway. He raised his eyebrow at me. "Are you sure you want me to do this?"

Both Kennedy and I felt Connor was a part of our family now, like a brother to us both. He'd been there with us, risking his life for us through all the past summer's drama. I couldn't think of anybody both of us trusted more to marry us than Connor. That's why I asked him to get ordained to perform weddings in Hawaii a couple of months ago.

"Fuck, Connor. Are you serious? It's a little late for this bullshit now. I already told you; you're who I want, and I know you're who she'd want, too. You're doing this."

Connor exhaled. "Okay, if you're sure, it'd be an honor to marry you guys."

I just nodded, glancing at the digital screen of my watch. It had been two minutes, and I looked up the aisle. I meant my threat. I knew Kennedy wanted to marry me, but I also knew she could easily get into her own head and overthink things. That was part of the reason I planned everything and did it spontaneously. Not having to deal with the stress of planning a big celebrity wedding would be a huge weight off of her shoulders, and I wanted to carry as much weight for her as I could.

I looked out into the friends and family that had assembled for our wedding. It wasn't a massive crowd like you'd expect for a wedding of someone that fronted one of the biggest rock bands in the world, but it was perfect for us. Everyone flew out here on the jet last night after the concert. Maddox and Jericho sat to the right of the aisle along with Montana and Harrison. Julian, too. On the other side of the aisle were True, Amara, Sebastian, and Grayson, when he finished walking Kennedy down the aisle.

Our group wasn't big, but we trusted and loved every single person here, and that was everything I wanted on my wedding day, and I knew Kennedy would feel the same. No paparazzi, no stalkers, just the woman I'd spend the rest of my life desperately loving and all our friends.

When I looked back at Kennedy, my world came into focus. The sight of her walking towards me, the ocean breeze gently lifting her hair and teasing it across her face was almost too much. I felt like I couldn't breathe but in the best way. I could keel over and die right here on Hawaii's warm sands, my vision filled with the most beautiful woman I'd ever laid eyes on. There was nothing I wouldn't do for her, nothing I wouldn't give to make her happy.

Her eyes were locked on mine, and I felt the sting of unshed tears. A surge of excitement washed over me as I realized this was the first day of my forever with her. She was officially trusting me with her heart, and I'd never fuck that up.

Kennedy and Grayson stopped when they reached me, Grayson handing her hand over to me. His eyes narrowed. "Break her heart, and I'll break your face."

I chuckled. If anyone could take me in a fight, it'd be Grayson, but I'd never admit that shit. "I'll never hurt her," I assured him before taking her hand in mine. She smiled at me warmly before tearing her eyes off of mine and looking straight ahead.

"Oh! Connor's marrying us?" she asked.

"I thought he was the best choice considering everything," I said with a shrug.

Kennedy's bright smile lit up the whole damn beach. "It's perfect," she whispered. "Thanks, Connor."

Wait, was he blushing? I was going to tease the shit out of him later for that. I chuckled.

Connor cleared his throat. "You're welcome." He took a moment to compose himself. "Ready?"

We both nodded at him, and he pulled out a stack of notecards and started to read. "Together, we are gathered here to witness an extraordinary ceremony, the union of Zen and Kennedy. Today we celebrate the power of your love and the strength of your bond. Before we begin, take a moment to look around at the many friendly faces before you. Know that all are here to offer love, support, and encouragement as you embark on this journey together."

We both turned and smiled down at our guests, who cheered enthusiastically back at us. "Speak for yourself!" Maddox called, and I heard Kennedy laugh.

Connor scowled at him before continuing. "There are few greater joys in life than finding someone who we truly click with. You've found that in each other as soulmates, each unveiling the best part of the other. You make each other come to life. You've found your safe haven in each other."

I locked eyes with Kennedy, our souls bared to each other on that Hawaiian beach in front of all our friends and family, tying ourselves together for eternity. It didn't feel real. It felt like a fucking dream.

"I hope Zen doesn't kill me for this, but if anyone objects, do it now and make it fucking quick," Connor said with a grin, eyes scanning the group behind us.

I glared individually at every single person present. "I dare you."

Kennedy's musical laugh rang out. "They couldn't stop me from marrying you if they tried."

I grinned, leaning forward and stealing a quick kiss.

"Hey, save it for the end," Connor scolded me, chuckling.

"Let's get to the end then," I countered.

"It's time for the vows. Kennedy, I know this was sprung on you suddenly, so just speak from the heart," Connor instructed.

She turned to me, a tear spilling out of her eye and running down her cheek. I gently wiped it away with my thumb.

"Zen, today, you become my husband. Who would've thought I'd be marrying a drunk bum I rescued from his kidnapper?" she wondered, and everyone laughed. "You turned a mirror on my life and showed me who I really am. You're the most thoughtful and caring person I know. You've always encouraged me to be my best self but also protected me when I needed it. You've given me the room to grow and been my best friend, there by my side, just in case I needed you. I have never loved and will never love anyone the way I love you. I'm yours now and forever."

Fuck, I was going to cry. I blinked a few times, trying to hold the tide of emotions threatening to make me look like a total pussy at bay. I brought her hand up to my lips, pressing a kiss to her knuckles before starting my own vows.

"Kennedy, you're so much more to me than just the love of my life, and being the love of my life is a huge fucking deal." Some of the guys laughed, and I continued. "I never dared to hope I could have the kind of love you've given me. You saved me from the darkness that was my existence before I met you. You inspire me and push me to be a better man. I didn't even know what love was until you found me and showed me what it is to truly care for someone. I'm going to spend the rest of my life making your dreams come true and showing you just how much I love you. I'm yours now and forever." I repeated her words back to her.

Tears ran down Kennedy's cheeks as she smiled up at me. I wanted to kiss every single tear away even if they were happy tears.

"Zen, do you take Kennedy as your wife and your partner? Do you promise to share her laughter during the good times and wipe her tears during the bad from this day forward?" Connor asked.

"I do."

He asked Kennedy the same.

"Hell, yes!" she said with a laugh, and everyone else laughed along with her.

"Who has the rings?" Connor asked.

"Me," True said, jumping up and running across the sand to hand them to us. I held Kennedy's platinum band in my hand while I waited to slide it onto her finger.

I turned to gaze into her eyes.

"Repeat after me. With this ring, I, Zen, commit my love to you, Kennedy, for all time, giving you all that I am and all that I will be," Connor said.

I repeated the words, sliding her ring onto her finger and giving her hand a squeeze. She grinned at me.

Kennedy did the same and slid my ring onto my finger. The weight of it would be a constant reminder that we'd tied ourselves together forever.

"By the power vested in me by the State of Hawaii and the internet," Connor began, and everyone chuckled. "I now pronounce you husband and wife."

Connor hesitated, a grin on his face. I was impatient. "Hurry the fuck up, Connor," I growled.

Everyone laughed. "You may now kiss the bride," he finished.

I wrapped my arms around my wife, dipping her back. I pressed my lips gently to hers at first before quickly deepening the kiss and dipping her low. Our friends cheered behind us, but my attention was fully on my wife. She wrapped her arms around my neck and tugged at my hair. I ran my fingers along the side of her neck, gently nibbling her lower lip before setting her back upright to more cheers and catcalls from our friends.

We turned to face everyone, matching smiles on both of our faces, my arm slung over her shoulders. Connor grinned at us. I'd never seen him smile so big before. I didn't know he had it in him honestly. Everyone closed in around us, congratulating us.

"Who's hungry?" Grayson asked. "We've got a bonfire and a traditional kalua pig roast down the beach." He motioned for everyone to follow him as he led the way.

True lingered behind, his eyes locked on Amara and I knew that look. Determination hardened across his face and I sucked in a breath, hoping whatever happened between them didn't fuck things up with our group.

I lingered in back, pulling Kennedy towards me. "Hey, wife," I said, smiling before placing an electric kiss on her lips. I couldn't wait to get back to our hotel to celebrate our wedding night.

"Hi, hubby," she giggled and scrunched up her nose. "I don't know if hubby suits you."

I wrapped my arms around her waist, kissing her nose. "Call me whatever you want. As long as you're mine and I'm yours, I don't give a shit what it is."

"I can't believe I'm somebody's wife," she mused, smiling softly.

"Not just somebody's wife, my wife. Mine," I said possessively.

She laughed. "Forever and ever, and you're mine, right, husband?"

I had staked the ultimate claim on her, and now I was her husband. My new title didn't feel weird to me; it actually felt perfect, like I'd always been meant to be hers.

"Forever and ever, wife," I said, before bending down and throwing her over my shoulder and wrapping my arm around her legs as she squealed and giggled. "Put me down!"

"No," I said, smacking her on the ass. "We're going to get some food to build up your energy, and then I'm carrying you off to bed." I had no intention of spending a lot of time socializing with everyone.

"Promise?" she asked, her voice hopeful.

"Promise."

THE END

ABOUT THE AUTHOR

For a full list of my books, see
www.heatherashleywrites.com/also-by

Stalk Me:
Facebook Group:
www.facebook.com/groups/thewildridecrew

Patreon:
www.patreon.com/heatherashleywrites

Website:
www.heatherashleywrites.com

- amazon.com/Heather-Ashley/e/B08663GYC3
- instagram.com/heatherashleywrites
- tiktok.com/@heatherashleyauthor
- facebook.com/heatherashleywrites

Printed in Great Britain
by Amazon